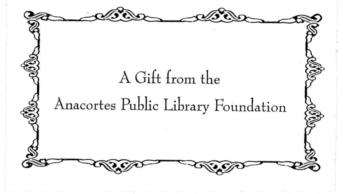

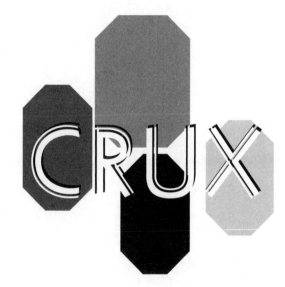

CRUX

Albert E. Cowdrey

A Tom Doherty Associates Book   TOR®   New York

CRUX

Edited by David G. Hartwell

Book design by Jane Adele Regina

A Tor Book
Published by Tom Doherty Associates, LLC
175 Fifth Avenue
New York, NY 10010

www.tor.com

Tor® is a registered trademark of Tom Doherty Associates, LLC.

Library of Congress Cataloging-in-Publication Data

Cowdrey, Albert E.
    Crux / Albert E. Cowdrey.— 1st ed.
        p.   cm.
    "A Tom Doherty Associates book."
    ISBN 0-765-31037-6 (alk. paper)
    EAN 978-0765-31037-8
        1. Regression (Civilization)—Fiction.   2. Assassination—
Fiction.   3. Time travel—Fiction.   4. Assassins—Fiction.   I. Title.

PS3553.O8975C78   2004
813'.54—dc22

                                                              2004055311

First Edition: December 2004

Printed in the United States of America

0   9   8   7   6   5   4   3   2   1

To Gordon Van Gelder

CHAPTER 1

Dyeva watched the Earth revolve beneath her, vanish into banks of icy cirrus, then emerge as a patchwork of blue sea and immobile, shining cumuli.

Bits of continents poked through the gaps as the airpacket swung out on a hyperbolic curve. She had a glimpse of North America, with the Appalachian Islands trailing into the Atlantic and the Inland Sea glimmering under the hot March sun. Then the sixty-one passengers were shrouded in the lower cloud layer and reading lights winked briefly on before they emerged again to flit like the shadow of a storm over the broad Pacific.

A light meal was served, and during dessert the glint of Fujiyama Island on the right with its attendant green islets announced that they were nearing the Worldcity. They flashed into the dark red sun, and the vast forest of China leaped out of the glittering wavelets of the Yellow Sea. Headwinds had already slowed them, but even fifty-five-hundred clicks were now too fast and one, two, three times the airpacket quivered as the retros brought it down to a sedate thousand.

They were speeding over the green savannahs of the Gobi, famous for its herds of wild animals. Of course, they were too high and moving too fast to see the herds, but the shadow box of a mashina in the forward wall of the cabin darkened, glittered briefly with pinpoints of light, and filled with solid-seeming images of wapiti, elephants, haknim, sfosura—animals native and imported from other worlds—shambling over pool-dotted green plains where the immortal Khan once ruled.

Dyeva's pale, high-cheekboned face concentrated and her

unblinking dark eyes glinted with reflected images. Nine-tenths of the Earth—humanity's first home—was now a world of beasts. The ultimate achievement of the man called Minister Destruction. Was it for this that twelve billion people had died?

2

In the sunset glow of Ulanor, the Worldcity, Stef sprawled on his balcony wearing a spotty robe and listening to the cries of vendors and the creak of wheels in Golden Horde Street. He loved to loll here smoking kif in the last light during all seasons except the brief, nasty Siberian winter.

A commotion in the street made him swing his bony legs off the battered lounge chair. He tucked the mouthpiece of his pipe into a loop of hose from the censer and shuffled in broken-strap sandals to the railing.

Down below, the traffic of trirads and vendors' carts had pulled against the walls and a long line of prisoners (blue pajamas, short hair, wrists and necks imprisoned in black plastic kangs) shuffled past like a column of ants. Guards in wide-brimmed duroplast helmets strode along the line at intervals, swinging short whips against the legs of laggards to hurry them on. The prisoners groaned and somebody started to sing a prison song in Alspeke, the only language that all humans knew: *Smerta, smerta mi kallá/Ya nur trubna haf syegdá . . .*

"Death, death, call me, I have nothing but trouble always. . . ." Picking up the rhythm, even the laggards began moving so quickly that the guards no longer had an excuse to strike.

A good song, thought Stef, lying down again, *because it goes in two opposite directions, endurance and despair. Those are the poles of life, right?* Of his life, anyway. Except for kif, which was close to being his religion, filling him during these evening hours with a distant cool melancholy, with what the Old Believers called Holy Indifference—meaning that what happened happened and you didn't try to fuck with the Great Tao.

And, of course, there was Dzhun. She meant a little more than lust, a good deal less than love. He whispered her name, which meant summertime in Alspeke, with its original English intonation and meaning: June.

Then he frowned. He was, as usual, out of cash. His money went for kif. Then how was he supposed to afford Dzhun? He brooded, puffing slowly, letting the aromatic smoke leak from his nose and mouth. He needed a case. He needed a job. He needed money to fall on him out of the sky.

3

Even blasé passengers who had seen Ulanor many times, perhaps even had grown up there, joined the newcomers in staring through the ports at the capital of the human race.

More than a million people! Dyeva thought. Who could believe a city so vast? Of course, compared to the worldcities of the twenty-first century, Ulanor was hardly a suburb. But this could at least give her a glimmering of the wonders that had been lost—a revelation of the once (and future?) world before the Time of Troubles had changed everything.

The shuttle was drifting along now, joining the traffic at the fifth level on the outermost ring, swinging around so that the city with its spoked avenues and glittering squares seemed to be turning. The copilot (a black box, of course) began speaking in a firm atonal voice, pointing out such wonders as Genghis Khan Allee, Yellow Emperor Place, where the various sector controllers had their palaces, and Government of the Universe Place, where the President's Palace faced the Senate of the Worlds.

"And then the Clouds and Rain District," said a man's voice, and the native earthlings all broke into guffaws.

The black box paused politely while the disturbance quieted, then resumed its spiel. Dyeva had turned a delicate pink. The brothel district (named for a poetic Chinese description of intercourse, the "play of clouds and rain") had been denounced in Old Believer churches ever since she could remember. And while she no longer was a believer herself, she retained a lively sense of the degradation endured by the women and men (and even children) who worked there.

She reflected that such exploitation formed the dark reverse of the civilization she loved and hoped to restore. Perhaps after all, there was something to be said for the near-empty Earth of today. Then, impatiently, Dyeva shook the thought out of her head. This was no time for doubt. Not now. Not *now*.

4

Stef was still frowning, with the mouthpiece between his lips, when his mashina chimed inside the apartment.

Irritated because somebody was calling during his relaxing hour, he padded inside, evading the shadows of junk furniture, stepping over piles of unwashed clothing. He told the mashina, "Say," and it flickered into life. Inside the shadow box hovered the glowing head of Colonel Yamashita of the Security Forces.

"*Hai, Korul Yama.*"

"I need something private done. Come see me now, Gate Forty-three."

No wasted words there. The image expired into a glowing dot. Sighing, Stef dropped his robe among the other castoffs on the floor and plowed into a musty closet, looking for something clean.

On the roof of the old building a hovercab with the usual black box for a driver nosed up when Stef pushed a call button. He climbed in and gave orders for the Lion House, Gate 43.

"*Gratizor*" (Thank you, sir), said the black box. *Why were black boxes always more polite than people?*

As they zipped down Genghis Khan Allee, Stef viewed the floodlit facades of Government of the Universe Place without interest. He had long ago realized that they were a stage set and that all the action was behind the scenes. Presidents were symbolic figures; senators had limited powers but spent most of their time talking; the great bureaucrats ruled.

Bronze statues honored the Yellow Emperor, Augustus Caesar, Jesus, Buddha, Alexander the Great, and, of course, the ubiquitous Genghis Khan. All of them Great Unifiers of Humankind. Forerunners of the Worldcity and its denizens. Genghis even had a pompous tomb set amid the floodlights—not that his bones were in it; nobody had ever found them. But yokels from the offworlds visited Ulanor specifically to gaze upon the grave of this greatest (and bloodiest) Unifier of them all.

Near the tomb foreshortened vendors were selling roasted nuts, noodles wrapped in paper, tiny bundles of kif, seaweed, bowls of miso and kimchi, and babaku chicken with texasauce. The scene was orderly; people strolled and ate at all hours and never feared crime. Breaking the law led to the Palace of Justice, off Government of the Universe Place, and the warren of tiled cells beneath that were called, collectively, the White Chamber. The formidable General Kathmann, Chief of Security, ruled the White Chamber and his reputation alone was enough to keep Ulanor law-abiding.

The cab turned off the main drag, nosed its way down back alleys at a level twenty meters above the street, and drew up at a deep niche in a blank white slab of a building. Stef flashed his ID at the black box and a flicker of light acknowledged payment. He stepped into the foyer and a bored guard in a kiosk looked up.

"*Hai?*"

"*Hai. Ya Steffens Aleksandr. Korul Yamashita ha' kallá.*"

His voice activated a monitor. The guard stared at the resulting picture, then searched Stef's face as if another, unauthorized face might be concealed beneath it. Finally he spoke to the security system, which silently opened a bronze-plated steel door.

In the public areas of the Lion House multicolored marble and crimson carved lion-dogs were everywhere, but here where the action was, the hallways were blank as culverts, slapped together out of semiplast and floored with dusty gray mats. Light panels glowed in the ceiling; doors were unmarked to confuse intruders. Stef, who knew the corridor well, counted nineteen doors and knocked.

He gasped as a stench that would have done honor to a real lion house hit him in the face. The door had been opened by a Darksider, and its furry mandrill face gazed at him with black cat pupils set in huge round eyes the color of ripe raspberries. The creature had two big arms and two little ones; one big arm held the door, one rested on its gunbelt, and the two little ones scratched the thick fur on its chest.

"*Korul Yamashita mi zhdat*" (Colonel Yamashita awaits me), Stef managed to say without choking. The Darksider moved aside, and he made his way through the dim guardroom followed by an unblinking red-black stare. He knocked again, and at last entered Yamashita's office.

"*Hai,*" said Stef, but Yama wasted no time.

"Stef, I got a problem," he began. Everything in the office was made of black or white duroplast, as if to withstand an earthquake or a revolution. Stef slipped into a black chair that apparently had been consciously shaped to cause discomfort.

"Why the animal outside? Can't you afford a human guard?" asked Stef, looking around for a kif pipe and seeing none.

"Everybody important has a Darksider now. More reliable, even if they do stink."

"You trust them more than people?"

"Absolutely. Now listen. This information is a beheader, so I hope your neck tingles if you ever feel an urge to divulge it. For months I been getting vague reports from the Lion Sector about terrorists who are interested in time travel. Now something's happened here on Earth. Somebody's pirated a wormholer from the University."

"Oh, shit." Since Stef hadn't even known that a real wormholer existed, his surprise was genuine.

"The people who were responsible for the machine are now with Kathmann in the White Chamber. They're undergoing *shosho* and I assure you that if it was an inside job the Security Forces will soon know."

"I just bet they will." *Shosho* meant torture.

"I don't have to spell out for you the danger if some *glupetz* gets at the past. Ever since the technology came along, assholes have been wanting to go back and change this, change that. They don't understand the chaotic effect of such changes. They don't see how things can spin out of control."

Yamashita sat brooding, a man who had devoted his life to control.

"They think they can manage the time process. They don't see how some little thing, some insignificant thing, can send history spinning off in some direction they haven't foreseen, nobody's foreseen."

His voice became solemn, almost religious. "The Great Tao loves irony. It loves to give people the exact opposite of what they're trying to achieve. It's a mean, laughing son of a bitch."

Stef nodded. He didn't give a damn about metaphysics; he

was thinking about someone monkeying with the past, suddenly causing himself, or Dzhun, or the genius who had synthesized kif to wink out of existence. It was hard to maintain Holy Indifference in the face of possibilities like that.

Yama's mood shifted from solemn to fretful.

"Why don't these *svini* do something useful?" he complained. *Svini* meant swine. "Why don't they try to change the future instead of the past, try to make it better?"

"Possibly because you'd execute them if they did."

Suddenly Yama grinned. He and Stef went back a long way; the academy, service on Io, on Luna. They had been rivals once but no longer. Yama headed the Security Service at the Lion House, a fat job; the Lion Sector, which it administered, was a huge volume of space with hundreds of inhabited worlds stretching up the spiral arm toward the dense stars of the galactic center.

Meanwhile, Stef was out on his ass, picking up small assignments to solve problems Yama didn't want to go public with. Like the present one: Yama had no authority on Earth, but suspected a connection between a local happening and one in Far Space. As an agent, Stef had two great advantages—he was reliable and deniable.

"It's true," Yama went on, "I like things as they are. Humanity's been through a lot of crap to get where it is. We need to conserve what we've got."

"Absolutely."

Yama looked suspiciously at Stef's bland face. He didn't like Stef to say things that might be either sincere or ironic, or might wag like a dog's tail, back and forth.

Stef grinned just a little. "Yama, I really do agree with you. There are things I like about my life. Now, how can I find this wormholer thief?"

Yama was instantly all business again. "I'll tell you everything you need to know," he said.

"And not a bit more."

"Absolutely," said Yama, who really did have a sense of humor, colonel of security or not. Reaching into his desk (petty cash, top right-hand drawer) he handed Stef a hundred khans.

"Down payment," he said. "A thousand total if you succeed. Get to work."

CHAPTER II

The University of the Universe filled a walled compound in the center of the Worldcity, its buildings a jumble of architectural styles imitating Greek temples, Chinese pagodas, Victorian factories, Moorish palaces, and mixtures thereof.

Poor students and poorer instructors lived inside the wall, in dormitories and the Faculty Warrens, or outside in a teeming slum of narrow streets and courtyards with high-sounding names—Jesus and Buddha Court, Confucius Circle, Aristotle Manor.

Safely remote from this shoddy enclave stood the big, heavily mortgaged house of Honored Professor Yang Li-qutsai, famous historian. About the time Stef departed from the Lion House and Yama set out for home and dinner, Yang was entering his study and preparing to lecture. Not, of course, to mere students—to his mashina, under staring vapor lamps.

His course at the University of the Universe, *Origa Nash Mir* (Origin of Our World) drew a thousand students every time he gave it. The reason was not profound scholarship—Yang plagiarized almost everything he said—but his brilliance as a speaker. At times, he seemed to be a failed actor rather than a successful academic.

His image included a long gray beard, a large polished skull, a frightening array of fingernails, and a deep, sonorous voice that made everything he said seem important, whether it was or not. A memory cube recorded his lecture for resale to the offworlds where dismal little academies under strange suns would thrill to the echoes of his wisdom.

Even as he began to speak, stabbing the air with a long thin index finger that ended in nine centimeters of nail, Yang was calculating what resale and residual rights on the lecture might bring him. Enough to buy a villa at the fashionable south end of Lake Bai? Peace at home, among his four wives? At least an expensive whore?

On the whole, he thought, *I'd better settle for the whore.* Half of his two-track mind dreamed of girls, while the other half was retelling the most calamitous event in the brief, horrid history of civilized man. The first lecture of his course was always on the Time of Troubles.

"Considering that the Troubles created our world," he declared, "it is shocking—yes, shocking—that we know so little about how they began. In two brief years (2091–2093) twelve billion people died with all their memories. Seven hundred vast cities were obliterated with all their records; three-hundred-odd governments vanished, with all their archives of hardcopy, discs, tapes, and the first crude memory cubes. No wonder we know so little!

"Where and why did the fighting start? Early in the century, violence had consisted only in tribal wars and terrorism. But when China and Russia reemerged as superpowers, a new arms race began. Blue Nile hemorrhagic fever and multiple-drug-resistant blackpox were raging in Africa as early as the 2070s, and genetic science enabled both small and great powers to engineer lethal strains as weapons. The Time of Troubles was well under way even before the outbreak of war."

Introductions were always troublesome: students, realizing

they were in for a long hour, began to sink into a trancelike state accompanied by fluttering eyelids and restless movements of the pelvis. A warning light on the box glowed green, and Yang headed at once into the horror stories that gave the course much of its appeal.

"But the war of 2091 produced the most spectacular effects: the destruction of the cities, the Two Year Winter, and the Great Famine. Let us take as an example the city of Moscow, where robot excavators have recently given us an in-depth picture—if I may be pardoned a little joke—of the horrors that attended its destruction. A city of thirty million in 2090 . . ."

Detail after horrendous detail followed: the skeleton-choked subway with its still beautiful mosaics recording the compassionate reign of Tsar Stalin the Good; the dry trench of the Moskva River, whose waters had been vaporized in one glowing instant and blocked by rubble so that the present river flowed fifteen clicks away; the great Kremlin Shield of fused silicon stretching over the onetime city center, with its radioactive core that would glow faintly for at least 50,000 years.

Observing with satisfaction that his indicator light was turning from unlucky green to lucky red, Professor Yang moved on to the horrors of London, Paris, Tokyo, Beijing, and New York. Then he spoke briefly about the closed zones that still surrounded the lost cities, of irradiated wildlife undergoing rapid evolutionary change in bizarre and clamorous Edens where the capitals of great empires had stood, only three hundred years ago. . . .

The interest indicator glowed like a Darksider's eye. Professor Yang strode up and down, his voice deepening, his gray beard swishing in the wind, his long fingers clawing at the air.

"Precisely how did it happen—this great calamity?" he demanded. "How much we know, and how little! Will it remain for the scholars of your generation to solve these riddles finally? I confess that mine has shed only a little light around the edges of the forbidding darkness that we call—the Time of Troubles!"

As usual, his lecture lasted exactly the time allotted, a one-hundred-minute hour. As usual, it ended with a key phrase reminding the drowsy student of what he had been hearing at the rim of his clouded consciousness.

The power light in the mashina winked off, and Professor Yang shouted: "Tea!"

A door flew open and a scurrying domestic wheeled in the tea caddy, the cup, the tins of oolong and Earl Grey.

"Sometimes," muttered Yang, "I think I'll die of boredom if I ever have to talk about the Troubles again."

Through the open door he heard voices raised, another quarrel among his womenfolk. He swallowed one bitter cup, then another. The voices came closer. He foresaw demands for money, and suddenly decided to settle the issue before it arose by spending his available cash on himself. A few hours in the Clouds and Rain District would be exactly what he needed, to escape his own Time of Troubles.

2

The clocks of the Worldcity that marked the end of the lecture were announcing twenty-one in soft atonal voices when Yamashita, dining comfortably at home with his wife, Hariko, heard his security-coded mashina chime.

Hastening into his den, he received a secret report from his mole at Security Central, a certain Major Yost. Yama listened to the report with growing dismay.

"Shit, piss, and corruption," he growled, breaking the connection. "Secretary!"

"Sir?" murmured the box.

"Contact Steffens Aleksandr. If he's not at home—and of course he won't be—start calling the houses in the Clouds and Rain District. Make it absolutely clear that this is a security matter and that we expect cooperation in finding him."

"Yes, sir. His home is not answering."

"Try Brother and Sister House. Try Delights of Spring House. Try Radiant Love House. Then try all the others."

"And when I find Steffens Aleksandr?"

"Tell him to wipe his cock and get to my office soonest."

"Is that message to be conveyed literally?"

"Yes!"

Back at the table, he had barely had time to fold his legs under him when Hariko told him to stop using bad language in the house where the children might hear him.

"Yes, little wife," said the man of power meekly.

"I suppose you have to go back to the office."

"Yes, little wife. An emergency—"

"Always your emergencies," complained Hariko. "Why do I waste hours making you good food to eat if you're never here to eat it? And why do you employ that awful Steffens person? He's a disgrace, a man his age who lives like a tomcat. Not everyone can be as happy as we are, but everybody can lead a decent life."

Yama ate quietly, occasionally agreeing with her until she ran out of words. Then he went upstairs, removed his comfortable kimono, and put on again the sour uniform he'd worn all day.

On the way down, pinching his thick neck as he tried to close the collar, he stopped in the children's bedrooms to make sure they were all asleep. The boys in their bunk beds slept the extravagant sleep of childhood. Looking at them, gently patting their cheeks, Yama reflected that adults and animals always slept as if they half expected to be awakened—children never.

Then to the girls' room, where his daughter Kazi slumbered in the embrace of a stuffed haknim. Yama smiled at her but lingered longest at the bedside of his smallest daughter. Rika was like a doll dreaming, with a tiny bubble forming on her half-parted pink lips.

He was thinking: *if someone changes the past, she may vanish, never have a chance to live at all.* To prevent that, he resolved to destroy without mercy every member of the time-travel conspiracy.

At the front door Hariko tied a scarf around his neck and gave him a hug; she was too modest to kiss her husband in the open doorway, even though they were twenty meters above the street. He patted her cheek and stepped into the official hovercar that had nosed up to his porch.

"Lion House, Gate Forty-three," he told the black box, and sank back against the cushions.

3

At Radiant Love House, Professor Yang relaxed from his scholarly labors on one side of a double divan in the high-price parlor and viewed 3-D images of young women to the ancient strains of Tchaikovsky's *Nutcracker*.

"Do you see anything that pleases you?" asked the box that was projecting the images.

"Truly, it is a Waltz of the Flowers," replied Yang sentimentally. The smell of kif wafted through the room, presumably from a hidden censer.

"The dark beauty of Miss Luvblum contrasts so markedly with the rare—indeed, unique—blondness of Miss Sekzkitti," murmured the box, going through its recorded spiel. "The almond eyes of Miss Ming remind us of the splendor of the dynasty from which she takes her *nom d'amour*. Every young lady is mediscanned daily to ensure her absolute purity and freedom from disease. Miss Gandhi is skilled in all the acts of the famous *Kama Sutra*. For a small additional fee, an electronic room may be rented in which the most modern appliances are available to heighten the timeless joys of love."

Professor Yang had already halfway made his selection— the most expensive of the "stable." Miss Selassie, a tall, slender woman of Sudanese descent, had been genetically altered into an albino. The box referred to her as the White Tiger of the Nile, and bald, bearded, long-nailed Yang, at ninety-nine reaching the extreme limits of middle age, found his thoughts turning more and more to her astounding beauty.

Her body is like a living Aphrodite of ancient Greece, he thought, *while her face is like a spirit mask of ancient Africa.*

"Miss Selassie, how much is she?"

"One hundred khans an hour."

"Oh, dear. And how much for an electronic room?"

Professor Yang rightly believed that all the appliances known to modern science would be needed if he was to spend his expensive hour doing anything more than enjoying Miss Selassie's company. Drugs, alas, had long ceased to work for him.

"Fifty khans an hour. However," said the box seductively, "for such a man as yourself, Honored Professor, the house gladly makes a special price: Miss Selassie *and* an electronic room for the sum total of—"

A brief pause, during which Yang felt himself growing anxious.

"One hundred and thirty-five khans, a ten percent reduction."

"Agreed," breathed Yang, giving himself no time to think. There was a brief flutter in the box as his bank checked his voiceprint and transferred another K135 from his already deflated account to one of the bulging accounts of Radiant Love House.

"You should've asked for twenty percent off," said a voice, making Yang jump.

A long, stringy, bony man holding a kif pipe rose from the other side of the double divan and stretched and yawned.

"I hope you haven't been eavesdropping," snapped Yang.

"No more than I had to," said Stef in a bored voice. "I've made my selection, but the selectee is popular and she's busy. I'm just telling you, if you've got the balls to bargain you can get them down twenty percent, sometimes more if it's a slow night. The ten percent reduction they offer you is just merchandizing."

Resentment at the stranger's intrusion struggled with economic interest in Professor Yang's breast. The latter won.

"Really?"

"Sure. I do it all the time. You could've gotten the whole works for a hundred twenty."

"Indeed. And the electronic room—is it really worth it?"

"It is if you have to have it."

Yang was just beginning to get angry when the door opened and a very tall naked woman entered. Her hair was in a thousand white braids and her eyes were oval rubies. The aureoles of her taut, almost conical breasts were much the same color as her eyes. A faint scent of faux ambergris wafted into the waiting room and mingled with the fumes of kif. Yang sat hypnotized.

"You the customer?" she asked Stef with some interest.

"No, I'm waiting for Dzhun. This guy's your customer."

"Figures," she sighed, and taking Professor Yang's thin and trembling hand in her own, the White Tiger led him away.

A few minutes later the box made two announcements: Dzhun was ready, and Stef was to wipe his cock and get to Yama's office soonest. Stef promptly did what he almost never did—lost it completely.

"FUCK THE FUCKING UNIVERSE!" he roared in English. The divan weighed a hundred kilos, but he tossed it end over end. At the crash the door flew open and a guard entered, pulling an impact pistol half as long as her arm. Stef calmed down instantly.

"*Ya bi sori*. My deepest and humblest apologies," he said, clapping his hands together and bowing. "I don't know what came over me."

Stef had seen a number of bodies killed by impact weapons. A body shot usually left very little except the head, arms and legs, plus assorted fragments.

"Straighten out the goddamn sofa," said the guard, watching him narrowly. She looked tough and Stef did as he was told.

"Incidentally," he said as he was leaving, "I'll need a rain check on Dzhun. I already paid my khans."

"Talk to the front desk," growled the guard.

Outside, Stef took a deep breath and ordered a hovercab. He felt that he now had a personal score to settle with the wormholer-snatching *svini* who had forestalled his session with Dzhun. Since the *svini* were the only reason he currently had money enough to buy her time, that was unreasonable. But Stef wanted to be unreasonable. That was how he felt.

4

"So the theft was an inside job," he muttered, trying without success to get comfortable in one of Yama's black chairs.

"Yes. According to my contact—a guy who works in the White Chamber—a trusted scientist turns out to belong to a terrorist group that calls itself Crux. He's been checked a hundred times. Living quietly, no extra money, no nothing. During lie-detection tests, brain chemicals always indicated he was telling the truth. Trouble was, the wrong questions got asked. Are you loyal? To what? He answers yes, meaning loyal to humanity as he understands it. Are you a member of any subversive group? Subversive in what sense? To the existing order, or to humanity? He gets by with a false answer again."

"What exactly do these Crux fuckers believe in?"

"Life. The absolute value of human life. The wormholer opens the way to reverse the worst calamity in human history, the Time of Troubles. Trillions of lives are hanging on the issue—not only the lives that were lost in the famines and plagues and wars but all their descendants to the tenth generation."

Stef growled, scratched himself, longing for kif, for Dzhun. "Bunch of fucking idealists."

"Exactly. People with a vision, willing to destroy the real world for the sake of an idea. We've gotta kill them all."

Yama jumped up—a springy man, muscular, bandy-legged. He was fifty and nearing middle age, but a lifetime of the martial arts enabled him to bounce around like a ball of elastoplast.

"Kill them!" he roared, chopping at the air.

Watching him tired Stef.

"And this was what you called me back for?"

"No. Or not only." Yama fell back into the desk chair. "The group that has this grand vision is, of course, organized in cells that have to be cracked one by one. But the guy who talked in the White Chamber knew one name outside his group, the name of a woman, an offworlder. She's called Dyeva. She's one of the founders of the movement and she was supposed to contact him."

Stef sighed. "Anything from IC on her?"

"No," admitted Yama. "No report yet from Infocenter."

"Call me when one comes in," said Stef, rising. "I'm extremely grateful for the way you took me away from my pleasures to give me information that, as yet, has no practical significance. Please don't do it again."

Yama saw him to the door, nodding to the Darksider who approached smelling like the shit of lions, owls, and cormorants mixed together. Stef pinched his nostrils and spoke like a duck.

"I love coming to your office, Yama. The place has a certain air about it."

Half an hour later, Stef was again sprawled in the expensive parlor at Radiant Love House, waiting. Another customer had taken Dzhun while he was away. Stef spent the time smoking kif and thinking about shooting Dyeva, whoever she was, with an impact pistol.

"*Phut,*" he said, imitating the uninspiring sound of the weapon. He made his long hands into a ball and drew them rapidly apart, imitating the explosion inside the target. Impact ammo vaporized in the body and formed a rapidly expanding sphere of superheated gas and destructive particles.

Dyeva v' átomi sa dizolva, he thought. The *svinya,* the sow, flies apart, turns to molecules, atoms, protons, and quarks.

"How happy I am," murmured the box, "to inform you, sir, that Dzhun is ready to receive you."

Instantly Stef was up and moving, his bloody thoughts forgotten. At heart he was a lover, not a killer.

5

In the blue peace of the electronic room, Professor Yang lay huddled under a sheet of faux silk.

Beside him, her hand still languidly resting on a gadget called an erector-injector, lay a statue of living ivory. At least he now knew the White Tiger's given name. It was only a prost's working name, a *nom d'amour,* yet for Yang it was what the old French phrase meant—a name of love.

"Selina," he murmured, and she turned her head and smiled at him.

"I'm afraid your time is up," she whispered. "But perhaps you'll come again, my dear. You were special."

"Selina," he said again. Around him monitors winked and a low electronic hum soothed with a white sound. Yang was all too conscious of the birth of a new obsession, one even less affordable than four wives and natural sugar.

"I *must* see you again," he said.

Detecting the urgent note in his voice, Selina smiled. *Ah, that enigmatic whore's smile!* thought Yang with pain in his heart. What did it mean? Pleasure in you, pleasure in your money, no pleasure at all but mere professionalism? Who could tell?

Wasn't this how he had happened to marry the most obnoxious of his four wives?

CHAPTER III

Dyeva sat quietly in the front room of a small but elegant suburban villa.

The windows were open and the morning sun entered through a screen of glossy leaves thrown out by a lemon tree. The room held all the necessities of rustic living, bare beams across the ceiling, lounges covered with faux linen, a glass table bearing apples and oranges and kuvisu fruit, and a mashina half the length of the wall to entertain the owner, a professor of rhetoric whose hobby was playing at revolution.

Relaxing on the lounges were the other members of the cell: two students and a dark and tensely attractive woman of middle age, who bore a painted mark on her forehead. The students were still talking about Professor Yang's lecture of last evening, tailor-made as it seemed for the members of Crux.

"Lord Buddha, but he makes you see it," said the boy, fingering a string of beads restlessly. He was an Old Believer. Dyeva had noticed years ago that such people were represented in Crux far beyond their numbers in the general population.

The girl was lovely: bronzed, yellow-haired, sloe-eyed, the perfect Eurasian. She called herself Dián and spoke in a throaty whisper that someone had told her was mysterious.

"Actually, he's a horrible old man. But it's as Kuli says, he has the gift of making the past live."

"*We* expect to do more along that line," said the owner of the villa in a deep, resonant voice, and the two young people laughed happily. All three of them loved the taste of conspiracy; the older man, whose code name was Zet, earnestly hoped to seduce Dián. Supposedly nobody in the group knew anybody else's real name. They had a vast and fundamentally childish panoply of measures to preserve secrecy—passwords, hand signals, ways of passing information in complicated and difficult ways.

Because cyberspace was a favorite hunting ground for the supermashini of the Security Forces, they avoided electronic contact whenever possible. Instead, they had oaths, secret meetings, symbols. Their key symbol was the looped cross of ancient Egypt—the ankh or *crux ansata*, the sign of life.

Kuli wore a crux on a cord around his neck; at meetings he took it out for all to see. The girl, Dyeva noted with amazement, had the symbol tattooed on the palm of one slender hand. Why didn't the senior members of the cell force her to have it removed?

People had often told Dyeva that she had ice water in her veins. That wasn't true: her emotions were intense, only deeply buried. Right now anger and alarm were stirring deep beneath her masklike face. Did her life, to say nothing of the lives of trillions of human beings, depend on these amateurs, children?

The dark woman, who called herself Lata, brushed a hand across her brow and said, "The essential thing is to speed our visitor safely on her way. And I must tell all of you something I learned last night. The theft of the wormholer has been discovered and there have been arrests."

"*Arrests?*" demanded Dián, in a scandalized tone. "Of someone I *know?*"

She seemed to think that the polizi had no right to arrest members of a secret organization merely because it was bent on annihilating the existing world.

"No," sighed Lata. "Fortunately for you. That beast Kathmann and his aide—a wretch named Yost—drugged and tortured both the guards and the people who were responsible for technical maintenance of the wormholer. Thus they learned that one of the scientists had been involved in the theft. Thank God, the device had already been turned over to another cell, and the poor man who talked didn't know their names or where it is at present."

The two young people seemed paralyzed. Zet was turning his head from side to side, looking at the furniture, the fresh fruit. Dyeva had no trouble reading his mind: the *glupetz* had suddenly realized that he could lose all this by playing at conspiracy. *Someday,* she thought, *if he thinks about it long enough, he will realize that he may lose much more.*

"I will go with you," said Dyeva, rising and pointing at Lata, apparently the only one of the gathering with any sense. "You will conduct me. I must not stay here longer and endanger these heroes of humanity."

Zet looked relieved at the news she'd soon be gone; Kuli and Dián were still absorbing the news of the arrests. He was stunned, she indignant.

"Oh, but the people who were tortured—they're martyrs!" she exclaimed suddenly and burst into tears.

"Yes," said Dyeva, "and by this time they are also corpses. Death is the reward the technicians of the Chamber hold out to their victims. I will be packed and gone in five minutes if you will lead me," she said to Lata.

"Of course," said the dark woman, and Dyeva hastened to the room where she had slept to gather her kit.

Later, in Lata's hovercar, Dyeva asked her how she had come to join the movement.

"I despise this world," Lata said quietly. "It's a gutter of injustice and pain. Nothing will be lost if this world suddenly vanishes at the word of Lord Krishna. Of course, if we manage to undo the Troubles, success will cost us our own lives. That is the splendor of Crux. If our movement did not demand the ultimate sacrifice I would not have joined it."

Another Old Believer, thought Dyeva, *only this time of the Hindu type. And I was brought up a Christ-worshipper, and the boy Kuli is a Buddhist. Are we all remnants and leftovers of a dead world? Is that why we wish to restore it?*

"What are you thinking?" asked Lata.

"Wondering why the movement contains so many Old Believers."

"Oh, I think I know. It's because we want to undo the death of our faiths. So many people simply stopped believing after the Troubles. They said to themselves, There is no God. Or, if there is and he allows this to happen, I do not care about him."

Dyeva glanced at her curiously. They were entering the airspace above Ulanor, and Lata paid frowning attention to the traffic until a beam picked up her car's black box. For an instant Dyeva had a powerful urge to continue this conversation, to talk about things that had real meaning. Then she remembered that the less Lata knew about her, and she about Lata, the better for both of them.

"We all come to it for different reasons," she said guardedly, and silence followed. The little car revolved above the Worldcity, bearing two women who hoped to change it into a phantasm that had never existed at all.

2

Stef and Dzhun were having breakfast in a tea shop deep in the Clouds and Rain District. Half the customers seemed to recognize Dzhun, and she waved and blew kisses to them. She had scrubbed off her white working makeup and with it had gone her nighttime pretense of lotus delicacy and passivity. She looked like and was a tough young woman to whom life had not been kind.

"Wild turnover last night," she said to a red-haired eunuch who had stopped by the table to shriek and fondle her. "I did ten guys."

"Oh my dear," said the *sisi*, "I do ten on my way to work."

"Seems you've got some catching up to do," Stef told Dzhun when the *sisi* had moved on.

"Oh, he's such a bragger. And old, too. When I'm his age I'll have my own house and instead of bragging about doing ten guys I'll be doing one—the one I choose."

"And that one will be me."

"Only if you get rich," said Dzhun candidly, buttering a bun. "I'm tired of being a *robotchi*, a working stiff. I've got a senator on the string now, Stef, did I tell you? Soon you won't be able to afford me at all."

She dimpled as she always did when saying unpalatable things.

"Is that why I'm buying you breakfast?"

"Oh, Stef, I'm just needling you. I love my poor friends, too. Look, why don't you take me to Lake Bai for a week or two? Get a cabin. I won't demand a villa. Not yet."

"Unfortunately, I'm on a big case right now. One that might even save your life."

Dzhun stopped eating and stared at him. "You're telling the truth?"

"Believe it. When the payoff comes, it'll be as big as the case. Then we'll go to Bai. Get a villa, not a cabin."

Stef spoke with the calm assurance he employed when he was in a state of total uncertainty. The investigation was dead in the water. The arrests had not led to the wormholer. IC still hadn't come up with a make on Dyeva. Mashini were combing passenger lists of recent arrivals from the offworlds—voice-prints, retinographs, DNA samples—turning up nobody with a record, nobody who fit the profiles. Stef's local contacts had nothing to offer.

"What's it all about, Stef?" asked Dzhun.

"Never mind. The case is a beheader. It's nothing you want to know about, so don't ask. It's a security matter and it'd be a hell of a shame if the Darksiders came and carted off a butt like yours to the White Chamber."

Their voices had fallen to whispers. Dzhun's face was so close that Stef's breath moved her long eyelashes. A delicate scent clung to her kimono, some nameless offworld flower, and the drooping faux silk disclosed the roundness of her little breasts like pomegranates. Stef could have eaten her with a spoon.

"I won't say anything," she promised. "If anybody asks what you're doing, I'll say that you never tell me anything."

Stef leaned back and sipped the bitter green tea he used to clear his head in the morning. Effortlessly, Dzhun put her whore's persona on again, screaming and waving at a friend who had just entered the tea shop. Towering over the crowd, the White Tiger of the Nile headed for their table.

She and Dzhun kissed and Selina sat down, nodding at Stef.

"Hell of a night," she said to them and the world in general. "I did a dozen guys."

"Oh, Selina," said Dzhun. "Honey, I do a dozen on my way to work."

3

Yamashita clapped his hands and bowed to announce himself to the *fromazhi*—the big cheeses who ruled the human-occupied universe. Today they were holding an emergency meeting to deal with the wormholer theft.

Yama's boss, Oleary, Deputy Controller of the Lion Sector, grunted a welcome, adding, "You know these people, I'm sure."

Considering that he was talking about the Controller, her deputy the Earth Controller, her Chief of Security, and Admiral Hrka, commander of the Space Service, that was inadequate to say the least.

The Controller was Xian Xi-qing, a small woman with a parchment face, tiny hands and dull gold and jade rings stacked two and three to a finger. She was famous for many things, her opulent lifestyle, her stable of male concubines, the ruthlessness and cleverness that had kept her alive and in power for decades as the State's supreme bureaucrat.

She glared at Yama and demanded abruptly, "We've heard from Kathmann. At least he's caught somebody. What are *you* doing about this wormholer business? I've heard rumors the conspiracy originated in your sector."

Yama took his time seating himself on a backless chair known as the *shozit*, or hot seat. The grandees faced him behind a Martian gilt table surrounded by an invisible atmosphere of power. Admiral Hrka, Yama noted, wasn't even wearing his nine stars. That was the ultimate sign of status. Nobody needed to see *his* rating.

Among these bureaucrats, the admiral looked and probably felt out of place. Hrka usually dealt with the arcane business of moving in Far Space—using inertial compensators and particle beam trans-lightspeed accelerators, navigating by mag-space forcelines and staging chronometric reentries where an error of a microsecond could put him deep inside the glowing core of a planet. He was accustomed to using atomlasers that could melt steel at half a million clicks, launching supertorps at near-light velocities and converting the enemies of his species into plasma thinner than the solar wind.

Now he found himself face-to-face with a threat that might enable one fragile human to undo his world and render all his knowledge and bravery pointless. He looked as if he longed to be in Far Space now, where even if he was a thousand light years from anyplace, he knew where he was.

Seated to one side was Kathmann. The Chief of Security resembled a files technician, with his pointed head and fat neck. He wore replacement eyes and the plastic corneas glittered blankly. Behind him, appropriately shadowed, sat Major Yost. Yama's eyes rested for a moment on his mole with a nonrecognition so total he could not even be said not to have seen him.

When his turn came to speak, Yama quietly laid out the steps taken so far to locate members of Crux. The notion that the conspiracy had grown up in the Lion Sector remained unproven, yet diligent inquiries were under way on all the Sector's 236 inhabited worlds. All available mag-space transponder circuits had been cleared for this one task. Enough energy to light Ulanor for six weeks had already been poured into the message traffic. The whole business was necessarily slow; even at maximum power, a message routed through mag space from the farthest planets of the Sector took more than seventy standard hours to reach Earth.

And so on. Actually he had nothing to report and his aim was to make nothing sound like something. When he was done, the *fromazhi*, who knew bureaucratic boilerplate when they heard it, just sat there looking bored. Only Kathmann spoke up.

"All your inquiries are on offworlds?"

"Certainly. That's where my authority begins and ends."

"You're not using unofficial agents here on Earth?"
Yama was shocked.

"Onor Ghenral, eto ne' legalni!" (Honored General, that's illegal!), he exclaimed.

Kathmann raised one fat fist and stared at Yama with eyes like worn silver half-khan pieces.

"Remember, Colonel, this hand holds the keys to the White Chamber!"

Yama raised his own much solider fist.

"And this one, sir, has killed a thousand enemies of the State!"

The spat had Admiral Hrka grinning.

"Simmer down, boys," he said, while the Earth Controller, a man named Ugaitish, muttered into his beard, *"Spokai, spokai."* (Take it easy.)

"What I want to know," said Oleary in a fretful tone, "is why anybody built this goddamn gadget in the first place. If it didn't exist, it couldn't be stolen."

"It was some idiots at the University," said Ugaitish. "They just had to see if the theory worked. They applied for a permit, all very legal, and some minor official gave them an *oké* for the materials, which are pretty exotic. There's no use putting them in the White Chamber," he added, waving a hand to shut Kathmann up.

Xian agreed. "Typical academics. Not an atom of common sense. All they know is what they know."

"Besides," Ugaitish added, "the academics were the ones who reported the theft. Except for that, nobody would know anything about it."

"They should be beheaded anyway," Kathmann growled, "to get rid of the dangerous knowledge in their brains. A laser can do it in five seconds, and there you are."

Yama's sharp eyes intercepted the glance that passed among

the *fromazhi*. Kathmann made them uneasy—a man who knew too much and executed too readily.

Yama filed away this insight for future reference. If there was one thing life in the Security Forces had taught him, it was that your boss was invariably the person blocking your own path to advancement.

"At this point, beheading is not the issue," declared Hrka. "Let me sum up. A woman, name unknown, took a commercial ship, probably somewhere in the Lion Sector—now there's a big volume of space to cover—and traveled to Earth, where she has, perhaps, contacted a group of terrorists who intend to obliterate our world by changing the past. The group has a functional wormholer, calls itself Crux, and in the most overpoliced human society since the fall of the Imperial Chinese People's Republic nobody knows who they are or where they are. Have I stated the situation clearly?"

Xian glared first at him, then at the two cops in turn.

"You'd better find them," she said, "or I'll put you *both* in the White Chamber."

She let that sink in, then said more formally: "Honored security officers, we permit you to go."

When they were gone, Xian told the others, "We need information now. Ugaitish is putting out a public call for help. We don't have to tell everything, just that a gang of terrorists called Crux is on the loose, planning to kill many innocent people."

"Is that wise?" worried Oleary. "Informing the masses seems like an extreme step to me."

"If we don't, the politicians will. I have to brief the president and the Senate today, and what do you think will happen then?"

"Much smoke, much heat, no light," said Hrka fatalistically. "Well, we'd better catch these bastards. The whole world order as we know it exists only because of the Time of Troubles. Without that, everything would be different."

The *fromazhi* stared at each other. "Great Tao," said Ugaitish, "if these scoundrels succeed—even if we continue to exist at all, we might be anything. Coolies, prisoners, offworld scum!"

"Ask for help," Oleary told Xian. "If necessary, beg."

4

After his night in the District, Stef needed sleep. Yet he spent a couple of hours at his mashina, checking his regular contacts for hints of terrorist groups. He heard gossip about lunatics who wanted to blow up Genghis's tomb, but nothing of interest to him. So he went to bed.

The daytime noises rising from Golden Horde Street had no power to keep him awake. He had slept away too many days, sunk in the half-light admitted from the roofed balcony, embracing rumpled bedcovers in the brown shadows of afternoon. In a few minutes he drifted off, but not for long.

He woke suddenly thinking he must have shit on himself. He reached for his pistol just as a crushing furry weight fell on him.

The ceiling light went on and the Darksider rolled Stef over and sat on his back. For a few agonized moments he couldn't breathe at all, while the creature, aided by a human Stef never saw clearly, thrust his hands into a kang and locked the wrists. Then the Darksider rose, bent down over its gasping victim, and lifted him so that the kang could be clamped on his neck as well. A four-fingered, two-thumbed hand gripped his hair and pulled him to a sitting position.

Spots drifted before his eyes in a red torrent that slowly cleared. Stef was sitting naked on the bed with a black plastic kang clamped on his wrists and neck. His faint hope that this might be a nightmare died. The Darksider was standing bow-legged by the bed and scratching its chest. The human seemed to be wearing a polizi uniform; he kept to the shadows just beyond the limits of Stef's vision. Head immobilized, Stef tried to twist his body to get a view of his captor, but without success.

"Who the fuck are you?"

"Your guide, Mr. Steffens," said a quiet, dry voice. "I'm here to show you something you never saw before."

"What?"

"The inside of the White Chamber."

At a gesture, the Darksider tossed a sack over Stef's head and pulled a cord tight around his neck. A hypodermic gun spat at his shoulder and he had a horrifying sense that his whole body was melting into a cold and lifeless fluid before darkness descended.

He would have preferred not to wake up, but wake he did. Still in the kang, still with the sack over his head. *Of course you're not comfortable,* he told himself. *You're not supposed to be comfortable.* He had no idea how long he'd been here, except that he was thirsty and hungry. No idea where "here" was, except somewhere in the warrens of the White Chamber.

He had urinated at some point and was sitting in the wet. The cell was so small that his knees were folded up against his chest. His icy toes pressed against metal that was probably the door. The cell was narrower than the kang, and Stef had to sit with his body twisted. There was no way to move, no way to rest.

As the hours passed, agonizing pains began to shoot through his back and side. Breathing became difficult. He began suffering waves of panic at the thought that the polizi would leave him here until he slowly suffocated. The panic made things worse; he started to hyperventilate, and every breath stabbed him like a knife. He tried to calm himself, counting slow shallow breaths that didn't hurt so much.

Then voices approached along a corridor outside the cell. Faint hope was followed by stomach-knotting fear. *They might let me go; it was all a mistake; Yama will get me out.*

No, Yama doesn't know anything about this. They're coming to torture me.

The voices came close. Two techs were discussing a "patient," as they called their victims. Voices neutral, atonal like the voices of two black boxes.

"Maybe twenty cc of gnosine would do it."

"I dunno. This patient is a tough case."

"Maybe skopal? Or needles in the spinal marrow . . ."

They were gone. A faint noise in the distance remained unidentifiable until a door in the corridor slid open. Then Stef heard a whimpering, sobbing sound that made all the hairs rise on the back of his neck. *Extreme agony,* he thought—*beyond screaming.*

The door slid shut again and the sound became a low meaningless murmur. Human footsteps approached again. Two voices.

"Just wonderful, Doctor. I never thought she'd break."

"Sometimes a combination of therapies is essential."

They, too, were gone. Doctors. Technicians. Therapies. Patients. The language of the Chamber. We are not sadists, we are scientists performing a distasteful but necessary function in the cause of justice. Try the gnosine, try the skopal, try the needles, try everything in combination. Promise the patient life; after you've worked on them for a while, promise them death.

When the polizi came at last, they came in silence. Without the slightest warning the door clanged open. Somebody yelled, "Get the scum! Get the piece of shit!"

A Darksider grabbed Stef's legs and dragged him into the hall and the wrench on his cramped limbs made him scream. Then the animal was dragging him down the hall by the heels, while boots kicked at Stef's ribs and head.

The kang knocked against the walls and floor. A human hand grabbed his testicles and twisted and he screamed again, louder than before. Then somebody, a crowd of them, human and inhuman, seized the ends of the kang and dragged him to his feet.

"Walk! Walk, you piece of shit! Walk!"

He couldn't and fell, and somebody kicked him hard in the groin and this time he did no screaming. He was unconscious.

He woke with intense light in his eyes. He was sitting in a hard duroplast chair and the sack was off his head. His eyes burned; agony rose in waves from his groin. Somebody in hard boots stamped on the bare toes of his left foot.

Stef wasn't thinking any longer, he was living in nothing but the conviction that every second some new pain would strike. *What next, what next?* Hands seized the kang and pulled it back. Other hands, some human, some inhuman, grabbed his ankles and stretched out his legs. In the blazing light he was half blind, absolutely helpless. Somebody touched his breastbone and he moaned and his stomach knotted, expecting the blow.

Nothing happened. The light dimmed. Gradually his eyes cleared. A man with a pointed head was standing before him. The man had plastic eyes that went blank when he moved his head. There was no crowd of tormentors, only two thuggi from Earth Security and one Darksider. One of the thuggi gave the other a piece of candy and they stood there, chewing. The Darksider scratched its furry backside against a wall.

"Mr. Steffens." His voice was unfamiliar—rasping, metallic.

"Yes," whispered Stef.

"I'm sending you home now. For the future, will you remember one thing?"

"Yes."

"From now on, Yamashita will continue to pay you from the accounts of the Lion House. In spite of that you'll be working for me as well as for him, and I'll expect to know everything you do and everything you discover about Crux."

Kathmann leaned forward and once again tapped Stef's breastbone.

"If you hide anything from me, I'll know it, and I'll bring you back here. Do you understand?"

"Yes."

"Next time you'll get standard treatment," added Kathman, straightening up. "Not the grandmotherly kindness you received this time."

To the thuggi he said, "Give him one more."

He left the room and a door closed. Behind the light the room flickered and a second Darksider Stef hadn't seen before approached him, holding a spiked club in its paws. *But that'll kill me*, he thought, and his eyes clamped shut on a final vision of the new Darksider raising the club for a smashing blow to his gut.

He sat there blind, waiting. Then he heard them laughing at him. He opened his eyes as one of the thuggi unlocked the kang. The other was grinning. The Darksider with the club flickered, evaporated. A three-dimensional laser image, created, Stef now saw, by projectors mounted high up on the walls.

"The boss likes to have his little joke," the thug explained with a wink. The real Darksider was still scratching its butt. Insofar as an animal could, it looked absolutely bored.

Outside was deep night or earliest morning. Wrapped in a blanket and shivering uncontrollably, Stef rode home in a polizi hovercar. Before dawn he was in his own bed, racked by pain from toes to scalp. Yet he slept, and by noon was able to creep to the balcony, dragging one foot behind him. He walked bow-legged, because his scrotum was the size of a grapefruit.

Slowly, very slowly, he prepared kif and lay down. He was starving but wouldn't have dreamed of getting up to look for food.

He smoked and the drug dulled everything, pain and hunger alike, and let him sleep. In all the world only kif was merciful. No wonder it was his religion.

By nightfall Stef was minimally better. He slept long, despite nightmares that left him drenched with sweat. By morning he was functional enough to bathe (he smelled worse than a Darksider) and dress. Then he called Yama on his mashina, hoping the polizi would monitor his call—he wanted to remind them that he had powerful friends.

"Stef. What's up?"

"I just wanted you to know that your boss Kathmann had me in the White Chamber. I'm working for him now, too."

"That son of a bitch. He hurt you much?"

"It wasn't a picnic. But I've been through worse."

"Yeah, I know you're a survivor. Well, I guess we got to share anything we find out. You got anything broken, like bones?"

"No."

"Well, at least the miserable bastard went light on you."

Stef next called a neighborhood babaku shop and ordered food. Then he found his pistol, made sure it was loaded, and returned to his kif pipe.

On the balcony he smoked and thought about ways to kill Kathmann. He had two people on his list now: Dyeva, because she wanted to destroy his world, Kathmann because he had—well, not tortured Stef; what had happened was too trivial to be called torture. No, Kathmann had simply been getting his attention in the inimitable polizi way.

This wasn't the first time in his life that Stef had been completely abased and humiliated. But he decided now that it was to be the last. He pointed his pistol at the wall and said, *"Phut."*

After Dyeva, Kathmann was next.

CHAPTER IV

That evening Professor Yang again stood before his *mashina*, which was set to Transmit and Record.

A memory cube nestled in the queue. Xenon lights arranged by his servant illuminated Yang against a background of ancient books that had been imprinted on the wall by a digital image-transfer process. (Real books were too expensive for a scholar to afford.)

Watching the interest indicator with a sharp eye, Yang launched into the second lecture of his course, "Origin of Our World." His subject today was the response to the Troubles: the slow repopulation of the Earth by humans and the reintroduction of hundreds of extinct animal species whose DNA had fortunately been preserved for low-gravity studies on Luna.

He spoke of the first halting steps toward Far Space and the gradual emergence of humanity from the cocoon of the Solar System during three hundred years of experiment and daring colonization. He spoke of the new morality that emerged from the Time of Troubles, the ecolaws that limited the size of families and prescribed a human density of no more than one person per thousand hectares of land surface on any inhabited planet. (Great populations tend to produce political instability, to say nothing of epidemics.)

He spoke of the Great Diaspora, the scattering of humankind among the stars to ensure that what had almost happened in the past could never happen again. He spoke of a species obsessed with security and order, and pointed out what a good thing it was that people had, for once, learned from the past, so that they would never have to repeat it. He spoke about the liquidation of democracy and explained the strange term as a Greek word meaning "mob rule."

He described the "magnificent tripod" on which the world order stood: the governing bureaucracy, the Security Forces, and the Space Service, comparing them to the legs of the ancient bronze *chueh* vessels in which people of the Shang Dynasty had heated wine. He ended with a kindly word about the Darksiders, friendly aliens who had joined humanity's march toward ever greater heights of stability and glory.

All across the city, students were recording the lecture. So were people who were not students but had a hunger for learning. In his apartment, Stef listened because he was still recovering from his night in the Chamber and had nothing else to do. His chief reaction to Yang's version of history was sardonic amusement.

"Onward and upward, eh?" he muttered. "Pompous old *glupetz.*"

In another shabby apartment, opening on Jesus and Buddha Court, Kuli—whose real name was Ananda—and the beautiful Dián—whose real name was Iris—also listened to Yang. Their reactions tended less to laughter and more to scorn.

"I like the bit about the Darksiders," said Ananda, fingering his rosary. "A bunch of smelly beasts our lords and masters use as mercenaries to suppress human freedom."

"You're so right," said Iris, shutting off the box. "How I hate that man."

"Oh well, he's just a professor," said Ananda tolerantly. "What can you expect. Look, is there a Crux meeting this week?"

"I don't know. Lata will have to message us, won't she? Nobody we know has been arrested. Maybe the excitement's over," she added optimistically.

"I thought Zet was getting spooked."

"Well, he's old. Old people get scared so easily."

She smiled and sat down on the arm of his chair. Ananda used his free hand to rub her smooth back. Not for the first time in history had conspiracy led to romance. The relationship had begun with talk and more talk; change the past, restore life to the victims of the Troubles, and at the same time erase this world of cruelty and injustice. Neither Ananda nor Iris could imagine that they might cease to exist if the past were changed; they thought that somehow they would continue just about as they were. Maybe better.

Growing intimate, they told each other their real names; that had been a crucial step, filled with daring trust and a quiver of fear—like their first time getting naked together. The fact that Ananda in the past had told other girls his name and had tried to recruit them for Crux was something that Iris didn't know.

Indeed, Ananda had forgotten the others, too, for he was floating in his new love like a fly in honey. In the middle of the dishevelled apartment, surrounded by discarded hard copy, rumpled bedding, a few stray cats for whom Ananda felt a brotherly concern, Iris of haunting beauty bent and touched her lips to those of the ugly young man with the rosary at his belt.

"I'd better go," she murmured. "I've got a lab." Her tone said to him, *Make me stay*.

"In a minute," said Ananda, tightening his grip. "You can go in just a minute."

2

A few streets away, in a less shabby student apartment occupied by four young women, the mashina was still playing after Yang's lecture, only now switched to a commercial program.

One of the women was insisting that she needed to make a call, but the other three were watching a story of sex among the stars called *The Other Side of the Sky* and voted her down.

"You can wait, Taka," they said firmly. Taka, who was twenty, had begun to argue when a news bulletin suddenly interrupted the transmission.

"Suppose I make my call now—" she started to say, when something about the bulletin caught her attention.

"Hush up," she told the others, who were bitterly complaining about the interruption of the story just as the hero had embraced the heroine deep in mag space.

"I want to hear this," said Taka.

After the bulletin the story quickly resumed. Taka thoughtfully retired to her bedroom and sat down on the floor, folded her slim legs gracefully under her, and reached for her compwrite. The compwrite transmitted through the mashina in the other room but gave her privacy to work.

"A letter," she said, "to—"

Who? she wondered. Daddy had always told her to obey the law but have nothing to do with the polizi, who were, he said, scum, *gryaz*, filth. How then to get her information to them without using the boxcode that had appeared on the screen during the newsflash?

"To Professor Yang, History Faculty," she began, rattling off the university address code from memory. "Send this with no return address, *oké?*"

"I am waiting, O woman of transcendent beauty," said the compwrite. Taka had taught it to say that and was now trying to make it learn how to giggle.

"Honored Professor, I am sending this to you as a person I honor and trust and admire," she began, laying it on thick.

"I have always been a law-abiding person and there was a news bulletin just now where the polizi were asking for information about a terrorist group called the Crooks. Well, a student named Ananda, when he was trying to climb aboard—scratch that, make love to me—a couple of months ago, stated that he belonged to this group and tried to make it seem incredibly important, though I had never heard of it myself up to that time. In any case my native dialect is English and I happen to know what Crooks means and I was angry that somebody would try to involve me in something criminal.

"Hoping that you will convey this info to the proper authorities, I remain one of your students choosing to remain anonymous."

She viewed this missive on the screen and then added, "PS, this Ananda is an ugly guy with a rosary of some kind he wears on his belt. I think he's an O.B. He is skinny and wears a funny kind of cross under his jacket. He says it is a symbol of something I forget what."

She added, "Send," and headed back into the front room, where the current chapter of *The Other Side of the Sky* had expired in a shudder of Far Space orgasms.

"Well, I suppose I can make my call now," she said, and did so, setting up an appointment for tomorrow with the mashina of a depilator who had promised to leave her arms and legs as smooth as baby flesh, which she thought would look very nice.

3

Professor Yang's infatuation with Selina was leading him deeper and deeper into debt. He tried to stay away from Radiant Love House, but instead found himself dreaming of the White Tiger all day and heading for the District by hovercab at least three times a week.

He told himself all the usual things—that this was ridiculous in a man his age, that he would lose face if his frequent visits became known, that he couldn't afford this new extravagance. No argument could sway him; he wanted his woman of ivory in the blue peace of the electronic room where for an hour at least he feasted on the illusion of youth regained.

He was again in the expensive parlor waiting for the White Tiger when Stef lounged in and collapsed on the double divan.

Ordinarily, Yang would have ignored the fellow, but when Stef said, "How are you, Honored Professor?" he felt he had to say something in return.

"Quite well." Brief, cool.

"I watched your last lecture," said Stef, who was inclined to chat, knowing that as usual he had time to kill before Dzhun could receive him.

"Really," said Yang, thawing slightly. He was paid .10 khan for every box that tuned in to his lectures. It wasn't much, but he needed every tenth he could get.

"Yeah. I'm not a student, but I am ill-educated and I occasionally try to improve my mind, such as it is."

Stef pulled over a wheeled censer, dumped a little kif into it from a pouch he carried, and turned on the heating element.

"Inhale?" he asked, unwinding two hoses and handing one to Yang.

"The waiting is tiresome," Yang allowed, and took an experimental puff. Finding the quality acceptable (local kif, not Martian, but pretty good), he took another.

"May I ask your profession?"

"Investigative agent. I'm also a licensed member of the Middlemen and Fixers' Guild."

"Ah." Yang looked at Stef sharply. "Are you good at what you do?"

"Well, I live by it and have for years. Why? Need something looked into?"

"Actually," said Yang slowly, "I received an anonymous letter last evening and I've been wondering how to handle it. It claims to place in my hands certain information that I, ah, feel somebody in authority ought to know. Yet I have no way of checking it or naming the sender, who claims to be a student of mine. It may be worthless; on the other hand, if it's useful, well—"

"You'd like to be paid for it," said Stef promptly. "I can handle that. Insulate you from the polizi. There are ways to handle it confidentially and at the same time claim a reasonable reward if the information's good. What's it all about?"

Yang thought for a moment and then said, "It concerns something called Crux."

All of Stef's long training was just barely sufficient to enable him to keep a *marmolitz*—a marble face.

"Ah," he said, clearing his throat, "the thing the polizi were asking for information about?"

"Yes."

Briefly he told Stef about the letter, withholding, however, the name Ananda and his description.

"What do you think it might be worth?"

"How happy I am," interrupted the box in the corner, "to inform you, honored guest, that Dzhun is now ready to receive you."

"Tell her to wait," said Stef.

To Yang he said, "Let me try to find out if the matter's really important. If so, I wouldn't hesitate to ask ten thousand khans in return for such information."

"Ten *thousand*?"

The kif pipe fell out of his mouth.

"It must be something major," Stef pointed out, "or it wouldn't have been put on the air. At the same time, I would recommend caution. This is clearly a security matter, and you certainly wouldn't want to expose yourself to the suspicion of knowing more than you actually do. That's a short path to the White Chamber and *shosho*. Luckily, I have a friend on the inside who's not polizi and can make inquiries."

"And your, ah, fee?" asked Yang.

"A flat ten percent of the award. I'm an ethical investigator."

"Good heavens," said Yang, who was perfectly indifferent to Stef's professional ethics but whose mind was engaged in dividing K9,000 by 120 to reach the astounding figure of seventy-five hourlong sessions with the White Tiger in the electronic room.

"What do you need?" he asked.

"Your chop on my standard contract, one sheet of hardcopy with the message, and about two days."

"You shall, my friend," said Professor Yang rather grandly, "have all three."

4

Yama and Stef sat at the duroplast desk in the Lion House staring at the hardcopy.

"One name. And what a crappy description. Maybe I should turn Yang over to Kathmann just to see if he knows anything more."

"An honored professor? Come on, Yama. Stop thinking like a security gorilla for once. Yang doesn't know a damn thing except that he needs money to rent his albino. What we need is to find this Ananda."

"How? Call in the polizi?"

"Hell, no. Get the credit yourself. First of all, access the university records. Tell your mashina to search for Ananda as both a family name and a given name. Let's say for the last two years. Do you have access to the polizi and city records?"

"That's Security Central stuff," said Yama with a cunning look. "It's off-limits to us. Of *course* my contact over there has access."

"When you get some names from the university, have the box start calling their numbers and checking the faces of these

Anandas. That'll eliminate some—they can't all be skinny, ugly guys—and meanwhile you can be having the names checked against the polizi records for arrests and against the city records for everything else—property ownership, energy payments, tax payments, everything. Then there's the Old Believer angle—"

Yama was already talking to his box. "I want confidential access to university records. Now."

He turned back to Stef. "By the way, how much is this costing me, assuming it leads to anything?"

"If it leads to Crux, I promised Yang fifteen thousand."

"Petty cash," said Yama. "If it leads to Crux."

The box chimed. "Sir, I have accessed the university central administrative files."

"Search admission, registration, and expulsion records for the name Ananda," said Yama promptly, "especially expulsion." He added to Stef, "Terrorists are often students, but very few of them are good students."

Dreaming of the money, Stef paced the room impatiently. The university records were voluminous and ill kept. There was no Ananda as a family name. Searching given names was just getting underway—"This baby does it in nanoseconds," promised Yama—when the whole university system went down. And stayed down.

After more than an hour of waiting and pacing and dreaming of kif, Stef lounged out, holding his nose until he was past the Darksider, and took a hovercab home. There he called Earth Central and reported to one of Kathmann's aides that he and Yama were following down an anonymous tip that a student was a member of Crux.

Then he called Yang and told him that the money was practically in hand. Yang was ecstatic.

"You don't know what this means to me, honored investigative agent," he bubbled. "I've had so many calls on my purse lately."

"I know what you mean."

"What do you think this Crux organization might be?"

"I don't have the slightest idea," Stef lied. "In English the word means, uh, the essential thing. Like the crux of an argument."

"Of course there's also the Latin meaning."

"What's Latin?"

"It's a dead language. The original source of the word. In Latin it means cross. Hence the crossroads, the critical point."

"Ananda wears a funny kind of cross," said Stef slowly.

"Yes. My informant thought he was an Old Believer."

"I wonder—"

Stef's box chimed. He quickly made arrangements to bring Yang his payoff and cut the circuit.

"Say," he told the box.

"Stef, I got the names," said Yama, abrupt as usual. "Got your recorder on? Here they are. Last year, Govind Ananda, withdrawn. This year, Patal Ananda, Nish Ananda, Sivastheni Ananda. That's all."

"Boxcodes?"

"Got 'em all except Govind. Like so many of those damn students, he may have a pirated mashina. I'm having the box call the ones we've got, and at the same time start running through the city records. Got any more bright ideas?"

"No," said Stef, "except I want a vacation when this is over. And my pay."

"Stop kidding me, I know you'll take your pay out of old Yang's reward money. Don't try to . . . wait a minute. Box reports Patal and Sivas-whatever don't resemble the description. Nish is away from home. Wait a minute again. Govind Ananda paid the energy bill on Number 71, Jesus and Buddha Court. Didn't the letter say something about a rosary? And about him being an O.B.?"

"Keep trying Nish, Yama, but send three or four of your

thuggi to meet me at J and B Court. I'm going to try Govind. I like the smell of that address. It's near the University and the names would echo for an Old Believer."

"You got 'em. Plus a Darksider in case things get rough."

"And a gas mask."

Stef rang off, plunged into a battered Korean-style chest on his balcony, and brought out his one-centimeter impact pistol. He touched the clip control and chambered one of the fat, black-headed rounds.

Action elated him, freed him from his memories of being beaten, his sense of uselessness. Suddenly he felt wonderful, better than when he was on kif, better than when he was drunk, almost better than when he was about to make love. A flutter of fear in his belly was part of the frisson. So was the taste of iron filings beginning to fill his mouth.

He rummaged through his closet, dragged out his most ample jacket, tore the right-hand pocket to give him access to the space between cloth and lining. Hand in pocket, he pressed the gun against his ribs to hide any bulge and slipped through the door, listening to it click behind him, wondering if he would ever unlatch it again.

He whispered a good-bye to Dzhun. On the roof he signalled for a hovercab.

"Jesus and Buddha Court," he said, when one drew up.

The cab's black box said, *"Gratizor."*

CHAPTER V

On Lake Bai in the evening the tinkle of samisen music mixed with the thrumming of a Spanish guitar, the notes falling like lemon and oleander flowers into the dark, cold water.

Half a click down in the huge lake—really a freshwater inland sea—glacial ice still lingered, surviving into the heat of an earth warmer than it had been since the noontime of the dinosaurs. Shrieking happily, goose-pimpled swimmers were leaping into the water from the floating docks of lakeside villas. Farther on, strings of Japanese lanterns illuminated teahouses and casinos and slider-rinks where the children of grandees cavorted on expensive cushions of air.

Back in the hills, spotlights illuminated palaces. Bijou villas lined the shores, and on the veranda of one of the smaller ones Stef and Dzhun idled, wearing light evening robes and not much else. Dzhun kept returning to Stef's account of the raid, trying to get the story straight.

"So these terrorists—did you shoot them?"

"Didn't have to. I've seldom felt like such a fool in my life."

Stef gestured lazily, and Dzhun disturbed herself long enough to pour champagne. The grapes of Siberia were justly famous, the flavor supposedly improved by the low background radiation.

"The terrorists weren't dangerous?"

"Pair of dumb kids. The boy wearing his funny cross and the girl with the same symbol tattooed on her hand, if you can believe that. The Darksider smashed the door in and let out a roar and they both fainted dead away. Then I jumped in yelling and the thuggi followed, and suddenly the four of us were prancing around waving weapons at two unconscious children. Ridiculous scene.

"I almost puked when I had to hand them over to the polizi. Not that there was anything else I could do, with the thuggi and the Darksider there. I was sure Kathmann would tear them limb from limb, but Yama says they woke up spilling their guts. The polizi have got 'em locked up, of course, but Security got everything they wanted in the first three minutes."

"Dyeva."

"Absolutely. Iris and Ananda said she'd come in by the Luna shuttle on such and such a day. That was enough. Kathmann called Yama. Yama has shuttle data at his fingertips, there were only four females of the right age on that one, and they all checked out except Akhmatova Maria from a planet called Ganesh, which is, just like it was supposed to be, in the Lion Sector. She stepped off the shuttle and vanished.

"So now they got her hologram, plus retinographs, voiceprints, DNA, all that stuff they take when you get a passport. The kids have positively identified her. Dyeva's been made, for whatever good it may do us.

"It was an eventful day. The kids had met Dyeva at a villa outside town, so the polizi descended on that and bagged the owner. He went straight to the Chamber and promptly gave them the name of another member of the cell, a woman who has so far evaded capture. A demand for information went out to Ganesh at maximum power and with the most awful threats that Yama could think of on the spur of the moment.

"He'd just laid all this information on Oleary's desk when another call comes in from Security Central. Kathmann's got the wormholer. Gadget takes a hell of a lot of juice, so his mashini were watching the Ulanor power grid for unusual current surges. Well, a surge of the right size occurred, and Kathmann's guy Yost arrived at the meter with half a dozen Darksiders to find the wormholer standing all by itself in a deserted warehouse in the northwest quadrant."

Dzhun was frowning. "Then that means—"

"You and I may vanish at any moment," Stef grinned. "Dyeva's presumably in the twenty-first century trying to prevent the Time of Troubles. I wish her luck. How's she going to do it?"

"And we're here."

"And we're here, relaxing, courtesy of the payoff to Yang. My success in cracking Crux convinced Yama that I'm the guy to stop Dyeva. He offered me a hundred thousand to go after her. I laughed in his face."

"Then who'll do the job?"

"Some thuggi from Earth Central who're under military discipline and can't say no."

"And what'll happen to her?"

"In the twenty-first century? Probably get killed by the surface traffic. Or catch a fatal disease. Or get lost in the crowds. I wouldn't trust Kathmann's idiots to find their peckers when they need to piss. Dyeva's safe enough from them."

Later, he and Dzhun wandered up the shingled beach to a waterside inn that served caviar and Peking duck and other edibles. People of the upper and underworld were crowded together at small tables, eating and drinking. Blue clouds of kif drifted from open censers over the crowd, relaxing everybody.

Dzhun, who had an indelicate appetite, was just piling into her dessert when the haunting notes of a synthesizer drifted like pollen across vast, cool Lake Bai. A band floated up in an open hovercar, and a *sisi* with a piercingly sweet voice performed a popular air, "This Dewdrop World," whose simple theme was eat, drink, and be merry, for tomorrow you die.

The crowd loved it; silver half-khans and even a few gold khans showered the car. Whenever a coin fell in the water, a musician jumped in after it like a frog and clambered back into the car with the coin in his mouth.

It was a fine end to the evening. When Stef and Dzhun left the restaurant the air had the lingering chill of spring and the scent of lemon groves that were blossoming in the hills. Dzhun pulled Stef's arm like a scarf around her neck and started to sing the song again. He leaned over her, hugged her close. It was at moments like this that he almost envied people who were foolish enough to fall in love.

"That's a wonderful song," she said. "It's so nice to be sad. Sadness goes with joy like plums with duck."

Didn't statements like that mean that she was, after all, a bit more than just a whore? Stef hugged her tighter, breathing in her offworld perfume with the chilly scent of the lemon groves.

They had an amorous night and spent next morning lolling on the deck with their usual strong green tea. They were supposed to start back to the city today, and Dzhun was looking abstracted.

"Can't wait to get back and go to work?" Stef smiled.

"Stef . . . there's something I have to tell you."

"What?"

"My senator wants to set me up in a little house in Karakorum. He's jealous, and it'll be the end for you and me."

That produced silence. Stef cleared his throat, drank tea.

"Ah. So this trip was a kiss-off."

"It doesn't have to be."

"Meaning?"

Dzhun said, eyes cast down, "I'd rather live with you."

"No," said Stef.

Dzhun sat down, still not looking at him.

"I thought you'd say that. I've never bothered you with my life story because I thought you'd get bored and angry. But let me tell you just a little. My family needed money, so they sold me into the District when I was nine. The owner rented me to one of his customers. The night he raped me, I almost bled to death.

"By the time I was twelve I was a registered whore, a member of the guild. It took me three more years to pay off my debts because in the District the houses charge you for everything, heat, water, towels, mediscanning, almost for the air you breathe. But I was beautiful and earning good money and I was out of debt by the time I was sixteen. Now I'm almost eighteen and I'm sick of it all. I don't want to be a *robotchi* anymore.

"I hear people talk about going to the stars and I've never been out of Ulanor. I can barely read and write and if Selina hadn't taught me some arithmetic so they couldn't cheat me, I wouldn't be able to add two and two. I don't know anything, all I do is live from night to night—up at sixteen, to bed at eight. I've had dozens of diseases—sida six times—and the last time it took me a whole month to recover. The house doctor says my immune system's collapsing, whatever that means.

"I've got to get out of the life, Stef. I want to live with you, but if you don't want me I'm going with my senator. He has some funny tastes and three wives and he's old, but he's also kindhearted and rich, and that's enough."

She stopped, still looking down at the floor. Stef was staring at Dzhun and clenching his fists. He felt as if a favorite dog had just bitten him. Twice, in fact—once by threatening to leave him, and once by demanding a commitment from him.

"I don't want anything fancy," Dzhun went on. "I want to live in a house with a garden. I want to get up in the morning and go to bed at night. I want to go to school before I'm too old and learn something about the world. I can see you're angry with me. Well, so be it. If you're too angry to pay my way back to the city, well, screw you. I'll get the shuttle by myself."

She stood up and walked somewhat unsteadily into the house, taking by habit the little mincing steps they taught the girls—and the boys as well—in Radiant Love House.

Half an hour later she came back out, dressed for the road. Stef was leaning on the railing, looking down into deep and black Lake Bai.

Stef said, "I'm poor. I'm a loner. I'm a kif head."

"So you can't afford me, don't want me, and don't need me because kif's better. Right? So, good bye."

"Can you fend off your senator for a while?"

"Not forever. He can buy what he wants, and I don't want to lose him."

"I guess I could set up housekeeping with a hundred thousand," Stef muttered. "But maybe I can bargain for more."

Dzhun collapsed rather than sat down and drew the longest breath of her life. She put her hands over her face as if she was weeping, though in fact she had stopped crying many years before and her face was hot and dry.

Her mind was running on many things, but chiefly on her friend Selina's brainstorm, the wonderful invention of the senator, who, of course, did not really exist.

2

"So you'll do it," said Yama.

"For a million khans. Paid in advance. I want something to leave to my heirs in the event I don't come back."

"That's a bunch of fucking money."

"There's one more thing I want. Get those two kids I captured turned loose. Otherwise Kathmann will sooner or later cut their heads off."

Yama frowned. "He'll never turn them loose. They're young and the girl's beautiful, so he'll want to mutilate them. In my opinion he's saving them for something special. That's the way Kathmann is—he's a fucking sadist, as you of all people ought to know."

"Try anyway."

"It's hopeless. But if I can save them I will."

When Stef had gone, Yama set out to sell his prize agent to the *fromazhi*. He expected trouble with Kathmann but none developed; the chief of Earth Security was assembling an assassination team under Major Yost to kill Dyeva, and viewed Stef's mission as a chance to test the wormholer. Ugaitish, Admiral Hrka, and Xian were ready to try anything and put their chops on the proposal without a murmur. It was Yama's own boss, Oleary, who objected because of the cost.

"Why don't you go yourself?" he demanded. "It'd be cheaper."

"Sir, I'll go if you say to. But I got a wife and four kids."

"That's two more than the ecolaws allow."

"I got an exemption."

Oleary stared at Stef's file, frowning.

"What's wrong with this guy? I don't trust him. Why did he have to leave the service in the first place?"

"Sir, he's a great agent. Brave, quick, adaptable. But he's got a soft spot in his head. He's sentimental. You can't be a cop and be sentimental. A long time ago he helped a woman thief who was headed for the White Chamber to escape. Well, I found out about it, so I did my duty and turned Steffens in."

Oleary kept on frowning.

"If he's sentimental about women, what about when he has to kill, what's her name, Dyeva?"

"Sir, she's different. She's threatening his whole world, including this little tart he seems to be in love with."

"Oh, well," said Oleary, shrugging. "Send him, I guess. Can't hurt. But take the money back if he doesn't succeed. How could I justify a budget item like that for a failure?"

3

"You go tomorrow," said Yama. "Here's some stuff to study tonight."

Stef took the packet of copy, caught an official hovercar, and flew straight to Radiant Love House. The long farewell that followed left Stef weeping, and Dzhun—once the door had closed behind him—smiling at prospects that seemed equally bright whether he survived his mission or not.

Back home, he settled down on the balcony to study the three items that Yama had provided him: a hologram of Dyeva, a summary of her life on Ganesh, and a map of ancient Moscow. The map got little more than a glance; he needed to be on-site to use it. Dyeva's hologram was another matter. Stef studied it as closely as if she, and not Dzhun, was his lover, imprinting on his mind Dyeva's round Tartar face, high cheekbones, and unreadable eyes.

Then her biography. To his surprise, the hard copy with its STATE SECRET/BEHEADER stamp had been written by Professor Yang. Liking the taste of polizi money, he'd gone to work for Yama as a volunteer agent, and his first task had been writing up and annotating Dyeva's life story.

Settlers of the Shiva system had been led by a devout Hindu who had hoped to establish a refuge for members of all the old faiths—Muslims, Christians, Jews, and Buddhists as well as his own people—where, far from corruption and unbelief, peace and justice and the worship of God could reign for all time.

"The actual results of this noble experiment," wrote Yang, "were not without irony." In the process of settlement three intelligent species had been destroyed, and among the humans religious wars and bitter sectarian disputes had constituted much of the system's subsequent history.

Akhmatova Maria was born to a devout family on the third planet, Ganesh. They maintained Christian belief according to the Russian Orthodox rite and hated both their neighbors of other faiths and the depraved and godless civilization of other planets. In time she lost her own faith in God, but adopted in its place the religion of humanity. Her private life remained austere; she had neither male nor female lovers, and the name she took in the movement which she helped to found, Dyeva, meant virgin in Russian, her native dialect.

She was attending the local academy when news of the technical advances that allowed invention of the wormholer, gave her the great project of her life. She was one of a group of people loosely connected with the academy who formed a scheme to undo the Time of Troubles by returning to the past. Some members of her group transferred to the University of the Universe in Ulanor, where they made converts to their views and laid plans to build—later on, learning that one had already been built, to steal—a wormholer.

Then came a part of the account that Yama had marked in red. Dyeva's theory that the Troubles could be prevented rested upon a verbal tradition among the Russian Christians of Ganesh: that a man named Razruzhenye, the defense minister of ancient Russia when the troubles began, ordered the first thermo-bio strike upon China and that this attack launched the Time of Troubles. Killing this one individual might well prevent the war and undo the whole course of disasters that followed.

"So," muttered Stef.

It seemed a little strange to him that Dyeva, who believed in the absolute value of life, was returning to the past to kill someone. But Yang in a footnote pointed out that such things had happened many times in the past: people who believed in freedom imprisoned freedom's enemies; those who believed in life murdered anybody who seemed to threaten it.

"I guess that's reasonable, in an unreasonable way," Stef thought.

He ate a little and fell into bed. He woke when his mashina chimed, stumbled through a bath, and confronted a large box of ridiculous clothing that had been prepared according to Professor Yang's designs, based on what men wore in the mosaics of the Moscow subway.

At 7:75, a government hovercar picked Stef off the roof and flew him to a neighborhood that he knew only too well, a cluster of huge anonymous buildings with vaguely menacing forms. The car flashed past the ziggurat Palace of Justice in whose cellars Stef had tasted the joys of interrogation.

This time, however, the huge pentagonal block of Space Central—Admiral Hrka's HQ, with the world's best equipped laboratories—was the goal. Since Kathmann had too hastily killed the builders of the wormholer, he now had to depend on Space Service experts to analyze and work it.

The hovercar descended through a well in the courtyard that wits called the Navel of the Universe. Yama met Stef as he climbed down from the car into a sunless areaway paved with black hexagonal stone blocks. He led him down one narrow blank corridor after another, past huge stinking Darksiders armed with impact weapons, into a vaulted underground room with a gleaming contraption standing in the center of the floor among a jungle of thick gray cables.

"So that's it," said Stef, interested by his own lack of interest. At the center of the wormholer was a two-meter cube with a round opening in one side, whose purpose he could easily guess.

Blue-coated techs helped him into a heavy coat with wide lapels and big pockets, slipped an impact pistol into the right-hand coat pocket, and slid a black power pack with a small control box into the left. Somebody stuck a chilly metal button into his left ear.

64   Albert E. Cowdrey

"Pay attention to the control," said Yama. "Take it in your hand. Now. Red button: job's done, bring me home. *Oké?* White button: I need help, send backup now. Black button: hold onto your ass, Dyeva's succeeded, and your world is finished. The power pack feeds a little tiny built-in mag-space transponder that emits a kind of cosmic squeak for one microsecond. The signal crosses time exactly the way it crosses space, don't ask me why. That's what we'll be listening for. Then we have to pull you back, send help, or—"

"Grab your butts. I see. But that also means you could just cut me off, leave me there, save yourselves a million."

"Yeah, we could but we won't. Hell, I really mean *I* won't. Not," he smiled, "for a measly million that isn't even my money."

They stared at each other, until Stef managed a weak grin.

"That's good enough. Any problems?"

"Yes," said Stef, "lots. I don't speak Russian. I've got no goddamn idea how to find Dyeva even if I land in Moscow at the right time. I—"

Yama took Stef's arm and began to walk him toward the wormholer.

"Don't worry about the language. That thing in your ear will translate for you. And don't worry about the time. A register inside the machine recorded the day Dyeva chose, the three hundred thirty-first day of 2091. So we're sending you to that same date in hopes she's close to the point of exit. If she's not, you'll have to find her."

"How?"

"Come on, Stef. I sold the others on you because of your adaptability. This whole world you're going into vanished in a cloud of dust. How much can anybody know about it? There's just no way to be systematic."

They stopped beside the huge glittering gadget.

"I really envy you," said Yama in a choked voice. "This is the most crucial moment in human history. You're the plumed knight of our world, like Yoshitsune, like Saladin, like Richard the Lion-Hearted."

Yama embraced him. "Take care, my old friend, and *kill that fucking virgin.*"

An instant later the techs had helped Stef into the wormholer and closed the heavy door, which looked like a nine-petal steel chrysanthemum. Yama stepped back, wiping his eyes. Kathmann had now arrived to observe the action and Yama joined him.

"Well, that's one less friend I got," said Yama. "This job of mine is hell. How are the preparations going for Yost's assassination team, General?"

"As fast as possible. Of course they're the ones who'll really do the job."

"There's a chance that Steffens might pull it off alone."

"Yeah," said Kathmann, "and there's a chance I might be the next Solar System Controller. *Svidanye*" (See you later), he added. "Some more members of Crux have been arrested and I got work to do in the Chamber."

CHAPTER VI

In the wormholer, seated as he had been instructed, knees drawn up, chin down, arms around his shins, sweltering in the heavy coat, feeling the pistol grate against his ribs, Stef tried to imagine Dzhun's face, but found that it, like everything else, was inadequate to explain to him why he was where he was.

The excitement he'd felt earlier was gone, replaced by mere dread. He could only suppose that his entire life had been leading up to one moment of supreme folly, and this was it.

Then a great violet-white light flashed through him, he felt an instant of supernatural cold, and he was sitting on a gritty sidewalk against a damp stuccoed wall.

He raised his face. The day was overcast, and a restless throng of thick-bodied people wrapped up against the autumn chill hurried past, not one of them paying him the slightest heed.

He looked higher. Behind the solid walls of elderly, three-story buildings with flaking plaster and paint he saw high polished towers of what looked like mirror duroplast. Immense crimson letters hovered just below the lowest layer of murk.

Since Alspeke was written in Cyrillic letters, he had no trouble reading *Moskovskaya Fondovaya Birzha,* and when he murmured the words aloud a soft atonal voice in his ear translated: Moscow Stock Exchange. Below the sign was a huge blue banner saying 1991–2091.

Slowly he got to his feet, staggered, caught himself against the wall. A pretty young woman paused, stared at him, then drew a pale furry hood around her face and hurried on.

A couple of teenagers stopped also, looked at him and grinned. They squawked to each other in seabirds' voices.

"What's this asshole dressed up for?"

"Must think he's Stalin or something. Hey, asshole—where'd you get that coat?"

A stout woman stopped suddenly and shook her fist at the kids.

"You leave that man alone! Can't you see he's crazy? He's got troubles enough without you hooligans pestering him."

A little man in a checkered coat stopped and joined her.

"Show some respect!" he shouted at the kids.

"What, for a guy dressed up like Stalin, for Christ's sake? Hey you," said a teenager to Stef. "You going to a party?"

Unfortunately, the translator didn't answer questions, and Stef just stared at him.

"My God, he's deaf and dumb, and you're harassing him," said the woman in scandalized tones.

By now a little crowd had gathered. Everybody had an opinion. It was the adults against the teenagers.

"You little bastards got no respect for anybody!"

"Not for you, Granddaddy."

"Call me Granddaddy? Yes, I've got grandchildren, but thank God they're nothing like you, you little pimp."

In the confusion, Stef managed to slip away, leaving them arguing behind him. In an alleyway he unbuttoned the coat and stared down at the tunic and coarse trousers jammed into boots. The clothes were *nothing* like what people were wearing on the street. Already the stiff, knee-high boots of faux leather were beginning to chafe his toes, and he hadn't walked more than a hundred meters.

Cursing Yang, he tried to decide what to do. While he pondered, he worked his way from alleyway to alleyway until he suddenly spotted, among the hundreds of small shops lining the street—Boris Yeltsin Street—a shop with a sign that said *Kostyumi*. He didn't need the translator for that.

Thirty minutes later, Stef emerged from the costume shop wearing acceptable clothes, short soft boots, baggy trousers, a faux astrakhan hat, and a long warm padded jacket. In his pockets were thirty ten-ruble notes, the difference between the value of the handsome and practically new theatrical garb he'd sold the shop's owner and that of the secondhand, ill-fitting stuff he'd bought from him.

He slipped into the crowd, which was denser than the center of Ulanor on Great Genghis Day. The street traffic was noisy and thick, everybody driving headlong as if their odd, whining little electric cars were assaulting a position. Above, the air traffic was thin, almost absent—a few primitive rotary-wing machines with shapes so bizarre that Stef thought at first that they were some sort of giant insect life. Jet trails streaked far above, making him wonder if airpackets already flew from Luna.

Between street and sky, strung on cables, hundreds of blue banners fluttered, all saying 1991–2091, and sometimes 100 YEARS OF THE DEMOCRATIC REPUBLIC, whatever that meant. He could see no mention of Tsar Stalin the Good.

His next stop was in front of a huge window filled with flickering mashini. Stef was surprised to see that the images made by the boxes were three-dimensional—he had expected something less advanced—though the technology was crude, merely a rough illusion created on a flat screen.

His eyes roved past a ballet and half a dozen sports programs. Russian *futbol* teams had dominated world play in the season just past, but what would the hockey season bring forth? Young people dashed around on grass or ice while the announcer talked.

Nobody at all seemed to be thinking about the danger of universal destruction. Stef shook his head, amazed at the ordinariness of this world, so close to its end. People who would soon be dust and ashes jostled him and he felt astonished at their solidity, their obvious confidence that they would exist for a long time to come.

A single screen was tuned to a news program called *Vremya* and he moved a few meters to watch it. A young woman with a fantastic pile of yellow hair spoke of the Russian-led international team now hard at work establishing the Martian colony and the problems it was facing. People on Mars, needing to communicate despite a babel of tongues, were developing a jargon all their own; the American members of the colony called it All-Speak. It was mostly Russian and English, with a flavoring of words from twenty other languages.

Meanwhile a new condominium development on Luna marked the transformation of that spartan base, barely seventy years old, into a genuine city, the first on another world. Space had never looked better; Russia's own program, after a long eclipse, again led the world. Here on earth things were not so encouraging. There were new outbreaks of Blue Nile hemorrhagic fever. The Forty Years' War continued in the Rocky Mountains; the weak U.S. central government seemed unable to conquer the rebels, and United Nations peacekeepers had again been massacred in Montana.

But the big worry was that border tensions continued to mount in Mongolia, where Chinese forces had occupied Ulan Bator. The name caused Stef to press his nose against the glass. He had heard enough of Yang's lecture to know that Ulan Bator was the origin of the name Ulanor, even though the city the announcer was talking about was now—now?—nothing more than a mound on the green forested banks of the River Tuul.

According to Yang, a few survivors of the Troubles had trekked northward, bringing the name with them and applying it to a cluster of yurts in an endless snowstorm. Later, because it had low background radiation, the place had become the site of the Worldcity—a strange fate for a Mongol encampment that had survived the Two Year Winter for no better reason than the sheer unkillable toughness of its people and an endless supply of frozen yak meat, which they had softened by sleeping on it and eaten raw for lack of firewood.

Another name caught Stef's attention. "Defense minister Razumovsky has declared that Russia, together with its European and American allies, will stand firm against further aggression by the Imperial People's Republic of China."

Defense minister Razumovsky? That wasn't the word he had learned, the name of the man Dyeva was supposed to kill. It was another Raz word, Raz, raz—*Razruzhenye.*

He must have said the word aloud without meaning to, for his translator murmured, "Destruction."

Stef nodded. Sure. In the folk memory, Minister Razumovsky became Minister Destruction. The name was wrong, but the tradition might still be correct.

Razumovsky suddenly appeared in a clip. He had a wide, flat face like a frog someone had stepped on. He seemed to talk with his fists as much as his mouth, pounding on a podium while he spoke of Russia's sacred borders and of China's presumption, now that it had conquered Korea and Japan, that all East Asia belonged to the Dragon Republic.

"They'll find out different if they mess with us!" Razumovsky bawled, and loud cheering broke out among a crowd seated in something called the Duma. "They think they can threaten us with their rockets, but our Automated Space Defense System is the most advanced in the world. I spit upon their threats!" More cheering.

Then a weighty, white-maned man came on, identified as President Rostoff. His message was of conciliation and peace. "As the leader of the Western Alliance, Russia bears a grave responsibility to act with all due caution. Our guard is up, but we extend as well the hand of friendship to our Chinese brothers and sisters."

Stef smiled; across the centuries, he recognized without difficulty the ancient game of good cop–bad cop. He moved on, meditating on a final line from the announcer: that the debate on the Mongolian situation would continue in the Duma tonight, and that the president and the cabinet would again be present. Was that why Dyeva had picked this particular day to return to the past?

2

Consulting his map, he walked down a gentle declivity where the street widened into an avenue called Great Polyanka and rose to the marble pylons of a new gleaming bridge. Beyond a small river he saw red walls, gold onion domes, palaces of white stone—the Kremlin.

Pleasure boats with glass roofs slid lazily along the river, which was divided here by a long island. In the boats Stef could see brightly dressed people dancing. Then the crowd swept him onto the other bank, past the Aleksandrovsky Gardens and up a gentle rise. Here the throng divided; most people passed on, but some joined a long queue that had formed at a brick gatehouse.

Stef continued with the majority along the autumnal garden and the crenellated wall into Red Square. He stared like any tourist at a cathedral like a kif-head's dream and then, feeling tired and hungry, crossed the square and drifted into the archways of a huge building that filled the far side, a market of some sort crowded with shops and loudly bargaining people. At a stall that sold writing paper, Stef bought a small notebook, an envelope, and an object he had never seen before—a pen that emitted ink.

The building held eating places, too. Hungrily, Stef found himself a place at a small table in one of them and ordered *shchi* without knowing what cabbage was. Soon a bowl of hot greenish soup lay steaming before him, along with a sliced onion and a chunk of dense and delicious brown bread and sweet butter. It was the first time he'd ever tasted butter from a cow, since all the Earth's cattle had died in the Troubles. It had a subtle, complex flavor and an unctuous texture quite different from the manufactured stuff he knew.

He devoured it all, licked his fingers as the other diners were doing, and paid with a few of his rubles. Then, still sitting at the table, he laboriously wrote a few lines, tore out the page, and sealed it in an envelope which he addressed to Xian in care of Yama. He thrust the message deep into a trouser pocket and left the eating place smiling grimly; in case something went wrong, this note was another legacy he hoped to leave behind him.

He returned to Red Square to find that in his absence it had become almost unbearably beautiful. A light autumn snow had begun to fall, streetlights were coming on, and the bizarre cathedral of Saint Basil floated in its own illumination, more than ever a dream.

Shadows, light, and snow turned everything to magic. Strolling past were young people with faces as white and pink as dawn clouds, and among them stout men in astrakahns and elegant women in faux ermine. Old women hawked apples that could have been plucked from their own cheeks.

A little band began to play somewhere as Stef slowly retraced his steps, out of the square and up to a floodlit gate in the Kremlin wall. People were streaming in, all talking excitedly, and Stef followed.

Inside, he moved with difficulty through the throng gathering at a big, anonymous new building with the words DUMA OF THE RUSSIAN PEOPLE in gold letters above the doors. Guards in hats of faux fur were trying to keep a roadway open here, pushing people back but, to Stef's surprise, using no whips. Considering what he had always heard about the Tsars, the mildness of this government was astonishing. He circled the crowd, his mind now centered on Dyeva's hologram, searching faces of which there seemed no end, countless faces, all different, none hers.

Away from the Duma the Kremlin grounds were more open. In the last light, huge rooks wearing gray patches on their wings like shawls flew from one bare tree to another, cawing their complaints about the human invasion. Where to look next for Dyeva? She'd been an Old Believer, hadn't she?

Stef wandered into a small church that looked like a glittering lacquered box. Gold-haloed saints ascended every wall and hung suspended in the red depths of the ceiling; ghostly notes of song showered down, although he could see nobody singing. He stood amazed, gawking, as if he'd wandered into someone else's dream. Was this the interior of an Old Believer's mind, this place of fantastic images and magical unity?

Around him people knelt, prayed or, like Stef, simply stood and looked on. An old woman rose, crossed herself, and jostled Stef on her way out. Another, and younger, woman wearing a fur hat and a long coat rose and turned to go. Either Dyeva or her twin sister passed so close to Stef that he could have touched her.

3

After a stunned instant of surprise he followed, out into the dry fresh-falling snow, the lights and shadows of dusk. The rooks had settled into their nests. She didn't walk, she strode, eyes straight ahead. He followed her along a winding path, keeping one or two people between them. He was looking for a place to kill her, a dark corner, a moment of privacy.

Then he realized that he didn't need privacy. Left hand on the red button of the transponder, he gripped his weapon with his right, raising the barrel a little in his coat pocket. He would kill her in the open and escape where nobody could follow. He only had to make absolutely sure that this was his quarry. He stepped off the path, the dry snow crunched under his boots, he hastened, he was directly behind her.

She had stopped to watch a wedding party ending a day's celebration here in the Kremlin at dusk. Holding wineglasses were a pretty girl in voluminous white, her new husband in an uncomfortable-looking suit of black, and half a dozen friends. One of the friends stepped forward with a bottle of bubbling wine and filled their glasses. Everyone was laughing. They had picked up a street musician someplace, an old man with a primitive instrument of some sort that he crushed and stretched between his hands. He played wheezy music and the young people toasted the couple while onlookers clapped, laughed, and wept.

"Dyeva," said Stef and she turned her head and looked at him.

Unquestionably it was the Tartar face he knew so well, with the high cheekbones and the angled eyes. Her face didn't change, yet she knew instantly why he had come.

"Look at them!" she said. Her voice was low, urgent, strangely musical in tone. "Look at them! Look at this world. Can you really let it destroy itself to save what we have—tyrants, fools, Darksiders, the White Chamber? These people are alive, they're free, they think there's a God and that he loves them. If they're deluded, what of it? They deserve to have a future. Whoever you are, take just one second before you kill me. Think about it!"

And for a lengthening instant Stef did. In fact, he had been thinking about it secretly for hours. To be here, now, seeing these people, this world—it wasn't theory anymore. Uncounted millions lived and breathed and wanted to keep on doing so. His own world seemed remote and for the moment unbelievable—the broken drains and babaku smells of Golden Horde Street, his dirty apartment and the kif pipe, Yama and his stinking guardian, his long day in the White Chamber, Lake Bai and the singsongers on the boat, the synthesizer and the *sisi* warbling the melody "This Dewdrop World."

For that instant he could have joined Crux himself. Then he thought of Dzhun and he was paralyzed by indecision. As he hesitated, Dyeva turned to face him squarely and he heard the soft sound *Phut!* as she shot him through her coat.

He felt—not pain, but an incredible, crushing pressure in his midsection. His upper body flew backward, almost separated from the rest of him and the back of his head struck the cold hard snowy ground. A last mechanical contraction of his right hand fired his pistol, sent the bullet up, up into the darkening overcast like a tiny missile. His left squeezed the red button, meaning: my job is finished, I have succeeded. Bring me home.

Dyeva turned and hastened away, boots squeaking in the fresh snow. People were gawking at the wedding party, yet in a few seconds she heard a single scream. She would never know that the reason was not only the sight of a dead man lying horribly mutilated in the snow, but the fact that, even as someone spotted him, he disappeared, evaporated into the gathering darkness.

4

She plunged into the crowd before the Duma building, her mind running now on the scheduled arrival of the president and his cabinet for a debate on the Mongolian situation. Running also on the fact that such schedules were almost never kept. Running on the fact that she still had fifteen bullets, and that any one would be enough. Running on the importance of stopping this Minister Destruction that she had been hearing people on Ganesh curse since her childhood—the man who had given the order that ended their world.

No, she didn't believe in God any longer. But she had had to try once more to recapture her faith in the Cathedral of the Annunciation. Who could have imagined that she'd ever have a chance to pray there, in a building long since vaporized and its atoms embedded deep in the Kremlin Shield?

Well, the experiment had failed; she could not recapture her own faith, but she would ensure that other people kept theirs. She would sacrifice herself as Christ had for the sins of the world. There was no heaven at the end of it, but this was how she wanted to die.

She squeezed herself through the crowd, murmuring apologies in her strangely accented Russian, a kind of Russian that wouldn't be invented, ever, if she could manage it. She wondered if her parents would still be born and meet and have a child and call it Maria. No, too unlikely; if they lived at all, they would meet other people and marry them. Everything would be different. She felt a strange, dark satisfaction in thinking that she would not merely die here in the Kremlin—in some sense, she would never have existed at all.

She had reached the front of the crowd and stood pressed behind a bulky policeman. Fortunately, when the first gleaming limousine turned in through the Gate of the Savior and slid to a stop before the Duma, the policeman moved a little to get a good view of the notables. On the far side of the car, President Rostoff emerged and turned to wave at the crowd. On this side, a young and apparently nervous security man emerged and glanced briefly at Dyeva's face. Other security men appeared, too, jumping from cars, stepping briskly through the snow.

Rostoff, instead of going inside, crossed behind his own car and came to the crowd, reaching out to shake hands. People were cheering, arms reaching out and waving like limbs at the edge of a forest in a windstorm. From a second limousine, Razumovsky approached, also smiling, but keeping a few steps back to avoid upstaging the president. Dyeva shifted the pistol in the deep pocket of her coat and prepared to fire.

Then a gaggle of odd-looking people ran up, carrying primitive cameras of some sort. A sudden spotlight flashed on the crowd and Dyeva was blinded by the light. The long barrel of the impact pistol slipped through the hole in her coat made by her last shot. Shielding her eyes, she aimed as well as she could at Razumovsky. The little sound *Phut!* vanished in the roar of the crowd.

But the young security man had spotted the gleam of metal, and without the slightest hesitation he shoved the president the wrong way, into the path of the exploding bullet. Suddenly half of Rostoff's large body was gone, shredded.

Unaware of the disaster, the security man raised his own right hand, which was holding the newest M91K police automatic, 7.8 mm and loaded with superteflon hollowpoints. The first of six bullets hit Dyeva. They were not impact ammo, but they were sufficient.

She toppled backward, firing a last round that skated upward and blew a meterwide hole in the marble facing of the new Duma building. The chips were still flying as she hit the snow, feeling nothing but a strange lightness as if she had become a woman of air that would shortly disperse. She looked up into the faces of the security man and Minister Razumovsky as the two bent over her.

But you're supposed to be dead, she thought. And died.

Razumovsky glared down at her Tartar face.

"The goddamn Chinese did this!" he roared, and turned away.

Half a dozen people in the crowd were down, bleeding and crying for help, because the young security man and the others who had rushed to help him had managed to hit not only Dyeva but everyone near her as well. Razumovsky ignored all that, the screams, the confusion. Roughly he shook off the hands trying to drag him this way or that way to safety. Alone of them all, he knew exactly what he wanted to do.

He plunged into the president's armored limousine and shouted to the driver, "Get me out of here!"

While the driver, weeping and blinded by tears and lights, tried to find the gate, tried to force a way through the crowd without killing anybody else, Razumovsky took a key from around his neck and drove it into a lock in the back of the front seat. A small steel door fell open and he pulled out a red telephone.

"Razumovsky here!" he roared. "Chinese agents have wounded the president! I relay to you his exact words: 'We are at war! You will launch now!' Code word: Ivan the Terrible."

He sank back on the upholstery and passed a shaking hand over his squashed-frog face. At least in dying, the *glupetz* Rostoff had inadvertently chosen the right policy—for a change. Had he lived, who could tell what might have happened?

CHAPTER VII

It's a question of evidence," Yamashita said. "It's true, we didn't watch the Troubles begin. But we do have evidence."

The *fromazhi* had assembled to hear Yama's report on Stef's mission. Xian, Ugaitish, Hrka, Oleary—they were all there but Kathmann. Major Yost had moved a little forward; a man of no special age with a long, pale, intellectual face, he now sat behind Yama, quiet as his shadow.

Except for Xian—who already knew the story—the *fromazhi* were leaning breathlessly over the gilt Martian table, listening to the story of how their world had been saved.

"First," said Yama, "we recover Steffens's body, dead, obviously shot by a modern weapon, *oké?* His own gun has been fired once. The world we live in does not vanish, but on the contrary looks as solid as ever, at least to me. Just to eliminate any doubts about what happened, we use the wormholer one more time. We pull back from Moscow, three hundred sixtieth day of 2091, an air sample full of intensely radioactive dust and ice particles.

"I ask you, Honored Grandees. What can we conclude, except that Stef and Dyeva killed each other, that with his last gasp, so to speak, he signalled us to recover him because his job was done, and that the Time of Troubles proceeded to happen on schedule?"

Xian turned to Yang, standing in the shadows, deference in every line of his big, weak body. "What do you think, Honored Professor?"

"I agree. The evidence is absolutely irrefutable, and I have spent my whole life evaluating evidence."

"Well, I guess we have to accept it," fretted Oleary. He still hoped to take back Stef's million, but he could see that it would be difficult now.

"I am obliged to add," Yama continued, "that a sealed envelope was found on Steffen's body containing a note to Solar System Controller Xian."

He glanced at her and she nodded.

"It reads as follows," said Yama, spreading a copy on the arm of the *shozit*.

Facing death, Dyeva states that Kathmann cooperated in the theft of the wormholer. He expected to win promotion by crushing the conspiracy afterward, but Crux was too clever for him. Ever since, he has been desperately trying to wipe out those few who know of his treason.
Steffens Aleksandr

The *fromazhi* drew a deep collective breath.

"Is it possible?" demanded Ugaitish. "The Chief of Security? What could he hope to gain from assisting a conspiracy, then destroying it?"

"He told me once," said Yama, who had been waiting for this moment for many years, "that he dreamed of becoming Controller."

"Honored grandees," said Xian, "you must know that at first I, too, found this accusation hard to believe. But the evidence is great. The paper, ink, and handwriting prove that Steffens wrote this note. In his own defense, Kathmann made the claim that Steffens was seeking revenge because he had been tortured. But

Kathmann's own record of Steffens's interrogation certifies that the questioning was 'exceptionally gentle.' This was a troubling contradiction.

"We all know that Kathmann, in spite of his many virtues, was too zealous, too ambitious. I ordered him to bring me the scientist who stole the wormholer for questioning. The man had been beheaded. That seemed an extremely suspicious circumstance to me. Was Kathmann trying to ensure his silence? All the builders of the wormholer were also dead. I questioned the only two Crux prisoners who were still alive, but they were mere children and knew nothing—which was probably why they had kept their heads.

"In the end, to resolve the matter I ordered Kathmann into the White Chamber. Major Yost conducted the interrogation most skillfully. With the needles in his spine, Kathmann made a full confession. Every statement made by Steffens in this note is true. Kathmann knew too many state secrets to be permitted to live, and so I had him beheaded."

She looked around at the others, as if waiting for a challenge. Yama smiled a little. Admiral Hrka remarked that he had never liked the fellow. Aside from that, Kathmann's harsh fate produced no comment whatever.

"Is there any other business, then?" asked Xian, preparing to end the meeting.

Yang had been waiting for this moment to step forward from the shadows. "Now that Crux is finished, Honored Grandees," he said smoothly, "I would suggest going public with the story and making Steffens a hero.

"The heroes we honor all lived a long time ago; they are almost mythic figures—indeed, some of them, like the Yellow Emperor, are entirely myths. But here we have a hero of today, one that people can identify with, one who brings the glory and splendor of the present world order home to the common man. It's true, of course," he added, "that certain aspects of

Steffens's life will have to be edited for public consumption. But the same could be said of any hero of history."

"Superb," cried Xian at once, ending any argument before it began. Raising a tiny, thin hand that looked with its many rings like a jeweled spider, she declared: "Steffens will be buried with full honors. Someone with talent will write his biography and Yang will sign it. Scenes from his life will be enacted on every mashina. A great tomb will be built—"

"Honored Controller," muttered Yama, "we've already cremated the body and disposed of the ashes."

"What difference does that make? Do you suppose Genghis Khan sleeps in what we call his grave? Now *bistra, bistra!*" (quick, quick!) "Get a move on. Remember that heroes are made, not born."

Professor Yang left the cabinet room with Yama and Major Yost. He was smiling, bubbling over with ideas.

"Wouldn't it be interesting, Honored Colonel," he said, "if time is, so to speak, absolutely relative—if this episode has been embedded in the past ever since 2091, and all our world is the long-term result of what, from our point of view, has only just happened?"

Though anxious to get on with his new duties, Yama paused long enough to stare.

"What complete nonsense," he growled.

Pending appointment of a replacement for Kathmann, Yama was combining Security Central duties with his own. His first action was to name Yost his deputy and recommend him for promotion to colonel.

Then Yama carried out a more personal duty: as he'd promised Stef, he ordered the release of Iris and Ananda from the White Chamber. He did not see the young people, and so never knew that their brief stay beneath the Palace of Justice had turned their hair the same color as the tiled walls of their cells.

It was past 19 and Yama was thinking of Hariko and his

children when a piece of copy containing two lines of script was hand-delivered to his desk. Thus he learned that the woman Lata, last survivor of Crux on earth, had been tracked down at a village near Karakorum. She had committed suicide before the polizi and the Darksiders arrived and had left this note.

"It is all over," she wrote, "and I know it. This world endures as if protected by a god. But what sort of god would protect *this* world?"

Yama slid the paper into a port on his mashina.

"Copy, file, destroy," he said.

2

On the next Great Genghis Day, Government of the Universe Place was crowded with people. From every flagpole hung nine white faux yak-tails in honor of the famous Unifier of Humankind. But the event of the day was not honoring Genghis—though President Mobutu burned incense on his grave—but the dedication of Stef's memorial.

As the veil over the statue fell, Dzhun and Selina stood together looking at an idealized Stef striding ever forward, holding an impact pistol in one hand and a globe symbolizing the world order in the other.

Since Dzhun was only semiliterate, Selina read her the epitaph that Yang had composed: "Like the Great Khan in Courage and like Jesus in Self-Sacrifice."

"Yang's been made a grandee, you know," Dzhun said. "They needed somebody to purge subversives from the University, and he just dropped into the slot. We're lucky he's our customer."

She had used the million Stef had left her, not to buy a cottage or get an education, but to open her own brothel. She called it House of Timeless Love. With clever Selina to manage it— and to serve a few select customers, such as the now famous, rich, and powerful Yang—it had rapidly become the most popular of the newer houses, with capacity crowds every night.

Selina smiled down at her friend and employer.

"Anyway, the statue's nice. Of course he never walked stiff-legged like that. Stef just lounged around."

"I think I preferred him as he was," mused Dzhun. "Alive."

"You loved him, didn't you?"

"I guess so. I really don't know much about love. I know that I love you."

She and Selina had been sleeping together for years. Sometimes they made love, but sex wasn't really the point. After the night's work was done and all the customers had gone, they lay together for comfort, holding each other close.

"Can I ask you something, Dzhun?"

"Anything. Almost anything."

"How'd you get Stef to leave you all that money? Was it just telling him that you had a senator on the string?"

"That was part of it. But also I made up a sad story about myself and fed it to him. You know, in spite of everything he was sentimental. That's why he was thrown out of the Security Forces. I was working for the polizi then, keeping them informed about my customers. When I reported that Stef was working on an important secret project, I got a bonus. Colonel Yost—he was just a major then—told me all about Stef's weakness," said Dzhun. "Even way back then I had powerful friends, Selina."

"*Tu nespravimy, Dzhun,*" said her friend, smiling and shaking her head. "You're incorrigible."

"What's that word mean?"

Selina told her. Dzhun smiled; she liked the sound of it.

"Well, honey, if you ask me, we live in an incorrigible world."

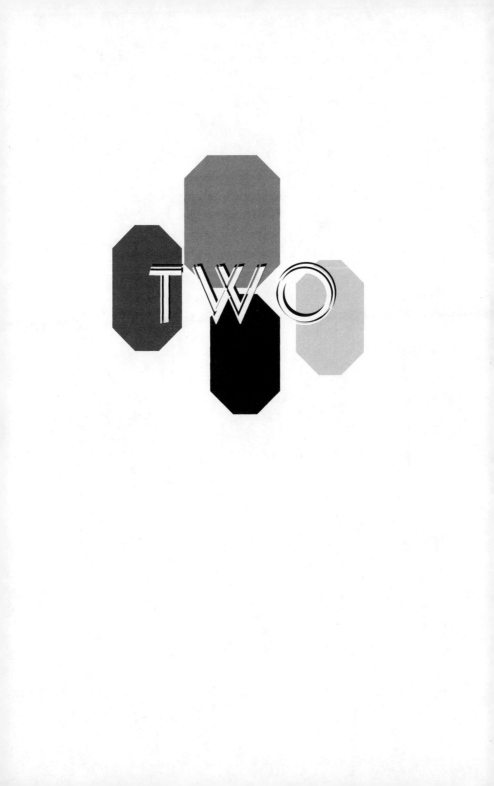

TWO

CHAPTER VIII

Her maid gave a last tug to Xian Xi-qing's robes of faux silk and rolled away. Stiffly seated on a throne of pale poured marble, the ancient Controller stared down the long hall and tried to resemble a goddess without feeling much like one.

Once she had actually felt unshakable, but no longer. Adept as she was at concealing weakness from others, the Crux conspiracy had frightened her badly. The very energy she'd summoned to destroy Kathmann had left her drained in the aftermath, terrified at how close treason had approached her unseen.

Her tiny hands clutched each other, stilling a tremor. *Ah,* thought Xian, *what good is all this stem-cell therapy if you lose your courage, if you age inside? I never used to feel I needed protectors. But now . . . have I found the man to protect me, protect our world?*

Gold-leafed doors at the end of the hall swung open and a tall, heavy man of Japanese ancestry strode forward, each step covering a precise meter of polished floor. Two Darksiders slouched behind him, spreading a stink that nine censers burning faux ambergris could not cover.

Yamashita halted, bowed. His face was like a brick, his head like sandpaper. The huge, ill-smelling, heavily armed beasts looked over his back, ready to destroy him or anybody else if Xian gave the kill signal. But she said only, "Rise, Honored Chief of Security."

She'd meant to conceal her new-found weakness and yet, when she began to speak, her voice shook and her words revealed deep-seated anxiety.

"General, extraordinary measures of security are needed," she began. "We trust the Space Service to deal with unfriendly aliens; they're quite insignificant. But here at home, ah here at home . . . "

Now her hands were trembling again and clutched each other tighter.

"Suppose someone builds another wormholer?" she almost pleaded. "We know now that it's possible; we know that terrorists exist ready to destroy themselves if they can destroy this world of ours! Can we ever be secure again?"

Yamashita needed his *marmolitz,* his marble face. He'd expected a mere formal welcome to his new job. And here the Controller, an unfamiliar quavering note in her voice, was demanding he reply to an unanswerable question.

Luckily, he was quick-witted.

"Honored Controller," he intoned, "I have given this problem much thought."

He paused—gave it the only thought he'd ever given it—then continued: "There is only one way. A new wormholer must be built under the control of the Security Forces. Reliable people must be trained to journey through time."

He paused, astonished at his own chutzpah, then thundered, "The Security Forces must police time itself! Absolutely! Only in this way can our world be secure!"

For a moment Xian was lost in admiration, thinking: What a marvelous bureaucrat! Imagine, working all this out ahead of time, then demanding such an immense responsibility, knowing what will happen to him if he fails!

She looked with new confidence into his face, seemingly impervious to heat, cold and pity. She nodded, extending a hand so thin the fingers looked like tiny sticks from a magpie's nest, each finger stacked with glinting rings of dull gold and green jade.

Her voice regained strength as she said, "Your proposal is approved. Succeed, General, and three hundred inhabited worlds will praise you. Fail—"

She let the word hang in midair, as Kathmann had hung toward the end of his interrogation, when the skills of Colonel Yost and the technicians of the White Chamber had made his treason clear. Then she said abruptly, "Honored Chief of Security, we permit you to go."

2

In his big new office, Yamashita grinned boyishly. He yawned, broke wind, sprawled back in a tall chair of black duroplast. His thick fingers drummed on the polished desktop, a massive slab of Martian petrified wood, a hundred million years old if it was a day.

He was thinking: *What the fuck. I deserve all this.*

Thirty years it had taken him to get here. Thirty years since those far-off days in the Security Forces Academy when he revealed his ambition to his friend, Cadet 1/C Steffens Aleksandr.

"You watch me, Stef. One day I'll be the fucking Chief of Security."

"Why would you want to be?"

A typical Stef answer. The man who had become a cop without believing the basic truths of cophood.

"Because, *glupetz*, that's where the power is."

"And the problems. And the danger of losing your head."

The difference between them. Between the man who won fame by accident and the man who achieved incalculable power by deliberate, long-headed effort and thought.

Time to use some of that power. Yamashita barked, "Secretary!"

Obediently, a large mashina whose memory was stocked with the world's most elaborate encryption software rose from a well in the floor. "Yes, Honored General?"

"Get me Yost."

An instant later a prickle of laser beams created the illusion of Yost's face hovering in the mashina's shadow box.

"*Hai*. Well, I'm officially in. So here's a few things for you to get started on. First, find the White Chamber new quarters. It's too small and the electrical system is antiquated. Also, change its name. It's got a lousy reputation. Call it, um, Special Investigations."

"You aren't abolishing *shosho?*" asked Yost, alarmed.

"Great Tao, no."

Neither man could imagine running a proper criminal justice system without physical methods.

"Oh, another thing. Xian wants us to build a new wormholer. Kathmann executed the guys who built the last one, so you'll have to assemble a new team. We'll need young, strong, expendable people to do the time traveling. It's no game for old farts."

"Chief, this is all damned expensive. Where's the money to come from?"

"Don't worry, I know where a lot of bodies are buried. I'll squeeze the Senate. But for a start, we can economize. The budget of the Penal Moons is way out of line. Release all offenders who've served ten years or more if they're fully rehabilitated. Execute those who aren't."

"Will do."

No order bothered Yost. He'd climbed to his present post over Kathmann's body, after all.

"In case anybody complains about any of my policies," Yamashita finished, "you're the designated motherfucker, understand? I set people free while you cut off heads. I abolish the White Chamber while you run Special Investigations. When you follow me into this office, you can mistreat your deputy the way I intend to mistreat you. Understood?"

"Yes, Honored General," sighed Yost, and his image evaporated.

Yamashita reared back in his chair and the boyish grin returned to his usually stolid face. He was going to enjoy his new job. A little *mosh*—power in Alspeke—was a pain in the butt. Ask poor Yost.

But a lot was heaven.

CHAPTER IX

On the nearby campus of the University of the Universe, a knot of students gathered in the warm Siberian sun around a kiosk plastered with notices and job announcements.

"Great Tao," said one. "Timesurfing. How's that for a job?"

"Tailbuster," said somebody else. "Beta test scores, alfa fitness, SECRET/BEHEADER clearance!"

Most of them drifted on. One who didn't was a tall, solid-looking young man who took a notebook from his beltpouch and read the announcement's boxcode into it.

"Gonna apply, Maks?" asked a friend.

"Why not? Nothing to lose."

Hastings Maks would not have dreamed of admitting how excited he felt. He loved history, loved finding out how things really happened. To explore the actual past sounded too good to be true.

And to do it under the leadership of General Yamashita, the security chief who'd gained everyone's love by closing the White Chamber and opening the doors of the prisons. Why, hardly a day went by without the news programs showing some tearful ex-convict returning home to his weeping family. Nobody in Ulanor the Worldcity was more popular than this strong man, who kept society in order through justice, not cruelty!

Next morning Maks woke up and faced reality. He was not exceptional in any way, mental or physical, and the likelihood that he could get into an elite program was small.

But he was bold enough to defy the odds. Sheer grit would have to substitute for special talents. He called the boxcode from his parents' mashina and registered for the first test—a gruelling athletic trial called the *Fizikál*.

2

For the next month he was up before dawn every morning, working out in the campus gymnasium with the young men and women who would be his competitors.

He deliberately chose the best of them to test himself against—for wrestling, a strong young Mongol with the torso of a lion; for running, a woman offworlder named Zo Lian.

Lian was definitely odd. Though human, she'd been genetically adjusted to her homeworld, Beta Charonis; her bones looked almost delicate but her muscles were long, tireless strings. Her chest—intended for use in air with a lower oxygen content than Earth's—was a barrel; her breasts small, and she made them smaller by binding them with an elastic bandage.

Lian told Maks that the only thing remarkable about her planet, aside from its rich lodes of metals and natural radioactives, was the fact that the ill-smelling, ferocious creatures called Darksiders came from there.

"When I arrived on Earth and saw a platoon of them guarding the Palace of Justice with whips and guns," she said wryly, "I felt at home right away."

Ambitious, she'd worked her way to Earth on a freighter, won a stipend to study at the University, then applied for the surfer program. Maks found her almost sexless form too strange to be desirable, but he admired her guts and her prowess as an effortless, tireless runner. If he could keep up with Lian, he could keep up with anybody.

After working out in the gym, they put on thin coveralls with cooling units and set out, running through the outskirts of the city and up the dry Butaeliyn Hills in the metallic dust of summer. Invariably, Lian led the way, Maks puffing behind, with the heels of her ragged old running shoes flickering like little mirages ahead of him.

One day after a ten- or twelve-click run they stopped to rest and drink at a cold spring. In the shade of bent pines Maks sank down, all his muscles quivering, his lungs burning as he gasped for air. Even Lian had found the long uphill run tough; she propped her skinny arms against her knees, lungs working like bellows.

When her racing pulse had quieted she walked unsteadily to the spring and knelt down. Maks joined her and they drank side by side like two weary animals. Then sat quietly on the ground and looked at each other.

Lian had a laconic, flat way of talking.

"We'll both get into the program," she predicted. "I'll make the first cut and you'll make the second or third."

"You know, you've got just the slightest touch of arrogance, Lian."

She plucked a stalk of dun grass and thoughtfully picked her long white teeth. At such moments she looked subtly unhuman, all her proportions just a trifle off the earthside norm. The fact that she had amber eyes heightened the near-alien effect.

"Not really. I'm smarter and quicker than you are, that's just a fact. But I've watched you almost kill yourself working out, Maks. You'll make it on guts alone."

That was the most encouraging thing he'd heard yet. As his breathing quieted, scenes from the past formed in his mind. He saw China's first emperor dip his writing brush to order the building of the Great Wall. He saw a troop of Crusaders ride down a dusty road in Anatolia, chain mail chinking like a pocketful of half-khan pieces. He saw naked whores dancing in the Red Room of the White House while one of the Decadent Presidents looked on, grinning and munching toasted pork rinds.

The past, the incomparable past, made up of so many presents forever lost, now regained.

Suddenly his fatigue was gone. Like a boy he took out his excitement by jumping Lian. For a few seconds they rolled over and over in the dust like playful puppies. This was one place where Maks's weight mattered; he found himself astride her, pressing her whip-thin arms to the dust. Her strange eyes stared up at him, bright as burning amber.

Embarrassed, he jumped up, helped her to her feet. They brushed each other off.

"Timesurfing—it's the only life, isn't it?" he asked.

"Yes," said Lian, "there is no other," and began to trot down the mountain, leading the way as usual.

3

That same summer—not that Earth's seasons meant anything in the tunnels of the penal moon Calisto—Convict Ya7326 prepared for the end of his term of imprisonment.

Sentenced for life, he now had a chance to be set free after only twenty years. Like all the men and women who dwelt in the tunnels, he was bald and muscular. Convicts were routinely depilated for hygienic reasons, and work at the Near Space Refueling Depot, for which the penal colony supplied labor, made you either strong or dead.

Inwardly Ya7326 was exceptionally intelligent, though his prison jobs as cleanup man, oiler, and subtechnician at the liquid nitrogen storage tanks had given him little chance to prove it.

As the "day" approached (days were marked by fluctuations in the automatic lighting) he seemed absolutely unaware of the coming change. Until a robot guard called him to the Out-Processing Unit he continued to make up his bunk, work in the tunnels, eat every mouthful of food allowed him—in short, to obey each and every one of the 92 Rules of Conduct he'd learned on arrival.

After passing a total radial scan to make sure he wouldn't carry diseases back to civilization, he reported to the psychiatrist's office. He sat down on a battered duroplast bench and waited without fidgeting. Memories passed through his mind.

His arrest and his time in the White Chamber would be with him as long as he lived. He'd run an identity-counterfeiting ring connected with the *mafya* and had spent a long time with the needles in his spinal marrow, screaming and twisting, his back arching until he felt it must break.

Then General Kathmann had entered the room. His grating voice said to the techs, "You've got all the juice out of this *kukrach*. Don't waste any more time on him."

Kukrach meant cockroach.

So he survived the White Chamber and became Ya7326 and traveled to Calisto in a freighter's hold. There things got rough again. He still remembered the blinding headache that followed insertion of his control chip and the little explosive sphere of synthetic neurotoxin. Then later in his cell, trying despite the headache to memorize the Rules of Conduct.

Breaking any of the first 12 (lack of neatness in the cell, failure of personal hygiene, etc.) brought punishment by hunger. Breaking the next 21 meant hunger plus sensory deprivation for longer or shorter periods. Breaking any of the other 59 rules brought death, which was so easy: a program running on the mainframe in Central Control reviewed the guard reports, assigned or deleted quality points, sent a signal, and a prisoner keeled over, untouched by human hands.

At first Ya7326 couldn't believe the prison authorities were serious, that there could be so many reasons to die. Then they began culling the new prisoners. First to go were the double-Y-chromosome types. He was glad of that—scary guys, good riddance. Then the incurably disruptive. A woman convict who threw wash water on a robot guard in an attempt to short it out went down like a poleaxed cow within a meter of him and the guard dragged her away by the ankles.

Yet Ya7326 had survived the culling, too. Why? he often asked himself. Was he reserved for some great destiny? Life in the tunnels gave him endless time to think about such profound and basic questions.

A light blinked above the door and Ya7326 got up, neither hurrying nor lagging, even though he knew that the critical moment was at hand. If he was judged rehabilitated, he would go free. If the psychiatrist penetrated his most profound thoughts, he would die like that woman, even now, even after twenty years.

"*Hai,*" the psychiatrist greeted him. "I see we have another candidate for release. Why should we set you free, Ya7326?"

"I feel that I'm ready to regain my freedom. Suffering has purified my inner self. I've had no demerits at all for the past five years."

The psychiatrist—a black box—checked his record and confirmed his claims.

"That is very satisfactory, Ya7326. Your cell sensors report no rule-breaking activities of any kind, and that is also good. Have you reflected on the errors that brought you to Calisto?"

"Yes," he said, "I often think about those errors."

Now they were getting to the heart of the matter. For the interview Ya7326 sat in a *senzit,* a chair that monitored a variety of physical reactions. The *senzit* was part of the psychiatrist—its lap, maybe.

"Meditation on one's past mistakes is a prerequisite to sound action in the future," it intoned. "Do you agree?"

Ya7326 had often noticed that black boxes were even more tiresomely moralistic than humans.

"Emphatically, Doctor, I do agree."

"Do you blame yourself or others for your crime of counterfeiting identities?"

"I blame no one but myself."

"Very good," said the box, after checking his reactions. "Now, this is a question you will need to answer with perfect honesty. Your answer will be noted purely for medical purposes and will not be reported to the prison authorities."

Despite everything, he felt increased tension that he knew the box was reading from the *senzit*. Of course it was lying—everything would be reported.

"Do you desire revenge against the authorities who subjected you to *shosho* and later sent you to prison?"

Ya7326 took a few seconds to compose himself.

"Let me be precise," he said. "I admit to hating General Kathmann. But he's dead. I have no desire whatever to become the kind of contemptible criminal I used to be. I don't want to harm any human individual."

A few silent seconds passed. Then the psychiatrist said, "Your involuntary reactions and brain-wave patterns, Ya7326, indicate that you have spoken the truth as you see it. It can therefore be said that your rehabilitation is complete."

Next day Ya7326 was sitting on the examining table in the dispensary, waiting for the surgeon to appear. A locked instrument cabinet stood in front of him; he looked at his reflection in the mirror duroplast and smiled, thinking of the psych interview. How stupid black boxes were!

No, he had no desire to commit again the acts he'd been

convicted of. If he had to commit them in furtherance of his plan, he would. But he had no *desire* to.

Yes, he blamed himself for being such a fool as to imperil his godlike self for the trivial rewards of petty crime. No, he wanted no revenge on any human *individual*.

He turned as the door opened. The surgeon bustled in, washed his hands at a little sink on the wall, and prepared for business.

"Had your mediscan?"

"Yes, sir."

"Psych interview?"

"Yes, sir."

"Ready to go, then?"

"Definitely, sir."

"Lie on your stomach. This will hurt a little, even with the local anesthetic—the back of the neck has so many nerves in it."

"I don't mind pain," said Ya 7326, truthfully.

During imprisonment his pain threshold had risen so high that he could hold his fingers in an open flame, smelling the flesh burn but feeling hardly a sting. It was part of the transition he'd undergone in the tunnels, an aspect of his entry into a new kind of being.

"Cut away," he said, and closed his eyes.

4

The first day of the *Fizikál* was devoted to gymnasium sports. Maks got along well enough, and Lian did splendidly until the candidates paired off for wrestling.

Then the powerful young Mongol who used to wrestle (and invariably throw) Maks sprang into the circle with Lian, seized her around her slender waist and with one violent contraction of the arms broke her back.

Maks, horrified, rode with Lian to the hospital. A few centuries in the past, so serious a spinal cord injury would have meant permanent paralysis. Now it meant an operation to replace the damaged section with nerve fibers from genetically altered embryo monkeys. Then it meant lying in bed for months, waiting for the regeneration to be complete, followed by more months of therapy to restore full function.

Maks paid as many visits to Lian as he could. But the first year of the timesurfer program—he'd barely made the third cut after screwing up a math exam—was especially arduous, designed to weed out anybody who couldn't take it. When Maks did visit the hospital he felt guilty to be talking about his progress.

"Now they're taping me with Archaic English," he said. "It's pretty easy; after all, I know the modern dialect. At least I get a chance to sleep while the mashina's on. Aside from that it's run, run, run all the time."

Lian sighed. As of today she'd been looking at the ceiling of the hospital room for seventy-three days. She knew every crack in the paint by heart.

"It'll take me forever to get back in shape," she muttered.

"I'll help you."

"You're a dear friend, Maks, but you won't have time."

That was true. The harder truth was that Lian's injury made things easier for Maks. One competitor less—and a tough one, at that.

"It's just something that can't be helped," Lian added.

Lying in bed she looked pale and yellowish. Her face had gone wan and ascetic and her normally thin body was a sack of bones. Maks was sitting in a chair by the bed, sleek with muscles, glowing with health.

"Well, I'll be back as soon as I can," he said. He pressed her hand and it felt like a fossil.

Maks meant what he said, but in fact he did not go back to the hospital. He was too busy. The place was too depressing.

People his age were not supposed to be left broken and helpless. He felt guilty about not going, but not guilty enough to go. Instead, he celebrated his twentieth birthday with his first trip through the wormholer—just a year to the day after the *Fizikál* that had been so disastrous for Lian.

Miniaturization had reduced the device to a cylinder encircled by two rings: the first held the gravitron accelerator, the second massive electromagnets wrapped with coils of superconductors cooled by liquid nitrogen to prevent meltdown when gigawatts of energy were poured in. Behind a shield, techs watched the monitors of the mashina that ran the show.

"Recite the Standing Order!" demanded Maklúan, a redhaired tech with an ugly face and an irritating manner.

" 'The past is not to be changed in any manner, however slight. No one can tell what effect a change may have upon the present. If I have to choose between changing the past and destroying myself, I must destroy myself.' "

"Let's go then. I don't have all day."

Carrying a small hand control to signal for his return, Maks relaxed and listened to the hum of the metal slide that carried him into the cylinder. He adjusted opaque goggles over his eyes to prevent retinal damage, and felt rather than saw the intense flash of light that marked the Big Bang-like burst of photons created by the sudden torsion of spacetime.

He removed the goggles. He was lying on the floor of an empty room in the academy. He got up and noted the time recorded by the clock on the wall: 1534.6/7/2465. A year had been subtracted. The door of the "receiver room," as they called it, was locked and sealed shut to prevent accidental contacts between now and then. But a square window, said to be mirrored on the outside, gave him his first sight of the living past.

For long minutes he stared down with some unsayable emotion at the world of a year ago—then saw something that almost stopped his heart.

Lian, carrying a gym bag, was hurrying toward the *Fizikál*. Waiting for her, Maks knew, was the Mongol wrestler.

Suddenly Maks found himself beating on the window, trying to attract Lian's attention, trying to cry a warning. But she hastened past, disappeared from Maks's angle of vision. Maks put his face into his hands. More time passed before he could pull himself together sufficiently to press the control and return to his own time.

When Maklúan helped him out of the wormholer, he was still pale and shaken. With a superior smile on his ugly face, the tech remarked, "A *glupetz* never learns."

One sandy eyebrow was raised; the tech seemed to be enjoying some joke that he alone understood. Maks suddenly realized that the path to the gym didn't go anywhere near the receiver room.

The "window" hadn't been a window at all; the scene had been a mashina-generated image. In an instant his grief turned to blinding rage.

"You fucking bastard," he gasped. "I ought to kill you."

"If you do," the tech said coolly, "you'll never be a time-surfer. Incidentally, this was a test. You flunked it."

Maks stared at him, his hands clasping and unclasping. Then he slammed out of the room.

For the whole of the ten-day week that followed Maks waited to hear he'd been plowed. But nobody said anything; gradually he began to breathe again. Maybe, he thought, you were expected to fail the first time.

Nevertheless, the experience had reminded him of Lian. One evening he looked her up. Since her discharge from the hospital, Lian had been living in a dormitory for offworld students at the University. The room, painted sickish green, was crowded with six folding beds and fragrant with moldy towels.

But Lian was looking better, as if the environment didn't

touch her. She smiled, tried to make Maks welcome. She wore shapeless overalls that sagged as if there was no body inside.

"I've started exercising again, but it's tough," she admitted. "I run half a click and get winded. Still, I'm hoping to apply again in the fall."

You'll never make it, thought Maks, somehow forgetting that he had succeeded by grit alone.

"I wish you luck," he said and put on what he hoped was an encouraging smile. He took her hands and squeezed them; if she hadn't looked so . . . odd, he would have kissed her, out of sheer pity.

CHAPTER X

Ulanor, the Worldcity, the capital of the human species, the arena where people struggled for boundless wealth and *mosh*, was blasé about visitors, even important ones. Heroes of the alien wars in Far Space returned to find themselves forgotten; off-world senators were ignored.

Perhaps no visitor had ever been as thoroughly overlooked as the former Ya7326. He reached Luna as he'd left it, in a freighter's hold. He dozed in the shuttle port until an empty seat came up and he could be thumbed aboard.

But at least he arrived back in the city of his birth carrying a passport with his convict ID exed out. He was now Vray Dak, the name under which he'd been arrested two decades before.

His first duty was to report to the polizi in the ziggurat Palace of Justice and sign in, giving his current address. Then he spent an hour walking the hard, polished corridors, gazing at carved dragons and snarling lion-dogs and quotations from that

Great Unifier of Humankind, Genghis Khan. Such as: "He who breaks my law will vanish like an arrow among reeds."

A recovered arrow, he ventured downstairs, the level of the former White Chamber. Now it held the offices of a small Security Forces agency. When a guard frowned at him, Vray apologized and departed.

He loitered for a time outside the building, standing by a tri-rad stand so that he'd seem to be waiting for a vehicle if anybody challenged him. In fact, nobody did—he was a casual, slouching figure, a bit overweight as a result of gorging himself on non-prison food. The only remarkable thing about him was his wig, cheap and often askew, that gave his head a faintly comic appearance. Some passersby smiled at him, and he smiled back.

Next day he found a legitimate job with the Water and Waste Monopoly, operating an autominer similar to the ones used on Calisto. He worked there patiently for a year, until he no longer had to report to the polizi. By then he'd made contact with some other graduates of what the underworld called *Kalist' akad*, Calisto Academy. With *mafya* help, he quit his job and entered the city's trade in stolen goods.

He was cool and cunning and seemed to draw on boundless supplies of energy, going sometimes for four or five days without sleep. A year of effort made him fairly prosperous.

With money in his pocket, he adopted new hobbies. He obtained a portable holographer, bought a license, and began to appear on streets around Ulanor, taking people's pictures against projected 3-D backdrops for a silver half-khan. One of his favorite posts was outside the Palace of Justice.

"So," said a guard who recognized him. "Got a new line?"

"Yes, sir. In business for myself, you see."

"Lemme see your license."

The license checked out. Rather reluctantly—he would have liked to run the bugger in, on general principles—the guard returned it to him.

"Quit your job digging sewers?"

"Well, sir, after you've lived underground for twenty years, it's nice to work where you can see the sky."

"Making a living?"

"Scraping by, sir."

"Well . . . watch your ass."

"Always, sir."

By offering free samples, Vray managed to capture the likeness of a number of civilian employees of the small agency that occupied the former White Chamber. Then he disappeared from the street.

If anyone had been interested, they might have found him at home in an apartment he'd rented in the Clouds and Rain District.

There he spent much time staring at a stolen mashina he'd kept for his own use.

He was studying an interactive book called *The Glorious Language: Archaic English for Beginners*. He read history, everything he could find on the twenty-first century, and mythology, memorizing stories of forgotten gods. He was fascinated by a book called *America in Decline: The Decadent Presidents*, enough so that he and the prosts at the cheap brothels he frequented tried out some of the games the decadent presidents had played.

Vray Dak had become a successful minor criminal, an autodidact and a self-made bore. That was how they knew him in the District; outside it, few people knew him at all.

2

Lian had astonished Maks by passing the entrance test, including the *Fizikál*, though just barely—36 candidates were admitted and her class number was 35. But that was only the beginning.

Slowly she'd made her way forward. At the end of her first year she stood 21st in a class that resignations and failures had reduced to 29. In her second year, Lian cracked the midpoint: 12th out of 24.

When she came to Maks' graduation, she was almost unrecognizable: a third-year student, confident of her future, marked out from her classmates only by her strange physique and amber eyes. Her class standing was now 6th out of 20. Maks's final standing had been 17th in his own class of 19 men and women.

"You see," Lian told him at the end of Maks's graduation ceremony, when they embraced amid a crowd of well-wishers.

"If you hadn't been injured," Maks admitted, "my class standing would've been eighteenth."

"That's true, it would have been."

Maks laughed helplessly at this blunt immodesty. But it was hard to be offended by the truth. After three years of training Lian made him think of a steel string on some strange instrument, perfectly tuned, perfectly taut.

She still didn't attract him, but she fascinated him. In spite of everything—her injury, her offworld birth, her poverty—he could see now that she was one of fate's darlings, possessing a bit more of every talent than most people could ever have or hope for.

"Lian," he said honestly, "I'm lucky to know you."

"Yes, my dear friend," she answered gravely, "you are."

3

On his postgraduation leave Maks took a girlfriend to Antartica for the summer skiing. On his return he reported to the grim step pyramid of the Palace of Justice and entered, brushing past a fleshy man in a wig to reach the guard station.

Pastplor, the Office for the Exloration of the Past, had been operating for only five years—the new kid on the bureaucratic block, distrusted by the uniformed thuggi whose idea of policing did not include time travel.

Maks had Pastplor's status forcefully brought home to him when he realized that its offices were on the first level underground, in space formerly occupied by the White Chamber of infamous memory.

Searching for the right room, he walked down soundproofed corridors lined with small tiled cubicles and occasional larger rooms. The steel doors were gone and desks had taken the place of metal tables with electrical attachments and blood drains. The narrow punishment cells now imprisoned only brooms and mops. Ceilings had been painted sky blue and there were no Darksiders about.

Yet Maks felt anxious and oppressed. He didn't need this atmosphere for his first day on the job.

Eventually—after asking twenty or so people and getting nineteen wrong answers—he found the room where his orientation was to take place. At once he relaxed. It was full of his friends and Maks forgot his first impressions of the place in happy gossip about how everyone had wasted the summer just past.

Then a black box at the front of the classroom beeped them to attention.

"What," it demanded, "are the Authorized Uses of the Past?"

The young surfers took out recorder disks, warmed them between their hands and started taking notes.

"The first," said the box, answering itself, "is to maintain everlasting vigil against criminals like the Crux conspirators.

"The second, newly imposed by the Controller herself, is to reach practical solutions to questions of scientific importance."

Maks now learned that weather stations the size of grains

of sand had been sent to a variety of times and locations to build up a reliable picture of temperature variations for the last 100,000 years. These tiny globules stuffed with nanomachines were unlikely to be spotted by baffled *stari* (the old ones, the people of former ages). They were also cheap to send and recover, and that was important: the biggest item on Pastplor's budget was energy. In time the globules would yield the finest database ever assembled on the world's weather, its past and probable future.

"The final Authorized Use," the atonal voice went on, "is to investigate the origins of the Time of Troubles. This great catastrophe—the war of 2091, the Two Year Winter, and the Nine Plagues—created our world; we can hardly learn too much about it. You, young ladies and gentlemans, will find in these endeavors your lifeworks.

"You must, however, be aware of the danger. Last year a surfer was sent—at the cost of a gigawatt of energy, chargeable to this agency's budget—to the Imperial Chinese People's Republic in 2041. A defective accent in Archaic Mandarin gave him away and he was arrested as a spy. His control device was taken from him before he could use it to escape, and when we attempted to recover him we got instead an officer of the Imperial People's Liberation Army. Interrogation of this officer revealed that your poor young colleague died while undergoing a torture called 'the points,' which I will not describe as you might find it too distressing.

"Remember that past times may be dangerous," the black box concluded solemnly, and dismissed them for lunch.

Maks followed his friends to an underground cafeteria filled with the clash and rattle of trays and people yelling at each other to be heard above the din.

"What fiendish torture, young ladies and gentlemans, was the captured Chinese officer compelled to undergo?" demanded a class comic, mimicking the blank, flat tones of the black box.

"The points?" asked Maks.

"No. He was forced to eat this soyloaf."

Everybody groaned in sympathy with the victim.

4

"You're getting beautiful," said the woman with whom Vray Dak had finally settled down. To the polizi she was a registered prost, but that only proved the headquarters mashini were behind the times.

Getting too old to live by whoring, she'd gone to a school that billed itself the Academy of Beauty and turned herself into a skilled cosmetician. Now she earned her living from the brothels in a new way, making up the inmates for their evening work. In one of the houses she'd met Vray.

He was rather proud of the fact that he'd lost six kilos lately. Most of the flab he'd added as a free man was now gone; his hairless body was sleek as a fish.

"Yet I have to lose a bit more," he said.

"Why? I like you the way you are."

"I have to get down to about seventy kilos before Great Genghis Day."

"Why?"

"If you don't stop asking questions, I'll kill you."

An odd duck, she thought. He talked about losing weight and killing in exactly the same tone of voice.

She looked at him narrowly. She was seventy, well into middle age, and hadn't been a beauty even when young. She had never quite understood what he saw in her, a younger man with good connections in the *mafya.*

"Loki, my love, I won't ask even one more," she promised.

That was the name he preferred to be called. He said it was

connected to his religion. He smiled, and she nestled into the crook of his arm.

"Oh, incidentally," he said.

"Yes?"

"I want you to get me some things. A new wig, some contact lenses. And I'll need you to make me up for a job."

Ah, she thought, *so that's what he sees in me.* But she was a realist; she not only didn't resent his making use of her, she was glad of it. It was another bond between them.

"Whatever you want, my dear," she said, and soon—his body reacting as it usually did to submissive words and acts—she had her reward.

5

Maks's first year as a surfer turned out to be frustrating, then infuriating. Instead of surfing, he found himself turning into a glorified technician and button-pusher.

People he knew went to the past, but not Maks. His own classmates returned to London, New York, Moscow. Then people from the next class started going. Even Lian: she had graduated No. 1 at the academy and from her first day at Pastplor everyone treated her with respect. With a stab of envy, Maks realized that she was regarded by Colonel Yost as the agency's great hope for the future.

When Lian was picked to visit New York in 2025, Maks decided to complain. He asked for an appointment with Yost and was refused. Too angry to be scared, he went to the top: asked for an appointment with General Yamashita himself. Somewhat to his surprise, he was granted five minutes, and for the first time entered the Security Forces' command suite, sixty meters down in the most secure part of the Palace of Justice.

His first breath let him know he was in another world. Darksiders were everywhere, and their numbers increased as

Maks approached Yamashita's office. Smelling atrociously, the beasts seemed to stand at every corner of the long, zigzag marble corridor, clanking in cartridge belts and fingering five-kilo impact weapons that looked like toys in their massive fists.

Sometimes in Pastplor Maks almost forgot that he was part of the Security Forces; down here, *mosh* in its nakedest form was on display everywhere.

A black box ordered him to stand at attention just outside the steel doors, where he remained immobile, his nose itching devilishly, for twenty-seven minutes by a large wall clock. Then, just as abruptly, the box ordered him into the sanctum.

The big office was clean as a Zen temple, hard as a tomb. In the center reposed a wide empty desk like a frozen lake, a huge mashina, and Yamashita himself, a bemedaled monolith in a tall black chair.

"What the fuck do you want?"

That didn't sound promising. Maks had not been invited to stand at ease, so he stared at a far-off blank wall and spoke as much like a black box as he could.

"Sir, I've been a timesurfer for two years and have yet to be sent into the past. If I'm an asset, I deserve assignment like the others. If I'm not, I want to know it so I can resign and look for a meaningful job elsewhere."

"You wasted my time with this?"

"General, you can settle the rest of my life in two seconds. Nobody else can."

Considering that the room was cool, Maks was astonished to find himself sweating in so many different places. One large cold bead was travelling down the furrow of his spine; he would have given anything to stop its ticklish progress.

Yamashita barked at his mashina, "Record of this T/S1 you gave the appointment to." Glancing at the record, he said, "Yost doesn't trust you because you fucked up on a test."

"Sir, I didn't know it was a test."

"Those are the only tests that matter. Do you want to stay with the program?"

More than I want to live, Maks almost said. But no, the general didn't deal in exaggerations.

"Very much, sir."

"You'll be tested again. Now—out. I got work to do."

Recovering his equanimity in a toilet outside the command suite, Maks thought with narrowed eyes of Maklúan, the red-haired tech who'd tricked him. The man now worked at Pastplor, and Maks had to see him almost every day. Maks wasn't a hater, but he made an exception for Maklúan.

Yamashita was as good as his word. New orders were received, and a few days later, in the company of Timesurfer Mogul Peshawar, Maks went back to Pastplor's offices as they had been just before the agency occupied them.

The outside doors were still sealed. The cells of the White Chamber stood empty, dark, and abandoned. Some of the light switches worked, some didn't. With Mogul beside him, Maks walked the echoing corridors, observing and describing, his handheld recorder disk growing slick with chilly sweat.

Dread invested everything. The thick cell doors, some covered on the inside with ratty carpet for added silence. The lingering smell of Darksiders. The graffiti in the holding cells, which he traced painfully under a light held by Mogul. Hundreds of dates, curses ("Fuck all thuggi"), questions ("Why am I here?"), prison names and boasts ("Red Pepper too tough, never break"), pleas ("Tell my wife Dzhimi still loves her"). But the commonest, repeated like an operatic theme, was *Smerta mi kallá* (Death call me).

"Why'd they send us here?" he whispered to Mogul.

"Still trying to toughen you up, I guess."

"I'm not a coward."

"No, you're just a sweet kid. History's a merciless process. That's why time travel's not for sweet kids."

While Mogul paused to take down an inscription that interested him, a seething Maks walked into what had certainly been a torture chamber. It was larger than most of the cells, and deep in shadow. His handlight showed nothing but the usual battered metal table, the dangling wires, the blood drains.

Skin crawling, he turned away. Then sensed a movement behind him.

He spun around to see an immense Darksider that seemed to have sprung out of the walls lurch toward him, swinging a huge spiked club over its head. He gasped, almost broke and ran out of the chamber, out of Pastplor, out of the whole goddamn business of dealing with the unspeakable past.

Then, inside his head, he heard his father's voice say firmly, *Once but not twice.* He stiffened, stared into the animal's red/black eyes. Realized suddenly what some deep part of his brain had already noted: He couldn't smell the Darksider.

Suddenly he began to laugh. As he did the image broke up, dislimned, evaporated. Around the ceiling a prickle of tiny lights in laser projectors darkened.

Mogul dawdled into the chamber. "I guess we can go back now," he said.

CHAPTER XI

By comparison with that test, Maks's first trip into what surfers called the "real past" was easy—at first.

He and Mogul went to Washington in 2052 and spent two weeks recording data in the Library of Congress. The aim was to discover America's role, if any, in bringing on the Time of Troubles.

For the first time Maks absorbed the sense of another age—the strange food, the metallic taste of polluted air, the babble of archaic words, the dizzying throngs on the streets. The *stari* were a strange bunch, with their odd hairstyles and odder clothes and their abrupt, informal manners. They talked about the Century When Everything Went Wrong, about savage terrorist attacks, about the party strife paralyzing the government, about the Chinese ambassador's public remark that he no longer bought congressmen because renting them was cheaper. Cynicism was in style.

The picture he and Mogul assembled from documents confirmed popular opinion. The long-dominant American economy had stalled. The gigantic Chinese industrial machine ruthlessly outproduced and undersold all rivals. Nature had been merciless—California devastated by the worst earthquake in history, the nation's other rich coastal regions flooded by a sea rising faster than anyone had predicted. The whole insurance industry had gone under with the coastline, and the stock market had followed.

As wealth declined, taxes soared and a small antitax rebellion in the West had been fanned by foolish policies into a major regional uprising, the first since the Civil War.

To Maks's surprise, the current president, Derrick Minh Smith, was a break from the long run of Decadent Presidents who disgraced the midcentury. Tough and able, he tried to suppress disorder while winning himself the nickname of The Peacemaker for his tireless efforts to avoid war with China. America seemed to have had nothing to do with fanning the rivalries that led to the Troubles.

Instead, the picture was of a great nation undergoing slow internal decay. The library building was still ornately beautiful but falling apart for lack of upkeep. Carpets were worn, tiles displaced. The quaint toilets overflowed. Bits of glass fell from mosaics and tinkled on the marble floor as Maks walked by.

Outside, the summer heat was stifling and brownouts and blackouts increased the tumult of the nights. Some merchants refused to accept dollars, demanding good solid rubles instead. Programs on the tivis—crude and brainless mashini—touted An Age of Gold: The Twentieth Century. Or the nineteenth. Or the eighteenth. Anytime but now.

Towards the end of Maks's visit, the disorder began to hit home. Political parties had multiplied, fielding private armies of agitators and thugs who battled each other in the streets. Rioting over some incomprehensible issue broke out one evening, and troops carrying big clumsy rifles and wearing primitive night-vision helmets trotted up to guard the library.

That evening the murmur of mobs sounded like summer thunder and fires glowed in the distance. Maks and Mogul climbed to the roof of their rooming house to watch. Odd-looking aircraft buzzed like big wasps, dropping an irritant gas that drifted with the wind and forced the two surfers to go to their room and sit there, sweating, with closed windows.

Next morning Mogul was too sick to work. During the day he got sicker, despite the so-called universal inoculations they'd had before leaving Ulanor. By the following day his condition had become so bad that Maks had to call for help; they were both returned early and immediately put into an isolation unit until the virus, an ancient and lethal form of influenza, could be identified and destroyed.

Maks got a promotion for saving Mogul's life. He'd done well in a simple assignment; other and better ones loomed. His time of waiting was over.

He called the girl he'd taken to Antartica. Her name was Steffens Maia; he'd early been taken by her ample body, her sharp wit, her flat disclaimer of fame ("I am not related to the Worldsaver in any way, shape or form!"). Now he hinted that like the man she wasn't related to, he'd had great adventures in time. He asked her to join him at Lake Bai for Great Genghis Day, and she agreed.

Suddenly his world looked rich indeed.

2

Great Genghis Day had expanded to a three-day midsummer holiday, and traditionally people went wild the first evening, which was called *pyatnit*, or Drunk Night. The second was for the fireworks display and patriotic oratory about humanity's forward march. The third was for recovery, with a workday looming ahead.

In the Clouds and Rain District, the morning after *pyatnit* was celebrated with bloodshot eyes, headaches, and hot cups of strong green tea. In the Four Seasons teahouse, however, a bore in a wig seemed to have no hangover at all. He was questioning a sleepy-looking man—pale-faced and red-haired—who'd spent the night in one of the cheaper brothels.

"So you're in time travel," said the bewigged one. "Tell me this: do you know what the basic factor of history is?"

"Don't ask me. As I told you, all I do is run the goddamn machine."

"Well, let me tell you, then. The basic factor is context."

"No shit."

The tech had put in a strenuous night. He lived alone and when he visited a brothel tried to make up for lost time. Last night he'd gotten drunk and ended up spending far beyond his means.

"Yes. Move an event from one temporal context to another and it changes like a chameleon moving to a new leaf. If Hitler had tried his tricks under Kaiser Wilhelm, he would have been sent to an asylum; if under the Federal Republic of Germany, to jail."

"Hitler who?" asked the tech, taking out a kif pipe and waving it at a waiter. He would have gotten up and moved away from the bore except that he felt so tired.

Thank the Great Tao today's a holiday, he was thinking. *One pipe and I'll go home to sleep.*

"Or consider the Time of Troubles."

"Must I?" asked the tech, stoking his pipe with a thin pinch of kif that the waiter had brought him.

He couldn't believe, looking back, that he had spent *every khan* he owned. Not a silver half-khan, not a copper tenth was left to chink in his pockets. His bank account was overdrawn. What would he eat on until payday? *Who* would he eat on? For he was not a man with friends.

"In 1950, nuclear war would have ruined a few cities and that's all. In 1970, it would have caused an immense but endurable catastrophe. In 2091, it devastated the Earth and almost annihilated humanity. But by then there were offworld colonies to resettle our lamentable planet."

The tech, never a polite man, was growing irritable.

"Mister, I've known sweeper robots that had more original ideas than you."

Vray gave no sign of being insulted. His quiet voice droned on—a white sound, not unpleasant. He signalled for more tea for both of them.

"My point is that there was a window—shall we say—a window of opportunity. A time when sophisticated weapons existed but the offworld colonies weren't yet self-sustaining. Let's say from about 1980 to 2070. If the war had occurred then—"

"We wouldn't be drinking green tea and three hundred planets would be empty of the human life that infests them," said the tech, puffing.

He bowed slightly to thank Vray for the fresh tea. Vray noted that his companion had already reduced his pinch of kif to ashes.

"Allow me to buy you a decent quantity of kif."

"Don't mind if you do."

By the third pipe they'd gotten quite chummy. The tech's name was Maklúan and his view of life was anything but cheerful.

"I work with the world's most complicated and most useless goddamn machine," he groused, "and I get paid peanuts for doing it. I keep thinking things will get better, my life will turn around. I wish I could go to sleep for a thousand years, wake up and see if things've improved. If not, go back to sleep again."

"A man of your intelligence deserves better."

"You're fucking right. By the way," said Maklúan, "what's your business?"

"Oh," said Vray, "I buy and sell. Electronics, mainly. Twice-owned mashini, calcs, and so on. I wonder, could you use some extra money?"

"Absolutely," said the tech, suddenly alert.

"It's a great piece of luck for me, meeting you this way. I'm thinking of adding certain sophisticated devices to my inventory, but I'm just not capable of understanding their fine points. I'd pay a thousand khans to have a man of your expertise advise me."

Maklúan tried to conceal his delight, not very successfully.

"It sounds quite, ah, quite interesting," he muttered. "When would you like me to look these gadgets over?"

"If you're free," said Vray, rising, "there's no time like the present. And please—allow me to pay your check."

3

After the long, long years of preparation, things were speeding up. *It's now or never,* Vray thought. *Before Maklúan's absence is noted at Pastplor. Before they make changes in the* wormholer codes that he so kindly gave me just before dying. *Now.*

Fierce lines of afternoon sunlight burned around the shutters of the small room where he sat, dreaming of what was to come. He returned to the present when the woman sitting across the duroplast table from him—dumpy, washed-out, utterly forgettable, but a genius at her trade (which, oddly enough, had once been his trade)—asked:

"Well, what d'you want me to do with this?"

"First, I want you to read the code. Can you do it?"

She frowned at the square of hard ceramic lamina he'd given her, at the stacked layers of dotcode, and the hologram of a pale-faced, red-haired man imprinted not on the ID but in it. She turned and snapped it into a monitor and dropped a pirated memory cube into the queue.

"Standard polizi code," she said. "Name, Maklúan Artur; Age, thirty-one; Height, two point-oh-one meters; Weight, sixty-eighty point five kilos; Profession, Wormholer Technician; Employer, Pastplor; Clearance, one-A; Police Record, None. Description . . . Well, that's the problem. You can't just insert your own picture and a new description to match yourself."

"Right. The mashina at the guard station would pick it up. Description and picture must match those in the system's memory. At the same time, a human guard will be looking from the ID to my face. He'll be looking casually, stupidly, the way those people always do. But he'll be looking. I want you to retain the hologram on the ID, but morph it until it closely resembles this one."

She took the new hologram, frowning. It showed Vray wearing, not the cheap wig he'd received from the penal colony, but an expensive red wig precisely the color of Maklúan's hair. Vray's darkish face had been made up to resemble the tech's reddish coloring, with a sprinkle of ginger freckles. Contact lenses changed his eyes' soulful brown to the peculiar blue-gray of Maklúan's.

"Huh," she muttered. "You're rather good-looking, he's ugly as a stump, and yet the bone structure is quite similar. And so is the height. Is that why you picked him?" She made a few quick measurements. "Didn't shut your jaws for the picture, did you? Bit your tongue. Lengthened your face a centimeter or so. Gave you that horsey look."

She nodded. "I can do it."

"Today?"

"That will cost you double. I've got a ton of work."

"Perhaps I can come back tonight, bring the money and pick up the card."

"Very well," she said. "Come about nineteen. It's none of my business, but I'm rather curious about your interest in Pastplor. I hope you don't mean to try and steal the wormholer. That's a beheader, and I don't mess with capital crimes."

"Hardly practical, since the wormholer weighs seven metric tons. I deal in small electronic devices of all sorts. The offices of this outfit are full of them and the security, once you're past the guard post, is negligible. By the way: if you ever need a new monitor, let me know."

She gave him a washed-out smile as he left. He almost regretted having to kill her.

"At 19 then," he said, and went away.

4

Arriving late for work the day after the holiday—he and Maia had become more than friends at Lake Bai, and parting even for a day had been difficult—Maks found a knot of polizi at the guard station and signs of strain among the technicians.

"What's the problem?" he asked Mogul, now back at work, a bit stringier and leaner than before.

"You know that red-haired guy, the wormholer technician?

Well, the polizi found his body early this morning. He'd been tortured to death."

Maks felt shock. Not that he wouldn't have liked to kill Maklúan himself, but—

"And there's been a security breach, too. Don't know exactly what. But the whole place is boiling like a teakettle."

In the hall, Lian grabbed Maks and pulled him into a vacant office and shut the door. One of the surprising things about her was her talent for picking up gossip.

"Maks, they've gotten back the medical examiner's preliminary report on the time of death for that son of a bitch Maklúan. You remember him, don't you?"

"Only too well," said Maks.

"Well, somebody used his ID to enter Pastplor a good twelve hours after he'd been killed."

Maks gave a long, low whistle.

"That's not the worst of it. The intruder might have been just a thief. But the wormholer's been tampered with."

They stared at each other.

"Another Crux?" whispered Maks. Lián shrugged.

"All I know is, someone totally unauthorized has gone into the past. Back before the Time of Troubles. Why, nobody seems to know."

By lunchtime other tidbits had been fed into the gossip mill.

"The polizi are finding other bodies," Lian reported to Maks and Mogul. They were eating together at a corner table in the noisy cafeteria. "They've found physical evidence to connect Maklúan's death with the murders of two women."

"It's a conspiracy," said Mogul.

"Either that or somebody who really gets around."

It was late in the afternoon of a stressful day when Colonel Yost called a meeting of the timesurfers. Because of the crowd, the white-tiled walls soon became steamy with moisture.

Maks had always vaguely liked and trusted Yost's long pale

face and his precise intellectual air. Stories that he presided at *shosho* sessions Maks dismissed as gossip. Maybe the polizi had to beat up an occasional criminal, but surely the savage *shosho* of the past was over for good.

Today Yost seemed undisturbed either by the heat or by catastrophic events. He repeated quietly the news that everybody already knew, then delivered some new tidbits.

"I must tell you that this incident has the makings of a major scandal."

He sighed, his most emotional reaction so far.

"Tentative identification of our intruder has been made from the DNA in traces of semen retained in the body of one of his victims. Though he sometimes went by the name of Loki, he is really a criminal named Vray Dak, who served time in a penal colony."

"Are we sending somebody into the past after him?" Lian wanted to know.

"That has not yet been decided."

But as the members of the agency filed out, Yost called Mogul and Maks aside. In a low voice he told them that, while Vray had erased his destination from the wormholer's memory, a backup memory retained it.

"I believe this may have been Maklúan's last contribution to Pastplor," he said. "To conceal the existence of the backup. Or he may have died before he could give the necessary code. The tortures to which he was subjected indicated a certain inartistic crudeness on the part of the murderer. Or perhaps simply haste."

Something about the quiet, pedantic way he said this gave Maks a chill. Then Yost's next words made him forget everything else.

"His goal is Washington, two years before you men visited it. We have his approximate 'landing zone' to within a square kilometer. Whether he's moved on, of course, I've no idea. You'll follow, prepare a hiding place, and guide the polizi when they arrive. My statement that no decision has been made," he added apologetically, "was not entirely true."

5

How splendid it all is, Loki was thinking.

He sat on a broad marble terrace gazing into the dense pollen-colored light of the setting sun. In the distance a battle was raging on one of the city's broad avenues—a scuffle of black beetles, it looked like from this hill. Primitive noisy firearms exploded here and there.

He smiled blissfully. He had discarded his useless and inappropriate former names once and for all. No more Vray Dak, the counterfeiter of identities. No more Ya7326 the convict. Instead the name of an ancient fire god, a malicious being whose business was destruction.

To lounge upon a high place, looking down on a world, knowing that its future and its fate lay in your hands—if being a god didn't mean this, what did it mean?

If he had ever doubted the fact of his deification in the tunnels of Calisto, he doubted it no longer. For this he had undergone torture and exile, to burn away the merely human, to make him the fated master—or the master of fate—he had become. He curled his fingers around empty air, feeling he held such *mosh* as no human had ever known.

Gas grenades popped and a column of masked soldiers double-timed toward the disturbance. They carried knives on the ends of their firearms and the points glinted and waved like a field of shining grain on the fertile fields of the Gobi.

He stood up and craned to see better, then ducked involuntarily as a bullet whistled overhead. He frowned at himself: as if a bit of metal could injure *him*.

Commands were shouted nearby and he turned to see a file of soldiers appear around the corner of an antique domed building looming behind him. A sergeant shouted at him and gestured coarsely with one thumb. Loki thought of killing him—he was carrying an impact pistol under a loose shirt he'd procured from the costume room at Pastplor.

No, he thought, retiring down a long flight of stained and worn marble steps, *better do nothing to call premature attention to myself. There'll be killing enough later on.*

That night was noisy and humid. Loki padded down a tree-lined street, reflecting on his first day here. The language was more of a problem than he'd expected. You couldn't learn much about the way real people spoke from a book, even an interactive book like the one he'd studied. Especially this ancient gobbling, mispronounced, full of allusions to things that had vanished centuries ago.

On the other hand, some things were unexpectedly easy about living in this world. The fact that he had an unintelligible accent didn't seem to bother anyone. The same was true of half the people in Washington. So far nobody had asked him for an ID. There seemed to be no checkpoints, no random arrests. The lack of social controls made him feel first giddy, then anxious.

Why, he thought, *you can hardly call this a society at all—everybody doing whatever they please!*

He was still brooding about the deplorable lack of order when he spotted an elderly woman who had come out to buy food. At once he forced her into an alley, killed her with a blow to the nape of the neck, and robbed her. For a little time he hovered over the corpse whispering to the woman (as he'd whispered to Maklúan and his lover and the woman who forged identities), *Welcome, welcome to my kingdom.*

Then he went to dinner.

He ate in a small food shop, paying 5,000 dollars from his store of stolen cash, and left the shop picking his teeth. Spotting a sign in a dimly lit window, he rented a room nine or ten blocks from the Capitol building. When the landlord tried to find out something about him, he relapsed into Alspeke.

"Ya kam' syudá vas destrukta," he smiled, telling the truth for once. (I came here to destroy you. You plural—all of you.)

"Oh, a Russian," said the landlord. Mr. Santana wore his gray undershirt and permanent stubble of beard like a uniform of his calling. "I guess your luggage'll be along later?"

"Yess," said Loki, with what he hoped was a friendly smile.

"One thing I got to say for you people, you know how to run a country," said the landlord, showing him to a bed-sitter three flights up. "Not like them fuckers down the street."

Left alone, Loki counted his money, checked the pistol he'd bought on Ulanor's black market, and went to bed. Sleep proved difficult, for the heat was oppressive and a brownout had reduced the bed-sitter's primitive aircooler to tentative gasps. He got up, sweating, opened a window, dragged his mattress onto a little halfmoon-shaped balcony and stretched out there. A bit cooler, though not much.

In the distance, a shot. Closer at hand, a scream. Just below the balcony, a laugh. *Ah, my people,* he thought. *They're all about, the hunters prowling the dark, rejoicing in the disorder that frightens everyone else.*

Eventually he fell asleep and dreamed of slaughter until he was awakened by the sun.

CHAPTER XII

On their second trip to Washington, Maks and Mogul found the city much as before. Sometimes it was hard to remember that they were two years deeper into the past than the last time they'd been here, since everything seemed just about the same.

President Derrick Minh Smith was completing his second year in office and his record so far was the subject of noisy debate. A big, solid, slow-talking politician, he had the necessary ethnic mix—part white, part black, part Latino, part South Asian. (South Asians were current favorites with Americans because of their heroic resistance to Chinese aggression.)

He came to power with a mandate for restoring order, but his use of force so far had been brutal and inept. In Idaho several National Guard units had gone over to the rebels; people were talking about a downward spiral, but nobody knew how to stop it.

As for Vray Dak, he was invisible in a disorderly city of nineteen million. Completely untrained in police work, Maks and Mogul had not a clue as to how to proceed, except to get a place to live and prepare for the arrival of the professionals who would manage the search. They found an apartment in the lower reaches of Capitol Hill near the Burned-Out District, in a 150-year-old redbrick row house owned by a slatternly widow named Mrs. Crane.

Here they laid out their small valises with a change of twenty-first-century clothing, impact pistols, their own wormholer controls and two extras—one to return Vray's body to their own time, one for backup in case a control was damaged. Then they went shopping, using a counterfeit cashcard manufactured by the Security Forces' digital imagers. They needed to be in electronic contact with this world, and so they bought first a tivi that received the local thousand channels.

"A thousand!" said Mogul, shaking his head. "Great Tao, Ulanor gets along with three channels. In the offworlds, there are whole planets that have exactly one. I don't see how the government can maintain control, do you? Why, anything might go out over the air! Do you suppose the polizi watch all thousand?"

Maks shook his head. This world grew stranger, not more familiar, the longer he stayed in it.

"It's no wonder everything's in such a mess," he had to agree. "Nobody's in *charge* here."

The day was hot, the walk long. The tainted air made them cough and the crowds were mind-numbing. Street-corner orators bawled their messages and small crowds of red-faced, sweating people shouted yea or nay.

In another electronics store they bought a second kind of primitive mashina. This one had a brain, and was called a kompyutor. They came in all sizes, from boxes with screens four meters square down to micros that dangled from charm bracelets or, set like gray sapphires into rings, answered questions in tiny voices like mice.

"Everybody's got one," a baffled clerk told them, "usually more. Where you guys from? No, you don't need a license to own one. What do people do with 'em? Well, they all send and receive whatever they please, including invitations to attend riots. It's up to you what you use it for."

They chose a cheap model with a medium screen, returned to their apartment weary, and soaked their feet, sitting side by side on the edge of a pink plastic tub that sported the hair of unknown people embedded in a greasy ring. Then they unboxed and began to examine the purchases they'd made during the day.

The tivi was a disappointment—just sex, sports, baffling comedies, ranting Old Believer priests. They set the kompyutor up on a battered plastic kitchen table and were just about to try a few commands when the room flickered.

A sudden hot wind rushed through the apartment, tossing their unpacked clothing against the walls. A figure condensed as if a billion pixels had rushed together from the far horizons to form a single image. The image moved, smiled—the woman was wearing the clothing of the twenty-first century and carrying an impact pistol in her hand—and she was Zo Lian.

2

At once the kompyutor was abandoned. For an instant Maks wanted to ask Lian how she'd found them so precisely, but then he forgot the question. Instead they embraced and laughed, and then they all went out for dinner.

The soy house had its own gasoline-run generator and a big fan that whipped the hot air into furious motion. Afterward they strolled a few blocks and sat down together on the grass in a small park while dusk darkened into breathless night. The heat was such that forty or fifty people were resting on the grass nearby.

They chatted softly in Alspeke, a language that only one other man in the city could have understood.

"Why'd they decide to send you, Lian?"

"Well, I do have an idea. Or rather I had an idea given me. I went to the university and spoke to Chancellor Yang, the famous historian, and I said to him: we think Vray Dak wants to change history, but how's he going to do it?"

"I've asked myself that question ten-to-the-tenth-power times," admitted Maks, "and I still don't know."

Lian had brought a *meshok*—beltpouch—of kif and three folding pipes with her. Since other people lying in the dark grass among the katydids were smoking various substances, the surfers lit up as well. Traffic rumbled on the nearby streets and polizi hovercraft buzzed and sputtered overhead, drawing white fingers of searchlights across the city.

"Here's Yang's suggestion," said Lian. "The one thing Vray has that could make him a man of influence in this world is his knowledge of the future. Suppose he tries to set himself up as a prophet?"

Maks smoked quietly, letting the drug relax and clarify his mind. It was Mogul who spoke up.

"That's an idea," he admitted. "And if you're right, I think I know how to find him."

"Ah," said Maks. "The kompyutor."

At this point a man lying on the grass nearby asked in Russian, "*Izvinitye, pozhal' sta. Vi govoritye po-russki?*"

"Not a word," said Lian, and the three surfers got up, stretched themselves, and strolled away into the night.

"I could swear," said the man querulously, "that those guys were talking some sort of Russian. I worked in Moscow for five years with our embassy and I recognized a word here, a word there. But it's not like any Russian I ever heard."

"Don't ask me," said a man who was lying next to him. "Not all so well I don't know Inlish mine self."

Then he rose and slouched casually away into the darkness, following the surfers.

The Russian speaker sighed and stretched out again, hoping for a breath of cool air but finding none. *What a city*, he thought. *Nineteen million people and no two of them can really understand each other. No wonder things are in such a mess.*

3

Working with the primitive kompyutor wasn't easy, Maks quickly discovered.

In spite of all their training in archaic English, it was always misunderstanding their commands—even Lian's, who spoke the language best. Though its cyberspace was limited to the Earth and Luna and ought to have been fairly simple to move around in, in fact it was more complicated than anything Maks had ever seen.

As the clerk had told them, all sorts of totally unauthorized people used it for every imaginable purpose and finding things required a knowledge of mysterious icons that meant nothing to the time travelers.

Maks was still confused and angry at the gadget when a thunderstorm swept in, relieving the heat but shutting off the electricity and blanking out the kompyutor. So they went to bed, waking only for the watch Mogul insisted they keep, sitting up one at time with their backs against the apartment's flimsy door.

Just after dawn, Maks, who'd had the last watch, again tried his luck on the strange mashina. He felt like a twenty-first-century navigator compelled to use an astrolabe, contemptuous of the primitive instrument yet baffled as to how to use it properly. Aside from offers for an array of sex services, the only thing of interest he found was an infopage called "The Moon Today," inserted by the International Space Agency.

The sound of the kompyutor's nonhuman voice woke first Lian, who was sleeping on a divan, and then Mogul, who entered from the bedroom.

"Things must be really crude up on Luna," Maks reported. "It's not a self-sustaining colony yet. They're just installing the first laser-fired pure-hydrogen reactor and it's a new technology and everybody's expecting it to blow up. They've found the deep permafrost beds under the Sea of Tranquillity, but they haven't figured out a way to extract the water efficiently. Everyone's living in domes half buried in the dust and drinking recycled urine."

"I think I had some of that with dinner last night," muttered Mogul, for the city's water supply was contaminated and resembled tea in color, though not in taste.

Maks continued to try his luck, wasting some time futilely looking for prophets.

"Try psychics," suggested Lian.

"I don't know that word. What does it mean?"

"Just try it."

Sure enough, the keyword yielded a directory of names and specialties. Some psychics apparently did nothing but find lost pets; some, lost children; some gave tips on the stock market; some helped with errant lovers. Apparently President Smith was a believer, for some psychics averred that they were "Often Consulted By The White House."

Many predicted the future, and here Maks concentrated his efforts. One advertisement followed another, every one rich in promises of better times.

"Poor bastards," he muttered. "I suppose I could tell them, 'The future won't only be worse than you imagine; the future will be worse than you *can* imagine.' But who'd want to believe that?"

Lian got up and stood behind him. Suddenly she said, "There!"

"Where?"

" 'The Future So Real. Firm tip on whats happening politicly.' Only our friend would be likely to write like that."

Maks tapped the screen. A face startlingly like the dead tech stared out at them. The come-on promised "Absolute tip on next year doing in high level political thing. Aks and you sall get all you wish to know bout Congress & Pres outcome world event cetera. Cost merely $12.5K per suces." A long string of symbols followed, concluding, "Futureman.psi."

"I wonder how many customers he's gotten with this," smiled Lian.

Mogul had joined them. "Can you ask him a question?"

Maks enunciated Vray's address in his best Archaic English and ordered, "Call."

All three tensed: for the first time they were about to speak directly to their quarry.

"How can I assist you?" asked a cool female voice.

They looked at each other.

"I would," said Maks slowly and clearly, "like to know Futureman's prediction for the outcome of the current fighting in Montana. Will the government be successful or will the rebels?"

"Please leave your E-address. Futureman will return your call within thirty minutes. Cost to you will be only twelve thousand five hundred dollars."

They looked at each other. Mogul was saying, "Well, of course we don't have an E-address," and Lian was saying at the same time, "It's some sort of answering service, don't you see," when they heard a scream from downstairs.

Then a small, dull sound on the staircase, more like a cough than anything else.

4

Lian recovered first, diving for her weapon as feet pounded up the wooden stairs. Maks, slower to respond, was just beginning to grasp the danger when the flimsy door burst open and a tall man with red wig askew stepped into the apartment, raised an impact pistol with both hands, and touched the firing stud.

The round hit Mogul square in the chest and flung him backward over the kompyutor. Maks was halfway to the floor by then and the second round clipped his flying hair and blew a small hole in the wall of the building. In the same instant Lian's answering shot struck the intruder in the belly and tore him in half.

Suddenly and with amazingly little noise the room had become a bloody shambles. Blood sprayed the walls and ceiling; dust drifted in the air, and a ray of sunlight entering through the crater blown by Vray's round illuminated a slow-swirling universe of motes. Maks raised a head whitened by plaster and stared uncomprehendingly at the ruin, the shattered bodies.

Lian got up quietly, gun in hand. Warily she approached Vray's body, turned its lower half over. She knelt and spent a minute or two going through the pockets. Maks turned his attention to Mogul, but the sight was horrible and trying to help was pointless. Mogul was dead, the center of his rib cage pulped, twenty centimeters of his spine missing.

Shuddering, sick to his stomach but unable to vomit, Maks turned away. He stumbled to the window and stared out. The street looked absolutely normal. The hole was in a side wall and would go unnoticed unless the neighbors happened to look up. The impact weapons spoke so quietly that even the birds in the small, heat-dried plane trees outside continued to flutter and sing in celebration of dawn as if nothing had happened at all.

Lian showed Maks her bloody gleanings. Vray had almost 80,000 dollars in notes—"Not much," remarked Lian, "he'd have had to start stealing again pretty soon"—and several important items of information as well.

Maklúan's ID was there, with the picture Vray had used to set up his page. Several stained and folded pieces of paper: a receipt from We Speak 4 U Arbot Service; another from the landlord of a rooming house on Capitol Hill not ten blocks from this one. Then Lian held up like trophies two metal keys for mechanical locks.

"Entry to his den," she said.

Maks was still full of shock and sickness. He felt like a child; he wanted to cry, but controlled himself.

"I guess I wasn't much good in the crisis," he muttered. He kept thinking that somehow he ought to have saved Mogul. Lian understood at once and spoke soothingly.

"You couldn't have saved him, Maks. Anyway, he was the senior member of the party and the fact that we were caught off guard was more his fault than yours or mine."

Maks nodded but felt no better. If not exactly a friend, Mogul had been his companion in adventure and they had trusted and depended on each other.

"I suppose we'd better be preparing for transit," Maks said. Then suddenly he turned and embraced Lian.

"Thank you. For saving me. I'd be like Mogul except for you."

Even in his distress he noticed yet again the oddness of her body's feel. She stood quietly, not responding to his embrace, just experiencing it. Then gently pushed him away.

"You're welcome," she said. "But we've got things to do. Before we go, we have to visit Vray's apartment and clean out anything that might show he was from the future."

"You're right, you're right," Maks muttered, wondering how he could have overlooked something so obvious. Lian gave him another gentle shove, this time toward the bathroom.

"You can't go outside like that," she said. "Wash off the blood. And get the plaster dust out of your hair."

Now she's treating me like a child, thought Maks resentfully as he scrubbed. Drying his head, he reflected on his career thus far. All his life he'd been a mediocrity, and Lian—cool and daring and inhumanly detached—had shown him only too clearly that he was one still.

He rejoined her looking clean, sober. They walked down the stairs, avoiding their landlady's shattered corpse, disturbing a few green flies. Out into the hot sunlight, where the air tasted like copper and the murmur of a mob could already be heard in the distance, preparing the day's demonstration.

"I'll be glad when we get home," said Maks. Lian raised her eyebrows.

"Oh yes?"

"Yes. I'm going to resign once this job's done," said Maks, and they walked the rest of the way to Vray's dwelling without speaking.

Finding a dour-looking, undershirted man seated on the front steps of Vray's building, they waited until he finished reading a crumpled piece of hard copy—the four-page "morning paper" that could be bought for a 500-dollar coin from containers at street corners—and shuffled away on some errand or other.

Then they used the two keys to enter first the house and—after much fruitless trying of locks—Vray's own room. It was big, airy, with odd pieces of hardware left over from earlier centuries. Pipes for illuminating gas dangled from the ceiling and ancient painted-over copper wiring was still tacked to the baseboards.

They quickly searched Vray's neatly made bed and closet, finding that he had carried his habits of deception and anonymity into the past with him.

"The only things he had that clearly say 'Future' we've already got," said Lian when the search was over. "I thought he might have some extra rounds of ammo here, but apparently what we found was all he had."

Maks shook his head. "I still don't really understand his plan. What was he after, committing those murders in Ulanor, coming to this place? What could he hope to accomplish?"

Lian shrugged.

"Yang thought the date—2050—might be significant. Tensions between America and China were high at the time, until President Smith made concessions to buy peace. Vray might have hoped to influence Smith to set off the Time of Troubles early, which would have meant the end of humanity. Rather a pathetic hope, considering he couldn't even speak the language decently. But then Vray may have been paranoid, with delusions of omnipotence. Whether he was born that way or driven around the bend by torture and isolation, who can say?"

Maks nodded slowly.

"It amazes me how some people can figure things," he said. "Well, come on, Lian. Let's clear out. We've got some messy work still to do."

Lian shook her head, smiling.

"Maks, Maks," she said, drawing her pistol. "It's too bad. You're such a nice guy, but so dumb. We're not going back. I'm going to carry out what Vray started. Only I'm going to do it right."

CHAPTER XIII

Improvising a kang was easy enough. Lian had Maks remove two slats from Vray's bed and cords from the window blinds and wet them in the sink.

Then Maks had to lie down with his neck and wrists on one board while Lian laid the second over his Adam's apple. She knelt on the second board, almost throttling him, and tied his wrists and head tightly between the boards. As a kang it was imperfect, but it served.

Lian tied his ankles as well. Finally, she gagged Maks with a torn pillowcase and left him lying on the floor while she returned to the other building to dispose of the corpses, sending them to the future. She was an efficient worker; forty minutes later she was back, carrying a bag with her personal items.

Her last job before resting was to call up Vray's web page and rewrite it in clear, elegant Archaic English. Then she removed Maks's gag and sat down on the floor beside him to have a chat.

"I sent a note with the bodies, explaining that Vray had a confederate and that you and I were going after him. I added that no backup would be needed. I think that our success in getting rid of Vray will impress them enough to trust our judgment. Kif?"

Lian held the pipe to Maks's lips to help him smoke. Then, like old friends, they talked quietly together.

"How long have you been thinking about destroying us?" asked Maks. His voice was still hoarse from Lian kneeling on his throat; it hurt just to swallow his spit.

Lian thought for a long time. She had turned on a small lamp. Sitting on the floor (she wouldn't sit on a chair, as if politeness forbade putting herself on a higher level than Maks), she looked even less human than usual.

Like an extinct beast—what was its name? Maks wondered. *Oh yes, the cheetah.* A kind of cat, skinny, long-limbed, with a great barrel chest and a killer's heart. Dimly, from some long-ago Earth Biology class, he remembered that the female of the species had been the most accomplished hunter.

"Do you know," Lian finally asked, "how the Darksiders became servants of humanity?"

"No."

"My planet, Beta Charonis, has an unusual motion: one side always faces its sun, the other always away. A civilized race called the Siat gradually won dominance of the warm side. The Darksiders were primitives—intelligent but mute, with a crude material culture—and they were forced back gradually into the penumbra, the twilight between the two hemispheres. Often, when they were under attack they had to retreat into the region of everlasting cold. They acquired the eyes of nocturnal beings, the fur of creatures acclimated to cold, and the howling winds that always blow between the two sides of the planet. They lived in nomadic societies that you might call either packs or tribes.

"Then came the humans, and their *mosh* changed everything. The Siat resisted their attempts to take land and mines. So the humans allied themselves to the Darksiders. Without fighting themselves, they supplied modern weapons to their barbarian friends, who proceeded to wipe out the Siat with unimaginable savagery. The Darksiders imprisoned their foes in pits and spent— I don't know how long; a long time—dragging them out a few at a time to flay and burn and eat. The humans took what they wanted from the planet, mainly ores, and in time they began to use the Darksiders as mercenaries."

Maks said, "That's a horrible story, but it doesn't explain your actions."

"It's hard to convey," said Lian, frowning. "There aren't any words for what I feel because there aren't any precise words for what I am. When the mining companies were looking for a way to adapt humans to Beta Charonis they borrowed a few surviving Siat slaves from the Darksiders and the *mediki* experimented on them. Of course our *mediki* weren't the best by any means, and they came up with synthetic genes that changed more than they were supposed to change. Sometimes I think I'm more Siat than human. Certainly I've never felt human. And if I can bring this off, the whole episode of the human invasion will never have happened at all."

"How can you hope to destroy a whole species?"

"It's very, very difficult," she sighed. "But I didn't come to Earth expecting it to be easy. In fact, until the timesurfer program was set up, I didn't have any clear plan at all."

At this moment the kompyutor chimed. Lian listened to the

query for Futureman—how would the coming congressional elections come out? She answered that the party split would be: National Union, 12 percent; Revolutionary All-American, 7.5 percent; Constitutional Conservative, 7 percent . . . and so on down to Democratic, 3 percent, and Republican, 1.8 percent.

"You have a remarkable memory," murmured Maks.

"I read your report on your first trip to Washington two years from now," said Lian. "It was truly informative."

They smoked a while longer, until Maks got up the courage to ask another crucial question.

"What do you intend to do with me?"

Lian let thin trickles of smoke exit her nostrils.

"I'd like to let you live for whatever time remains," she said. "Killing you would be . . . painful. It's not what I want. I've had such an awful life and I want to be happy. Once. For just a little while. We could . . . we could spend the time together."

She coughed on the smoke. Maks twisted against the cords. Stared at her. *Great Tao*, he thought. *So that's it.*

She turned away, unable to look at him as she whispered, "It's either that, or you have to die now."

She turned back then, her face as still as a stone lion's.

So, he thought, *I'm the window in the wall the experimenters on Beta Charonis built around her. All this has been inside her—hate, love, everything. And I never guessed.*

"I can't set you free now," she explained. "Obviously. But if we—if you agree, well, I'll set you free as soon as I can. After I've accomplished what I want to do, I'll destroy the controls, all of them. I'll untie you then. I don't care if you kill me. I have to die anyway. But if you don't, then we can have a little time together before the end of everything."

The kompyutor chimed, making both of them jump. The voice of the answering-service arbot said, "The customer you just replied to wishes to know how you can make such precise predictions?"

Drawing a deep breath, Lian steadied her voice. "Because I am not a psychic. I am a messenger from the future, come to prevent dreadful things from happening. President Derrick Minh Smith is the key figure, the pivot upon whom the ages turn. If he chooses right, the whole human species will live, and if he chooses wrong they will all perish. I'm here to give him such help as I may."

Lian smiled at Maks. "That should attract the idiot," she remarked.

The kompyutor chimed again.

"Yes," said Lian.

"The previous customer has now paid 37,500 dollars," said the service. "His new question is this: What will be the outcome of the present fighting in Idaho and Montana? Will the federal forces win, or will the rebels?"

"Neither," answered Lian promptly. "Both will still be engaged in pointless conflict when the Chinese attack occurs."

Apparently the cool-voiced arbot wasn't prepared for phrases like "Chinese attack."

"I beg your pardon?"

"Repeat my words exactly as I have said them," said Lian, and smiled at Maks.

"We have a fish," she said. Then sighing, she stretched out on the floor beside Maks.

"Can you make love to an animal?" she asked.

Can I? he wondered. But the way to survival, the only way, was plain to see. His voice roughened.

"I'm supposed to fuck, tied up like a pig?"

"Oh, it can be done. But only if you want to."

"The polite rapist."

She shivered. "Don't use that word. And don't say fuck. I know the love's only on one side, but don't insult it. Even if you hate me, don't hate the love."

He closed his eyes. *I can think of Maia.* He pictured her as she had been at Lake Bai when they lay down together, the Siberian wine running in their veins. Tasting each other—above, then below.

"If I've got to die with you," he said, "I might as well do some living first."

She smiled, and unless he was crazy, her smile was *shy*. "You'll have to tell me what to do. I've never done it. Will it hurt me?"

"Yes," he said.

2

Night came on with a sudden shower of rain, unexpected coolness. Lian washed herself in the pink tub, sitting a long time in the warm water. He heard her crying softly. Then she washed Maks, pulled up his trousers, and fed him.

When he complained of pain in his shoulders, Lian massaged him gently. When he demanded to be untied, she pointed out that she couldn't do that.

"You ought to practice patience," she admonished. "Pain is only pain, after all. With the proper attitude, one can endure anything."

She sounded now like one of Maks's childhood amahs.

For the night, Lian dragged and lifted Maks onto the divan, made him as comfortable as possible, then put out the lamp, and curled up like a cat on the floor. A little while later, he heard the regular breathing of deep sleep.

In the darkness, immobile in the kang, Maks tried to review the astounding events of the last twenty-four hours. But instead of trying to plan an escape, he saw her again, her long strange body mounted on him, impaling herself, sweating and wincing and finally crying out because she was trying to take him in too deeply.

Pain was only pain, after all.

He smelled again the curious odor of her sweat. Of her blood. Then exhaustion fell on him like an assailant and wrapped him in thick blankets.

He woke when the kompyutor chimed. Tall windows had turned gray and slow rain was falling. Lian spoke quietly to her caller, jotted something down on a scrap of paper. Then she kissed Maks on the lips and donned fresh clothes.

"Someone important wants to interview me," she told him. "I'll try to be as quick as I can. Perhaps you'd like a drink before I go?"

Maks drank the water. He didn't bother to mention that he hurt, that he was stiff. Lian would simply tell him to practice patience. He also needed to urinate, but shrank from having her touch him again. He looked at her with hate.

Just before she gagged him, he said, "I guess you *will* come back?"

"Oh, yes, my dear. And I hope I'll be able to set you free."

Then Lian was gone. Quietly, checking the stairs first to be sure the landlord was not about, then locking the door behind her. Distantly the front door closed.

The rain fell like the slow drumming of bored fingers. Maks tried to keep his circulation going, clenching and unclenching his fists, wiggling his toes. His skin felt as if it had been sandpapered; he itched intolerably. A cockroach climbed ticklishly up one leg, explored his face, and fed on fluid oozing from his nose until he sneezed and sent it scuttling away.

He needed to urinate, to defecate, tried to hold it, couldn't. He had heard about prisoners who were forced to lie in their own excrement, but he had never thought he could be brought so low.

In a sudden fury, he twisted and wrenched at the cords until his neck and wrists bled. It was hopeless. He began to sob and the tears ran out of the corners of his eyes and down his cheekbones.

Thunder muttered a long way off. The rain stopped, then started again.

Footsteps were ascending the staircase. At first he thought Lian had returned, then realized that the steps were too heavy and too slow. A key rattled in the lock, and a weighty middle-aged man backed in. His arms were full of sheets, pillowcases, and towels. It was change-the-linen day.

He turned, displaying the permanent bristle of gray beard, the permanent undershirt. A cigarette was sutured to his lower lip. When he caught sight of Maks, his jaw dropped, but the cigarette clung to its place.

"*Sheeeee,*" he muttered. "Who's this?"

Maks made incoherent sounds as he approached, wrinkling his nose. He pulled the gag off roughly and repeated his question.

"I own this joint," he added. "Name's Santana. Now talk."

"Your tenant kidnapped me," gasped Maks, his speech unusually thick because the gag had dried his mouth.

"Good Christ, another Russian. What is that guy, Mafia?"

"Yes, *mafya*," said Maks.

"Well, I'll be goddamned. They know you at the embassy?"

"Yes. Could you please untie me?"

The landlord frowned, debated the question in his mind. What if this guy was Moscow Mafia, too? On the other hand, he looked different from the tenant; a different kind, more like a college kid. Slowly and reluctantly, he began to untie Maks.

"The Mafia must be like the Boy Scouts."

"Why?"

"Teach 'em to tie good knots. What'd he want from you?"

"Money and cashcards," said Maks promptly. "He's out right now, trying to use my cards."

"We'll call the cops as soon as I get you loose."

Just sitting up was agony. Every muscle seemed to have frozen and rusted in place. Maks's arms were dead white, his feet and ankles swollen. At first he couldn't stand. Santana helped him, but with obvious reluctance.

"I can see you've had a rough time, young fella, but frankly, you stink pretty bad."

"Sorry."

"Don't apologize. Go wash."

Maks did, while the landlord shook his head over the stained and fragrant bedding he'd left behind. He took the sheets with obvious distaste and threw them into the hall.

Somewhat restored to decency, Maks rejoined him, wearing a set of Vray's clothing with only moderate discomfort at armpits and crotch.

"You call the polizi," he told Santana (the Alspeke word just slipped out). "I'm going straight to the embassy to report this. My name is Ivanov Nikolas—pardon me, Nikolas Ivanov—and I'll be there when they want me."

"What if he comes back?"

"Go stay in your apartment until the polizi come. Have you a weapon?"

"You bet I do. The most illegal one I could find."

"Shoot him if he tries to come in. Oh, and he has a confederate who's even worse than he is—a young woman with weird-looking eyes. Stay completely out of her way. Tell the poliz—police that she's armed with a new type of exploding ammo the Moscow Mafia's been trying out. Tell them she's extremely dangerous."

Suddenly the forgotten cigarette burned the landlord's lip and he cursed and flung it away.

"Christ, that thing cost me twelve bucks on the black market," he muttered and lurched away into the shadowy hall.

Maks waited at the head of the stairs until he heard the door of Santana's first-floor apartment close and four separate locks snap into place. Then he called the answering service on Vray's kompyutor.

"I've lost my note on that address you gave me," he said. "Would you please repeat it?"

"Room 3657B, Executive Office Building."

His last chore was to unplug the kompyutor and wrap it in an extra shirt. A minute later he was on the street, hungry and tense and happier than ever in his life just to be free, to be moving, to be capable of action again. The blood pumped deliciously through his whole body, erasing the last traces of stiffness.

The rage remained. *Lian, Lian,* he thought. *You should have killed me when you had the chance.*

3

He smiled grimly. Adrift in a disorderly city centuries before his birth with no money, no weapon, and no way to communicate with his own time or return to it, he was recalling Mogul's remark that time travel was not for sweet kids.

Yet he had a plan. Maks was searching for the kind of shop where small loans were made. The Alspeke word was *zlog,* but for the life of him he couldn't remember the Archaic English; all he could think of was, for some reason, the game of chess.

He plunged into the streams of people flowing past the Capitol, with its peeling iron dome and mellow stone walls and small groups of soldiers idling near the autogun emplacements on the weedy lawn.

He'd walked nearly three clicks when the word "pawn" suddenly registered in his mind. It was painted on a small windowless building equipped with a steel door and two hired thuggi lounging on a bench outside. Each man had a pistol stuck in his belt. They looked at Maks with the eyes of bored dogs as he entered. A few minutes later he emerged, richer by a thousand dollars—enough to buy breakfast, which he did at a greasy food kiosk down the street.

With food in his belly and vengeance on his mind, he found the rest of his walk to the White House easy. *All that running and wrestling and swimming is paying off,* he thought. But the White House was easier to look at than to approach. The streets that ran by the Treasury were blocked off and patrolled by uniformed thuggi and by others in civilian clothes, each with a little button of a jabber mike stuck in his ear. They were, Maks decided, probably more dangerous than the uniformed types and he gave them a wide berth.

He had to circle wide, up 14th Street to Franklin Park, where more soldiers were encamped under spreading green trees, then along Eye Street to 17th and south again, giving Lafayette Square a wide berth. *Must have been a riot there,* he thought, eyeing the throng of soldiers and polizi and the meat wagons from the Medical Examiner's office and the *mediki* removing bodies.

It was 1 PM—that is to say, 13—or a little past when he reached the old multicolumned Executive Office Building. On the rooftop, batteries of television cameras and laser-activated automatic weapons turned slowly from side to side; within the building, Maks assumed, kompyutors were watching for suspicious behavior. Farther down 17th Street smoke was rising from the hulk of the Corcoran Museum, recently torched.

Intent as he was on finding Lian, he loitered for long minutes in this dangerous region, fascinated by the sight of his own world, the world of the Darksiders and the Security Forces, already— more than forty years before the war of 2091—beginning to emerge from the decay of what textbooks called the Democratic Century.

Getting into the building seemed hopeless. Only one entry was open and people going through it were being checked and scanned. Lian had passed through that door at the invitation of someone within. But nobody had invited Maks, and if he lingered too long the kompyutors would spot him as a suspicious person.

For an instant he considered getting himself picked up for questioning; at least it was a way in. But a shudder went through him just to think of it; he knew now what being a prisoner meant.

Instead, he drifted with a passing group of federal workers, all equipped with metal ID collars, back to Pennsylvania Avenue and up it toward the northwest. He could not get at Lian inside the building, but he could wait for her to come out. Assuming, that is, he could tolerate waiting at all.

CHAPTER XIV

For Lian, the morning went first well, then badly.

The presidential aide who'd vouched for her at the guardpost was lowly, a young man worthy of nothing more than a tiny office in a deep basement. The aide had dandruff and pinkish eyes and even a trace of acne, as if he'd finished with adolescence only last month. A youngster whose life was a long series of putdowns from his superiors, he glared at her with defensive arrogance.

"So you're from the future?"

Lian smiled. "Just so."

"I'll try to explain in simple terms why I'm wasting time with you. We've got these arbots, little bundles of artificial intelligence with complicated algorithms that can carry on lengthy conversations. We put them into cyberspace to entrap subversives by drawing them into conversations where they give themselves away . . ."

"I'm familiar with the technique in possibly more sophisticated form," said Lian patiently.

The aide frowned. "Well, false prophecies are politically useful in some instances but dangerous in others. So we have arbots check the psychics and draw them out. The odd thing about you is that your data on the next election's quite close to some highly classified computer estimates done for the president. We'd like to know where you got your information."

"From a history," said Lian, "that will not be written for three hundred years. If your estimates are in basic agreement with my data, I'd say they're quite accurate. May I make a suggestion?"

The aide raised sandy eyebrows.

"Certain objects were taken from me when I passed through the checkpoint. If you ask to have them brought here, you may find what I'm saying a bit more believable."

Sighing, the aide touched a button and spoke to a small, shiny intercom. Then he took some papers out of his desk and ostentatiously worked on them until the door opened and a uniformed guard placed in front of him a ceramic disk and two oblong devices with metal studs and cyrillic lettering.

Lian picked up the disk and warmed it in her hands. "Say," she told it.

"What time you get your break?"

"Ten to."

"Long time to go."

"Tell me 'bout it."

"Fuckin' Redskins lost that preseason game."

"Deadskins, I call 'em."

The sparkling conversation at the guard post continued to unroll. The aide took the disk and examined it for controls, finding none.

"So you just talk to it," he said with mild interest. "Neat."

"Do you have anything similar?"

Immediately the aide's face became blank.

"Maybe and maybe not."

"Perhaps," said Lian, losing patience, "you'd be kind enough to direct me to someone less stupid than yourself?"

The aide spoke again to the intercom. "Send a guard. I got somebody who's leaving."

"Do you have something like this?" asked Lian. Playing her trump card, she handed over one of the controls.

"I'm not touching one goddamn thing," said the aide, rising. "You, lady, are a nut and this thing I bet is a bomb."

The door opened. A fat guard stood in the doorway, the one, Lian remembered, whose break was scheduled for ten-to. Without hesitation Lian handed her other control to the guard, who took it with a baffled look.

"Watch out!" yelled the aide.

Lian touched the return stud and jumped back, shoving the aide against the wall. The guard's plump body flickered, they saw his guts, they saw his bones, they saw nothing at all. The doorway was empty.

Lian pushed the aide into his chair, closed the door, and sat down across from him again.

"Do you know where he's gone?" she asked, taking back the remaining control.

"To the future?" asked the aide, weakly.

"Yes."

They sat looking at each other for the greater part of a minute. Finally Lian's patience ran out again.

"Hadn't you better notify your superiors?" she asked.

"Oh," said the aide. "Yeah. I guess so."

2

In the ammoniac fumes of a men's toilet, Maks bent over the recumbent body of a federal worker he had followed in and rapped lightly on the base of the skull.

He examined the ID collar closely, then stood up with a curse. There was no way to remove it except to saw it through or cut off the man's head. He was tolerably certain that cutting the collar would inactivate it, and he wasn't willing to decapitate anybody but Lian.

With a muttered apology, he took the man's money—120,000 dollars, he carried a fair sum—and his cashcard and slipped out of the toilet and the restaurant it belonged to, unobserved.

So now I'm a thief, he was thinking. *I wonder if they have penal colonies in 2050. My guess is they do.*

3

How true the saying is, Lian reflected, *that government is a system devised by geniuses to be run by idiots.* It was as true in the twenty-first century as in her own; no doubt it had been true in the Venetian Republic, in the Tang Empire, in thrice-ancient Ur of the Chaldees.

The dandruffy aide's superior was indeed that: superior. Paranoid, perhaps, but not to be accused of stupidity. He examined the ceramic disk and simply nodded. Nobody needed to tell him that it was the end product of a technological evolution that had hardly begun.

"I suppose if I have it X-rayed there won't be anything showing inside," he muttered, adding with a faint smile, "I'd like to have seen the business with the guard."

He was a small man, balding, his flesh burnt away by a lifetime of trusting nobody. His name was Gray.

"Unfortunately," Lian told him, "I've only got one control device left. If you need to see it work, call in another guard."

"You wouldn't mind being marooned in this goddamn century?" asked Gray, continuing to smile bleakly.

"I can help you to make it better. Better than you might believe. Because, unlike anyone else now living, I know what happened."

Gray put up a tent of thin bony fingers that were stained with some drug, probably nicotine.

"Tell me what 'happened,' as you put it."

"China will soon take advantage of America's distress to attack you. Your Russian and European allies will express horror, but do nothing."

"Of course," said Gray, who looked as if he could believe anything about anybody, especially allies. "You won't have heard yet, but China's sending a peace delegation to discuss our outstanding differences. Quite a suspicious act in itself. What better time to start a war than while you're talking peace? Please go on."

"A brief period of peace will be bought by the sacrifice of roughly ninety-two million American lives. But it's only a breather. In circumstances that remain unclear, general war breaks out in 2052 with a thermo-bio exchange so massive as to create a two-year winter while launching lethal epidemics of genetically enhanced influenza viruses that decimate the survivors. Twelve billion people will die."

Gray nodded. "About in line with projections. Every once in a while one of our engineered viruses gets loose and there's hell to pay."

"I have been sent to urge you as strongly as I can to take the only action that can forestall this terrible catastrophe, which is known to our small community of survivors as the Time of Troubles. I refer to preventive war."

Gray said slowly, "That possibility has been . . . discussed. May I see that gadget?"

Lian handed over the control. Gray sat back and looked at it, then, with a wry smile, said to his intercom, "Call the guard station and tell them to send in Harry."

To Lian he added, "He's the one I can spare best. I hope the people in your time don't mind being sent another idiot."

The door opened and a hulking man entered. Harry looked like a Darksider without fur. Lian waited for the new experiment, her mind dwelling with amusement on the astonishment at Pastplor as still another bewildered stranger came through the wormholer.

"Arrest her," said Gray, and Harry grabbed for Lian.

She reacted without thinking, jabbed the big man's Adam's apple with karate-hardened fingers and hurled him back a step into the hall with a gargling sound in his throat. Then Lian turned on Gray, only to find herself facing a crude pistol the man had pulled from some recess.

There was a sound of thunder.

4

"Whatever the truth may be," Gray told the president, "I could hardly have allowed this person into your presence until she was rendered helpless and thoroughly scanned. We've had too many cases of suiciders swallowing plastic microbombs, passing through the screens and blowing up everything in sight."

Smith, staring at the control, merely nodded.

Of course they weren't in the Oval Office: that light-flooded room, for all its triple-paned bulletproof glass, was occupied only by a robot resembling the president, which moved about, conferring with other robots, appearing to drink coffee. It was there to draw fire. Recently a maniac had tried to crash a small plane into the office, only to be stopped in midair by a missile.

Thirty-six meters below, the president kept to his bunker, a complex of offices and guard posts, communication centers and dispensaries, dining halls and dormitories. This comfortable room was his favorite, its walls decorated with trompe l'oeil images of rare books. The furniture was deep-cushioned Victorian; the pictures on the walls, historic portraits.

A rosewood armoire and the walls of creamy old plaster hid the electronic spiderweb that connected the president to the outside world. Overhead, faux candles flickered in a chandelier with one hundred prisms. An imitation fire burned in an imitation fireplace.

"Still, it's too bad she's dead," said Smith in his deep, heavy voice. "I'd like to know just what her game was."

"Well, the ME's working on the body now," said Gray. "DNA's still being analyzed, but parts of the genome have been replaced with sequences that are either nonhuman or else artificial. Her body's undergone some kind of modification, possibly for life on another world."

"That doesn't seem to fit the story she told you."

Gray looked at his leader gratefully. He liked working for somebody who was almost as smart as he was.

"Exactly, Chief. If there's to be a general catastrophe, if nothing's left three hundred years from now but what our visitor called a small community of survivors, how did she happen to get modified for life on another planet? For that matter, how did such a community manage to produce the sophisticated technology that brought her here? Something's wrong."

"And," said the president, shaking his head in wonder, "she came here to persuade me to wage a preventive war."

"Ironic, isn't it?"

The two enjoyed a quiet smile together, members of an exclusive club of less than a dozen who knew the great secret.

"So," Gray murmured, "our woman of the future died never knowing that her mission was needless, perfectly needless. Well, that's luck of a kind, I suppose."

5

Maks had seen a meat wagon draw up to the executive office building, turn in through steel gates and vanish down a ramp. He had seen it reappear with a screaming motorcycle escort. The thought that Lian might have overplayed her hand occurred to him, but he had no way to be sure.

By three o'clock—that is, 15—he was inclined to think that the body removed by the wagon had in fact been Lian. Either that, or she'd penetrated to the very center of power and was at this moment trying to persuade Smith to launch a war. In either case, Maks was clearly wasting his time.

"Either she's succeeded or she's dead," he thought.

Time for plan two, except that he had no plan two. In fact, he could imagine only one line of action, though it seemed to promise little. Vray's house was clearly off-limits to him, since the landlord would long since have called the polizi. But Mrs. Crane's house might still be empty, and he had a key to the front door. He could at least search the place.

There had been four controls for the wormholer remaining after Lian dispatched the pile of bodies, and four pistols. He couldn't imagine Lian carrying such a load of hardware into the executive office building, where everything might be confiscated. And where could she have left what she did not take but in that house?

Maks caught a decrepit subway back to the Hill. The tunnels were defaced with slogans urging war, peace, offering sex, recording the names and initials of unknowns. There was no aircooling and the trains moved at about three clicks an hour. The crowds were stolid, silent, each person sweating and giving off organic fumes. At a station called Capitol South Maks exited, climbing escalators that were immobile and rusted into place. Hastening past the Library where he'd do his research two years from now, he reached the back of the Supreme Court, or what was left of it after a recent riot.

He found Mrs. Crane's house, all dull redbrick and rusty ironwork, and for a few minutes loitered outside. Looking up, he could see the hole in the side wall where Vray's shot had gone through. Yet no polizi showed themselves and the block was deserted except for plastic cylinders of uncollected garbage. Perhaps nobody had noticed the violence of yesterday, or the missing woman.

Taking a deep breath, Maks climbed the iron steps to the front door, inserted his key, and opened it quietly.

The house was silent. He poked around downstairs, in the part of the house Mrs. Crane had kept for herself. Battered furniture, a convex mirror with a gilt eagle perching on it, paper doilies on the backs of the chairs. The kitchen was clean, bare and shoddy. Just outside the back door flies buzzed around a garbage can that had not been put out.

He closed the door, returned to the hallway and climbed the stairs. On the step where Mrs. Crane had died was nothing, not a stain, not a questing fly. He was surprised that Lian had found time to clean so thoroughly. On the second-floor landing, the door to the apartment he'd shared with Mogul was closed. He turned the knob. Locked. He sniffed an unpleasant smell and concluded that Lian had failed to get rid of the bodies, after all.

He pushed his key into the lock and the door swung open. As it did a huge two-thumbed hairy hand reached out and seized him by the shoulder and dragged him inside.

The Darksider transferred his grip to the back of Maks's neck. Its three other hands gave him a rough search. Meanwhile, from the bedroom emerged two thuggi in blue-gray uniforms and the crossbone insignia of a mysterious unit called Special Investigations. Behind them came Colonel Yost, his long gray face bleak and frigid.

"So," said Yost, "Hastings. Perhaps you can explain why—as Zo Lian reported—you chose to betray your comrades, murder one of them, and join forces with the criminal Vray Dak."

CHAPTER XV

The story that Maks told did not go down very well.

"Zo Lian is in every way a rising star of our organization," frowned Yost. "We granted her a secret commission in the Security Forces. She passed every test of loyalty we could devise."

"Just as Vray passed every psychological test the penal colony could devise," Maks pointed out wearily.

The Darksider was standing just behind him, enveloping him with its indescribable aroma. He was thinking of the image that had attacked him in the White Chamber. Well, this one was real enough.

"It's true," Yost conceded, "that no test has yet been devised that can penetrate the most secret places of the mind. But tell me, do you have a single shred of evidence to back up your version of what happened here?"

Maks's head fell slowly forward as despair gripped him. Was there anything? Then he slowly pushed back the sleeves of his shirt and stared at his wrists. The red lines of the cords that had bound him were still visible. Along each red furrow ran, like a small rosary, dark beads of dried blood.

He held out his wrists. Then he raised his hands—one of the thuggi reached for a gun—and opened his collar. Yost leaned forward, staring intently at the bruises.

"I see," he said. "Yes, this is evidence—of a sort."

"Do you think I did this to myself?"

"No. But I don't know how it happened. Perhaps when Lian discovered your treason she tied you up."

But there was now uncertainty in his eyes. As he meditated, a point about Maks's story suddenly registered with him.

"You say that you saw Zo Lian enter the Executive Office Building," he muttered. "One of our wormholer controls returned to us with a very astonished fat man who was unable to give any coherent account of what had happened to him. But he claimed to be a guard at that building. That's why I came here myself—to see what the devil was happening."

Suddenly he made his decision. "Can't you see that Time-surfer Hastings has no weapon?" he snapped to a thug. "Arm him at once."

He gestured at the Darksider, which freed Maks. An instant later, an impact pistol was in Maks's grip, and he hefted it, feeling a profound urge to kill somebody. Almost anybody, though Zo Lian headed the list.

Sweet kid, eh?

"Now we must find the traitor," said Yost, "and try to undo whatever trouble she's causing."

"How can we reach her?" asked Maks, envisioning an assault by Darksiders on the White House, an event sure to attract unwelcome attention.

Yost smiled less bleakly than before. "Via the Worldcity," he said. "Via your time and mine. Every control device contains a tiny homing device no bigger than a grain of sand, but packed with nanomachines. We got the idea from the weather stations. We'll follow the signal to the place where Lian is, after a detour of eighteen thousand kilometers and three hundred years.

"Surely our trip will give a new meaning to the old phrase about the shortest distance between two points."

2

In the presidential bunker, Smith and Gray sat in overstuffed chairs smoking long cigars.

The doors to the armoire stood open; the TV glowed. In three dimensions and a variety and depth of hue as rich as the portraits on the walls, a semicircle of bemedaled officers sat around a table.

Smith liked the new TVs, with their built-in receiver-senders and the near-perfect illusion of depth that enabled him to feel the presence of his subordinates without actually having them in the room with him. He distrusted his generals, just as other politicians as varied as Lincoln and Stalin had distrusted theirs.

"I take it, then, that the majority of the Joint Chiefs advise against attacking the Imperial Chinese People's Republic," said Gray quietly.

"We consider it excessively risky. Our space defense system remains untested in actual combat," said the chairman, Admiral Simms.

"How is it to be tested in combat if we never go to war?"

Gray enjoyed this kind of fencing. Besides, as National Defense Advisor, it was his role. By posing as the advocate of a war policy, he enabled Smith to give the appearance of sitting in impartial judgment on a matter he had already decided.

"Simulated attacks—"

"Have given excellent results, according to your memorandum of 23 January 2049," said Gray. "Shall I read it to you, Admiral?"

The admiral looked uncomfortable. Of course the JCS always claimed to be ready for war: that was their business. To be in the position now of claiming that, after all, they actually weren't created a problem in logic that they were not subtle enough to solve.

General Shabazz spoke up. Tall and slender as only a descendant of the Watusi could be, she owned a brace of doctorates in addition to her stars. She might have been chairman of the JCS, except that it had been the Navy's turn.

"I would remind you, Mr. Gray, that as a result of treaty commitments American forces overseas are largely under the command of Russian generals, and that Russia has not given prior assent to our unilateral attack on China."

Smith bestirred himself at that.

"Balancing diplomatic and military considerations is the job of the president alone," he growled.

"Absolutely," said Gray. "Besides, once our common enemy has been pulverized it's the judgment of the Foreign Policy Adviser that the Russians will follow our lead."

"Surely that's intolerably risky—"

"May I say," put in Gray smoothly, "that until today I never knew that military officers were so averse to risk?"

That produced an uncomfortable silence. Gray smiled inwardly. These people, he reflected, spend their lives convincing themselves and others that they're daring. For them to urge caution goes against their own self-image.

General Pozniak of the Air Force spoke up.

"In my opinion, preventive war is by far the best policy in the long run," he declared. "China will only get stronger. We control our own strategic forces—or to be precise, the Air Force commands them. I'm convinced that a decisive attack on China will not only win support from the Russians but spark a general uprising against Chinese occupation forces in Japan, Korea and Vietnam as well. I hope that the president will opt for war."

"When do you recommend we attack, if the president decides upon that option?"

"The first window will occur this afternoon between 1340 and 1920 hours, when our killer satellites will be in optimum position vis-à-vis the enemy's orbital launch platforms. Here's a schedule of other such windows for the next year."

Something hummed in the comm system as a decrypt fax sent a long piece of hardcopy whispering into Gray's hand.

Smith stirred again.

"Pending my decision I wish Condition Yellow to be instituted throughout the United States on the grounds that a new offensive is getting underway against the western rebels. Thank you for giving me your views, and have a good evening."

Gray closed the doors of the armoire on the now silent and dark TV screen, then resumed his seat. For a few minutes he and Smith smoked in silence. The decrypt lay on a small eighteenth-century table, neglected. They weren't interested in any launch window but today's.

"At last we're at the point of action," the big man remarked. "Congress can debate the war after it's won. I don't like the attitude of the Army and Navy chiefs. Simms thinks of nothing but his pension and I never should've appointed that bitch Shabazz. Well, we won't need land forces anyway for what we've got in mind."

Gray nodded. "I've covered all the bases I can think of. Of course, things could go wrong. We might lose a few cities ourselves."

"No pain no gain," said the president philosophically. "We're going to revise this old world, Gray. Stop the downward slide. Save the good, and as for the bad—"

He blew a smoke ring. Gray nodded. There was no need for the president to complete the sentence.

3

Yamashita stared at Yost while Maks waited outside.

What! The prison release he'd ordered had set this Vray Dak loose? The surfer program for which he was responsible had allowed some semi-alien to go through the wormholer to destroy the world?

He thought of Kathmann's end and knew that Yost would use the needles on him without hesitation if the Controller gave the order.

"And where is the missing control—the one that's beeping out this message?" Yamashita demanded.

"It's gotten very faint," said Yost. "It's underground, we think, in or near the White House in the lost city of Washington in the year 2050."

He added, "Maybe it's been put away in a vault or safe. If so, an arriving surfer might have his atoms jammed into a mass of solid steel. That's why I'll send young Hastings first."

Yamashita hardly heard him. He was turning his head slowly, eyes panning the big, gleaming office toward which he'd been striving for most of his life. Was anything in the world so fluid as *mosh*, so apt to slip out of your hands?

He stood up, strapped on a pistol. Better to die in some god-damn primitive city than sit around here waiting for the laser to take off his head. He would trust nobody to handle this except himself. Absolutely no one!

"Yost," he said, "take over while I'm gone." Outside, in the marble corridor, he collared Maks.

"I want a volunteer to lead the way," he said. "You're my volunteer."

4

The two of them hastened to the nearest lift, up to Pastplor, down a long corridor to the transit room. Along the way they were joined by the rest of the task force, two thuggi and one Darksider.

Yamashita viewed the wormholer with deep distrust that

verged on loathing. He was remembering how his friend Steffens Aleksandr, the Worldsaver, had entered the capsule of a bigger, cruder version of the device and returned as a shattered corpse.

Then he shook himself and gave Maks final instructions. "Press the signal stud on your control when you arrive. As soon as we get the message I'll be right behind you."

Maks jumped on the slide, pressing an opaque black cloth over his eyes to shield them from the flash. The instant he felt something hard beneath his feet he pulled the hand away and the cloth fell to the floor.

The haste was needless. He was alone in an elegant and quiet room filled with furniture of a type he'd never seen before. He signalled as Yamashita had ordered, then began to explore. Almost at once he spotted the missing control and Lian's recorder disk on a small table and put both into his beltpouch.

A fire seemed to be burning, but when Maks approached it he saw that the back of the fireplace was a 3-dimensional screen broadcasting a fire. The books that lined the walls turned out to be fakes, too. Yamashita materialized behind him, tore off his goggles, and looked around with astonishment.

"Where are we?" he demanded.

"In a house of illusions," said Maks.

While the thuggi materialized, followed by the Darksider, Maks opened the armoire. A row of studs with icons lined the big screen inside; recognizing some of them, he touched On. Elegantly convincing, the image of President Derrick Minh Smith sprang into view, speaking to the nation in a firm sonorous voice:

". . . like 7 December 1941, like 11 September 2001, this day will live in infamy. Without warning at 12:53 this afternoon, Washington time, our nation's space defense system began to intercept incoming missiles. Computer calculations left no doubt of their origin: we were under attack by the Imperial

People's Republic of China, even as the diplomats of that aggressive nation were arriving to negotiate with us!

"Was ever any nation so betrayed as ours? But I assure you that this dastardly act has not gone unpunished. Within seconds a counterstrike by our missiles destroyed the enemy's orbital launch platforms! At the same time, our Space Defense System intercepted the approaching enemy missiles and—"

The picture flickered, the sound went out. Maks darted a glance at Yamashita, who stood erect, staring at nothing. The air in the room was still disturbed by the materializations and papers overflowing Smith's wide desk whispered to the floor.

Then a deep shudder passed through the bunker. Portraits rattled against the walls and a fine snowfall of creamy plaster dust descended on the scattered hardcopy and the Persian carpet.

"Oh Great Tao," whispered Maks. "Lian succeeded."

5

His knees buckled and he almost fell, not from the impact of whatever weapon had exploded outside but from the dreadful realization that his world and every human world, past, present, and future, was ending. The war was coming forty years too soon; the earth would be ruined, the Luna colony would perish when its lifeline was cut. Maia's face flashed across his mind, and he clung to her image, the last his brain would hold.

"Bullshit," snapped Yamashita, shattering his tragic mood. "She didn't have time—Wait. I see! Good for Zo Lian! We'll have to put her statue next to the Worldsaver's!"

Suddenly he was pounding Maks's shoulder with a karate-hardened fist. Maks retreated a step, wondering if the General had gone insane.

"Glupetz!" he shouted. "Don't you see? These people went to war for reasons that have nothing to do with Lian. But by bringing us here she gave us a chance! We have to get back to Ulanor, quick, quick!"

He pressed the return stud on his control and Maks followed so fast it was a wonder their atoms didn't mingle in a horrific explosion in the wormholer. But in fact Maks collided only with Yamashita's big feet as the general flung himself off the slide, shouting: "Send us back! Four hours earlier! Send us back!"

He jerked Maks out of the wormholer, threw himself back onto the slide, burying his face in his hands as the violet-white light flashed. Maks followed, and suddenly they were standing together, dizzy and disoriented, in the same office as before. But not the same.

The false fire burned quietly and the armoire stood closed, its mahogany front dully gleaming. On the walls the portraits of gentlemen in white wigs or high gleaming leather stocks and black coats and spotless shirtfronts hung quiet. Then the room's heavy steel door—in appearance, richly paneled wood painted a creamy enamel—slid abruptly into a slot and a big man strode in.

CHAPTER XVI

Smith was talking, his head half turned to direct the stream of words at a smaller man following him. Smith's impetus carried him two full strides into the office before he saw what was awaiting him.

By then Yamashita had a pistol to his face. The smaller man

suddenly hared off down the hall with Maks pounding in pursuit. The man stopped suddenly, whirled, and raised one hand in a strange gesture, as if his empty palm were holding something, and then Maks slammed into him, a young heavy body hardened by training crashing into an aging bureaucratic wraith.

Gray collapsed on the floor, and Maks dragged him unceremoniously back into the office by the heels.

He found Smith seated in a leather chair behind his desk, staring at Yamashita. They were about the same size, and Smith had never seen an impact pistol before, but he seemed to have no doubt that his best course in the circumstances was to sit still.

Maks felt Gray's pockets, found nothing; checked his breathing, found him alive though unconscious, and left him lying on the carpet. As he turned, President Smith blinked twice and growled, "How'd you find me? Traced that damned gadget, did you?"

Maks tried to imagine himself walking into such a situation and realizing almost at once what it meant. The world, he felt—not for the first time—seemed to be full of people who were smarter than he was.

"I'd like to smoke," Smith muttered.

Only Maks knew what he meant; Yamashita looked around for a kif pipe but saw none. Maks opened a gold-chased humidor on the desk and presented their large captive with a cigar.

Smith fished out a gold lighter, snapped it, and puffed slowly.

"It kills you," he remarked. "We've known that for a hundred years. Are you people friends of the creature?"

"Not friends," said Yamashita. He spoke so deliberately, with such emphasis, that translating was easy for Maks. "We'll get to her in a moment. The crucial thing is this: you must rescind your order for preventive war, and do it now."

Smith frowned. "Suppose I refuse?"

"Do I look like a man who'll take no for an answer?"

Two more puffs on the cigar. "In short, I can have my war, but only if I die for it."

"You'll die for it anyway. Your defense system will not work adequately. You'll die in your bunker, however deep it may be."

Maks watched, under a curious impression that each man was holding cards, and that they were dealing them one by one. But there was no doubt who held the aces.

Smith sighed and looked at Gray stretched out on the floor. "He was the one talked me into it," he said. "A very brilliant man. He killed that creature, too. Still, if you say the war policy's unsuccessful . . ."

He gestured at the armoire. "Open the doors, young man. If I must countermand the order, I must. Please stand back, the two of you, out of the picture."

Yamashita turned away, but the corner of Maks's left eye caught a slight movement where no movement should have been. Gray had raised himself slightly and a pistol slid into his hand so suddenly that it seemed a magic trick, as indeed it was—like a stage magician, he'd had it up his sleeve.

Then his small body seemed to explode, almost noiselessly, like a rodent struck by a meteor. Hand steady after the shot, Maks turned his gun on Smith, who once more proved his intelligence by sitting absolutely still.

So, thought Maks without surprise, *now I'm a killer, too.*

2

He bent and checked the weapon in Gray's hand, pulled up his sleeve far enough to expose the piston-and-cylinder device and the trigger that ejected the gun when Gray pressed his right elbow to his side.

Yamashita turned on Smith, his eyes like jet reflecting flame.

"I didn't tell him to do it," the president pointed out hastily. "He heard enough to know he was out of power, and for him that's worse than death, so he played his last available card." He puffed and gazed steadily at Yamashita. "Would you have done any different?"

Maks touched the On icon that in a previous time-stream he wouldn't touch for another three hours. The screen sprang to life, bland and blue this time, awaiting orders. Smith edged his chair in front of it and spoke a series of commands with code words the machine wouldn't have recognized in any voice but his.

Maks and Yamashita stood to either side against the wall, while the president reversed his orders, to the delight of the Army and Navy and the fury of the Air Force.

Still, Maks and Yamashita could not return to their own time. Maks knew by now that cleanup was as much a part of the job as the job itself. So hours elapsed, while Smith ordered the medical examiner to deliver Lian's body and all specimens taken from it to the White House bunker. Empty time ticked on and smoke rose and turned the room blue, until baffled guards wheeled a big metal casket fuming with frozen carbon dioxide into the hallway outside the bunker and withdrew, leaving it behind.

Things stretched out so far that a rush of hot wind swept away the smoke of the president's cigar and again set papers whirling off the desk. Smith had something new to stare at as two thuggi and a Darksider materialized in the room, plus translucent images of Maks and Yamashita that instantly faded and disappeared.

"Good gravy," he muttered, adding to Yamashita, "I can honestly say that you, sir, have given me a day like no other in my life."

Yamashita stopped supervising his minions in dispatching two ruined bodies to the Worldcity and turned to Smith.

"I regret to tell you, Mr. President, that the day isn't over. We have one more interesting experience for you. We're going to another time."

"By 'we' you mean—"

"By 'we' I mean us." With triumph assured, even Yama relented, though only a hairbreadth.

"Don't worry, you'll be returning to your White House very shortly. But—trust me—you'll return a different man."

3

Gilded doors swung open and Maks stepped back to allow Yamashita to enter Xian's reception hall. He followed and stood at rigid attention while the general advanced and bowed from the waist.

"Rise," said Xian. She stepped forward and extended a tiny hand. Yamashita bowed again, this time to kiss it.

"General," she said in a voice unsteady with emotion. "How can the State repay you? As I read in your fascinating report, you learned of a new and grave danger, an impending war in 2050, and sent agents to explore the situation."

"Yes," said Yamashita coolly. "That's exactly what happened."

Maks stared at him, thinking with a cynicism new to him: so this is how history is invented. The losers die, and the winners make up stories to suit themselves.

"And then you yourself led an expedition that ended the menace!"

"Yes, Honored Controller."

"And how did you deal with this—this President person?"

"Our *mediki* inserted a control chip and an exploding poison pellet in his head, just as we do with convicts. If the nanoma-chines we've scattered across his world report a sudden increase in radioactivity *from any source whatever* the chip will blow his head off. The same if anybody tries to remove it. I advised him strongly to become his century's most ardent advocate of peace. And I know from the documents this young man"—he gestured at Maks—"saw in the Library of Congress two years later that he followed my advice."

Xian clasped her hands as if in prayer. "Profoundly mysteri-ous is the Great Tao!" she exclaimed.

For the third time Yamashita bowed. "So all the sages have taught, Honored Controller."

A robot servant rolled in a wagon with a tea caddy, and Ya-mashita and Xian drank a ceremonial cup together. Then she pinned on new stars, until he had seven on each shoulder.

"I chose well when I chose you," she congratulated herself.

"Honored Controller, if I were the Senate, I would vote you the titles All Wise and Ever Victorious. Who but you made this triumph possible by commanding me to build the new worm-holer?"

Xian's thin face now held a porcelain smile. She remem-bered perfectly well that the idea had been his. But how clever of him to present it as a gift to his superior!

In the same spirit she accepted it.

"I'll have them do just that," she murmured. "I haven't had a new title in some time. And now, Honored Chief of Security, we permit you to go."

4

Back in the Palace of Justice, in Yamashita's office, Yost pinned the insignia of a lieutenant in the Security Forces on Maks. Lian's death had opened a slot, and Maks was the only candidate given serious consideration for it. Meanwhile Yamashita was cleaning things up again, barking orders into his mashina.

"Contact Calisto. All prisoners, regardless of sentence, will be held for life. Contact Admiral Hrka of the Space Service and inform him of the Controller's order to liquidate all 'modified humans' on Beta Charonis and anywhere else where that misbegotten experiment has been tried. I want a goddamn clean sweep, understand?"

"Of course, Honored General. The orders have been sent, Honored General."

At last Yost was able to lead Maks before the big desk to salute his commander. Yamashita rose slowly and saluted back.

"I like you, Hastings," he said. "Not real bright, but reliable, and character means more than intelligence. Look around you. Once I was a young guy like you, and I knew where I wanted to end up—here. It took me a while, and it'll take you a while. Others' turns will come first."

He nodded at Yost. "But keep at it, and one day you may sit here and hold incalculable *mosh* in your hands.

"Meanwhile, accept my congratulations and the thanks of all loyal people. You've helped to save this world of ours—Xian and me and Yost and the whole Security Forces and the World-city and the Darksiders and everything else besides."

Maks saluted and marched out of the room as Yost was saying, his normally soft voice raised a little so that Maks couldn't help but overhear, "A fine young man."

Outside, a little crowd had gathered, Maks's fellow surfers, ready to hug him, pummel him, pour congratulations on him with a delicious mixture of joy and envy in their voices. Maia waited at the edge of the crowd, ready to reward him with a kiss, perhaps more.

Then why was he suddenly tasting blood? Why did he have to bite his lips to keep from shouting, No, No, No?

THREE

CHAPTER XVII

Fifth Avenue, November 2091: a gray day makes the armored facade of Tiffany-Cartier look even steelier than usual. Led by motorcycles with screaming sirens, a fourteen-meter limousine zips south on Fifth Avenue, past the leafless tangle of Central Park, past Grand Army Plaza and the vast bulk of the New Plaza Hotel.

On the steps of the hotel, holographic cameras are recording a model clothed in a brilliant smile and a body stocking as she runs to the golden doors, pauses, loses her smile, descends, and runs up again. Later, software will morph various costumes onto her image.

A small crowd gawks at the model; her bodyguard hefts a machine pistol and eyes the crowd. At the curb gray rats swarm over a heap of uncollected garbage. The rats ignore the people; the people ignore the rats.

The driver of the limousine ignores everything, the rats, the model, the burned-out hulk of buildings torched during a recent riot. Another block and the car slides to the curb in front of the jewelry store. A guard jumps out and waves back the sidewalk vendors of hashish and roast chestnuts and the beggars displaying surgically implanted scars and hand-lettered signs that say Veteran of the War in Idaho.

When the way lies open, plump Benjamin Kurosawa, glossy in a $200,000 Armani suit, leaves the car.

A famous Wall Street bear who made trillions from the collapse of the market, Benjo (as his ex-wives and the tabloids call him) likes to sock solid chunks of his wealth into gems whose supernal glitter hypnotizes him just like other people. Only last month he made the news by adding the most famous of stones, the Hope Diamond, to his collection.

Gawkers accumulate, as if to warm themselves by gazing at so much wealth. Stringers for news organizations appear from nowhere, looking for a sound bite. A tall youngish man sprints up and reaches out an odd-looking microphone. The guard frowns but hangs back; the financier revels in fame as he does in wealth.

"*Cybertattle*, Benjo! You adding to your famous diamond collection?"

The young man thrusts the gadget so close to Kurosawa's face that Benjo automatically puts up a hand and pushes it away. There's a strange flicker, a little whirlwind blows up a microstorm of paper and plastic scraps from the sidewalk, and somebody begins to scream.

Another stringer—a young woman who works for the Times-Enquirer Syndicate—is babbling into her jabber mike, "Instant news! The world's richest man has just been kidnapped! How? Nobody knows. Why? For the ransom, stupid!"

The news hits the airwaves just as an incoming thermal cluster aggregating 2,000 megatons puts an end to the city and everybody in it. Three centuries will pass before anyone will know how right the newscaster was.

For Benjo Kurosawa is being held to ransom—in a way entirely new to human experience.

2

"Congratulations to you, Major Hastings!" exclaimed Xian Xiqing.

The ancient Solar System Controller fondled an exquisite pectoral of nineteen ginger-colored diamonds. Autominers gnawing through hard gneiss strata, their tunnels awash in brine and eerily lit by radioactive fires, recently recovered it from a vault deep beneath the fused silicon of the Great North American Shield.

Hastings Maks bowed. Xian made him uneasy, partly because of her incredible *mosh* and partly because her appetite for jewels was matched only by her well-known appetite for younger men. With a new wife waiting for him at home, Maks much preferred to satisfy her itch for jewels.

General Yamashita, the Chief of Security, looked proudly at his protege, the bold timesurfer whose rise in the Security Forces dated back to the conspiracy of Zo Lian. Together, he and Maks had saved this marvellous world, sharing great peril and forging a personal bond almost as close as the long-ago friendship between Yama and the Worldsaver.

Deeper in the shadows, standing next to a heavily armed Darksider that was one of Xian's guards, Colonel Yost looked on, pale, immobile, and silent.

"You say this Kurosawa person directed the miners to this marvel?" Xian asked.

"Yes, Honored Controller," Maks replied. "He's been a fine source. The twenty-first century was a time of disorder and the rich buried many of their possessions and Benjo knows where. Wonderful things have come to light in the vaults, curious inventions, rare books, archives of secret documents, ancient timepieces, works of art. Mediscans of our captives have allowed the *mediki* to do statistical studies of changes in the human genome—"

"Yes, yes," she said. "I'm sure someone will find all that very interesting."

She extended a tiny hand heavy with glinting rings. Maks was allowed to kiss it, a rare privilege.

"Keep him busy," she told Yamashita. "And now, Honored Chief of Security, we permit you to go."

The three officers bowed and retreated in reverse order of rank: Maks first, then Yost, then Yamashita, who was privileged to enjoy Xian's presence longest. When gold leaf doors at last closed behind him, the Controller was still playing with her baubles.

"Great Tao," the general muttered, "she's in her second childhood."

"What a pity!" Yost said. "Such a great leader in her time! Now all she wants are pretty jewels and young lovers."

"Luckily, we only have to supply the jewels," growled Yamashita. "The Security Forces aren't pimps."

"At least not yet," sighed Yost. "Who knows what we may come to in time?"

3

Far from the Controller's palace, in a cramped apartment of the Faculty Warrens at the University of the Universe, Steffens Maia ordered her mashina to show the public information channel.

Actually, she only wanted to sleep—she was young, and yet everything seemed to tire her since Maks had left her for his new wife. For a while, anger had sustained her. Then anger subsided into a long, dull depression. The news meant nothing to her, but she found the flat, atonal voice of the journalistic software hypnotic, soothing.

Today the program began as usual with a shot of the pompous tomb of Steffens Aleksandr, the hero who had saved the world by defeating the infamous Crux plot. That Maia (and several thousand other people) shared the Worldsaver's name was a minor though irritating irony of her obscure life. Then the camera rose until the white-marble surroundings of the tomb—the President's Palace, the Senate of the Worlds—lay revealed like a dinosaurs' graveyard.

Brief clips of important personages and events followed, ending with a shot of smiling people boarding one of the slow, comfortable Earthliners that departed the Worldcity every day for vacation spots like Antartica and the North American Game Preserve.

"Oh, Great Tao," Maia breathed and sat up.

All the travelers had the oiled, glowing look of success; among them were Honored Senator So-and-so and Honored Monopolist Such-And-Such. Last came Major Hastings Maks, brave timesurfer, and his new wife, Sherí.

The couple paused to smile at the camera, Maks solid, handsome; Sherí smiling shyly, her flame-colored hair piled up in fashionable disarray. Maia devoured every detail of her replacement, from Sherí's stunning physical beauty to the little gap between her upper front teeth.

Then a dark, slender man in Security Forces uniform glided up and presented her a blazing armful of peonies.

"On behalf of General Yamashita," said the flat voice, "Captain Pali of the Security Forces presents a bouquet to the happy couple. In other news—"

"Oh, fuck," said Maia. "Shit. Off!"

She threw a pillow at the now-silent mashina and stretched out wearily on her lumpy divan. Yamashita's fair-haired boy. Maks, Maks, she thought for the thousandth time, what happened to you?

"You didn't have to surrender *unconditionally*," she told him once, when their marriage was falling apart.

"I didn't surrender. I grew up."

"When we met you were ready to ditch the Security Forces, get out, live some other kind of life. Now you want to be a general. Keep this up and you'll be conducting *shosho* sessions next."

"That's not funny."

"Torture's not funny? I thought all you thuggi enjoyed it."

Maia had a gift for the cutting phrase. At the University she taught Ancient Poetry. Many of her poets had possessed the same dangerous gift, and some had been executed for indulging it. Their fate should have warned her that the wrong phrase can cost your head—or your happiness.

"You think you're going to run the Security Forces one day," she couldn't resist adding. "Well, you won't. You're not mean enough, and you're not smart enough, either."

Maks had given her a dead-level look that reminded her uneasily of the fact that he'd killed at least one man. Then he went on another of his perilous transits to the ancient world on the eve of the Time of Troubles. When he returned, he moved out and sent her an electronic Message of Divorce.

He didn't take their son, Sandi, away from her; in fact, Maks came to see him often and provided well for him. The last trace she could find of the old Maks, a little dumb but sweet-tempered and generous and a wonderful lover.

Later she heard he'd married a gorgeous woman from the frontiers of space, from some rock in the infinitely remote Dragon Sector. Undoubtedly an adventuress who'd come to the capital in search of exactly what she'd found—a handsome husband on the way up.

Time traveler finds happiness with space traveler, Maia thought. *Like goes to like. It's an old story. All the most painful stories are old ones.*

4

Sighing, she laid her head back on a pillow made in the shape of a haknim. Those gawky, giraffelike creatures had been favorites of hers since childhood. Sandi, of course, preferred stuffed

Darksiders carrying toy guns . . . *how like a male,* she thought, eyes fluttering shut . . . *especially an eight-year-old one . . .*

She woke up feeling refreshed. Sleep: great nature's second course; the death of each day's life. The ancient poets had a line for everything. She sat up on her bed, yawned, glanced at the clock. And gasped.

Seventeen. She'd slept for 140 minutes—almost an hour and a half. Where was Sandi? Had he come home from school, let himself in?

Anxious, she rose and hastened through her small apartment overlooking the campus. Sandi was not in his room. Nor the kitchen. Nor anywhere.

She hurried to her small, battered mashina and said, "Call." It flickered into life and she gave the boxcode of his school. After a lengthy wait the nightguard answered.

"Damn," she muttered.

The guard was a black box. When she had asked for a trace on Sandi it beeped and spent a number of minutes doing, apparently, nothing at all. Then its atonal voice announced:

"Doorguard reports Hastings Aleksandr, eight-point-five years, male, firstform, left school fifteen-fifty-five as scheduled. School vehicle sensors report him not present. Report forwarded to Master's office but not received as Master himself left at fifteen-sixty-one. Can I in any other way assist you, Madam?"

"*Where is my son?*"

"Shall I repeat my previous report?"

She cut the connection and headed for the lift. *Oh, if the little bastard's just playing a trick on me,* she promised, *I'll kill him.*

In the street she hastened to the nearest gate in the campus wall. The gatekeeper—another black box—informed her that, no, Sandi had not come in.

She wondered if he might have squeezed through one of the many breaks in the wall and was playing on campus; if so, he would come home when he felt hungry. For the moment, she'd better consider the worst possibilities.

Outside, she rejected a hovercab as too expensive and hastened down the broken and rutted street to a trirad stand. She paid half a khan to a driver and climbed into the dirty vehicle. He revved the whining motor and they set out for Sandi's school.

Dusk was approaching when they arrived. She questioned the gatekeeper, which repeated that Sandi had left at 15:55.

"Did he climb on the bus?"

"That is the concern of the vehicular sensor, Madam."

"So there's a break in observation as the kids leave school—between the time you stop watching them and the vehicle starts?"

"I am not able to answer that question."

"Fuck you very much."

"That phrase is not in my vocabulary, Honored Mother."

At least the trirad was run by a human. She explained that she wanted to retrace the route to the campus slowly, keeping an eye out for a small boy in a school uniform.

"Your kid go missing, lady?"

"Yes. I'm terribly worried."

"I would be, too, lady. They sell little kids to the houses in the Clouds and Rain District. Some guys will pay a lot for a kid."

"This boy's father is a major in the Security Forces."

"Oh, lady, I'm so glad I ain't the one stole your kid. The bastard did it will get *shosho* for sure."

The trirad was at best a clumsy vehicle. Its three-wheel base was unstable and Maia began to feel seasick as she scanned the rising and falling faces to either side of her.

The streets were crowded. Kif sellers, peddlers of babaku chicken with texasauce, of miso, of combs and brushes, of incense. Everywhere she saw places where Sandi could have disappeared from view. A small boy could be anywhere, playing, skylarking, visiting a friend, eating a plate of noodles. Or being drugged, sold, raped, killed.

Back at the University she paid off the driver and almost ran to the gatekeeper. No, Sandi hadn't come back that way. Back in her apartment, she found silence, the same quiet small rooms with nobody in them.

At last she collapsed in front of her mashina and said, "Call."

It waited politely, then prompted: "Boxcode, Madam?"

"I don't know," said Maia. "Tell the Security Forces operator I must contact Major Hastings Maks. Say it's an emergency. Say that his son is missing."

CHAPTER XVIII

Maks and Sheri shared an outside compartment on the earthliner. Touching a stud turned the whole exterior wall transparent. Maks rested with his head on Sheri's lap.

"Great Tao, but that last transit was a bastard," he sighed. "I misjudged the time and got out just minutes before the Troubles started."

"You was so brave, Maks," said Sheri automatically.

Smiling wearily, he corrected her grammar. Admittedly, she'd grown up in a primitive world, but she just didn't seem to be a very fast learner and you couldn't get along in the World-city without a good command of Alspeke.

She frowned. Didn't like being corrected, even (or perhaps especially) when she was wrong. She had a sharp tongue, thought about using it on him, then changed her mind.

No, you catch more flies with honey than vinegar, Mama used to say. Besides, the sights passing below the earthliner were genuinely fascinating.

The Polar Ocean, creamy with whitecaps, flecked with blood by the lowering sun. Vast Hudson Sea. The broad Sanlornz River, foaming as it rushed over submerged rocks that had once been the Thousand Islands.

Maks napped and Sherí stroked his head, gazing down at the panorama. The earthliner slid silently down the Atlantic coast, where lines of silvery breakers washed against the foothills of the White Mountains.

Maks sat up, sleep clearing from his eyes, and smiled at her, enjoying her beauty profiled by the sunset glow. The pale skin with rose highlights, the burnished hair, the gray eyes—the meeting of fire and ice. He kissed her white shoulder and the smell of her flesh reminded him of the cakes that Tartar women pressed from curds of milk on the herd-rich Gobi grasslands south of the Worldcity.

Suddenly the sun was gone beyond the rim of the world.

"What be that down below, Maks?"

"The Great Shield."

He pulled her close and they gazed down, cheek touching cheek, as a river of dull, yellow-green lights rose from the sea and slipped by beneath them. Once the lost city of Baztan, with its endless suburbs, its centers of learning, its eleven million people.

"I can't believe it be so big," she whispered.

"This is only the edge."

Sometimes the lights fused into a broad, fuzzy glow; sometimes little separate spots winked like a galaxy of fireflies. Where the sea had intruded, the shield was a rash of little glowing islands marking forgotten hills and highlands. Beyond lay the profound darkness of the continent-wide North American Game Preserve.

"All those people gone," she whispered, her voice breaking as she slipped into her native dialect, English. "Millions and millions and millions of them."

The river of luminescence broadened. At the same time the glow at the center concentrated, spreading over a peninsula, part of an island, and swatches of mainland—Manhattan. Maks touched the stud and the wall became dark.

"Let's not watch. It's too grim."

"Oh, Maks," she said, "couldn't you save just a few of them? I mean real people, not these characters like Benjo what's-his-name."

"No. It'd cost me my head. I've taken a lot of risks already. And Sherí, we agreed to talk Alspeke until you're handling it perfectly."

"Oh yes, I almost forgotten," she said bitterly.

A chill descended as she turned away from him. Later, when the robot attendant made up their bed, she signalled unmistakeably that she was in no mood for sex.

Day was breaking over North America (and Maia, back in Ulanor, was making her sundown call to the Security Forces) when the earthliner coasted to a landing near the ancient town of Vizburkh on a bluff overlooking the eastern shore of the Inland Sea.

The morning seemed to have dispersed the touch of frost. Sherí was delighted by the inn, by their room so old-fashioned it had glass windows.

She was laying out clothes and humming to herself when a small robot of antique design knocked and politely informed Maks that he had a call from his headquarters.

"That's what I get for being an executive," he grumbled, but followed it into the hallway. He returned frowning.

"My son's gone missing," he told her.

"You mean he's run away?"

"Probably. Maia's so goddamn hysterical. I called Pali and asked him to have somebody check it out."

"He take care of things. He been so nice to me."

They bathed together in a quaint shower, and it was easy for Maks to forget any disappointments in the warm rosy touch of her body amid the steam. He sank to his knees, laughing and blinking under the torrent, and kissed her belly just above the tiny lank twist of coppery pubic hair. They grappled like teenagers in the heat of the drying lamp, made love again and again.

Afterward they dressed and breakfasted and strolled on the sun-dappled shores of the Inland Sea. Maks was full of ideas.

"We'll have a real vacation. We'll take the underwater tour of the fish ranches. And a hovercar ride to the High Plains to see the bison herds. And there's a mountain somewhere that's been carved with the faces of ancient gods . . ."

But that evening the mood darkened. Captain Pali called to say that Sandi hadn't turned up. He added that General Yamashita had ordered Colonel Yost to take charge of the investigation. That meant Sandi's disappearance must be a kidnapping.

In the small, old-fashioned room, Maks lay on his back and stared at the ceiling. His tension was palpable.

"Maks," she said, lapsing into dialect again.

"What?"

"Please take a pill and go to sleep."

"I can't. Pali might call."

"Well then, turn over and let me rub your back."

He had just begun to doze off when another knock rattled the room's quaint wooden door. As a result of that message, dawn found them groggily filing into another earthliner for the return flight to the Worldcity, their vacation over almost before it had begun.

2

"You said you wanted me," said Maks.

Pali nodded. A thin, dark man of quicksilver moods, he had been Yost's deputy when he headed the time-travel unit; now he was Maks's. A pliant, agreeable man, he didn't seem to care that Maks's influence with the general had enabled him to jump over his head.

"A message was combed out of cyberspace by one of our arbots. Obviously sent randomly from one public mashina to another on the assumption we'd pick it up. It said, 'If Maks wants to see Sandi he must wait for a message at home.' "

They sat togther in the Hastings apartment. Maks had taken a pill that eliminated jet lag but was still feeling somewhat leaden and depressed. Sherí sat in a corner smoking kif, her gray eyes distant.

"Have you talked to the boy's mother?" asked Pali in a low voice.

"Yes. Through the mashina. She had a wonderful idea—I was supposed to go back in time and stop the kidnapping."

They shared a faint smile. "Did you point out that changing the past is a beheader?"

"Wouldn't have done any good. She'd have wanted me to go anyway. So I tried to explain that as you approach the present, the logic circuits get confused over what's 'then' and what's 'now.' I said, 'Do you want me to wind up with atoms of myself scattered at random here and there over the past year?' That got me off the hook, though for how long I don't know."

Suddenly Maks's big mashina chimed and he snapped out, "Say!"

Maia's head appeared, hovering in the shadowbox.

"Maia, the instant I know something definite you'll know it, too," he said irritably.

"Oh, don't hand me that crap. You'll tell me what you think I ought to know when you think I ought to know it."

"Well then, here's something indefinite. We may—or may not—have a message from the kidnapper. If so, he's supposed to contact me here. Now please cut the circuit before I do."

"*Oké*, I'm going to sign off. But please, Maks—as soon as you know."

Again Pali began to chat quietly, in his soothing voice. He gave a brief account of how the *stari* the timesurfers had brought back were faring. They all wanted to start new lives in the here and now; they said they'd paid their ransom and wanted to be free.

"I tell them we've all got to wait for orders. In plain fact I don't know what the Controller wants done with them. I try to keep up their spirits while we milk them for information, but it's not easy."

Maks hardly heard him. "Thanks, Pali. I'll see you tomorrow."

Pali saluted, smiled at Sherí, and left the apartment. Two thuggi and a Darksider waited in the hall outside. The animal displayed its long fangs and scratched its fur in boredom. The thuggi were shooting dice.

Reluctantly they scrambled to their feet and saluted. Pali returned the gesture, walked to the end of the hall and signaled for his hovercar. When he glanced back, the thuggi were playing dice again; the Darksider had gone to sleep.

"Why does crime flourish in the capital city of the human species?" he asked himself with a wry smile. "Just look."

3

The mashina chiming woke Maks at a little past 3. He stared with gummy eyes at a double cone hovering in the shadowbox.

A flat voice, probably an arbot, said, "I want to speak to you entirely alone. Sandi sends greetings."

The message was over, but the lasers didn't go off. Instead, the boxcode from which the message had been sent floated into the shadow box. The Security Forces were at work.

Half a minute more, and he was watching a street corner scene shot from a hovercar in which a dozen polizi rushed a lighted public mashina set in the outer wall of a bank. One reached into the queue with a gloved hand and pulled out a memory cube.

"Delayed transmission, of course," said the cop. "Analysis of the cube will begin at once, Major Hastings."

"Thank you."

They're watching over me, he thought. *If only they weren't watching so closely I might be able to contact this guy—as he says, "entirely alone."*

Four twenty-five came and went with no further message. Maks checked the bedroom, where Sherí slumbered, thrust an impact pistol into his *meshok,* and at 4.65 stepped out of his door. The Darksider opened one raspberry-colored eye, but Maks raised a finger, then held up a palm.

Quiet, said the gestures. *Wait for me.* The animal made no move but watched him hurry down the hallway and step into the lift.

Another minute and he was standing in the lobby. He flashed his ID at the building's security monitor and when it opened the door, hastened into the shadowy street.

At this hour the northwestern suburb slept, locked away behind steel doors and flickering security eyes and silent sensors. The city center with its contradictory clutter of giant public buildings, anonymous apartment blocks, and crowded, lively slums, lay far away to the south.

Here everything was quiet. A few hovercars slid by overhead, gravity compensators chugging, but the streets were empty and dead.

Maks walked slowly down the well-swept sidewalk, avoiding the jut of buildings, sometimes stepping into the street of poured stone. Luminous circles set in walkways ten meters overhead cast an arctic glow that alternately gave him many shadows and none at all.

So, he thought. *Here I am, alone. Where are you?*

4

He heard a whining, rattling sound behind him and turned. An old trirad lurched into view, the driver's bearded face dimly reflecting the lights from his dashboard. It clattered past and disappeared around the next turning.

So nothing, he thought, and stood uncertainly at the curbside, looking sometimes up the curving street, sometimes at the blank-faced buildings and the third-stage walkways. *Maybe,* he thought, *I should be up there?*

Then he heard, far behind him, a small shrill motor. Maks eased his right hand into his *meshok.* He stepped back into an angle of a building just as a small black robot of the type used to carry packages rolled into view. One wheel was loose, giving it a wobbling motion. It stopped facing him.

"Major?"

"Yes."

"*Hai.* May I respectfully request that you show me your ID?"

Maks used his left hand to show the ceramic square with its hologram and the robot blinked at it.

"Do you have a message for me?" he asked.

"Indeed, yes."

"Well?"

"Nine ninety-nine Subotai Street at nine."

"That's easy to remember."

"Come absolutely alone. Otherwise—"

Without the slightest warning Sandi began screaming, again and again and again. Maks's heart paused, gave a bound. Then with a sudden cough and flare of blue light the robot disintegrated, scattered tinkling parts over the street.

An instant later Maks heard the old trirad again, whining somewhere up the street in the darkness. He whirled and pursued it around a bend and between a high stone wall and a fence of twisted steel. A dim light appeared and drove straight at him. He pulled his impact pistol and took a two-handed grip and a solid stance, feet a meter apart, prepared to demolish the driver with a shot through the windscreen.

The awkward vehicle squeaked to a halt and the driver jumped out crying, "Oh, Mister, don't shoot, don't shoot!"

Maks still had the weapon raised when a woman eased out of the trirad's back seat and hurried toward him.

Maia said, "Where is he, Maks? I heard him scream."

Slowly and almost regetfully he lowered the pistol. If he'd ever needed somebody to shoot, it was now.

The thuggi were still snoring when Maks and Maia quietly entered his apartment. They talked in low voices.

"So you still don't trust me," he said.

"Oh, Maks, I just didn't know what you really knew, what you were really up to. What's been going on?"

He told her what had happened, keeping to himself only the address. She seized on that at once.

"Where are you meeting him? I want to know."

"At a place where you won't be. Nor anybody else."

She digested that, then said dully, "It's so strange to sit here, just talking. I died a little when the screaming started."

"I've thought about that," he told her, "and I don't believe that was Sandi. I heard it up close and the sound lacked the overtones of the human voice. The whole thing, the message, the screams—it was all mashina-generated. They probably took a voiceprint of Sandi talking and created the screams from that."

She looked at him, frowning. "You're not just saying that?"

"No."

"Did you see where the robot came from?"

He shrugged. "No. My guess is somebody gave it a recognition code and parked it in a doorway to wait for me."

They looked at each other. Maks's mashina chimed and he turned wearily and told it, "Say."

It was a tech at headquarters. "Major? We've been analyzing that memory cube—you know, the one that sent the message for you?"

"Yes?"

"Well, sir, it's a standard one-cc, thousand-laminate, ten-trillion-byte cube. But it's kind of odd, because it has an electronic signature on it . . ."

Maks shot one glance at Maia, as much to say, "This may be what we're looking for."

"What kind of signature?"

"Well, sir, it's a Security Forces signature. It's our own issue."

CHAPTER XIX

So, how did she take that?" asked Sheri over breakfast.

Beyond the transplast window, just as in verses by one of Maia's ancient poets, dawn was coming up like thunder out of China. An almost cloudless sky promised a typically hot Siberian summer day.

"Not well," said Maks. "She jumped to the conclusion that

Sandi was snatched in some kind of internal polizi intrigue."

Sherí frowned as if she found such a notion hard to grasp. Maks went on:

"I told her that we buy these cubes by the million. They're not even accountable property. People take them home to use on their own mashini. Anybody can latch onto a polizi cube."

"Oh, well, I'm glad of that."

Why, Maks wondered, did he find Sherí's easy acquiescence as annoying as Maia's skepticism? He continued to talk, arguing now with himself.

"Actually, it's the most probable explanation. But . . . I have to be sure. I'm going to that meeting, and I'm going alone, and I'm not telling anybody, not Pali, not the General, not anybody. Just in case."

He hesitated, then added: "And Maia's going to help me."

Where another woman was concerned, Sherí's mind worked as well as anybody's. "I don't think I like that."

"There's nothing between her and me and never will be again," Maks told her. "But Sandi's our son and she's going to help me find him."

For an instant their eyes dueled. Then Sherí touched his hand lightly.

"I'm sorry, Maks. I know you're so worried. I'll help you to get what you want, and you'll help me to get what I want. Deal?"

He was too wary to fall for that one, so he said with false warmth, "It's wonderful knowing you're on my side."

Sherí smiled, restored to good humor.

He changed into old clothes. The message had said nothing about weapons, so he took three, one in his beltpouch, one hung in his armpit under a loose-fitting jacket, and the smallest thrust into his right boot. Armed to the teeth, he kissed Sherí and stepped out of his door, wondering when or if he'd return to her.

2

"I want the animal to stay here and watch my place," he told the thuggi as they came to attention. "You two come with me. My ex-wife has some materials that may be useful to the investigation."

At Maia's building, Maks entered at the sixteenth stage and left the thuggi hovering outside. Maia let him into her apartment, gave him a slip of hardcopy, and told him what she'd learned from her students about the secrets of getting out of the campus compound without using the gates.

"Sounds good," he said, and hesitated.

"Maks, you don't have much time," she pointed out.

"I'd like to look at Sandi's room before I go."

She nodded quickly and stood in the doorway behind him while he looked at his son's scruffy bed, the clutter of toys—the *futbol*, the plastic atomlasers, the collection of stuffed Darksiders with toy impact weapons in their furry hands.

A hundred other things, some bright, some battered. The boy's paintings hung on the walls among pictures of Maks and Maia that curled at the edges. Maks turned, blinking his eyes, and almost ran into her. He put his arms around her, his face sank into her dark hair, and he sniffed the shampoo she'd always used, with its vague lemony scent.

Her body felt the almost the same—maybe thinner. He was conscious of her breasts tight against his lower ribs, those breasts he had once seen as lanterns of desire, later as comforting pillows to rest against in bed. Maia had always had a good backside and his right hand, as if guided by its own will, slid down her spine and gently traced the familiar shape of an inverted heart.

It was really embarrassing, he thought—while she was removing the hand that had gone too far—how, after all that had gone wrong between them, he still responded to her touch by getting an erection. Half an erection, anyway.

"It's too bad, isn't it?" she whispered, and he nodded, knowing exactly what she meant.

"Oh, I wish I could go with you," she murmured as he left the apartment. "I know I'd be in the way, I've got no training and I'm afraid of guns—but oh, how I wish I could go with you."

He smiled and gave her a brotherly kiss. "Back soon," he said, and hurried down the hallway to the lift.

He took it all the way down to the cellar. Maia had supplied him an electronic key, which he used to open an external door without setting off its alarm. Trash bins stood in a weedy little courtyard. He slipped through an open gate into the campus grounds and headed for the wall.

Movement detectors watched the top, but down below, in a dank patch of high grass among some stunted pines, shielded by a warped sheet of semiplast he found a hole that he could just crawl through.

He emerged into a clump of coarse brush. A rutted street lay just beyond. Maks turned right, walked a hundred meters, and found the trirad parked where Maia had paid the driver to leave it. The slip of hardcopy gave him the lock code; he punched it in and the door popped open.

The vehicle creaked and swayed under his weight. *Hard to remember,* he thought, *how many people in the Worldcity couldn't afford a hovercab and got where they were going either on foot or in such rattraps as this.* He kicked a pedal and the whine of an electric engine started up. He tried the hand brake and shook his head over the steering lever. This thing would have seemed quaint in America 300 years ago. But it moved.

Down a gentle hill and into the noisy traffic of a busy street that emptied into Government of the Universe Place. Maks maneuvered through a couple of near accidents and turned into a broad avenue that ran beside the Senate of the Worlds. Darksiders were everywhere around the building like huge furry caterpillars. Senators in their purple sashes of office strolled alone or conferred in small conspiratorial groups, just as if they held real power.

A narrow street full of peddlers ran off the avenue and Maks turned into it. *Strat Subotai,* said a battered sign.

3

The houses were the usual banal jumble of styles. A woman came out of one, waving at Maks, and he almost stopped before realizing that she wanted to hire his cab. He passed her by and she shook a fist at him.

The numbers on the houses didn't seem to run in order; maybe they'd been numbered according to the order they were built in. Just when he thought he'd have to stop and ask, he saw 999.

He got out and locked the trirad's door behind him. The woman who wanted a cab ran up and began yelling at him.

"*Glupetz!* didn't you see me wave?" she demanded. "I gotta uncle in the polizi and I'll report you!"

"*Glupetz* your own self. I gotta fare," he said, pointing at the house.

"Like hell you do. That place is empty."

"If there ain't nobody there, I'll take you," he growled and left her standing by the trirad and kicking furiously at the front wheel.

Maks was not surprised to find the door unlocked. It opened noiselessly, too, as if somebody had recently squirted the hinges with defrictioner.

The entry hall was dim but not dark. Maks moved on to the

atrium with hand on weapon. A dirty skylight shone on an empty pool. Faux Roman had been in style when the place was built; a statue of cast stone viewed him with blind eyes.

Beyond the atrium was a large room, wide as the house, with a built-in circular dining table at knee height. A broken chandelier dangled by a chain. A low humming began and Maks noted that the vacuum vents and electrostatic filters around the baseboards were working, drawing away the dust.

"*Hai,*" said an atonal voice, making him jump in spite of himself.

Then he understood. Somebody had started the building's automatic systems working—including the intercom. In another room an arbot was preparing to converse. He seated himself on the circular table and waited.

"I bring you greetings from Sandi."

"Let me hear him."

"In just a moment."

The temptation to find and blast the speaker was almost irresistible. Instead, he crossed his legs and waited.

"You may be interested to learn that I am not seeking money," said the voice.

"I see. You want a service performed."

"Precisely. The service is one that would be impossible for anyone else, but should be simple for you, the famous time-surfer."

"I will not send an unauthorized person to the past, no matter what," said Maks, thinking of Dyeva, of Loki, of Zo Lian.

"Don't worry. I want you to bring someone from the past to the present—someone who would otherwise die only a few hours afterward. Surely *that's* possible."

Even through the impersonal voice he seemed to hear an overtone of irony. *How much,* he wondered, *does this bastard know?*

Maks frowned, uncrossed his legs, crossed them again. He

waited a few seconds, choosing his words, wishing that he could make his voice as flat as this artificial one.

"Possible, yes. In theory. But who and why?"

"Daddy, I don't like it here."

Maks shivered. It was Sandi's real voice, with the genuine overtones of anxiety, uncertainty, boredom, perhaps fear.

"Please come and get me. I want to go back home now. I don't like it here."

Silence. Maks sighed. *Yes, well, I know who's holding all the cards.*

"If I can't know why," he said, "I must at least know who."

"An absolutely harmless person, I assure you. A child not unlike your own. One who can't grow up unless you save him. He lives in the city of Washington in 2091."

"The date's right," muttered Maks. Suddenly he felt a dawning sense that a deal might, after all, be possible.

Hit early in the Troubles by a massive thermal cluster— roughly four times the explosive force of the one that hit New York—Washington had been so completely destroyed that robot excavators never had been sent there.

The aim of the Chinese had been to kill America's military and civilian leadership inside their refuge, a massively reinforced tunnel system beneath the city. So far as anybody knew, the attack, a classic of overkill, had achieved its aim. *No one* had survived.

"Unfortunately," the voice went on, "his parents and teachers will not know that your aim is beneficent. You'll have to kidnap him in order to bring him back."

Maks had often heard the phrase "a mirthless smile." That was now his expression as he contemplated the deal he was being offered.

"In short, to regain my son, I must become what you are."

"Say rather that my wish to save a boy's life is not unlike your own."

"I suppose you know that bringing an unauthorized person through the wormholer can cost me my head?"

"I am well aware of the risk."

"And you absolutely refuse to tell me why you want this particular child?"

Silence.

"Very well. Now I'll give you my minimum conditions. I must speak to my son directly, not to a recording, not to a mashina-generated image. I don't want virtual reality in this, I want reality reality."

"Agreed."

"One more thing. If you injure my son, either now or later, for any reason whatever, I will devote the rest of my life and all the resources of my office to hunting you down. When I find you I will personally direct your *shosho* and execution and I will watch you die."

Maks had never been able even to watch a *shosho* session, but his heart was hardening by the hour.

"Your message is understood."

"When will I hear from you?" Maks asked, rising stiffly to his feet. He was soaked in sweat, as if he'd been running a long race.

"When I choose."

Outside, the neighborhood was as nondescript as ever. The woman who wanted a cab had presumably found one. *Unless,* he thought wearily, *she was the one who planted the memory cube and turned on the intercom.* If he called Colonel Yost now, asked for a raid, had the Darksiders tear every one of these houses to pieces, would he find his boy? Of course not.

He climbed into the trirad and kicked the starter. The little motor whined. *I ever get through this and Sandi survives,* he thought, *I can endure anything.* Even *shosho* would be a vacation.

4

In Maks's absence Sherí summoned a hovercab and headed off to the far northeast quadrant of the city.

As honored guests of the state, the *stari* that Maks and the other timesurfers had brought back from olden times lived in a luxurious Security Forces safe house. Around the curling eaves of the faux Chinese roofs stretched formal gardens enclosed by a high stone wall. In other compounds nearby stood palaces belonging to senators, monopolists, top bureaucrats, generals, and guildmasters.

Sherí's cab sputtered down, avoiding the dangerous airspace above the compound. She saw the guard post at the main gate, the kennels lining the street, the Darksider guards lounging around scratching their fur and hefting impact weapons in double-thumbed hands. The cab's arrival caused a dozen big mandrill faces to look up, staring through blue sun visors and displaying long yellow fangs.

Then they were gone. Landing in a quieter street to the rear of the compound, she paid off the cab's black box and walked to a postern gate no wider than a man. Pali stood there waiting for her. She wasn't supposed to come here, and she sometimes wondered about Pali's motives in letting her in. Was he just being kind? He seemed like such a nice man! *Or,* she wondered, *does he think he'll benefit in the long run by making a friend of his boss's wife?*

Whatever, this was their secret, and they shared a conspiratorial smile as he used an electronic key to shut off the gate's sensors.

"Where's the boss, Madame Major?" he asked as they passed through into the garden.

"Business," she said vaguely. "Poor Maks, he's so terribly worried about his little boy."

Pali shook his head. "I don't really understand it, a thing like that happening in a society as well policed as ours. Do you want to go direct to the teahouse?"

"I think I'll say hello to some of the others, too."

"Fine. I like it when you come and visit. You're good for their morale."

While he returned to his duties she spoke to three or four of the *stari* who were strolling the garden. Most of them she liked—a darkly handsome Orthodox Jew from Manhattan's diamond center, a Tiffany-Cartier executive, a curator from the Met. She avoided a tall, imperious woman who seemed to think she still owned a billion shares of the Dotcom Cartel, even though it had vanished in a cloud of smoke three centuries ago.

Then Sherí crossed a curving wooden bridge and made her way by a path soft with emerald moss through a stand of giant bamboo. A little artificial waterfall murmured and chuckled, and beside it stood a plain small wooden house with shoji screens instead of windows and doors.

Inside, Benjo Kurosawa rose and put out his hands and smiled. Then he sat down crosslegged on a kapok cushion and gestured for her to do the same. She folded her legs and sat gracefully, noting with a thrill how his eyes followed her movements. A little robot entered and began to prepare tea.

She couldn't help smiling at the contrasts—a man of twenty-first-century New York wearing an Armani suit to an ancient tea ceremony taking place in the remote future.

"Right," he nodded. "All times and places meet here."

She laughed delightedly. "You're a real mind reader!"

He smiled. "Tell me about your adventures outside the wall, Sherí."

"It's not all gravy. The language is dreadfully hard and, frankly, I'm scared all the time. Benjo, are there *kloppi*—sorry, bugs—in this place?"

"No. Take it from me. I've searched it myself."

"It's just that I'm always so worried about being discovered."

"It must be tough. Yet—Jesus!—how I envy you."

"Oh, I know. It's so, so deluxe here, isn't it? But it's still a prison anyway."

He sighed. "Don't remind me. Whenever I can, I come out here by myself and think about the long ago and the faraway . . . You remember them building the Fifth-Level Highway?"

"Sure. I was living with Mama in a building near Rockefeller University and the hospital center. The noise kept us awake for two years. What it did to the patients I can't imagine."

"Well, I built it," he said. "That was when I was still getting my hands dirty by making things instead of just making money. In those days Channel 3500 called me the Japanese-American Robert Moses."

"Oh yes?" she said vaguely. "Who was he, some Israeli?"

Benjo smiled. Often in the past he'd met dim minds housed in magnificent bodies.

"Tell me about this Maks of yours," he said, changing the subject. "How'd you meet him?"

"Well, it started so simply. I had a fling with this good-looking, rather odd man I'd met romantically by running head-on into him on 57th Street. He had a funny accent, and his underwear! I'd never seen anything like it. But he was sexy and had, obviously, a big secret and that fascinated me, trying to get it out of him. Then one day he asked me if I'd like to visit his home, and I said yes, and he said, well, let's have a drink first. When I woke up here, I thought I'd gone crazy."

Benjo nodded. "I know how you felt. How'd Maks explain it to you?"

"He told me about the Time of Troubles and the Russian Defense Minister and China and so on. It was all so complicated and weird and I'd never paid any attention to politics, anyway. So at first I didn't believe him."

"Took me a while to believe it, too," he assured her.

"See, you do know how I feel. Oh, I'm so glad I met you, Benjo. And the others, too. When I heard you were here, I simply couldn't stay away."

His eyes probed her. She wondered if he was reading her mind and the thought made her uneasy. She didn't want him to know how much he fascinated her.

"You're a good friend," he said, and touched her hand, gently. "So please, Sherí. Do me a favor. Try to persuade Maks to get us released. I want to have a life again, a real life."

"I've promised you and I will. I want Maks to bring Mama here. I just can't think of her dying in some dumb war. I want him to set you and all the *stari* free, too, and I'm going to get everything I want, sooner or later. I can be pretty persuasive."

"Oh, I bet you can, Sherí. I've never met a woman like you."

How proud it made her feel to have this fascinating man say that to her! She raised a cup of the hot, fresh-brewed tea to her mouth and thought suddenly how like a magician Benjo looked, with wraiths of steam rising like incense around him.

CHAPTER XX

Maks returned as he'd come, telling Maia that a deal might be possible, picking up his escort—the thuggi grinned at him, pretty sure in their own minds why he'd been so long in his ex-wife's apartment—and at last heading home.

Sherí had just gotten back. She listened to his adventures, his hopes of a deal, then began to talk up her own projects. But he merely growled, "Not now," and headed out to his office. That evening he worked late, trying to catch up, and she had gone to bed when he returned.

Maks looked in on her, wondered briefly how this sleeping goddess could irritate him so much, then settled down with a sheaf of hardcopy from his office.

The mashina showed no calls for him since the morning. "When I choose," echoed through his mind, with the accent on "when." He was sharply aware of the clock on the wall. When it said, "Twenty-two, Honored Major," he stopped work and sat like a statue for several minutes. When it announced twenty-three, he had to go fetch his silver censer and inhale some kif before his nerves quieted enough so that he could resume work. And when it said, "Twenty-four, Honored Major. A new day is beginning," he gave up all pretense of work and sat smoking while its advancing numbers glowed and faded with the passing minutes.

At one he called Maia long enough to tell her that nothing more had happened.

"I think I'm getting tougher," she whispered. "You know, I didn't even try to follow you today."

She sounded strained and tired and clearly hadn't been sleeping. But she was in control of herself. Maks cut the connection, wondering if evolution had equipped women better than men for waiting. Over the eons, they'd had to do so much of it.

Not wishing to disturb Sherí, he made himself a nest of cushions on the floor, pulled the censer close, and settled down to wait. He must have fallen asleep again when, in a dream, a mashina chimed. First in the dream and then in real life, he said, "Say."

2

The double cone was shimmering again, the kidnapper's logo. What did it mean? he wondered. Then Sandi appeared and he forgot everything else.

The boy was sitting on an unmade bed, rubbing his eyes. Looking reedy, but no more so than usual; dark hair uncombed, with the widow's peak and the small shaved spot at the crown that all the kids were wearing. Suddenly he gasped, staring at an image of his father.

"Son, it's me. Are you all right?"

"Uh huh. Are you coming to get me?"

"As soon as I can."

There was a very brief time lapse between question and answer.

"I don't like these guys."

"Have they hurt you?"

"N-no. Grila won't let them. I just don't like them."

Suddenly Sandi was in a mood to issue orders.

"Daddy, I want you to come here and get me *right now.*"

When Maks said he couldn't, he started to cry and then to rage. Maks didn't care. He was talking to the real Sandi, that was the main thing, and the boy, though he was tired, scared and having a tantrum from sheer frustration, seemed to be unharmed.

Suddenly the communication ended. Another instant and a handheld vicor was showing him a shoddy room with a mashina standing on a table by a window.

A polizi tech walked in front of the vicor, rapped the mashina with his knuckles, and stared out the window. Then he turned and said, "Sir?"

"Yes?"

"Message originated somewhere in those tall buildings out

there. Probably sent by laser. A transceiver attached to this set converted the information impressed on the beam into a mashina image that was rebroadcast to you."

Sighing, Maks cut the circuit. He called Maia, told her the story, asked her not to cry. When she did anyway, he cried with her. It was his first breakdown since the ordeal began, and Maia seemed to like the proof he cared.

The sounds had waked Sherí. She emerged from the bedroom rubbing her eyes, made him tea, spoke quietly and sensibly while they waited.

"Have you checked out this 'Grila'?" she asked. She made no effort to talk Alspeke; they chatted in Archaic English.

"Sure. The techs ran it through Files. There's an old farmer living in Karakorum, whose name is Grila Simyon. He's a hundred-and-one and has no living descendants. It's probably a nickname or an alias for one of the kidnappers."

The message traffic continued. The polizi were searching the buildings where the broadcast might have originated. No hope of finding Sandi, of course—he'd undoubtedly been spirited away. But they wanted to find the room in hopes of coming upon physical evidence left by the criminal.

In fact, they would need two more days of patient legwork to find in a ninety-stage apartment block the room where Sandi had sat on a rumpled bed talking to his father through a mashina. Almost at once a disturbing new pattern began to develop in the investigation.

3

The mashina was there, the bed was there, the laser communicator was gone, Sandi was gone. The owner of the flat was gone, too—a hydroponics expert giving guidance on growing lettuce and carrots in the tunnels of Ganymede—and thus not a factor in the drama.

Polizi robots proceeded to vacuum the entire flat and carried off the dust in sealed and labeled bags. The bed, the sheets, the mashina followed to the laboratories of the Security Forces under the Palace of Justice. But the dust proved to be the most important gleaning.

In the lab a filter-separator began pulling out fibers, dust mites, bits of nail paring, coiled pubic hairs, flakes of dandruff, fallen eyelashes, navel fuzz, and similar detritus and parading 3-D images through the shadowbox of a mashina. Two techs of the sort that gun-toting polizi called white mice examined the images as they floated by.

"That hair's probably from a kid," commented the head mouse. "Too fine for an adult."

"Mark for examination," said the assistant mouse to the mashina. Then both gasped. What looked like an anaconda was writhing past.

"Oh, Great Tao," said the head mouse. "Rotate."

The image paused, rotated on various axes. When the head mouse ordered enlargement, the microscope zoomed in on curiously long, coarse cells that were almost big enough to be seen by the naked eye.

He looked at his assistant. The assistant looked at him.

"Was there a Darksider in the task force that entered the apartment?" asked the assistant.

"No," said the mashina, after a few seconds. "Humans only."

"Well," said the assistant, "maybe a hair adhered to somebody—"

"Look," said his chief. "This hair was entangled in stuff from under the bed. It was there for a while. I mean, it's like hunting dinosaurs. You find a bone embedded in a Cretaceous stratum, it wasn't dropped yesterday."

The head mouse ordered the anaconda separated and marked. Then he called the Chief of Research. She was deep in a saliva sample and answered the call in no good humor.

"Well? Well?"

The head mouse told her what they'd found. Almost a minute of absolute silence followed.

"I'm coming over," she said at last. "If you're right, bonuses for both of you. If you're wrong, kiss your asses good-bye."

The mice grinned at each other. They knew they were right. One of the kidnappers was a Darksider, and they, of course, served only the agencies of government.

Yamashita had ordered Yost to report to him personally on the kidnapping, and their daily session took place little more than an hour later.

"So you don't think it was *mafya*?" said the general.

"No. We've made arrests, of course, run a dozen suspects through Special Investigations. Two died, so I don't think they were lying. Nobody in the city's heard a whisper."

"Get any names from the *kukrachi*?"

"Yes, but they led nowhere. You know, when the needles are in somebody's spine, they start naming people. Any people, innocent or guilty. It's regrettable, but it happens."

Yost sighed over this evidence of human weakness. Yamashita peered at him and frowned.

"There's obviously something else. What is it?"

"A report—a rather disturbing report—has just come in from the laboratory."

He outlined the finding made earlier by the mice. Yamashita for once was too startled to fly into a rage.

"What? What? They've got a Darksider?"

"So it seems. The possibility has to be faced that one or more of our own people are somehow involved in this."

"Why would a cop get involved in a kidnapping?"

Yost shrugged. "I don't know. It's distressing to think of

such a thing. I hope there's some kind of mistake. But it does give us another line of investigation to follow."

"What?"

For answer, Yost took from his beltpouch a plastic envelope containing what looked like powder, but was in fact tiny spheres of dull metal. "Micromonitors," he said.

Yamashita made an impatient gesture. "Obviously. So what?"

"Well, they've been so miniaturized by now that they can be inserted by a hypodermic gun along with an aerosol serum. Then they circulate through the body with the bloodstream. If you approve, I'll order booster shots for everybody in the organization, human and animal. The mainframe mashina will track the monitors, and if anybody turns up where they're not authorized to be—"

"Good!" roared Yamashita, recovering his usual temper. "I like anything that improves top-down control! Do it!"

"Would you like to take the first shot," asked Yost politely, "or shall I?"

4

By this time another report was percolating upward toward Yost's desk. It was even more—in his word—distressing.

A private citizen reported to the polizi that sounds were coming from a supposedly empty apartment next to his own. Among the voices was that of a child.

The report was routed through various mashini and eventually landed on the desk of a sergeant named Blin, who decided it was one more false lead. Even so, she ordered a pair of thuggi to check it out on their way back to barracks from an interdepartmental *futbol* game.

The thuggi approached the door in a blank gray hallway on the nineteenth stage of another residential block. Then they paused, sniffed, and looked at each other. One mouthed the word, "Darksider," and the other nodded. They beat a hasty retreat.

Their report brought Sergeant Blin, six more thuggi, and two Darksiders, all armed with impact weapons, while a guncar nosed up to the exterior of the suspect apartment. Blin, almost spherical, 1.6 meters tall and 80 kilos heavy, rolled into the hallway hefting a pistol half as long as she was wide. She had a round face, small round dark eyes, and a cap of short gray hair. She took all crimes against children personally, and she was absolutely fearless.

"Is that the door?" she whispered.

"Yes, ma'am."

"Darksiders forward, one to each side. Right. Now stand back and *yell*, goddammit, all of you!"

"*POLIZI! Tor otkrit!*"

Impact slugs blasted through the door from inside and shattered the wall opposite. Suddenly the hallway was dim with dust and floating fragments like the dark spots that drift before the eyes after a blow to the head.

Blin's Darksiders poked their own weapons into the holes and fired into the apartment. Sounds of explosion, disintegration and collapse followed. Then they smashed in what was left of the door and the thuggi followed, roaring.

They found nothing. Blin led the way through a ruined parlor and into a bedroom. The window had been broken out; a hovercar lifted out of view just as she reached the shattered duroplast and stared out.

Blin was not the brightest star of the Security Forces, but she knew why a polizi guncar that hovered a hundred meters away wasn't firing at the fugitives. The escaping car was broadcasting a signature key that automatically immobilized all polizi automatic weapons and missiles.

Blin turned back, stunned, to face her gaping subordinates. The kidnappers were escaping in a polizi car.

CHAPTER XXI

Maks, knowing nothing of these developments, went through the days like an automaton. That was the style of the Security Forces: nobody ever told you anything unless you absolutely had to know it to do your job. In this organization, paranoia equalled policy.

He did his job at Pastplor, dealing with ordinary things, disciplinary hearings, efficiency ratings, budget numbers. He sent young timesurfers to the past and collated their reports. At one point he was called to the nearest dispensary to get a booster shot, baring his right arm amid a crowd of other grumbling officers.

That afternoon he sat in his office listening to the clock announce the passage of time. He tried to work on his budget for next year, but even with his mashina doing the math he somehow managed to get every number wrong. Finally he gave up and stared at a clock that stared back at him. Thirteen seventy-five. Every second was a minute long.

He called home, but Sherí was out. Her image politely informed him that she had gone shopping. He had a flash of rage at her, then drank some tea and tried to settle down.

He called Maia, but she looked so stricken when he said he still had nothing to report that he was sorry he'd disturbed her. He was sitting, brooding, disconsolate, when an alarm light on his mashina warned him that his secretary software judged a message to be urgent.

"Say," he muttered, hoarsely.

"Your Honored Wife is at Barrier One and wishes to be admitted."

"Let her in."

Ten minutes later the door to his office slid open and Sherí rushed in, breathless. Maks had long ago warned her never to speak English in headquarters, and her words tumbled out in a torrent of confused Alspeke.

"Oh, Maks, I goed by Fresher Market to buying plums, and a man handing out slips of hardcopy—you know how they doing—"

For a moment he thought she had gone mad.

"I thought somebody announcing a special on fat ducks or something, and I doesn't"—she gave up on Alspeke, disregarding all his warnings—"didn't pay him the slightest attention and I almost threw the paper away."

"Sherí—"

"It has instructions on it, Maks. For you. And a little picture a couple of inches—I mean five centimeters—square."

2

"One second."

To his mashina he said, "You will institute a complete information blackout of this office until further notice. You will record nothing yourself. You will allow no one to enter. Normal conditions will resume in ten minutes."

"Yes, Honored Major."

He leaned toward Sherí. "Read it to me."

" 'John Hammer, aged twelve, Venerable Bede Cathedral School. Tell him his father wants him back.' "

He was writing it down when he heard her say, "Oh, my God."

"I wish you'd stop saying that," he said automatically. "Not many people believe in God anymore. Someday you're going to give yourself away."

When he raised his eyes she was staring transfixed at the note. "This is the ransom?"

"Yes."

"Why does the kidnapper want this boy?"

"I don't have the slightest idea."

"Where's this school?"

"Washington."

"And the time?"

"Autumn 2091."

"Just before—"

"Yes."

"And you're going back to get him?"

"Yes."

She sat absolutely still for a moment, then said, "I thought you wouldn't save anybody else."

"This is my son we're talking about."

"What about my mother? You said no, you wouldn't go back for her. Why's your son different from somebody I love?"

Maks just stared at her. For the life of him, he couldn't think of a logical reason why Sandi was different. He took refuge in getting angry.

"Goddammit, Sherí, I saved your life! I invented a background for you and embedded it in the official files. I taught you how to live in this world. I tried to teach you the language, without much success, I admit. I don't owe you any apologies."

"Yes, I owe you my life, that's true, and thank you so much for reminding me."

"Honored Major," said the mashina, "the ten minutes are up. You are again in contact with the world."

It was a bad parting. Sherí walked out, face white with anger. Not until she was seated in a hovercab leaving the Palace of Justice did she remember the danger Maks would soon be facing.

My God, she thought, *suppose Maks dies in Washington?*

What'll happen to me? What'll happen to Mama and Benjo and all of us with him gone?

She almost ordered the black box to take the cab back where she'd come from. Then realized that Maks would be gone before she could reach his office.

"Oh, hell," she muttered.

"I beg pardon, honored passenger?" asked the black box. "Do you still wish me to take you to your home?"

"No," she said on impulse. "Taking me—take me to Imperial Mansions Sector, northeast quadrant."

The cab banked and began a slow turn. Of all the people in this strange world, the only one she could turn to for advice and comfort was Benjo Kurosawa.

3

How many, many times, thought Maks, lying inside the wormholer, he'd waited here with shielded eyes.

He'd grown so expert in using the device that he no longer needed technicians to aid him; he simply gave the controlling mashina its orders plus a five-minute time delay, and went. That was fortunate, considering the number of illegal things he'd done with the wormholer.

He tensed, felt the instantaneous flash of energy, the sudden supernal cold, then the ordinary brisk windy chill of an ancient autumn day.

He sat up among trees fluttering the red and gold flags of mid-November. This hillside in Rock Creek Park was a favorite "landing site" for the timesurfers, close to everything yet shielded from view.

Maks stood up shakily, then almost fell down again. The body of a murdered woman was lying facedown a couple of meters away. Her blood-dabbled red hair reminded him of Sherí. Averting his eyes, he hastened past the corpse and strode downhill, in a hurry to get away.

Little electric cars were scuttling along the parkway. He paused a last time to be sure he was properly dressed, then crossed a graceful pedestrian bridge and paused by a jogging trail to let a group of runners go past. Their guards, trotting at the rear with Biretta machine pistols slung casually across their shoulders, eyed him narrowly but did not stop.

Maks breathed easier; he always felt better after he'd passed his first inspection from the *stari*.

Just beyond the park was a burned-out neighborhood. The ruins were nearly forty years old and did not smell any longer. It was early morning and peddlers were putting out small stocks of rubbishy goods in stalls built of waste lumber and plastic.

They reminded Maks of the Worldcity's people, a little darker on average than the prosperous folks downtown, with a predominant type that was not unattractive, pale chocolate skin, large dark or greenish eyes, and black or red hair. They shouted cheerfully at one another in the dialect of the neighborhood, which Maks could barely understand.

He hastened on, his shadow fleeting before him. An ancient bus burning something that smelled like charcoal was marked CATHEDRAL. He swung aboard, paid 120 dollars, and sat down by an open window.

Time was, he thought as the bus labored up the avenue, *when this must have a been a row of palatial homes*. The baronial buildings were warrens of apartments now, and kids were climbing the old cornices like monkeys and swinging from the carved pilasters on dares.

In sight of the cathedral, he jumped off the bus. It had reached the end of its run anyway; steel gates closed off the rest of Massachusetts Avenue and guards lounged inside, chatting to their handphones. A steady stream of poorly dressed people passed through the gates, pausing to show their IDs and be patted down—servants, headed for work.

Maks joined the line, showed his fake ID, stated that he worked at one of the big co-ops on Wisconsin Avenue. When they patted him down, they found the wormholer control. At the same instant Maks realized that in the excitement he had forgotten to personalize the chip in the control—it would respond to anyone.

A guard stood fondling it for a moment, almost touching the activating stud.

"What the hell is this thing?"

"It's a handceiver for the building's intercom. They just installed a whole new system. It never works right."

The guard's index finger passed a millimeter from the bump that would have projected him three centuries into the future and stranded Maks in Washington.

"They never do, do they?" he said and handed it back. Maks moved on, a little stream of cold sweat coursing down his spine. In his pocket, he fingered the familiar controls until the gadget had memorized the unique pattern of microbloodvessels in his thumb. Then, breathing easier, he lengthened his stride.

The cathedral, fake Gothic and less than 200 years old, did not interest him and he hastened past it. Venerable Bede was new-old: reinforced concrete buildings with precast columns, architraves, plinths, caryatids, and whatnot glued on the outside to simulate age.

He paused at a wrought-iron gate in a mossy gray wall and peered inside. Beyond the school buildings stretched bright green playing fields where boys dashed about, kicking a white-and-black ball. Wire sensors of a crude sort ran along the top of the wall, half concealed in masses of English ivy. A couple of big-bellied thuggi stood chatting by a building marked LIBRARY in ornate lettering. They wore heavy pistols, and probably, Maks reflected, had received special training in protecting their charges from kidnappers.

Sighing, he concentrated on his memorized image of young John Hammer. A thin face, hollow-cheeked, with a shock of black hair and a hard, wary alertness about the round, dark eyes. But no child in sight resembled him. Maks moved on, glad that the avenue was bustling this time of the morning with streams of the little electric cars whining south to Georgetown, or north to the National Medical Complex that had swallowed Bethesda.

Now, he thought. *How exactly do I go about stealing this boy?*

4

"Tell you frankly, Sherí, I based my whole financial career on the infinite corruptibility of men. And, of course, women. The sexes are absolutely equal in that respect."

Sherí smiled. The odor of perfectly brewed tea, the rustle of wind in the bamboo outside, the sound of unseen water tumbling over rocks. Yes, this was what she needed.

Benjo, well aware that she was troubled, was saying outrageous things in the brisk nasal accent of New York, which brought back—oh, so much. A whole world.

But his basic sadness soon overtook him. "You know, honey, I never thought *everything* I did would disappear."

She nodded. "I know."

That was the point of their friendship, wasn't it? She did know.

She asked, "Did you have family, Benjo?"

"Yes. Four wives, four divorces. One child."

"Boy or girl?"

"Boy. His mother took him away from me when we split. She was really bitter, maybe with reason. I'd played around a lot, I admit. She remarried and got a tame judge to change my son's name. I was furious when I heard about it. Even had his eyes operated on so they didn't look oriental! Anything to erase me from his life."

Sherí frowned. "I seem to remember something in *Cyber-tattle* about it. She married—what was his name—a feelie star, was it?"

"No, an industrialist. Very rich man, from a famous family. His name was Hammer."

A long moment passed and Benjo looked at her curiously. She met his eyes steadily, without blinking.

"I see."

"Ah," he said. "You have a bad effect on me. I've said too much."

"How could you?" she whispered.

She wasn't quite sure what she meant by that—was she asking him how he could betray Maks, and in such an awful way? Or was she asking him how, a prisoner himself, he'd managed this extraordinary crime?

Naturally, Benjo assumed she was asking him how, not why, he'd done it.

"It wasn't hard," he said, refilling both cups. "Policemen are just as crooked today as they were in our time."

He smiled a little, his eyes distant. "I know you think I'm totally amoral, Sherí, but that's not true. I've got a sense of justice. It amused me to arrange the kidnapping of the son of the man who kidnapped me. And later force him to take my son as I'd taken his."

"Maks saved your life!"

"Oh, honey. Spare me. He brought me here as a living treasure map, nothing else. Drink your tea. It'll get cold."

He sipped his own. "You want to know how I managed it

when I'm a prisoner? The answer is bribery. I've given some useful information to the government about hidden treasures. But I know so much more. Nobody in history ever had the means of bribery that I do.

"Think of all the wealth going into the public treasury, which really means into the hands of this old woman, Xian, and her favorites and those dumb senators. Nothing left for the poor policemen! A river of wealth passes through their hands, and though very thirsty they're forbidden to drink. No wonder they become sadists. They've a lot to be sadistic about."

She whispered, "The little boy, Sandi. Is he all right?"

"Of course he is. When you're playing chess and you capture your opponent's pawn, you don't destroy it. You merely take it off the board."

"And the polizi helped you do this."

"A few of them, yes. A small, well-organized group within the Security Forces. See, honey, what I want is simple. And stop frowning, it's not criminal, not basically. I want to be set free to live in this time, to regain my son and reestablish my family. That's all."

He seemed to be pleading with her for understanding, and suddenly Sherí saw, under the ruthless conniver, a man who wanted very much what she wanted herself. He read her expression and pressed his advantage.

"And I want to marry, this time for the last time. Can you guess the name of the bride?"

She stared at him. She'd never been good at guessing games, not since she was a little girl and the kids at Rudolph Giuliani Elementary School No. 1 used to call her Dim Bulb.

"The bride?" she asked, baffled.

He smiled. "Think about it. Your life is in my hands, because I know you're here illegally. My life and my son's life are in yours. We three can truly understand one another; this Maks of yours can never be anything but a stranger to you, and the better you get to know him the more alien he'll seem. Once I'm free, you and I and John can be happy together. Unless I've lost my touch, and I don't think I have, we can be grandees in this world just as I was in the old one.

"Now, to quote one of my favorite old 2-D movies: Have I made you an offer you can't refuse?"

CHAPTER XXII

Sandi hated the new room where they'd put him even more than the others. It was like a jail, with a light in the ceiling, green walls, and a drain in the floor. A box in the corner held a chemical toilet smelling of disinfectant.

True, he'd been given books to read, dinosaur books, books that showed the Pleistocene mammals and the African animals and the North American animals and so forth. The food wasn't too bad—better than school, anyway. But he was desperately lonely and nobody except Grila seemed to understand that. And today Grila was late.

Sandi missed him. Of course Grila couldn't talk, but he stared fascinated at the pictures in the books, and Sandi read to him, never knowing how much he understood or whether he understood anything at all.

On this particular day, even emptier than the others, so empty that Sandi would almost have preferred doing lessons, he was sitting in a hard duroplast chair reading, when suddenly Grila's coming announced itself as a faint whiff of nose-wrinkling scent. The door clicked a few times as it always did when somebody was punching in the code, then swung open, and Grila came in carrying a bunch of grapes for him.

"Thanks," he said, and ate them while his friend sat down on the floor and looked at him in his quiet, undemanding way, not waiting for anything in particular, just waiting. He had a vet's tag clipped to one ear certifying that he'd received a booster shot. So that was why he was late.

"The grapes were good," said Sandi. "Look, Grila. Come here."

Grila just looked at him until Sandi gestured, and then he hunched himself along the floor, not bothering to rise, until he was next to the chair.

"Don't they make you take baths?" asked Sandi, holding his nose. Grila just looked at him, and Sandi reflected that he'd been without a bath so long himself that possibly he smelled as bad to Grila as Grila did to him.

"I guess we're just a couple of stinkers," he smiled and scratched his friend's head. Then he opened the book he'd been reading and pointed to a picture of a huge furry beast that was labeled in large clear print, *Afrikana Gurila*.

"See?" said Sandi as Grila touched the page with a sausage-thick hairy finger and scratched at the picture with two centimeters of yellow talon. The beast's extra arms reached for the book and helped to smooth it out on the boy's lap.

"That's where I got your name from," he told it. "You're Grila the Gurila, see?"

Great raspberry-colored eyes, too intelligent for an animal, not quite equal to the human, looked from the picture to Sandi and back again. The jaws opened, showing splayed fangs and a throat like a chasm. A burst of fetid breath emerged but no sound except the rush of air.

Steffi covered his nose and said reprovingly to his friend, "Don't they make you brush your teeth?"

2

Leaving the teahouse, Sherí almost staggered. The secret she knew seemed about to make her head explode. Pali spoke to her as he was letting her out of the gate, but she didn't know what she answered.

At a nearby pylon she called a cab, climbed in, and soared above the neat geometrical quarter of walls, palaces, and gardens. Sherí looked down, feeling like a passenger in a little boat tossed around by a storm.

At one moment she hated Benjo for his betrayal of Maks, at the next she hated Maks for refusing to do something so decent, so simple for him, as to save a few more lives from the Troubles—refusing, that is, until someone threatened his own flesh and blood.

Then it was different. Oh yes, then it was different. She thought of her mother vanishing in the firestorm, her atoms dispersed and buried inside the Great Shield. The marrow of Sherí's bones seemed to ache with grief. Benjo was a crook, but at least she could understand him, understand his needs, his yearning to re-create the core of his own life or die trying.

With the force almost of hallucination her mother's face rose before her. So many could be saved, a kind of Underground Railroad across time could be established, and Maks with his power as head of Pastplor—Maks was the key . . . What he wouldn't do willingly, perhaps he could be forced to do.

Benjo had discovered that. He was a compeller, not a persuader.

Suddenly she leaned forward and almost shouted at the black box, "Take me back!"

Sherí hardly noticed the landing. She called Pali from an intercom at the main gate, trying to hold her breath against the smell of the Darksiders. One approached her, curious and wary by its body language, like a dog meeting a visitor. She could see her white face reflected in its blue eyeshield.

Then Pali approached, smiling his courteous smile, his large dark eyes moist. He put out a slender hand and took hers.

"Ah, Madame Major. I didn't expect to see you again today."

"I'm afraid I may have left my—" *What?* she wondered, groping for a lie she'd failed to prepare in advance. "My comm-disk. With Benjo. He wanted to know how it works," she babbled, quite aware that Pali was aware that she had no idea how a commdisk worked.

But he said only, "I think he's still out there. Will you excuse me, Madame Major? I'm sure—after so many visits—you can find your own way."

Even in her mixed-up emotional state she caught something in his tone. Irony? She'd always resented people being ironic because it usually went right over her head. She tried to read his face but his expression was mild and bland and somehow sweet, like a chocolate rabbit.

The teahouse stood as before, a graceful small structure deliberately contrived to echo another time. The stream dashed and chuckled over round stones and a breeze stirred the stalks of giant bamboo and made them click and rattle.

Inside, Benjo rose, gripped her hands and kissed her for the first time. There was nothing tentative about it; his kiss was insistent and deep.

"I knew you'd come back," he told her.

"Oh," she whispered, clutching at the lapels of his elegant suit. She really needed something to hang onto.

"Benjo, I want to—to discuss what you said—"

But he didn't seem to be in the mood for discussion. He hugged her and she was surprised by his strength. He was as strong as Maks and more demanding. He kissed her deeply again and her knees seemed to give way beneath her.

They sank to the floor holding each other. She couldn't

decide whether to hold him off or pull him close. But he was deciding for her, grappling with her more like a wrestler than a lover, using his mouth to seize her lips, then her throat, while his hands stripped her with ruthless efficiency.

Oh Christ, she thought as he pressed her knees back against her breasts, *is this how the samurai did it?* The floor felt gritty under her bare bottom. She clutched at his head, bit his ear, tasted blood. Then she screamed.

Nothing made any difference. He had no patience, gave her no time, did not care whether she felt pleasure or pain. His semen jetted inside her like molten wax.

When it was over he stood up, gazed at his stained, limp trousers, and shook his head ruefully. The rapist subsided; the debonair businessman reemerged. He even apologized.

"Sorry, honey. It's been a long time. I didn't mean to be so abrupt."

"*Abrupt,*" she sobbed. "You're a goddamn animal. I'm bleeding."

"Let me see. Oh, that's nothing. You're hardly the Virgin Mary."

"You bastard."

She started to cry. He knelt, embraced her, comforted her.

"Sherí, try to forgive me, please. honey? Come on. I just wanted you too much, that's all. Share my life with me. Make me a better man than I've ever been before."

How many idiots have you used that line on? she wondered. Yet when he began kissing her, she kissed him back. When he pulled her close, however, she shivered and tried to get away.

But this time he was kind, gentle, almost submissive. The bamboo shadows lengthened as they enjoyed a slow, sweet lovemaking. She whispered her commands, and to her amazement he obeyed; he seemed to stay hard forever, and a hot expanding sun rose and set inside her, rose and set. When it was over her body was humming with violinlike overtones of sorrowful joy.

They left the teahouse arm in arm, walking down the little crooked path of emerald moss beside the bright water. Like young lovers they hardly watched where they were going, looking into each other's faces, trying to read their futures there.

"If only I could've found you long ago," he murmured. His voice was husky, dark. "I'd have showed you a life you can't imagine, Sherí. Now we'll have to start from scratch, build it from the ground up in this strange place, because our own world's gone. Together we can do it."

And somehow, even though her mind screamed warnings, her feelings swooned into belief that Benjo could accomplish anything, anything at all he wanted to do.

3

Maks had delivered a package to the school, making no effort to see John Hammer, remembering not to call him Hammer John.

The package was from a shop he'd discovered down the avenue among a cluster of expensive little stores. He'd selected a garment woven of wool, a natural fabric with a texture he'd never felt before. According to the sign, it was designed to make people sweat, though why they should want to Maks couldn't imagine.

The clerk told him that all the boys at Ven Bede's wore them and showed him how the garment was decorated with an embroidered shield showing the Latin word VERITAS, meaning truth.

Then to a shop that sold creamy paper for writing and pens that bled either wet or dry ink, whichever you desired. Maks inserted a note into the box with the sweater and rewrapped the gift as neatly as he could, sitting on a rustic bench under a rustling golden tree.

"Who's Hammer?" asked one of the fat guards when he handed it through the iron bars of the gate.

"One of your kids, I guess," said Maks in his best idiomatic English. "All I know is, some lady came into the store, bought it, and asked me to hand-deliver it. I gotta get back to work, so here it is."

Now the waiting began.

Maks ate lunch, stared into shop windows, bought a book of psychic predictions whose theme was that the next century would be incomparably better than this one. Smiling sadly, he tucked the book into a metal basket labeled *LITTER*.

He sat on the rustic bench and watched the traffic flow in bright primary colors along the avenue until his watch said 2, meaning 14. Then, in the distance, he saw a white-trousered leg thrown over the gray wall of Ven Bede's, followed by a hand, a rumpled blue coat, and a tousled dark head.

The boy dropped to the sidewalk and merged into a stream of pedestrians. When he reached a point across from Maks he paused and squinted at the strange man sitting quietly on the bench and waiting for him. The boy looked this way, that way. Maks understood that he was telling himself: nothing can happen to me with all these people around.

Maks quietly took the wormholer control from his pocket and toyed with it, as if it was a handceiver. When he looked up again the boy was standing on the curb on his side of the avenue and staring at him.

"Are you the guy—"

"Yes," said Maks. "Your father sent me to get you."

"You're a liar. He hates my guts."

The eyes were black and ice cold.

"Is that what you've been told?"

"Yes," said John. "Mama says it and for once she's telling me the truth. He's all over the tivi. He's rich. He could come and get me if he wanted to."

Briefly Maks racked his brain for someone named Hammer who might somehow be entangled with the kidnapping. He could think of nobody.

"Well, he wants to now."

He raised the control.

"You can talk to him through this. Christ, John, I don't expect you to believe *me*. Come talk to your father. I won't listen in. I'll cross the street if you want me to. It'll be totally private."

John edged closer. "Who are you anyway?"

"A private detective. He hired me to contact you. Come on, ask him. Stop talking to me, I can't tell you anything more anyway."

John's eyes were glued to the control. "I never saw a handceiver like that," he muttered.

"It's a new model. Nobody but detectives are allowed to own them."

Clearly, that was a big attraction.

"Reach it to me," the boy said cautiously. "I got to be careful. Lots of rich kids go to that school and one of 'em got snatched last month. Cost his family a billion to get him back. I never figured he was worth that much."

Maks stretched out his arm, the control in his hand. John edged toward him again, ready to break and run at the first false move.

"That was slick, the way you got over the wall," Maks said conversationally. "Why didn't the sensor pick you up?"

"Oh, that fucking gadget. I got myself ticketed for being in the hall without a pass. The ticket got me into the headmaster's office. He was busy, so I shut off the sensor in there, ducked out, and climbed the wall. Kids," he said, stretching out his hand, "always have ways of getting out."

"Ah, yes," said Maks, his thumb hovering over the activating stud. "I know that from personal experience."

John's fingers, one of which sported a small dirty bandage,

closed over the end of the control, and Maks touched the stud.

The next sound was an unhuman scream, the sound of an animal suddenly caught in a trap. Maks grabbed the boy, there was an instant of wild struggle, and John went limp.

They were lying side by side in a darkly gleaming metal tube. Automatic doors opened, and the shelf beneath them slid them soundlessly forward into the muted light of the transport room at Pastplor.

Maks checked the boy's pulse and heartbeat and carried him through the inner door and down a private corridor to his office and stretched him on a divan. He fetched a hypodermic gun from the dispensary and gave John two shots: the so-called universal, to knock out ancient diseases he might be carrying, and a sedative to keep him asleep for a few hours.

Then he began going through his pockets. Somehow this boy held the answer to the intricate conspiracy that had begun with the kidnapping of his own son, and he meant to find out what it was.

Boys' pockets turned out not to have changed much in 300 years. Maks found a knife, a ring with mechanical keys, a condom—how old was the boy, twelve? Must be starting young—plus assorted rubbish. His limp wallet contained ticket stubs to something called the Kennedy Center, a picture of a girl with Oriental features and wires on her teeth—why? wondered Maks. Some kind of communication device? But why on the teeth? A thousand-dollar bill, much folded—probably his allowance—and, hidden in a crude secret compartment, a picture clipped from the hardcopy version of *Cybertattle*.

Maks stared at the picture. Gasped. Turned it over. Scrawled on the back were the words, "My old man the bastard skum."

Finally he found his voice and said aloud, "But how?"

He was still facing this unanswerable question when his mashina chimed.

"Not now," he said. "Tell whoever it is that I'm out."

"Honored Major," said the atonal voice, "I have the honor to bring you a direct order from General Yamashita."

"Great Tao. All right, what is it?"

"Quote: tell Maks to get his fucking ass to Yost's office in the command suite and do it now, unquote. Is there any reply?"

CHAPTER XXIII

No human face showed in Captain Pali's mashina with its multiple secure channels. Instead, a double cone hung suspended in the shadowbox.

Benjo had selected that logo for the operation, as those involved called the conspiracy. He said it represented an hourglass, and when Pali asked what that was, he answered with a smile that in the past the hourglass had been a symbol of time.

An arbot's voice began speaking. "Have you received the new monitors?"

"Yes. I understand we're to insert them in the *stari* now?"

"Yes, and quickly. The general's decided that our guests as well as members of our organization must be traceable, for improved top-down control. The general is very strong for control."

"We'll begin at once. Twelve insertions by hypodermic gun—that won't take long."

"Be quick. You'll be having visitors from headquarters soon. Matters may be coming to a head."

"Do I understand that the 'operation' is almost ended?"

"I am not authorized to discuss that."

The double cone shrank to a glowing dot and vanished. The prickle of lasers in the shadow box ceased. The mashina shut itself off.

Smiling his gentle smile, Pali removed a major's insignia from the drawer of his desk and polished the bit of gold against his chest.

He deserved the promotion he saw coming. As an honest cop and an honorable man, he had helped to unmask a swindler—one who had dared to try to corrupt the Security Forces. As an ambitious guy, he'd incidentally proved that Maks, the man blocking his advancement at Pastplor, deserved demotion if not something worse.

Not that he really approved of kidnapping, but internal polizi politics were rough. It was by proving you were rough, too, that you won the respect of your superiors.

Of course, the teahouse was full of *kloppi*. Silly Benjo thought he could find the "bugs," as he called them, by looking for them. But these days, *kloppi* might look like grains of sand or even particles of dust, each one packed with nanomachines. By now they were ground into his clothes, packed under his fingernails, engrained in the very pores of his skin.

And what a tale those tiny devices had picked up and recorded on the memory cubes now resting in the queue of Pali's mashina!

Smiling, quick and gentle of aspect as ever, Pali left his office and went about his duties.

The day had advanced by an hour or two when a delegation of five thuggi arrived. Informed by Pali's arbot secretary that he was walking in the garden—actually, he was headed for the teahouse to fetch Benjo, the only one of the *stari* who hadn't yet received a monitor—one of the thuggi drew an impact pistol and went after him.

After some consultation among themselves the others decided to go ahead with the rest of their assigned task. Someone had neglected to inform Pali that the monitors inserted in the *stari* were like those inserted in prisoners—that is, they carried attached neurotoxin pellets. When activated, the pellets almost instantaneously shut down the entire motor nervous system.

The thuggi stood in a group around Pali's mashina while their leader punched in the activating code.

2

Bees had never buzzed so loudly—well, perhaps they weren't bees; some sort of modified fly the scientists had developed to pollenate flowers in a world where all the bees had died.

Anyway, they buzzed. And the sky was blue, and this unbelievable man was walking by Sherí's side, talking about his future plans when, without warning, she stumbled and fell.

Quite suddenly she was kneeling on something soft. She was kneeling on Pali's stomach. She looked down into what was left of his face and screamed.

He had been shot by an impact weapon. Or had shot himself. He still held a gun in his hand. Above her, she heard Benjo make a strangled sound.

His eyes were wide and staring. Over his head passed a sleek bluish shape, a polizi hovercar. The gravity compensator shut down and the rotary landing engines began to howl. In the distance she heard other engines, and somebody was shouting.

"Christ, Christ, they're onto me," he gasped in the hoarsest voice she'd ever heard.

He seized her hand, jerked her to her feet, and began to run, dragging her behind him. Then stopped so suddenly that Sherí cannoned into him. Stunned, frightened, she saw what Benjo was staring at.

More corpses. The *stari* were lying here and there. The woman who thought she still owned a chunk of the Dotcom Cartel had fallen on the path. An elegantly coiffed wig had fallen off; she was bald. The executive from Tiffany-Cartier had died inspecting a blossom. The young Orthodox Jew with connections to the diamond trade had slumped over on a rustic bench, a Hebrew devotional book in his hand. A spit curl of dark hair still clung to his ear.

Sherí let out a faint cry and clutched at Benjo, waiting for whatever had killed the others to strike her, too. But the seconds ticked by.

Then Benjo shook her, hissed, "Sherí, you got to get us out of here."

For another moment she stood staring at him.

"The key," she said.

"What?"

She ran back and knelt by Pali's corpse. His wound was horrible, the head half-blown away. Averting her eyes, she searched his beltpouch and seized the electronic key, a slip of silvery metal six centimeters long.

Meantime, Benjo was taking the weapon from the dead man's hand, hefting it, eyeing it curiously.

The noises were coming closer. Clearly, the polizi had missed Benjo when they counted the dead and now were systematically quartering the garden in search of him.

"This way," she said, and led him back past the teahouse, heading for the postern gate. She added, "You can't fire that thing yet. Put your thumb there—that's the recognition stud. Hold it tight for one minute."

"Lucky," muttered Benjo, "you being married to a cop."

A few minutes later they were on the street behind the compound. Beyond the wall, human shouts mingled with the roars of Darksiders.

She told him, "Those clothes are impossible, Benjo. You'll be picked up in no time."

"Wait a minute."

Down the street a man in workman's attire was trundling a cart of gardener's tools toward an open gate in the wall of a private villa. Benjo quietly approached him. Sherí saw the gardener half turn, then gawk at the strangely dressed fellow. His mouth was still half open in astonishment when Benjo karate-chopped him on the side of the neck.

Benjo came back, pulling the man's dusty coveralls over his Armani suit. The legs were too long and gathered over his polished shoes in dusty bundles like the feet of an elephant.

"Don't laugh at me," he warned her—a fop to the end.

At a pylon Sherí called a hovercab, and a few minutes later they were soaring. Down below, they could see squads of thuggi fanning out into the streets to begin a house-by-house and garden-by-garden search. Nothing had saved them but the time the polizi had lost searching for Benjo inside the compound.

"I'd always hoped to see the city," he muttered, staring at the skyline of Ulanor. "But not like this."

"I wonder if that man was badly hurt," she whispered.

"What man?"

Clearly, gardeners counted even less than most people in Benjo's world. In fact, his extraordinary self-confidence was flowing back into him. He told her he was not impressed by Ulanor.

"So that's the Worldcity? Is that all? It's not as big as Brooklyn."

Sherí sank back against the dusty upholstery. She'd given her own address to the cab's black box. Where else could they go? And what would they do when they got there?

As usual, he knew what she was thinking and took her hands in his.

"Look, honey, you got to be brave. We don't have any other option."

"But what's going to happen to us?" she asked helplessly.

"Don't worry. I got a plan. Say, how many bullets are in this thing?"

Cautiously he spread the flaps of his coverall and let her see the back end of the pistol.

"See there?" she whispered. "That's the counter. That little window—like an old-fashioned camera. Two shots left."

"Christ, that's not much. Still, how many bullets do you need to shoot yourself?"

"Why would Pali shoot himself?" she asked blankly.

"Because, obviously, he was my contact in the Security Forces. He set up the whole deal in return for the information I gave him. When the scheme collapsed he shot himself. Or," he added thoughtfully, "that's how it's meant to look."

He relapsed into silence, frowning. He was still brooding when the cab drew up to the twelfth-stage doorway in Sherí's building.

Getting Benjo into the apartment was surprisingly easy. The thuggi were dozing, as usual; when one of them opened his eyes, she said simply, "This *robotchi's* doing some cleaning for us."

The thug glanced at Benjo's coveralls, nodded, and closed his eyes again.

Inside, with Benjo trailing her, she searched the rooms, the bath of poured stone, the dining-cooking area with its round table and crescent benches and polished hotspots behind blue duroplast shields. Finally the bedroom.

"Where's my son? Will Maks bring my son here?" Benjo demanded, his voice sharp.

"Where else can he take him?"

He paced up and down. "Then maybe I can still straighten everything out. Hey. Anything to drink around here?"

"People nowadays usually smoke kif to relax. It's synthetic pot mixed with some other drugs."

"Impair the reflexes?"

"No."

"Then let's get lightly stoned. I have to admit that getting fucked by you and chased by the cops on the same day is tiring. I'm not as young as I used to be."

She threw a handful of kif into the censer and turned on the heating element.

"And when Maks gets home?" she asked.

"Then," said Benjo, "we'll all have a heart-to-heart talk."

3

Maks arrived breathless in Yost's office to find Yamashita there ahead of him.

The room was small and nondescript, with walls of dull whitish semiplast and a jumble of leftover furniture. Unlike his chief, Yost put up no front, projected no image of power; that was his great strength—also his weakness.

He and the general were standing in front of Yost's big mashina, staring at a schematic of the Palace of Justice. Maks had no trouble recognizing the intricate structure with its maze of rooms and corridors and glowing red spots that denoted guard posts.

This schematic also showed hundreds of small blue and greenish yellow dots that reminded him of the lights of the Great Shield. Some clustered in the command suite, some around the courts of law and the corridors of Yost's kingdom, Special Investigations. Some of the dots were still, some in motion.

Yost saw his bafflement.

"Blue indicates polizi," he explained. He pointed at a group of three blues. "The general, you, and me, for instance. The others are Darksiders."

Yamashita's thick finger stabbed a cluster of one yellow and two blue dots.

"See that, Maks? The mashina spotted it and Yost called me at once. Empty storage unit—supposed to be locked. What the fuck are a Darksider and two thuggi doing inside an empty storage unit?"

Maks's first thought was that both his superiors had gone crazy at the same moment. Who cared whether two men and an animal were dozing or shooting dice in an empty room?

"Come on!" Yamashita barked, and led them into the corridor. More Darksiders lounged around the command suite; he gestured, and three of the great beasts joined them. All were heavily armed and the metal of impact weapons and bandoliers clanked as they followed the humans with bowlegged strides.

Thuggi stared and clerks shrank back into offices as the strange parade moved at doubletime through the well-lighted marble hallways, then plunged into a maze of anonymous passages.

Corridors, corridors. The Palace of Justice was a honeycomb without sweetness. Gray walls, gray matting, gray doors with no identifying marks. Corridors that met at right angles, at wrong angles, at any possible angles. Ramps rising to the next stage, moving walks that had long ago rusted into stillness. Guard posts stuck seemingly in the middle of no place. In public areas, employees of the courts carrying sheafs of hardcopy, glimpses of courtrooms with accused men and women kneeling before the bar of justice while onlookers gawked. The smell of *mosh* and misery hung heavy in the air.

They turned into a corridor so narrow they had to string out in single file behind Yamashita. At the end was a dimly-lit atrium with one dusty luminous panel in the ceiling and three low metal doors with security locks. One stood ajar.

"The boy's gone," said Yost. His deskbound lungs panted with his recent exertion but his voice was as toneless as ever. "They've moved him again."

Yamashita must have had the same thought, for he uttered a curse as he kicked the door wide open. But now Maks knew what they were looking for, and suddenly he was pushing past his superiors, shouldering Yamashita aside without regard to his rank and stars.

He stumbled into the cell and an agonized howl burst from his throat. Against the wall stood a small rumpled bed splashed with blood.

Two human bodies in uniform lay pulped and battered against one wall. Beside the bed crouched a gigantic Darksider holding an impact pistol. The barrel swung toward Maks.

Then Sandi squeezed out from under the bed and ran past the Darksider into his father's arms. The creature lowered its weapon; Maks squeezed his son in a rib-cracking hug. After a moment, Sandi wormed free, and grasped one of the Darksider's free thumbs.

"Papa," he said, "this is Grila."

Maks felt he was in a dream as he scratched the monster's ears. His son a prisoner here in the Palace of Justice? Sandi's life saved by a Darksider? His hiding place brilliantly uncovered by Yost, of all people?

Maks slowly turned to the colonel, reached out, and shook his hand. The hand was long, cold, bony, and damp, and the eyes that met his looked like tea stains. But there it was: between them, a torturer and an armored beast had recovered his son for him, alive and unharmed.

"Take the boy to his mother," said Yamashita, after blowing his nose.

Staring at the general's face—usually impervious to heat, cold, and pity—Maks received a final shock. Yes, he knew that on his days off Yamashita was the doting father of four. But to see something glimmering in his small jetty eyes was as great a surprise as any the day had brought forth.

CHAPTER XXIV

Maks knew he was facing bad times, but being able to deliver Sandi to Maia almost compensated for them. With her he could do what would have been out of the question in the Palace of Justice—cry, laugh, and finally relax.

He felt that he had strayed a long way away from himself, from his true nature, from everything that mattered to him. What had Maia said to him once? He wasn't mean enough to head the Security Forces, and he wasn't smart enough, either. Had he really divorced Sandi's mother because she told him unpalatable truths?

As he watched her hugging their son, he knew with sad finality that they would never be reunited. Between them lay that time in New York when, nursing a bruised ego, he had met an impossibly beautiful woman and had fallen in love like a boy. That was a fact. He'd saved Sherí's life and forever changed his own.

That didn't prevent friendship with Maia, even a kind of love free from passion. When Sandi was asleep in his own bed, Maks had a few quiet minutes alone with her.

"Poor Maks. You're looking completely used up," she said. "Well, I know how you feel. I feel the same way."

"There's still a lot to be done," he sighed. "I wish I could go to sleep for about two months, but I can't."

"Do you know who did it?"

"I know one of them. I still don't see how he managed it. He had to've had help. Help from inside the Forces."

"Oh, Maks, I was afraid of that. And you don't know who his accomplice was?"

"No. I've wasted a lot of time suspecting Yost. He's got the power to pull a thing like that, also the brains, and I'm sure he views me as a threat to his position because the general thinks so much of me. But Yost found Sandi for us—that's a fact. I can't believe he'd have left the boy alive if he was involved in the kidnapping. Sandi might have noticed something, some clue that would lead back to him. He's too careful to leave a loose end like that."

"So you still don't know?"

"No." He smiled wanly at her. "I'm just not smart enough, that's all."

"Poor Maks," she said. "Don't you know there are enough smart people in the world? What we need are more brave and decent ones. That's your strong suit. Why don't you play it?"

He hugged her before leaving. "If anything happens to me, Maia, take good care of the boy."

"What could happen? Maks, what aren't you telling me?"

"I have to go home and get some sleep. Then I'm going back to the office and turn over some evidence to Yamashita. He and Yost have to crack this case, because I can't. And when they ask me how I got the evidence, well—I'll have to tell them."

"Oh, Maks, this isn't a beheader, is it?"

"Frankly, my head's feeling a bit wobbly. There, you've always been after me to tell you the truth. I just did, and now look, you're unhappy. What is it you want, anyway?"

She tried to match his sardonic smile and failed.

"Oh my dear, what a jungle we're in. How will we ever get out? Can't we all go back in time, back beyond the Troubles, to Wordsworth's England or Whitman's America, someplace where Sandi will be safe?"

"Ssh," he said. "Don't say things like that out loud."

"Well then, is it all right to think them?"

"Yes," he said. "Just . . . think them."

2

Maks entered his apartment feeling leaden, exhausted. The first glance showed a *robotchi* in dusty coveralls, probably there to haul trash.

Ignoring him, Maks went straight to Sherí and embraced her.

"Oh, Maks, what happened?" she whispered. "Did you find John Hammer?"

"In a minute," he said. "Bring me kif and don't make me talk for a while."

To Benjo he added: "Whatever you're doing can wait."

Benjo shuffled to the door and paused. Maks sprawled on the divan while Sherí loaded a pipe for him with shaking hands.

She heard Maks say to Benjo, "You waiting for your pay? How much do I owe you?"

"A lot, Honored Major," Benjo smiled. "My son, to begin with."

Maks stared at Benjo's pistol, then slowly turned his eyes to Sherí.

"Has he hurt you?" he asked.

"No," she whispered.

It was on the tip of her tongue to say, "Yes, he raped me, he's been holding me prisoner," but she didn't.

Benjo was not a gentleman. He'd either kill her at once or betray her to the polizi if he was taken prisoner. No, there was no way out of this one. She'd made her choice and there was no going back.

Benjo spared her one cool glance—he'd read her mind again—and then turned back to Maks.

"Where is my son, Major?"

Sherí was amazed to see a slight smile begin to lighten Maks's face. What could he be thinking?

"In the Palace of Justice, surrounded by a hundred Dark-siders. On the other hand, my son's free. Stick that up your nose, you piece of shit."

During his adventures in time Maks had had plenty of chances to use Archaic English. But he had never enjoyed doing so as much as in that last sentence.

Benjo sat down rather suddenly. Eyeing him narrowly, Maks felt reluctant respect. There he sat, alone, confronting a whole hostile world, yet the pistol in his hand never wavered.

"Have you ever heard the phrase 'Mexican standoff'?" Benjo asked.

"No."

"Neither side can win, but each can destroy the other."

"Is that our situation?"

"I believe so."

"What do you propose?"

Now it was Benjo who was smiling. Sherí winced, knowing what was coming.

"To allow you to live, provided you send Sherí and me back through the wormholer."

Maks whitened. He stared at Sherí, but didn't need to ask a question. Her face was a study in fear, defiance, and above all, guilt.

"She's been visiting me for months," said Benjo, twisting the knife. "Your friend Pali arranged everything, including the kidnapping."

Maks tried to speak once, twice, and failed. The blow to his ego was savage; why then did he feel so little surprise? For whatever reason, Sherí had gone back to her own kind, and he could find nothing to say.

Suddenly he wanted only to be rid of both of them.

"Where do you want to go?" he asked quietly, so quietly that Sherí stared at him in surprise.

"Back to our own era. But with enough time—that word

keeps coming up, doesn't it?—to get ourselves from the Earth to Luna before the Troubles begin. And to transfer some assets. Say a year. Send us back to November 2090."

Maks looked at Sherí. "Is that what you want?"

She had trouble meeting his eyes. "Yes. You won't believe me but I'm feeling terribly, terribly guilty and miserable about what happened."

He shrugged. He seemed to dismiss her entirely.

"And your son?" he asked Benjo.

"When we get back I'll snatch John from his mother and that goddamn school no matter what I have to do—get him out before you arrive to kidnap him—and take him to Luna with us. That's the only thing I can think of."

Maks rose. Benjo got up, too.

"Then let's go."

Maks had to pull rank to get Benjo, wearing his disguise, into Pastplor; fortunately, he had rank to pull. In half an hour the businessman was in the transport room with Maks and Sherí, staring at the device he had seen only once before, and then in such a state of confusion and rage and fear that he hadn't seen much.

Maks made them lie down on the metal slide, and gave them eyeshields to wear. Benjo held his a little raised. The pistol that had entered Pastplor in his pocket was now in his hand.

"Pay attention to the orders he gives that goddamn gadget," he warned Sherí. "I don't want him sending us to the Ice Age or something."

He watched narrowly as Maks spoke to the control mashina in Alspeke, rattling off 4-dimensional coordinates in a rapid sequence of numbers and coded commands.

"Any last words?" Maks asked.

"Yes," said Benjo. "You may not believe it but I'm sorry about your kid. I'm sorry about your wife. I'm sorry I had to hurt you."

"Oh, I am, too, Maks!" cried Sherí passionately. "Oh, I am, too!"

"Activate," said Maks to the mashina, and at the same instant Benjo touched the firing stud of his pistol.

3

Standing among the red flags of autumn trees on the slope above Rock Creek Park, Benjo smiled at Sherí.

"You killed him!" she cried. "You killed him, you—you bastard!"

"Oh, honey," he said. "How inadequate."

"You told him those lies about being sorry just to put him off guard, and then you shot him!"

Benjo shrugged. "Had to. If I hadn't, he'd have come after us. Instead, here we are and nobody from that world knows where. Nobody to pursue us. Nobody to interfere while we find John and get ourselves to Luna."

He pulled off the dirty coveralls, rolled them up, and flung them into the trees. His Armani suit was stained and smudged with the dirt of another world. But Benjo radiated power.

"Think about it!" he bragged. "Even with everything I've done in my life, I never managed a thing like this. A whole fucking world against me, and I won and they lost!"

As she had so often before, Sherí yielded again.

"Oh, Benjo," she sighed, "you appall me, but—but—yes, here we are. And you did do it. You're incredible. And as for us—when we go to Luna we'll take Mama with us, right?"

"Sure, honey. Whatever you want."

She threw her arms around him. "Oh God," she whispered, "I can't believe it. To live out our lives now—in our own time—"

A little sound, somewhat like a cough.

Sherí's body flung backward, striking the ground, rolling

over as it went down the slope. Benjo looked down at her bloody corpse.

He said softly, "Sorry to do it, but I really have no intention of spending the rest of my life with an asshole."

He slipped the impact pistol back into his pocket and eyed the swift flow of bright-colored cars down the parkway. Yeah, one of them would do to take him to Reagan National—

Then a disturbance made him turn his head. A little whirlwind? Leaves blew up, revolved. In the center something like an eddy of multicolored snow took form, solidified into Maks himself.

"He survived! He's come after me!" was Benjo's first thought, and he automatically leaped among the trees to hide himself.

Then he realized that Maks was simply on his mission, the mission Benjo had assigned him, to kidnap John Hammer.

Benjo watched Maks as he spotted the mangled body of a woman, averted his eyes, and strode quickly away. Benjo steadied his pistol against the white trunk of a young aspen and prepared to fire.

"To think," he whispered. "Killing the poor son of a bitch twice!"

A party of runners was approaching along the jogging trail. Not much time. Benjo touched the firing stud.

The pistol emitted a small apologetic beep. An instant later the runners, accompanied by their armed guards, were close at hand. Benjo lowered his sophisticated and entirely useless weapon. Not another round of the proper ammunition existed anywhere on Earth, or would exist for centuries to come.

Maks crossed the path, striding swiftly, and soon disappeared.

Benjo tossed his gun away, far away into the deep leaves, and set off in pursuit. Almost half a minute elapsed before he realized the meaning of this encounter.

Maks had taken John on the very eve of the Troubles, late in the autumn of 2091. So he'd tricked Sherí when he was reeling off that sequence of coded commands to the wormholer.

"Oh, you fucking dumb broad," Benjo muttered.

Christ, he thought, *I don't have a year to snatch my son, arrange passage to Luna, transfer assets, prepare for the coming storm. I've got days at most.*

Maks was now far ahead of him, moving with the speed of a younger man to do exactly what Benjo had commanded him to do—kidnap John and take him back to Ulanor, far out of reach of anyone in this dying world.

Benjo groaned and grasped his head in both hands. He lurched down the slope in pursuit, wading in the deep leaves of the last autumn that Earth would know for years to come. His foot struck a log hidden in the drifted gold and scarlet and he fell headlong. Dry leaves billowed up around him, and his right ankle twisted with a white spark of pain.

When he tried to get up he knew the injury must be a bad sprain. He tried to curse, but nothing he could possibly say seemed adequate. He had a vision of Maks striding on like fate, far ahead and lengthening the distance with every stride, taking his son where Benjo could never follow.

He groaned and began to crawl back up the slope, searching for a fallen limb sturdy enough to use as a temporary crutch or cane. As he worked his way along his mind continued to function, almost independently of him, secreting ideas as automatically as his gall bladder went on making bile.

By the time he had found a limb that met his needs and risen to his feet with its aid and that of a pine sapling, he knew what he must do. The only thing, in fact, that he could do.

He hobbled down the slope, in pain and cursing at every breath, but no longer confused or despairing. Kidnapping Maks's son had failed. Taking John from the school and escaping to Luna had failed. Come hell or high water, he had now formulated Plan Three.

A taxi was proceeding sedately along Rock Creek Parkway in the curbside lane when Benjo deliberately stepped in front of it. The cab squealed and shuddered to a halt at the very toes of his shoes, and the driver, an Iranian, leaped out screaming colorful oaths in Farsi and English.

Benjo threw up one palm, interrupting the flow, and said, "My name is Benjamin Kurosawa. I have more money than anybody in the world. I just escaped from kidnappers. Take me to Reagan National and I'll make you rich beyond your wildest dreams."

The cabbie stared at him from behind a bristle of black beard. Other cars had squealed to a halt, drivers were cursing, and the sound of crumpling metal told of rear-enders stretching into the distance. The driver waved at his passenger, an alarmed-looking old lady.

"Meester, I got a fare—"

"Tell her to shove over," said Benjo, and crowded into the back of the cab.

CHAPTER XXV

My God, Mr. Kurosawa, where've you been?"

His bodyguard stared at the rumpled, filthy man who had just passed through the scanner at the front door of the Kurosawa palace on Park Avenue.

"Riding a goddamn helicab from Kennedy. Why?"

"Well, sir, we been looking for you. Couldn't find you anywhere in the house, and we didn't know you'd gone out."

"Is Penrose here?"

"Your valet? Yes, sir."

"Well, call him on the house phone and tell him I need everything, beginning with a hot bath."

Interesting, thought Benjo, ascending to the top floor in a small, silent elevator. *So two versions of me can't coexist at the same time. At the time I arrived back the earlier version must've evaporated.*

He emerged into the main hall of his living quarters on the fourteenth floor. Windowless, of course, for security. Penrose met him, and Benjo entered his bedroom shedding clothes, which the valet gathered up, *tch-tch*ing over the state of the $200,000 suit.

"Forget it," said Benjo. "Lay out some travelling clothes. Where's LaJuan?" He meant his private-private secretary and part-time mistress. "In the office downstairs? Well, tell her to book me through to Moscow on the 6 PM SST. What's the date?"

"November twenty-third."

"And just remind me—the year?"

"Twenty ninety-one," said a baffled Penrose.

"Oh, Christ. That's what I figured. Gimme that robe. And call LaJuan now. I want some stuff from the vault. And get me an elastic bandage. I sprained my ankle pretty bad."

Half an hour later, somewhat cleaner and dressed in modish traveler's gear that included plaid socks, plus fours and a vicuña coat, he was seated in his private office, talking into a viewphone.

"Goddammit, Alexei, assassins are gonna try to kill the mayor of Saint Petersburg tomorrow night, your time. Don't ask me how I know. I just do."

A Russian-English translator program put through the reply, delayed a few seconds while the lips of Alexei Dromov, a colonel in Russia's Internal Security Directorate, moved soundlessly.

"We have received no indication of any such plot. What's your evidence?"

"I heard it from a source I'm not at liberty to divulge. But it's a solid source, a really solid source."

"Huh. Pretty thin. Anybody but you, my old benefactor, I'd just hang up."

Benjo had paid Dromov well over the years for a variety of services, and the radiance of shared corruption still warmed their relationship.

"So what're you gonna do about it? You know I wouldn't risk my credibility unless there was something going on."

"The president's planning to address the Duma here in Moscow, so we've committed just about all our assets to the Kremlin. Including some guys we've pulled in from Petersburg. If you're sure about this, I can send them back and tell the mayor to stay indoors."

"I am sure. Absolutely, totally sure. You won't regret this, Alexei. There's a promotion in your future, sure as shit."

Satisfied, Benjo cut the connection just as Dromov was mouthing, *"Do svidanye,"* which the software translated as "Bye-bye."

2

LaJuan knocked and entered as Benjo sat drumming his fingers on his desk. She had café-au-lait skin and golden hair and eyes so deeply outlined by kohl that they resembled Egyptian tomb paintings. Her exotic form concealed relentless efficiency.

"Tickets," she said, presenting them. "Harry's at the door with the armored limo. Here's the stuff you specified from the vault. I guess something big must be up. Got time for a kiss?"

"No. Yeah. There, that's enough. When my dick gets hard, my brain goes soft."

Unpuckering, she asked, "Your appointment to look at

diamonds at Tiffany-Cartier tomorrow—I guess you won't be keeping it?"

"Good Christ, no. Cancel it. Cancel it forever."

In the limo, crouched behind the bulletproof glass, Benjo again hit the phone. This time he called a man named Korovin, also in Moscow.

"Hey, Pyotr, how you been?"

"Keeping busy."

Speaking eight languages, Korovin needed no translators to serve as chief lawyer for the Moscow Mafia. The contrast between him and Dromov underlined Benjo's belief that people in the private sector were always smarter than bureaucrats.

"Listen, Counselor, I got some work to be done. It's big. So's the payoff. I'm coming to your town now, landing at Vnukovo on the 2400 SST. Can we talk?"

"My man will meet you," said Korovin, and communication ceased.

Well, thought Benjo, trying to relax, *I've done what I can to divert attention from Moscow so Korovin's men will find it easier to kill this defense minister who's going to start the war. If they succeed, there won't be any Worldcity. My son will be back studying useless shit in Georgetown. Little what's-her-name, Sherí, won't cannon into a man with a strange haircut on 57th Street, because he'll never have existed. She can have her two-bit life with Mama in some dump on York Avenue, and welcome to it.*

More to the point, I'll live out my life here in this world I know so well. And oh Christ, will I become a pacifist. I'll hire an army of hitmen and knock off anybody who even thinks about war.

"You got a big grin on, Mr. Kurosawa," ventured Harry.

"Yeah, I'm done being a hard-nosed bastard, Harry. I'm gonna become a great philanthropoid, or whatever they call it."

"That's good, Mr. Kurosawa. Doing good is kinda nice, once in a while."

3

Meeting night just east of Long Island, the SST soared into starlit darkness, the ruddy smudge of sunset gleaming on its six-story tail. Unearthly quiet surrounded it; the roar of its engines had been left far behind.

Benjo sat in one of the first-class modules—comfortable, anodized-aluminum half cylinders that gave their inhabitants an extra measure of comfort on chairs that stretched into beds, plus an agreeable sense of separation from passengers who couldn't afford them. A VR headset hung above his head, ready to supply sixty channels of entertainment, but Benjo was in no mood for pornography, video games, interactive horseplay with the Three Stooges, or the ten most popular movies of the day.

He needed to relax. His chair shaped itself to his body and began a quiet massage. On a small table rested a dish with crackers and caviar, a snifter of Rémy Martin, and a viewphone he didn't dare to use because none of the channels were secure.

Instead, Benjo sipped liquid fire and munched salty beluga roe until a charming, dark-haired flight attendant stopped at his seat to murmur, "Dinner, Mr. K."

"What you got tonight, honey?"

"The best thing is the *coq au vin.*"

"What, again? I had that last time I flew. Oh, hell, bring it anyway."

He turned on the soothing strains of neo-heavymetal and pressed deeper into his seat. The massager worked away. The odors of food drifted through the cabin. The cognac exhaled its own fragrance.

Cautiously he took from an inner pocket a small, tightly wrapped package. One by one he squeezed small pouches of soft cream-colored faux leather onto the table. Glancing suspiciously to left and right, he opened them one by one and gazed briefly at the jewels they contained.

Forty carats in brilliant-cut white diamonds. A ginger-colored stone that outweighed them all. Tiny lights twinkled in faceted depths, as if the stones were lenses leading the eye into a world of perfect, serene beauty. The payoff he would offer Korovin: ransom for a world.

He thought of the stories Pali had told him about Xian Xiqing's obsession with jewels, and how as a result Maks had been sent to kidnap Benjo, accidently giving him the knowledge and opportunity to save his world and destroy Xian's. Great jewels were more than stones, they were myths and legends and tales of greed and suffering, none more incredible than the fantasy he was now living.

He took out another stone—this one bluer than any sky, than the eyes of any blonde beloved. Benjo groaned aloud. Not the Hope!

When the expenses of the war in Idaho and Montana caused the government to cut back, the subsidies to the Smithsonian had fallen to the budget axe. At the same time, private contributions had withered and the stocks in the endowment had crashed, largely because of Benjo's operations on Wall Street.

As a result, the treasures of the Jewel Room had been sold off and the Hope had come to him. Mysterious in its origins, more fable than stone, this 45.5-carat chunk of crystallized carbon was the heart of his collection. Was it worth saving his son, saving his life, saving his world, if Korovin demanded the Hope as payment?

He slipped the blue diamond back into its pouch and tucked it into a different pocket from the rest.

If I have to, he thought. *But only if.*

4

An hour later the dinners had been removed and the plane's interior had darkened. With seats reclined, most passengers huddled under blankets. A few wore headsets from which faint buzzes and beeps suggested video games in progress. Six miles beneath the plane, the white jigsaw of the Arctic ice sheet slipped by, unnoticed.

In the semidarkness a few people moved about, going to and from the toilets, seeking a drink or a snack from the lighted galley in the tail. In the first-class modules attendants responded to occasional signals, but by and large the wide aisles were empty. Benjo tried to sleep, but finally admitted that the possibility of the world ending tomorrow made rest unlikely.

"Not as young as I used to be," he muttered, and left his module to stretch and yawn.

"Can I assist you, Mr. K?" asked the pretty flight attendant. For an instant Benjo considered doing something really wild, just for the hell of it—offering a total stranger a five-carat diamond for a blow job.

Then he dismissed the thought. You never knew when a little *jeu d'esprit* like that might cause a commotion. Tomorrow night—if there was a tomorrow night—he'd celebrate.

"No, honey," he said, and limped down the aisle between softly glowing luminescent lines, headed for the first-class toilets.

Inside, he did his business, then stood viewing himself in the 3-dimensional mirror. *Getting baggy eyes. It's all this goddamn worry. What I been through, it's enough to kill a young man. Got to try stem-cell therapy. Didn't work so well during the experimental phase, but now I hear the lab boys are getting the process down right.*

He sighed at the passage of time, washed his hands and face, shut his eyes when the warm wind of the drier cut on. He rubbed a little fragrant oil from a dispenser into his skin, turned, and opened the door.

The light fell full on Maks and the impact weapon in his hand coughed once, flinging Benjo back into the restroom. Maks stepped in, bent over him, then straightened up and closed the door, turning on the OCCUPIED sign outside. He touched the stud of a wormholer control in his beltpouch.

The SST soared on, passing inland over Archangel and the snow-powdered fields of Russia. A half-hour later at Vnukovo International Airport, Korovin's man found nobody to meet.

But perhaps the Moscow Mafia had some people among the *militsiya* who crowded into the plane when a shattered body was discovered in one of the first-class toilets. For, while most of the diamonds were recovered, the Hope had disappeared.

CHAPTER XXVI

Maks swung his legs off the slide of the wormholer, stood up shakily, and handed over his pistol to Colonel Yost. Resistance didn't occur to Maks; he was dead on his feet. In any case, he'd given his word to the man who had saved Sandi.

"You see," he muttered. "I did come back."

Yost nodded. His feelings about Maks had never been so mixed as at this moment. The monitor circulating in Maks's body—of which he knew nothing—would have enabled Yost to pursue and kill him. Despite his annoyance at Maks's failure to do the logical thing, try to escape in the past and so provoke his own destruction, Yost felt reluctant respect for someone so—so what? Brave, foolish, old-fashioned? Or merely so unexpectedly hard to kill?

The arrest proceeded in impeccable style. One of Yost's thuggi did a hasty pat-down, just to make sure the prisoner wasn't carrying another weapon.

While this was going on, Yost gestured at a meterwide crater blown in the wall of the transport room. "Kurosawa tried to shoot you, then?"

"Yes," said Maks. His own voice seemed to resonate, now loud, now soft. He had a feeling that time was slowing to a stop.

"I knew he would. The shot had to come just after I gave the mashina its orders. And while I may not be the brightest kid on the block, I do have excellent reflexes."

Yost nodded. Armed with evidence from Pali's mashina, he and his thuggi had forced their way into the room just as Maks rose from the floor, his hair full of dust from the shattered wall.

Quickly he'd explained about Benjo, about sending him back to the verge of the Troubles, about the possibility that a ruthless trillionaire might somehow contrive to stop them from happening. Then Yost proved what a great chief of security he might make, if Yamashita ever stepped aside and allowed him to show his stuff. In a few seconds he'd grasped the danger and seen the opportunity of ridding himself of both Benjo and Maks.

It had been an astonishingly bold act—arming his captive and sending him back in time, telling him about the *kloppi* Benjo still carried in his body, giving him a commdisk and the frequency so that he could track his quarry. And Yost had been justified by the results.

"I may have underestimated you, Major," he said as the party left Pastplor.

Terrified workers stared at their boss being led away under arrest, but Yost ignored them. He was honestly trying to understand how Maks's mind worked, and for once his acute intelligence faltered. He could only suppose that Maks had come back to make one last foolhardy effort to save his career.

As for Maks, he was too tired to notice either his subordinates or his captors. He shuffled along, unconsciously imitating the habitual gait of prisoners whose loose, soft slippers would fall off if they lifted their feet.

Through his mind ran only his last picture of Sherí, crying out how sorry she was just as Maks sent her back to the Troubles. The difference between *zvan novan* (twenty ninety), and *zvan novanda* (twenty ninety-one), had escaped her. On such minute points destinies turn. If he had not been so weary, he would have wept.

2

When they arrived at the general's office, Yost murmured a few sentences in Yamashita's ear, then absented himself without waiting to be asked.

Yamashita sat at his immense desk looking much more dangerous than when he raged. Like the Martian petrified wood, he seemed to have fossilized into some substance more unyielding than mere flesh. A long, silent minute passed with Maks at attention and the general looking at him without blinking.

"Got anything you want to say?" he asked at last.

This was standard polizi tactics. The prisoner was invited to accuse himself before hearing the charges against him. Often in making a statement he incriminated himself further.

Maks knew the routine and said nothing. Instead, he took the Hope from his beltpouch and dropped it on the desk.

"Something to make the Controller happy," he said, adding, "And I've killed Benjo. He was on his way to prevent the Troubles, but he won't do it now."

Slowly Yamashita's eyes traveled down to the diamond, then back to Maks. He grunted.

"Now tell me now about this woman you brought forward and married."

"She's been returned to her own time."

"You're good at cleaning up the messes you make," Yamashita acknowledged. "Who is this boy Yost tells me he found in your office?"

"Benjo Kurosawa's son. He was the ransom demanded for mine."

"Very interesting. That's two unauthorized people you brought through the wormholer. I understand you also embedded a lot of fake information about your wife in the mainframe mashina to create a false identity for her."

"Yes, sir."

"I guess you know that if you sneeze, your head will fall off."

"Yes, sir."

"Anything to say in your own defense?"

"No, sir."

"Then Colonel Yost will show you something you've never seen in all your years with the Security Forces—the inside of a cell in Special Investigations. If it turns out you've lied to me about anything whatever you'll be sent to *shosho* and then bow to the laser. Clear?"

"Yes, sir."

Maks was conscious that the routine which followed was gentler than normal. Being strip-searched was demeaning, but at least he didn't have to stand at attention for six hours with bare feet in a pan of ice water and his nose touching a wall. Wearing paper pajamas, he was put into a narrow holding cell, but at least he wasn't wearing a kang. Nobody punched, kicked, or jabbed him with an electric prod. By Special Investigation standards, it was almost a vacation.

At first he slept—impossible to say for how long. Then, during the long, long hours that ensued he had plenty of time to reflect on what a mess he'd made of his life. He had time to imagine torture, and that was only less harrowing than torture itself. He had time to remember Maia and Sherí and wonder when or if ever he'd see his son again. He had time to imagine the life he might have lived if he'd done this, that, or the other thing instead of what he actually had done.

If.

In the narrow, cold cell the ghosts of people alive and dead crowded around him, and his own ghost, the image of the man he now never would be, but might have been if he hadn't been such a goddamn fool, haunted him most insistently of all. The man who might have quit the Security Forces and taken his wife and son to live on some offworld where hard work and common sense meant more than brilliant scheming. The man who—

Without warning the steel door grated outward and Yost's pale, expressionless face, like the face on the crescent moon, looked down at him. His eyes were empty as craters. With him were two of his thuggi carrying black duroplast batons.

"Come along," he said quietly, and Maks, all his joints feeling rusted, creaked to his feet. The thuggi took him by both arms and helped him shamble along. He didn't breathe easily until they had left Special Operations.

At the general's office he was thrust inside and the door closed behind him. Yamashita sat in his usual place. Several silent minutes passed before something odd about him caught Maks's attention.

Usually a culprit standing before Yamashita was impaled by his gaze like a moth on a pin. Now he seemed to be hardly looking at Maks. Looking through him, rather. Looking at something, or at nothing, occupying empty space behind him. When he spoke at last, his words were absolutely unexpected.

"You remind me of my friend the Worldsaver," Yamashita said.

His voice was strong, but strangely distant. He was remembering the incomprehensible past—time travelling, so to speak.

"Like you, Steffens Aleksandr was gifted but erratic. He ruined himself, lost his career in the Security Forces. And what's a man without a career? A walking corpse. Yet in spite of that he became the Worldsaver, though exactly how I never understood."

He paused, brooding.

"What gets me about both you and him is the way positive results develop from your stupid fucking blunders. I guess it makes sense in terms of the Great Tao, but it makes no goddamn sense to me. Take this kid, Khamr Dzhon."

He gave John Hammer's name the Alspeke way, growled deep in the throat and with the last name first.

"He's in the dispensary, still out. I had the *mediki* run his DNA through the mainframe like we did the other *stari*. I was checking your statement, making sure he was who you said he was. Only instead of just doing statistics like before, I told them to check for individual relationships. Didn't tell them what relationships, because I didn't want them finding what they thought the general wanted instead of what was there.

"Well, those goddamn white mice in the lab, they turned up an amazing thing. An almost unbelievable thing. This boy's not only Benjo's son. The two of them are ancestors of people now living."

For the first time in a long time, Maks forgot his troubles completely, overcome by astonishment.

"John Hammer survives the Troubles? But how? Washington was totally destroyed in the war."

Yamashita sighed. "If you weren't so goddamn slow on the uptake, Maks, you'd realize that we don't send him back to Washington. We send him someplace else, like Luna, where he survives and grows up and starts a family."

"Why? Whose ancestor is he?"

"Mine, for one," said Yamashita. "Benjo didn't just beget a son. He started a whole family of motherfuckers. And you're looking at one of them."

Yamashita took a deep breath. "Since by violating regulations and bringing this boy into the present time where we could save his life you accidentally made it possible for me to exist and my children and their children, I guess I owe you something. So here's your life. And since you seem to have this weird fucking genius for doing important things by accident, you can even keep your job.

"But from here on out, you'll be on a leash. You'll be injected with a neurotoxin pellet. I alone will have the activating code and if you ever break the rules again, if you so much as spit on the goddamn floor, I'll show you what it feels like to have your whole body come to a stop all at once. I'll show you what it's like to stand there for a microsecond, a dead man waiting to fall.

"Any questions?"

3

When Maks returned to Special Operations with his discharge order, Yost congratulated him.

He lingered while Maks put on his uniform, including his major's insignia. Yost was puzzled, but since Maks didn't volunteer to explain his survival, he politely avoided comment.

For his part, Maks couldn't decide whether Yost was glad or sorry he didn't have to put him through *shosho*. They made brief arrangements for Maks to take John Hammer to Luna through the wormholer. They agreed that the appearance of a strange boy in that small colony would cause comment. But minor mysteries would be forgotten when the Earth exploded into the Time of Troubles.

Then they parted, neither man comprehending the other.

In his small, cluttered office, Yost sat for a while silent at his desk. How the devil had Maks gotten the general to set him free? Why were they sending this boy to Luna? Because he had no need to know, Yost hadn't been told.

Still, he'd accomplished the main thing. Ending Maks's special relationship with the general, eliminating him as a possible rival in the future. The thing he'd been angling for ever since Pali first came to him and told him about Benjo's ridiculous proposal to exchange data on the ancient treasure vaults for help in saving his son from the Troubles.

What an idiot, Pali had said. *Can you imagine his arrogance? You'd think we were his prisoners instead of the other way around!*

How does he propose to make Major Hastings bring this boy forward? Yost had asked.

I've been letting Hastings's wife in to see Benjo as you advised, Honored Colonel. Well, Sherí told him that Hastings has a son living with his previous wife. So he wants us to kidnap this kid and hold him to ransom!

Even Yost had enjoyed a good chuckle over that one. And then he'd shocked Pali by saying coolly, *Why not? I'll send over a few trustworthy guys. We'll put maximum pressure on Hastings and he'll dig himself in deeper and deeper. You do want to get your well-deserved promotion to head Pastplor, don't you, Pali?*

Yes, Honored Colonel.

Well, you manage this well, and I can promise you that whenever I succeed Yamashita, you'll find that Pastplor was only the beginning.

Before resuming work, Yost permitted himself one of his bleak smiles. By now Pali and everybody else involved was dead—Pali fingered as the villain, the others as his accomplices. Sandi was supposed to be found dead, but the two thuggi Yost had sent to kill him had been done in by the Darksider. Admittedly that was a glitch, totally unexpected. But Yost had taken good care all along that the boy never saw anyone but his keepers, and in the end it didn't matter.

Yost was sorry to lose the men he'd sacrificed. People he'd trained himself. Good subordinates were worth a lot.

But keeping open his path to succeed the general as chief of security—that was worth much more. Anybody who ever worked in a bureaucracy would understand that.

4

Maks had no trouble getting Maia and Sandi into Pastplor. He brought them in, tagged as visitors, just before the end of an evening guard rotation, and later deleted the memory from the guard station mashina.

In the transport room he prepared them with faked IDs, money, and clothing of the ancient world.

"You know what to do, Maia?" he asked her a dozen times, and she patiently answered yes.

Sandi was squirming in Maks's arms. He didn't understand why he had to be held like a little kid, but Maks gripped him strongly.

"Oh, Maks, you're sure you can't come, too?"

"No. I've got—well, you might say I've caught something. A kind of bug. It's circulating in my system somewhere, and I can't go because of it. If I came with you I'd soon be dead, and I'd be no good to you then."

She touched John Hammer's cheek. He slept on the metal slide, an IV in his wrist, a bottle of nutrient solution taped to his arm.

"Are we going somewhere?" asked Sandi.

"Yes. You're going to be a timesurfer, just like I am."

The boy stopped wriggling. "Really?"

"Yes. If it's a little while before I join you, you won't forget me, will you, Son?"

"N-no."

As he helped them onto the slide, he told Maia, "Watch out for John Hammer when you get there. He's a mean kid. He won't remember this place, but he'll be plenty confused. And he's already learned to be hostile."

Maia clung to Maks's hand. "You'll come when you can?"

"Yes. If I can. What was that ancient poet named Snow or Ice or something—you used to bore me reading his verses—"

"Oh, you mean Frost."

"There was something about two roads—"

"Two roads diverged in a yellow wood."

"That was it. Now lie back and cover your eyes. Sandi, do what your mother tells you."

"Good-bye, Maks."

"*Svidanye*, until—until—"

An hour later he was sitting in his office, staring at nothing in particular, when Yost called on the mashina.

"I see you took that boy to Luna," he said.

"You're monitoring my use of the wormholer, Colonel? Somehow I thought you might be."

"At the general's orders, you understand. I don't think he trusts you as he used to. But look here, Hastings, that's no reason to wear such a grim face. After all, a lot of people were out to get you, and yet you survived."

"Oh, did I?" asked the hollow man, thinking again of everything he'd lost. "Are you sure of that, Colonel? Did I?"

CHAPTER XXVII

Yamashita seated himself in the backless *shozit*, or hot seat, and faced the *fromazhi* without a quiver of anxiety.

After all, who were they? With one exception, nonentities or newcomers. Only Xian Xi-qing, the ancient Controller, merited his full respect.

Yes, she had her weaknesses, her great age, her greed, her famous sexual appetite for young men, but he could forgive anything for her wisdom, her sound judgment, her sure grasp of power.

The others? Bearded Ugaitish was Xian's mouthpiece, nothing more. Oleary ran the Lion Sector like a petty merchant, watching his bottom line. Admiral Dluga of the Space Service—well, who could tell? She was a newcomer among the *fromazhi*. Looked like a warship in a wig: stout and tubular, her bust a prow gilded with medals. Too bad old Admiral Hrka had found death where he'd fought so many battles, in Far Space.

Yamashita presented them a face untouched by heat, cold, or pity. Twenty years in power, he felt as invulnerable as he looked.

Some trifling business was quickly dispatched. Chancellor Yang of the University of the Universe had died—Yama knew, if the others didn't, that he had perished at the grand age of 119 in an electronic room of the House of Timeless Love. Announcements glorifying his memory were approved for the news programs and a new chancellor selected.

"He also left a document called his testament," Ugaitish

added, handing a piece of hardcopy to Xian, who spared it one glance.

Then the gathering got down to business. "Chief of Security, report," said Ugaitish.

Yamashita did so, rarely referring to the notepad that lay humming on his lap. No threats of subversion existed in the Solar System. Crime in Ulanor the Worldcity was down. The number of executions was up, but that was a consequence of rigorous policies designed to enhance the security of the State. Close monitoring of the past with the wormholer indicated no danger from that quarter. Any questions?

"I want to discuss Luna security," said Admiral Dluga. "The current arrangement has got to be changed."

She had a harsh voice and an overbearing manner. Yamashita took only a microsecond to recognize a bureaucratic foe.

"The Security Forces ought to be confined to Earth," she declared. "They're not set up to deal with another world. The Space Service ought to take charge of Luna."

Xian turned a tiny, withered face to look at Dluga.

"Luna belongs to the Security Forces," she said in a small, distant voice, "because they're responsible for Earth, and Earth can be dominated militarily by whoever controls its moon."

"I want to submit a memorandum supporting my view."

"Submit anything you like, Admiral," said Ugaitish as Xian relapsed against the back of her throne and gazed silently into the middle distance.

Yamashita's face continued to show as much expression as the backside of a brick. Inwardly, he glowered.

"Honored Chief of Security, we permit you to go," said Ugaitish. Yamashita rose, bowed, and left the conference room.

Wants Luna, does she? he thought. *I'll see she gets something. But it won't be Luna.*

2

In his office he snapped a command at his mashina, and the face of Colonel Yost duly appeared.

"I want *kloppi* planted in the Space Service Headquarters," Yamashita said. "Especially in the war room—the most secret place they got."

Yost frowned. The lapse of years hadn't much changed him; he was one of those people who never seem to age. His thin, gray, intelligent face had grown thinner and grayer, that was all.

"That won't be easy, Chief."

"I don't call somebody with your kind of goddamn rank to do the easy stuff. Infiltrate their technical staff. Blackmail somebody. Insert one of our guys in their security apparatus. It's not impossible. Those space types don't know shit about policing. I want a report on this matter every twenty-four hours."

"Sir, I don't know if—"

"Just salute and get the fuck to work."

Alone in his big office, Yamashita relaxed for a moment in his chair of black duroplast and smiled. *Poor old Yost,* he thought. *Been taking my crap for twenty years, always hoping I'll drop dead so he can get my job. Well, I'm in no hurry to go.*

Yamashita's morning was, as usual, busy. Informers' reports proved as nonsensical as usual; if he believed them, everybody in the Worldcity would be in jail. Yet he had to read them all. Plus reports from the arbots listening for subversive murmurs in cyberspace, plus input from thousands of *kloppi* listening to conversations around the Worldcity.

Elsewhere in the Palace of Justice, criminals were being tracked, prisoners were being beaten up, and subversives were undergoing *shosho,* needles in their spines. A policeman's work was never done.

At 13 his clock murmured, "Honored General, your wife is expecting you for lunch."

Gratefully he rose and made for his nuclear-steel office door, which slid noiselessly into its slot. Outside, a heavily armed Darksider ceased scratching its furry chest and came to attention. The door whispered shut behind Yamashita.

Already he was beginning to feel like a different man. In the maze of carefully fenced enclosures that made up his mind, he passed from supreme enforcer to devoted husband and grandfather without any sense of discontinuity whatever. In his own way, he was a homebody.

3

On the nearby campus of the University of the Universe, the cool voices of clocks were announcing the hour. Students on campus walkways passed each other like ants going to and from the nest.

In the *bukrum* of the university's Infostor, a statuesque young woman wearing the black cap of a science major leaned toward a handsome, thick-bodied man in Security Forces uniform.

Something in their postures suggested . . . lovers? No, not exactly. Maybe soon-to-be lovers.

"I'm thinking of getting out, Sandra," murmured Major Hastings Maks.

She looked stricken. "Out? You're going offworld?"

They'd met when one of her seminars had visited Pastplor, the Office for the Exploration of the Past. As its chief, Maks had given a brief lecture about time travel. For the first time in her life, the blue-gray uniform of the polizi hadn't frightened her. Besides, she seemed to sense some kind of mysterious affinity with him that was all the more fascinating because she didn't understand it in the least.

She'd heard, in fact, an almost audible click in her mind at the sight of him. Perhaps she was drawn to older men because the disappearance of her father had left such a gap in her life. And Maks was intelligent and brave and, with a touch of gray at his temples, looked impossibly romantic as he talked about his adventures in time.

And now he was getting out, just when things between them had been—well—about to happen.

They'd been spending an hour looking at the ancient books, many printed on real paper, some hand-sewn, secured in the *bukrum* in helium-filled cabinets. Maks read her some of the titles: gardening guides, children's stories, forgotten novels, pornography, cookbooks, a treatise on the biochemistry of algae. Random survivors of the Time of Troubles.

Only one title struck Sandra, a book called *My Father, My Self.*

"I'd like to be able to read that," she'd told him.

"Why? Because yours skipped out before you were born?"

"Yes."

He looked dubious and said something about it being long ago. She told him, "If it had happened to you, you'd understand. It's not something you get over."

They paused by a tall window looking out on the campus. It was then he told her about wanting to get out. His next words relieved her, but only a little.

"There are problems, but it's an idea that's been with me a long time. Getting out, going away."

"It always seemed strange to me, you in the Security Forces . . ."

He nodded. "Time travel's under the Security Forces because it needs such strict control. So I live in the belly of the beast."

"But where would you go?"

He looked at her steadily, searching her face. She knew that something important was about to be said. Maks cleared his throat and began, "Sandra, do you think—"

Muted by the sealed window but still gratingly loud, a scream of metal interrupted him. They turned and stared out. A flat gray oblong shape was descending, gravity compensator shut off, howling rotor blades raising a storm of dust.

"Great Tao," gasped Sandra as uniformed men hit the poured-stone walk, impact pistols in their hands, gas canisters on their belts. A Darksider followed, its mandrill face half-hidden by blue sun goggles.

Sandra was a strong young woman but she shrank against Maks. She never saw the damned thuggi without feeling they'd come for her. Maybe that was what had happened to her father; everyone knew that sometimes people just disappeared.

Students were scattering, trying to get away without looking guilty of something. But the thuggi knew their target. They'd grabbed a dark-haired young man and were wrestling with him. The sergeant bellowed, "Down, *kukrach!*"

Instead the "cockroach" broke loose and sprinted away. He ran in a widening circle of emptiness as everyone tried to escape his presence. The Darksider pounded after him, threw him to the ground, and dragged him back by one ankle, cursing and twisting.

"Oh, Maks, I know that kid!"

"Not a friend, I hope?"

"No. I've had a few courses with him. His name's Kai."

The thuggi were locking the wrists and neck of their prisoner into a black plastic kang and pushing him into the hover-car. The Darksider followed and the car lifted off, flailing dust. The whole incident had taken only two one-hundred-second minutes.

Sandra hated her own weakness, yet she wanted to start screaming. She hit Maks's chest with her fists, beating against the uniform.

"What did that kid do? Why'd the thuggi grab him?"

"Grow up, Sandra," he said, holding her. "There doesn't have to be a reason."

But in that Maks was wrong. This time there was an excellent reason.

CHAPTER XXVIII

Old as she is, Xian's smart," Yamashita was saying over lunch.

It was his habit to tell his wife about the events of his day, listen carefully to her advice, and then do exactly what he pleased.

"Of course she's become arrogant, too. Thinks she's the empress of China with her young men, her jewels, her palace. Still, she's somebody. The other councillors are just a bunch of shits. Especially this Dluga bitch."

"You must stop using bad language," Hariko scolded him. In public, she kept to the ancient custom of walking three paces behind him, eyes lowered. At home she was a different woman.

"You're a man of great importance," she went on. "You kept our world from destruction not once but twice. The Worldsaver was your friend. Everybody goes in awe of you. You must learn to be more dignified."

"My thuggi expect rough language," he protested between mouthfuls of briny sea cucumber and sweet baked eel.

He loved to sit here, legs crossed under the low table, holding forth to the one person he trusted completely. He loved eating good food and gazing through the window of missileproof transplast at the sunlit vista of Ulanor against the backdrop of the purple-blue Butaeilyn Mountains.

My city, he thought. *I feel every twitch, I know every secret. That's mosh. Mine is so great sometimes it makes* me *tremble.* He smiled a little and continued his good-natured bickering with Hariko.

"I have to stamp and roar a bit at work—"

"No, you don't! You gain more respect by being firm, immovable, like a Zen saint or a great rock."

She was expanding on this theme when the security-coded mashina in his study chimed. Swallowing a rich morsel of eel, he rose grunting from the floor, wrapped the old kimono he wore at home around him, and hastened to answer it.

Colonel Yost was smiling sadly. Yost took all his pleasures sadly. "I've found a volunteer," he said.

"Volunteer?"

"After we talked I had my mashina scan the dossiers of a few thousand people we've been keeping an eye on. It came up with a university student—been shooting off his mouth about freedom and revolution, all that sort of thing. Normally we'd ignore it, but this boy's father is a captain over at Space Service HQ. I had the boy picked up, and now I'll call Papa."

Yamashita was delighted. Yost was a bore, but he knew his business—how to be a useful Number Two without threatening Number One.

"Quick work!" he approved. "When you talk to this kid's father, point out to him that the best way to ensure his son's safety is to work voluntarily for the security of the State."

"Will do, General."

On the way back to his interrupted lunch, Yamashita stopped to see his granddaughter. His children were grown now, scattered across the Solar System, but tiny Rika, daughter of another Rika, was visiting: she was taking her afternoon nap, watched over by a robot amah.

What a big girl she's becoming! thought Yamashita, touching her cheek. Soon she'll be five.

He felt in his heart an odd kind of pleasurable pain. He loved his grandchildren, yet they reminded him how old he was getting. *Hell,* he thought, *I'm only seventy. Fifty years still to go in an average lifetime—with luck I'll live to see my granddaughter as a woman on the verge of middle age.*

That was a comforting thought. The tiny child was obviously so far from middle age. *I've a long way to travel,* he thought, heading back to his interrupted meal. *I can easily be Chief of Security for another thirty years!*

He seated himself again cross-legged by the table and expertly transferred what was left of the eel to his mouth with chopsticks.

"You see," said Hariko, whose sharp ears seemed to pick up every word that was said in the apartment. "You didn't have to shout at Colonel Yost."

Lucky she can't hear what I say in the office, he thought.

"Little wife, you're right as usual. I'll watch my dirty tongue hereafter."

After that the click of chopsticks alone disturbed the lunchtime peace. Yamashita's mind lingered on the *kloppi,* wondering what he'd learn from them about Admiral Dluga's secrets.

Wants to take Luna away from the Security Forces, does she! I'll kill the fucking bitch, he thought.

"We have green-tea ice cream for dessert," said Hariko, signalling to a robot servant standing in a corner of the room.

Yamashita grinned boyishly, and for the time being put thoughts of murder aside. He never mixed business with pleasure if he could help it.

2

Toward sundown, in the sleazy apartment she called home, Komesh Sandra prepared with special care for her date that night with Maks.

She knew it would be important. When they'd parted earlier that day she'd been deep in gloom, wondering what, if anything, would come of their friendship. Then at her lab she'd received a call from him inviting her to a new opera.

Now she was equally full of hope; the opera was expensive, he must be setting the stage—the little pun made her smile—for something.

Her mother would make no trouble. A confirmed kif-head, Komesh Inez lay on the divan, snoring. The whole apartment reeked of the drug. That meant Mama Inez had received her monthly stipend of 500 khans, and probably had spent most of it already. The money was a sore subject between the two women. It was enough for both of them to live decently on. But most of the money went, quiet literally, up in smoke. The source of the money was another issue, one that fascinated and baffled Sandra. Who in the world would support Inez, and why? But the older woman guarded her secret well.

Sandra hurried to her bedroom—cubicle might have been more accurate—snatched up a towel and clean underwear, and headed out for a shower-massage at a public bath. By a quarter to 20 she'd returned and put on her one respectable nonworking garment, a dress coverall with evening T-shirt. (Maks's time-surfers had brought back some ancient garments and retro styles were all the rage.)

Wearing her finery, she ran up two steep flights of stairs to the roof of the old building. After the heat of the day, the cool Siberian dusk was welcome. In the distance blue shadows were creeping eastward from the mountains and twinkling lights were performing their familiar magic of turning an ugly city into a chest of jewels.

For a time the evening traffic crept by, compensators chugging. Then Maks zoomed down in a hovercab and handed her rather grandly into the back seat. A few minutes later the avenues of the Worldcity were spinning like the spokes of a wheel as the cab banked and turned over Government of the Universe Place.

Sandra had few chances to join the air traffic above the rutted streets. She pressed her nose to the port and gasped as they buzzed the spotlighted statue of Steffens Aleksandr the Worldsaver.

Weary laborers paused in their homeward scurry to gawk. Noisy peddlers crying their wares of kif and miso and babaku chicken with texasauce waved and grinned. A fat woman laying flowers at the base of the statue stared upward, and Sandra briefly glimpsed the white-painted face of a licensed prost.

What a strange thing for a whore to be doing, she thought, and then forgot the incident as the opera house hove into view.

3

The cab left them near a crowd rising on a sliderramp toward one of the ornate entrances and a black box flickered once at the tickets Maks waved.

Then they were struggling across a vast lobby through a crowd of opulent-looking people. Senators in purple sashes, top bureaucrats wearing the chains of office, monopolists from the great cartels, officers of the Security Forces and the Space Service. Sporting a gold swagger stick, Admiral Dluga Suzana lorded it over a circle of fawning officers.

Then a gilded door opened and Xian Xi-qing, the ancient Controller, entered on the arm of a startlingly handsome young man in a captain's uniform. This unlikely couple—he was about a quarter of her age—moved slowly and regally through the crowd, which shrank back like semiplast burned by a laser.

All around her, Sandra heard people muttering at the spectacle.

"Who the devil is it?" asked a senator loudly. "Who's the *babochka*?"

The word meant butterfly; in slang it meant gigolo. Somebody knew, because as he and Xian vanished through an inner door, a whisper spread: "It's Captain Dluga. The admiral's son."

Maks looked at Sandra and gave a low whistle.

"Hadn't you better call somebody?" she whispered.

He chuckled. "Every Security man in this place already has."

He added more soberly, "Who's in the Empress's bed? That's the big news of the day. That's the world we live in."

Aided by a little usher robot, they found their seats at last. They had unobstructed views of a huge monitor hung from an ornate coffered ceiling. In an open box nearby, Admiral Dluga sat like a gleaming scarab, proud of the trump she'd just played in the ceaseless game of power.

Then gilded dragon lamps darkened and laser projectors sprang to life and another kind of spectacle took center stage. Ornate Cyrillic letters floated like passing clouds, announcing the title, Mir Tsava ("A World to Save"). From unseen synthesizers, music gushed in a flood.

A digital actress, a woman of light looking realer than real, rushed onstage. Sandra knew at once the character she was playing: the infamous Dyeva, leader of the Crux conspiracy.

She wore a cape three meters long. Her opening aria was harsh, atonal, full of threat. She sang of her desire to destroy the existing world in order to restore another world she'd never known. While she sang, a chorus of demons pranced and shrieked.

Sandra relaxed against Maks's solid shoulder and he turned

to smile at her. For an instant the performance was forgotten. Their hands clasped, fingers interlacing. Something passed between them, sudden and palpable as a spark, and though nothing was said Sandra knew that tonight they would make love.

4

Half a click distant and sixty meters down, Kai, the arrested student, was having a different kind of evening.

His efforts to learn why he'd been arrested so far had brought no answer except a vicious burn from an electric prod. Indeed, there must have been some sort of mixup: Kai's father wasn't an officer of the Space Service, he was a pharmacist still blissfully unaware of what had happened to his son.

Perhaps it was all a mistake. Nobody in the depths of the Palace of Justice could have told Kai what he was accused of, because nobody knew. But procedure was procedure.

A few minutes past 13 he'd been taken down nine levels in a clanking elevator and put through a routine the thuggi called "the short course." They also provided "the long course" for professional criminals, and for subversives "special handling," which few survived.

First, Kai had stood at attention, in silence, no visits to the toilet allowed, for five hours. Initial processing—stripping, searching, and scanning—followed. Then his neck and wrists were relocked into the kang. Body rustling in paper pajamas, he shuffled in loose slippers along a damp corridor between a warren of tiny cells. The prod mark on his shoulder blade ached and stung.

A thug pushed him into a cell. A door grated shut, leaving him in darkness except for the centimeter-wide line of dim light along the floor.

Kai sat with his knees under his chin, his body twisted side-ways because the kang fit the cell only on the diagonal. Outside he could hear the heavy tramp of thuggi, the peculiar scraping shuffle made by the hairy feet and long blunt claws of Dark-siders. Technicians padded down the corridor, talking in atonal voices.

"That patient's a tough case . . . Gnosine's no good. If skopal doesn't work, use the needles . . . sometimes you need a combi-nation of therapies to reach a good outcome. Promise him life. After you've worked on him a while, promise him death."

Kai shivered uncontrollably. His feet turned to ice. His ribs stabbed at him if he took a deep breath. From time to time, off in the darkness, a door grated open and someone screamed. Was that real, or a bit of mise-en-scène contrived by the Secu-rity Forces to wear their prisoners down?

If so, he thought dolefully, it was working. He'd just wet himself. He'd never been so scared. *Oh Great Tao,* he thought, *what is it they want me to confess? Will they tell me, or will I have to just start confessing to everything?*

What can I tell them that they'll want to hear?

5

To a crescendo of gongs the chorus of demons wheeled out a vast machine, all cables and flashing lights—the famous wormholer.

Finishing her song, Dyeva sprang into the machine and vanished in a burst of fireworks just as the Worldsaver came bounding onto the set, followed by a ferocious chorus of Dark-siders. Together they slaughtered the demons, but were too late to stop Dyeva from vanishing into the past.

Machinations followed. The evil Kathmann was introduced, a corrupt officer of the polizi who arrested and tortured Steffens in an attempt to make him join the Crux conspiracy. Instead, aided by the chorus of Darksiders, he escaped and leaped into the wormholer, vanishing in another brilliant burst of fireworks that was followed at once by intermission.

In the lobby, clouds of kif were as thick as the aftermath of the fireworks. Everybody buzzed with the news about Xian and Captain Dluga while standing in long lines at the toilets. Sandra and Maks managed to find an alcove between two gold-leafed pillars where they could sip plum brandy from a bottle that Maks had brought in his sleeve.

"What do you think of the opera?"

"Oh, I love it. As history goes it's probably a lot of crap, but it's wonderful."

He laughed, leaned close, and said, "Right on both points."

"And you've really gone through the wormholer yourself?"

"Yes. Often. It's not much like the thing on stage. Would you . . . like to go through it, too?"

She looked at him, startled. Then the lobby lights began to flicker and a gong summoned the audience back for the second and climactic act.

The monitor showed a vision of the Kremlin in the twenty-first century. Here Stef and Dyeva met. Overcome by her beauty, Stef made love to her instead of shooting her. The two then sang a long duet about their plans for returning to their own century as loyal servants of the State.

But the evil Kathmann, fearing that Dyeva would denounce him for his complicity in the Crux conspiracy, destroyed the wormholer and marooned the lovers amid the horrors of the Time of Troubles. United in love and singing madly, Stef and Dyeva perished together as thermo/bio weapons exploded in the background, the golden domes of the Kremlin were vaporized, and the first snows of the Two Year Winter began to fall.

Sandra, weeping happily, joined the rest of the audience in a standing ovation. Then mirrored doors enclosing Xian's box opened and the audience was permitted to cheer the Controller. The *babochka* was gone, to everyone's disappointment.

"No doubt," said Maks, "they'll be reunited in her bed."

In the lobby, people were fairly groveling to Admiral Dluga, and she was giving out brief, cold nods of recognition like favors. Maks and Sandra slipped past, caught an unoccupied cab, and headed for Maks's small apartment.

There they drank a bottle of good Siberian champagne from the vineyards on Lake Bai, undressed each other, and went to bed as if they'd done it dozens of times. They made love, parted smiling, and rested before trying it again.

Drowsy in the afterglow, Sandra let her fingers settle gently on Maks's arm, like sleepy dragonflies at dusk.

She murmured, "I feel like we're still doing it."

"Umm."

"Maks?"

"Umm?"

"Do you really want me to go through the wormholer?"

"Sure. With me."

"To visit the past," she said dreamily, her mind full of the opera.

"No," he said. "To live there the rest of our lives."

CHAPTER XXIX

In Special Investigations, shifts of technicians relieved each other, those who went off duty showering and donning clean clothes so as not to carry the smell of prison home with them.

Strangely enough, when not at work they lived quite ordinary lives, sleeping beside their spouses, playing with their children, watching entertainment programs on the mashina. Their jobs seemed to drain all cruelty out of them.

Just after midnight a newly arrived tech put on clean white working coveralls and consulted a clipboard.

"What does Colonel Yost want out of this guy?" he asked the thug-on-duty.

"Goddamned if I know."

"So just wing it, eh?"

"Yeah, I guess."

A few minutes later the tech arrived at Interrogation Room No. 5. Kai awaited him, strapped facedown to a metal-topped table between the blood drains.

The room stank of Darksiders, human sweat, blood, and excrement. Above the prisoner a many-armed device hung from the ceiling. Each arm ended in a long needle. One needle had already been inserted into a large vein in Kai's left forearm.

In a quiet, toneless voice, the technician, standing out of sight in the shadows, explained what happened when the other needles were inserted into the spinal marrow. The waves of agony. The tetanic arching of the back, sometimes until one or more vertebrae cracked.

As he talked, the IV dripped five-percent skopal—a powerful synthetic version of scopolamine—into Kai's veins. The drug was a new addition to the interrogator's arsenal; intensely psychoactive, it dissolved inhibitions.

"I know you didn't intend to do anything wrong," the quiet voice went on. "I don't want to hurt you. Actually, I'd like to have your help. Take it from me, helping us is the best service you can possibly do yourself. You'll be surprised how easy it is, once you start."

"What do you want?" Kai whispered.

He was terrified, and yet he also felt a growing sense of bizarre excitement, as if he was really free for the first time in his life. He thought of murdering his parents, of raping young girls, and he felt no sense of horror. *Anything.* The sky was the limit.

"Suppose you tell me," suggested the tech. "Just let it flow. Just think about anything you need to get off your chest. You help me, and I'll help you."

A hand emerged from the shadows and patted his shoulder. A towel mopped sweat from his brow.

"I'm sure," the tech's voice murmured, "that there's lots of subversion at the University . . ."

That was all the hint Kai needed. A problem with skopal was the strange sense of power it gave some users. They began to think that if they said a thing, it must be true.

"I can give you names," said Kai confidently. "Lots of names. All subversives."

And he began to name everybody he'd ever met on campus, every one he could remember.

2

That was a long night for Yamashita, too. With Hariko bringing him fresh cups of smoky Lapsang, he worked at his mashina, bringing up all the scraps of information the Security Forces could command on Admiral Dluga and her son.

Unfortunately, the admiral had a clean record. Respectable parents, both in the military, both dead. Service in the Third Alien War, this decoration, and that promotion. Married Commodore Dluga Petr, commander of the Deimos squadron that guarded the spaceways of the Solar System. One son, Ion. Her publications included "Tactics for Combat in the Vicinity of Large Gravitating Masses" and "Can the Accuracy of Faster-Than-Light Missiles Be Improved?"

Nothing vulnerable there. Maybe the Space Service records showed more, but surely by this time she'd have purged them of any adverse material. Trying to penetrate the military files seemed hardly worth it.

Her son was a lowly captain, and the Security Forces had only one item on him: the Space Service kept a liaison officer in Xian's secretariat, and Dluga Ion had been appointed to the job. No doubt a calculated move on his mother's part—pimping for her son. That must be when he came to Xian's notice.

Cursing inwardly, dripping tea on his kimono, Yamashita was staring at this item when a few more words unfurled in the mashina's shadow box. A new item had come in; the Honored General's mashina was being updated. Thus he learned that Captain Dluga Ion had just been appointed Special Aide and Private Secretary to Xian.

"The position of Special Aide—who held it before?" Yamashita rapped out.

"Nobody," the mashina answered. "The position has just been created."

"Bloody fucking shit," said Yamashita, and for once Hariko, wheeling in more hot tea, didn't tell him to mind his mouth.

3

On a vast bed supported by carved gold-leafed phoenixes, Xian lay under a purple sheet of faux silk, idly reading Chancellor Yang's testament. Meanwhile, Captain Ion poured two glasses of Siberian wine—and added a sleeping drug to one.

"Who was Yang?" he asked, not caring.

"Nothing but an academic," she murmured, touching the hardcopy with nine centimeters of fingernail. The nails of his ancient mistress had left long pink scratches on Ion's muscular back.

"But," she went on, "he was loyal, fairly intelligent, and sometimes useful."

"What does he say?"

"Oh, he starts with a bunch of compliments . . . 'Ever victorious Controller and most honored *fromazhi*' . . . and so on, and so on. Yang had a grovelling instinct I rather liked. Hmm. Wants to make us a final gift of his humble thoughts regarding the future security of the State. Lucky for him he's dead—he wasn't authorized to think about such things."

Ion handed her a glass, clinked it lightly with his own. Sipping, Xian continued to read.

" 'How noble is our State!' Yes, that's true. 'How firm it appears! How strong! Yet other States no less imposing have quite suddenly perished through the inscrutable workings of the Great Tao.' Pompous ass. Whenever people can't explain something they say it must be the work of the Great Tao. Just once I'd like to know what the damn word means.

"Well, here's something a bit more solid. 'Even the stablest regime may alienate its own young; may be injured by terrorists who willingly sacrifice their lives to bring it down; may be undone by the corruption of harem politics; or may be destroyed by internal war among the armed forces.' Or may be hit by an asteroid, I suppose. And I can't say I like that line about harem politics—maybe he was thinking about his own life.

"This last paragraph's absolutely subversive. 'Even you, most honored grandees, ought to remember the ancient Roman question, *Quis custodiet custodes?* Who watches the watchers? Our State is indeed well guarded; but can you trust the guards themselves?' That's a slur on the Security Forces or the Space Service or both. Yes, the old fool's lucky to be dead."

Ion collected her empty glass and put it away with his own. His heavy body dropped at full length on the bed, shaking the gold phoenixes. He smiled and touched Xian's withered face with his strong young fingers.

"Anyway, Empress," he whispered, "we've better things to do than listen to nonsense."

Xian turned to him, smiling. Quite suddenly and unexpectedly, she'd begun to feel sleepy. Yet sleep had become so much a part of her life that she suspected nothing.

"*Bistra, bistra!*" she whispered. ("Be quick, be quick!")

During the action that followed, the hardcopy slipped unnoticed to the floor.

4

By dawn everybody in the Worldcity knew what was happening. Even trirad drivers knew that the Space Service and the Security Forces were locked in a bloodless battle for control of Luna. Even unlicensed prosts as they idled on corners were making jokes about Captain Ion and his improbable mistress.

Gamblers throughout Ulanor began quoting odds. Hostesses in the great palaces of the northeast quadrant launched all-out searches for guests with possible secrets to spill. Inventing absolutely reliable facts suddenly became a major artistic endeavor, for creators of good stories could expect to dine out at the fanciest tables in town.

The city had always lived by whispers. But never had the mix of sex and power been as delicious as now. Handsome Captain Ion in the Controller's bed! And Xian was over a hundred years old! Stem-cell therapy was all very well, but how did she—how could she—how could *he*—well, do it?

As yet, Maks and Sandra knew nothing of this. Dawn found them still discussing the fantastic proposal he'd made. Deep in the privacy of pillows and heaped bedclothes they whispered, inhaling the milky smell of each other's mouths, feeling the sudden bursts of warm breath against a listening ear.

Holding Maks's big hand between her breasts, Sandra made endless objections.

"But, Maks, we'd have to leave everyone we know."

"Would you be sorry to leave your mother?"

"No, but—"

She hesitated. Ever since she was a little girl, she'd played with a fantasy. She'd be walking down a street, her mind a thousand clicks away. Then someone would tap her on the shoulder. She'd turn and see a man in youthful middle age—gray-haired, about sixty or seventy—and he'd say, "Excuse me. I've been in Far Space a long, long time. Aren't you—aren't you my lovely daughter, Sandra?"

Just suppose he was alive and he returned only to find her gone forever? But the dream that meant so much to her was too far-fetched to admit to Maks.

"I don't know if I could handle life in the past, Maks. We'd be living before the Time of Troubles and everything we do—we'll know in advance it's all going to be destroyed. If we have children, we'll know they're going to be killed."

"Not necessarily. The colonies on Luna and Mars will survive. In fact, pockets of people will survive here on Earth. As far as I'm concerned, there's only one real problem. It's—a kind of medical problem I have. Until it's taken care of I can't go. It's been holding me back for years."

"Oh, Maks. And medical care back then was so primitive."

So they debated with themselves and each other, believing as people will that they had control of their lives.

5

Yost had found his volunteer. The Admiral had placed her son in Xian's bed. Point counterpoint.

What Yamashita badly wanted was information that might turn the Controller against her young lover. An alert went out to his army of informers, and new software briefed the arbots to detect any whisper of Dluga Ion's name in cyberspace. A code word was assigned the case: inevitably, it was BABOCHKA.

For once the information he needed came in search of him. At 9:70, his mashina chimed.

"What?"

"Honored General," murmured its atonal voice, "a reliable source requests to speak with you regarding case Babochka."

"What source?"

"Whoremaster Dzhun of the House of Timeless Love."

He relapsed into his chair, muttering, "Say."

She had a round face painted with prost's white makeup, a small pink mouth, and slanted greenish eyes. She spoke with the hollow music of a wind chime.

"Honored General, we had a visitor early this morning, just as we were closing. A young man who insisted on service and paid well. I was intrigued by his air of power and the fact that he wore a mask, a very expensive one made of dermaplast."

This porous skin-substitute could be worn anywhere, like a contact lens, detectable only by its faint unnatural sheen under oblique light.

"Did you penetrate his disguise?"

"Well, we secured a semen sample."

"Ah," said Yamashita. "A car will pick up the sample within five minutes. Anything else?"

"Of course I never listen in on my clients except when the security of the State absolutely requires it—"

"Go on."

"He was quite brutal to my young woman, very energetic, insisted on entering her by what we call professionally 'the three portals,' if you know what I mean."

"I do."

"He'd had more than enough kif, babbled a bit, made noises like a horse, et cetera, all that's on a memory cube I'll be sending along with the sample. But he also used certain phrases you may find interesting. He told my prost that he was 'sick of fucking a mummy,' if you'll excuse my language, General, and he also said, 'Thank the Great Tao, it'll soon be over.' "

Dzhun produced a little simpering smile she'd learned long ago as a young prost. It was meant to please customers without cracking her makeup.

"I hope, Honored General, that I haven't wasted your time?"

"No," said Yamashita, "you haven't. I suppose I can rely on your absolute discretion?"

"General," she said, her voice sinking an octave, so that for an instant Yamashita recalled the charm she'd had twenty years ago when the Worldsaver had loved her, "General, do you think I've ceased to value my head?"

Even Yamashita had to smile. In his heart he believed that Dzhun could survive anything, even a new Time of Troubles.

"You've deserved well of the State," he said. "I won't forget you."

He cut the connection. His ever-efficient mashina had dispatched a hovercar at the instant he'd mentioned it. Now Yamashita sat drumming his thick fingers on the Martian petrified wood that formed his desk. His lips stretched very slightly in the kind of smile usually called mirthless.

Fucking a mummy, eh?

The young idiot!

6

Sandra's chemistry lab was dull as ever, an inescapable part of her training in offworld geology, a profession that in itself bored her. When the State paid your tuition, you took what you were told to take.

Today her work consisted of putting prepared samples of Centauran rock into a spectral chromatographer and saying,

"Report," which in time it would. At least she had plenty of time to think about escaping to the past, which at this particular moment looked truly attractive.

A few centuries back, she thought, *I'd be a genius, knowing all this cookbook science I've learned. I could be rich and famous.*

The thought of being a genius amused her and she was smiling as she strolled to the canteen for tea. Here the buzz of gossip was not about Xian but about the student arrested yesterday. What had happened to him? What would happen next?

A group of very young people were trying to come up with the most gruesome scenarios possible. None of them seemed to have any idea that the fate they were imagining for Kai could just as well happen to them.

"I bet he gets sent to Europa. What a dump. A methane sea and worms a thousand meters long in the depths."

"Uh-uh. Not if he's a subversive. He'll have to bow to the laser. My uncle's in the thuggi and he witnessed a traitor's execution. The heat of the laser sealed the carotid artery and the jugular vein so there was practically no mess. My uncle made a bet that it'd be a clean job and he won ten khans."

"Boy," said another young man, impressed. "There's no shit about those Security guys, is there?"

Escape's looking better and better, thought Sandra, sipping her tea.

Two polizi strolled into the canteen and began chatting with the manager. To her surprise, he pointed at her. The blue-gray uniforms headed for her.

Great Tao, she thought, her insides turning to ice. *They've found out what Maks wants to do. They've arrested him and now they're coming for me.*

"Name?"

"Komesh Sandra," she whispered.

"ID."

She handed over a disk of ceramic lamina with an embedded hologram and dotcode stacked in geological tiers. The thug glanced at it, then tucked it into his uniform beltpouch.

"Please come with us."

Suddenly they were walking away together. The two polizi were wide, solid men with impact pistols on their belts. Trying to run didn't occur to her. She was terrified.

"Where are we going?" she whispered. Students and professors looked at the three of them, then dropped their eyes and turned away. That was a good citizen's automatic response to the polizi.

They didn't answer. Outside the lab building stood one of the oblong gray hovercars.

"Get in," said a thug. They boosted her into the back, slammed a door with no inside handle, and climbed in the front. A minute later the car was banking over the architectural jumble of the University of the Universe.

Where, Sandra thought, her hands and whole body trembling, *nobody's ever taught me one essential lesson: how to survive in the hands of the law—which is to say, in the hands of the lawless.*

CHAPTER XXX

At the Palace of Justice the hovercar descended onto the third stage. Sandra was assisted out none too gently and pushed through a doorway lined with scanners. A bored functionary at a small table took her ID, gave her a receipt.

They marched her down a gray corridor. None of the doors had names or numbers on them. One of the polizi counted audibly to thirteen, then pushed her into a small office with duro-plast furniture.

"Wait," he said, and the door shut.

So now, she thought, *I'm supposed to sweat, feel guilty, start imagining all the things I might have done wrong. Is this Special Investigations, where they torture people? If I listen, will I hear screams?*

No, I've heard that's underground, deep down at the bottom of the world.

She forced herself to sit, though every chair seemed about as uncomfortable as every other. She counted her breaths, deliberately slowing her pounding heart. With despair, she thought: *when they ask me about Maks, what do I say? How much do they know already?*

Nearly an hour went by. Sandra found herself checking her watch at shorter and shorter intervals that somehow seemed longer and longer. She deliberately made herself ignore the time for what she thought must be fifteen minutes, then looked, only to find that exactly two and a half minutes had passed.

She was just uttering a curse under her breath when the door opened. She jumped. Then stared.

A tall, heavyset man of Japanese ancestry entered. He wore a general's stars on his tunic.

"I am Yamashita," he said, and sat down.

"The Chief of Security?" she asked weakly, thinking there must be two Security Forces generals with the same name.

"Yes."

She knew then that she was lost. Soon masked technicians would be at her with needles and drugs, demanding answers she didn't have.

The most terrifying thing was that Yamashita was saying nothing, merely staring at her. She flinched as he reached out and touched her arm.

"Don't be afraid," he said.

Then he added something amazing: "When I learned of your detention, I came down to apologize."

Apologize? Sandra simply stared at him. The epicanthic folds over his eyelids drooped, making his small, bright jetty eyes even more unreadable than they would otherwise have been. She did not know that he was equally intrigued by her Eurasian eyes, slanted like his but hazel in color.

Yamashita was thinking: *After so many years. This is what she looks like.*

Sandra was thinking: *One of the most powerful people in 300 occupied worlds has apologized to me. Now, that's just impossible.*

He smiled, said, "I see you're no fool," and stood up, adding, "The same men who picked you up will take you back." He walked out, leaving her with her mouth open.

Her ID was returned by the same functionary who'd taken it. She found herself clutching the square of ceramic as if someone had restored her soul to her after it had been lost.

A final, happy shock came when she emerged into the open air, followed by two remarkably chastened thuggi, and found Maks waiting for her. They hugged, letting the polizi wait.

"They didn't hurt you, did they, Sandra?"

"No. Oh, Maks, you're—"

She was about to say, "You're free, and I thought they'd arrested you." Instead, she closed her mouth with a pop.

"It's all right," he told the waiting thuggi. "I'll take her home. I've got an official car."

"Sir, the general told us to take her."

"Wait a minute. I know him personally. I'll call his office and we'll see what he says."

"Take her."

Shortly afterward, Sandra was soaring again, this time in the front seat of an official vehicle.

"Maks, what was that all about?"

"They drugged that kid they arrested yesterday and he started naming everybody he'd ever met at the University. A mashina issued an automatic order for a mass arrest, and it's just been countermanded by Colonel Yost. Now," he added, "let's not talk about it anymore."

Of course he meant that an official hovercar was certain to be full of *kloppi*. She sat quietly, clasping her hands, letting the tremors flow out of her body. She was afraid she smelled—of what? Body fluids? Fear?

Not until they were safe in Maks's apartment did she tell him what had happened.

"The general said that?" he asked, baffled. "He said that to you?"

"Yes. And I don't have the least idea why."

2

Why? Suddenly it seemed the most important question Sandra had ever asked herself.

In the shadows of her background stood somebody who was important, powerful. Since the person couldn't be Inez, it must be her long-vanished father.

Once again she thought of that old fantasy, the mature yet youthful man who touched her shoulder, calling her his lovely daughter. But the figure she had seen in her dreams since she was a small child no longer sufficed.

First Maks had crowded in, and now another figure, less definite than Maks but clearer and more powerful than her dream, was emerging into view. High in the government, in the monopolies, even in the polizi, there was a real protector so important that even Yamashita trembled before him.

How so great a man could ever have taken an erotic interest in Inez she couldn't imagine. But sex made both men and women do the damndest things.

She spent the night with Maks, trying to sleep, but without success. She lay wide-eyed until the blue clockface announced 3:90. Then she got up, slipped on a robe, and sat down in the darkness on the floor in the cross-legged posture of meditation.

She spent half an hour relaxing and then allowed her mind to play almost randomly with the problem. Since she had no data, only intuition could help her.

My father must be one of the fromazhi, she thought. The crowd at the opera flashed before her mind, the senators, the monopolists, the officers of the Space Service burnished and glittering like beetles—and she thought: *perhaps I saw him there that very night.*

Perhaps he had looked at her, too, and she wondered if he'd recognized her. Probably thought she dressed so elegantly every day, from the money he sent Inez.

By morning Sandra had made a decision. When Maks was dressing she borrowed a few khans from him. After she had seen him off, she hastened to the nearest pylon, caught an avtobus to Inez's apartment and let herself in.

She could hear snores even before she got the door open. Nothing had changed since her last evening here, the brown shadows, the harsh burnt smell of old kif that saturated even the gray semiplast walls.

For a long minute Sandra gazed down at Inez, wondering that any man could ever have found her attractive. Then shook her awake.

"Well, I thought you'd walked out on me, young lady," Inez greeted her, blinking. Her breath was bad; her mussed, slept-in clothes and unwashed body had a musky smell. Reluctantly, Sandra sat down beside her.

"You've been missing a lot lately. I suppose you're sleeping with a man again," she went on querulously. "You've never been very good at keeping your knees together."

"Thanks for the kind words, Mother. I brought you some money to—to help out."

Sandra gave her the khans. Inez smiled, took the money, and looked at her with bleared but crafty eyes.

"And in return . . .?"

Sandra sighed; Inez had never believed in gifts. Give or receive, there was always an ulterior motive. And how often she was right, as she was now. It was depressing.

"Tell me the name of my father," Sandra demanded bluntly.

"That's none of your business. He never even knew you. He doesn't care about you, even if he's alive, which I doubt."

"He got me out of the hands of the thuggi yesterday. General Yamashita himself came and apologized to me."

"Oh, what a liar you are."

Suddenly Sandra leaned forward and stared into Inez's eyes, stared so deeply and fixedly that she stirred, blinked, dropped her gaze. At that moment Sandra realized that this sodden woman did not know who her father was—and that could only mean . . .

"Inez," she said, grasping her thin wrists. Inez gave her a nervous glance.

"You're not my mother, are you? You're a *svinya*. That's right, isn't it?"

Svinya meant sow; in slang it meant a woman who made a living by bearing children for others. The profession had become popular decades back when in vitro pregnancies were banned because "bottle" children invariably emerged as emotional cripples.

"No, I'm not! You're the only one I ever—"

Briefly Sandra gave the Great Tao thanks for kif. Cold sober, Inez would never have given herself away like that.

"*Who was the egg donor?*" Sandra demanded.

"I'm your mother," Inez whined, trying to pull away. "I've

shown you the scars often enough. To say nothing of all I did for you when you were a kid."

Never had Sandra used force on Inez. But now she felt ready to do anything to this harpy who had brooded over her childhood. Her hands contracted until Inez winced and struggled.

"I'll scream," she warned.

"Not more than once, you won't! Who was the donor? Who paid you to take care of me? Who's been supporting us all these years?"

Inez sat silent for a moment, then whispered, "I can't tell you. It's too dangerous."

Sandra relaxed her grip and took Inez's hand instead. It felt dry, cool, and brittle. At sixty Inez was barely into middle age, yet her hand felt like a centenarian's. Sandra's anger ebbed; hating Inez was absurd; she wanted nothing but to know the truth.

"You say it's dangerous. My mother, is she—is she one of the *fromazhi?*"

The fear faded from Inez's face; sly malice took its place. "Don't we have dreams! No, she is *not.*"

"Will you at least ask her if she'll see me?"

"Sure. For a thousand khans."

Sandra's strong hands contracted again until Inez winced and tried to pull away.

"Stop it! I know you'd like to kill me. It's the thanks I get for all those months being sick, for the time I spent in hospital and then all those years of taking care of somebody else's nasty squalling brat. But you'll never find her except through me. So there it is. You pay me the money and in return I'll make one single call. Period. You can take it or leave it."

Sandra slowly opened her hand, then stroked Inez's. *Poor Maks,* she thought. *What a leech you acquired in me.*

"I'll take it," she said.

Back at the apartment she was sitting nervously, hands in

her lap, palms clammy, thinking of many things, when the mashina chimed.

"Say," she whispered, and Inez's unlovely head appeared. She didn't bother with a greeting.

"The egg donor is a prost. I used to work for her. She used to be just an ordinary whore, but now she owns a big house and has a lot of contacts, gangsters, polizi, everybody. That's why I had to be careful. She calls herself Madam Dzhun and you can reach her at the House of Timeless Love."

She hesitated a moment. "Sandra, I'm sorry we never got along better," she said. "Please send the money quick."

The image disappeared. Sandra sent her the money, and never saw her again.

3

In the hard afternoon light the poetically named Clouds and Rain District slumbered behind unfurled shutters, behind gates of duroplast and steel.

It had never looked less rainy—or less poetic—than it did now. At the House of Timeless Love a bullet-headed doorman gave Sandra a professional once-over while speaking to an intercom.

"No, she ain't a pro. Just says she wants to see Madame Dzhun. I guess she wants a job . . . wha'd you say your name was?"

"Komesh Sandra."

He repeated the name, listened a moment, then spoke to the armored door, which obediently clicked and opened. Under the sharp stubble that crowned the doorman's head two small round eyes like black buttons followed her inside.

The passage had walls covered in crimson faux velvet. A tall, rangy woman took Sandra's hand; she was an albino, with eyes like rubies. Feeling she had entered another world, Sandra followed meekly until she was thrust through sliding steel doors that grated as they opened and closed behind her.

Dzhun's boudoir was as brilliant and overstuffed as anything the younger woman could have imagined. *It's uncanny,* thought Sandra as she wended her way among small inlaid tables and garish Martian brocades, *how exactly a madam's bedroom looks the way it ought to.*

Hanging rose lamps had been turned off and slotted sunlight entered through long shutters and sealed windows. Lying in a nest of cushions embroidered with phoenixes, Dzhun was looking a bit overstuffed herself.

"My daughter!" she cried, rising in a flutter of faux silk and advancing with hands outstretched. They kissed; Sandra was enveloped in a cloud of expensive offworld perfume.

"Sit, sit," Dzhun exclaimed, drawing her down into the cushions. "What started you looking for me after all this time?"

Sandra, voice shaking a little, told her the truth. That she had never liked Inez, had never really felt she was a mother. That after Yamashita's visit, she realized that she must have a protector somewhere.

"And now," she finished, "I think I understand. You're Yamashita's mistress, and he saved me because I'm his daughter."

But Dzhun began laughing, a musical laugh like the hollow note of wind chimes.

"Oh, my dear—Yamashita? He's the *most* boring straight arrow. Absolutely a slave to his dowdy little wife. No, if Yamashita took a personal interest in you, it could only have been on account of your father. What a shock it must have been when your dossier flashed up on his mashina and he saw that Stef's daughter had been detained!"

"Stef?" she asked blankly.

"Steffens Aleksandr. The Worldsaver, as they call him now. I named you for him, Aleksandra."

Sandra did not faint—she was proud of the fact that she had never fainted in her life—but the garish room dimmed and quivered and several minutes passed before she could speak again.

"Tell me about him," she whispered.

Dzhun called for wine, and a servant trotted in with a fine Siberian vintage that was wasted on Sandra. Dzhun tossed off a whole glass, then rested on the cushions, twiddling jeweled fingers, a distant look in her greenish eyes.

"I was a simple young country girl, new at my job, when one night a tall, skinny man dressed in shoddy clothes came into my room. Well, I always tried to be a good whore, so I did my best to make him happy. And do you know, he fell in love with me!

"He was offered a lot of money to go into the past, and for my sake he accepted the challenge. The next thing I knew, his death was reported. I was desolated! Then came the lawyers with the money. And suddenly Stef was everywhere, you couldn't get the musical programs anymore because it was all Steffens, Steffens, Steffens. And the silliest stories about his life! Making him out a kind of Buddha or something. *Ha!* The stories I could tell. But won't! Oh no, my dear. I'll die one day and the truth will be buried with me!"

Sandra stared at her. *Great Tao,* she thought, *this one's a harder case than even Mama Inez.*

"And my father," she asked, "did you . . . love him?"

"I had a feeling for him, yes. But I'll tell you, my dear, the one thing a whore can't afford is to get emotionally wrapped up in a customer. Business is business, you see."

Sandra left as quickly as she could, enduring a good deal of kissing and fluttering in the process. Outside, the bullet-headed doorman grunted sympathetically, "She didn't want you, eh?"

For a moment Sandra steadied herself against the wall of the House of Timeless Love. Then she straightened her back and looked him straight in his little button eyes.

"No," she said, "and now I don't want her."

CHAPTER XXXI

Even with the burden of the Dluga business to occupy him, Yamashita thought about Sandra from time to time.

Her image comforted him, for it brought to mind his old comrade the Worldsaver and their triumph over the Crux conspiracy. *I'll win this time, too,* he told himself.

Then Yost sidled in with a memory cube containing the latest information from Admiral Dluga's headquarters. His "volunteer" had successfully placed *kloppi* in the War Room of the Space Service. But so far Yama had learned nothing useful.

Today's batch was the same. Officers chattered about all sorts of technical questions, excessive drawdowns at the refueling depots, the Deimos-based squadron and its pursuit of smugglers, and so on. Mere rubbish. Yamashita could have learned as much by intercepting the headquarters message traffic.

From time to time Admiral Dluga's unmistakable voice was raised, ordering, demanding, reproving. Yamashita, no slouch at chewing people out, listened with reluctant admiration to her tirades. *Tough,* he thought. *Dangerous.*

"Yost," he said.

"Sir?"

"Where does this bitch live?"

"While her husband's on Deimos, she stays in the command suite of the BOQ at her headquarters."

"Well, I want a *klop* installed in her private quarters."

Yost shook his head. "I'll see what I can do. But I can tell you, General, that nobody gets in there except her son and her closest cronies. Our spy is not among those invited."

"Well, we gotta do something. This goddamn stuff I'm hearing, I could make it up myself. Say. What did you do with this guy's son, the one you arrested?"

"Sent him to the reeducation center on the White Sea. He's safe there but still in our clutches."

"Well, take good care of him."

"Sir, he's the apple of my eye."

As a matter of fact, Kai's ashes had been delivered to his parents about an hour earlier. An official document showed the cause of death as a recreational drug overdose. Kai's parents were devastated; they tried to make inquiries, but could get no further information from either the University or the polizi.

Yamashita knew nothing about that. His major worry now was that another meeting of the *fromazhi* had been scheduled.

He felt uneasily that Xian might seize the occasion to take Luna away from the Security Forces. His contacts inside her palace reported that her infatuation with Dluga Ion showed no signs of weakening.

"How," Yamashita demanded querulously, "can somebody so old be so cock-happy? Wasn't eighty years of getting fucked enough?"

Yost shook his head.

"Sex isn't my weakness," he pointed out, perhaps needlessly. "Yet how difficult our jobs would be if it weren't so many other peoples'."

Well, that was true, of course. Yamashita sent him away and gave himself over to thought. He had one bit of crucial information that Yost knew nothing about—the man who had used the phrase "fucking the mummy" at the House of Timeless Love was indeed Dluga Ion. The semen sample had proved it.

Trouble was, Yama was by no means sure of how to play this card. Suppose he gave Xian the information and she said, "What mummy is he referring to?" would Yamashita then have to reply, "You, Madam"?

Or suppose Dluga simply told her that he'd never been to the brothel, that the lab report was a fake, the voice on the cube mashina-generated—would she, obsessed as she was, believe him? For witnesses, Yamashita had only a few prosts, people who notoriously would say or do anything the polizi wanted them to.

Once again he played Dzhun's memory cube and listened, frowning his disapproval.

A lot of grunting and groaning. Ion did make noises like a horse. Listen to that hooker squeal—in pain, not pleasure. The guy was a fucking sadist with women. Was that because of life-long domination by his mother, who was also his commanding officer? Did he take out his suppressed rage on other women? Or was he just a natural-born bastard?

Suddenly all the moral and psychological cliches went straight out of Yamashita's head. He was listening to Dluga Ion's voice make the remark about the mummy, then add, "Thank the Great Tao, it'll soon be over."

How'd I miss the significance of that before? thought Yamashita. *Wouldn't these two connivers want to keep the relationship going as long as possible? Why will it soon be over?*

His mashina chimed. He snapped, "Hold!"

"Sir," said the infallible device, "this should be heard. It concerns Case BABOCHKA."

It was Dzhun. "Honored General, I'm preparing a little party tonight for a certain individual. He must have enjoyed his last visit, though I can't say the same for my girl—I'm having to buy two replacement teeth for the ones he knocked out."

"Entertain him well," said Yamashita.

"Oh, whatever he wants. And perhaps—if he asks for kif, as he certainly will—skopal is such a useful drug, but so hard to obtain on the open market because the Security Forces take it all—"

"I'll send you a supply."

"What a pleasure it is to assist you, Honored General, in your noble task of preserving the State!"

Once again Yamashita sat in silence, brooding. Preserving the State. Yes, that was his prime duty. How convenient it would be if he could prove that the Dlugas were *threatening* the State!

If anything like that was up, surely the Admiral's husband would be in on it.

"I want a most secure channel, interplanetary link, Security Forces Central on Mars. Route through the mag space transponder."

Ridiculously expensive for a call to a neighboring planet, but secure and fast. While he waited, he formulated his question carefully. In a little under six minutes an old comrade of his, Colonel Medved, appeared in the shadow box.

"General. To what do I owe the pleasure?"

"How's the old Russian bear these days?"

They chatted briefly; then Yamashita said, "Tell me something. The Deimos squadron. Anything unusual happening there?"

"Not. Deimos Base is empty as a bucket. There's been a routine redeployment."

Yamashita felt a little catch in his breath. He couldn't recall anything being said at the Space Service HQ about a redeployment, routine or otherwise.

"Where's the squadron being deployed to?"

"Luna Base. For refitting. Or so I hear."

"Luna Base?"

"Yes."

"Arrival date?"

"Sometime next week. Want me to get a precise time for you?"

"Get me everything you can on it."

"Something up?"

"Who knows?"

When the shadow box was empty, Yamashita sat silently, his big fists clenching and unclenching. How could he get more information, the kind he needed?

Suddenly Sandra's face flashed across his mind. Her dossier contained a note that she was living with a Security Forces officer who, of course, had had to report the connection.

Major Hastings Maks, he thought. *Pastplor. The wormholer. Yes.*

2

Sandra told Maks, "I've had a rough day."

Her hands lying in her lap like small dead animals, she told him Dzhun's story. She was too tired and distraught to follow the changing expressions on his face.

She watched dully when he went to his mashina and dialed up a life of Steffens Aleksandr, scrolled the pages, and printed out a hologram. He knelt in front of Sandra and held the portrait up to her face.

Then they looked at it together. Her face was fuller than Steffen's and her eyelids had the epicanthic fold while his didn't. But underneath, the bony architecture was the same.

"You're the Worldsaver's daughter," he whispered.

"Yes. And hers. That woman's. I'm going to lie down."

When Sandra emerged from the bedroom an hour later, he'd gotten together a scratch meal and a pot of fragrant tea. He had kif pipes ready, and Sandra gratefully sipped and smoked before downing a slice of bread and a wedge of synthetic cheese. Then she patted his hand.

"Bless you, my dear. Now, there's something I'd like to talk to you about. Why don't we take a stroll?"

His neighborhood was sufficiently upscale to boast covered walkways at the third-stage level. On this bright afternoon the ways were crowded with strollers and shrieking children.

A hundred meters on, the walk broadened into a little park with artificial trees and duroplast benches. Lovers sat together, whispering; old people did tai chi exercises or minded their grandchildren. Sandra and Maks found an empty bench and sat down.

"Now," he said quietly. "What's on your mind, *mi dori*?"

"I do want to get away," she said quietly.

He nodded. "You probably had the shortest and easiest imprisonment on record. But . . . now you know, don't you? What our world's really like. Nobody's safe."

"It's not only that."

He raised his eyebrows slightly and waited.

"Maks, I want to see my father. Even if only for a few seconds. I want to see him in real life, and then I'll be content, I'll go anywhere with you."

He thought about it. "I've had a project on the books for a long time. To go back to the Kremlin that night and see what really happened. Routine business has always gotten in the way. Besides, it's terribly dangerous. Anything could go wrong. We could get caught like those people in the opera. And taking an unauthorized person through the wormholer is absolutely forbidden."

As I know well, he thought, his mind on the micropellets of neurotoxin still circulating in his bloodstream. Knowing nothing of that, she nodded soberly, assuming the two of them ran the same risk.

"If you're willing, I'm willing," she said.

For a long moment Maks meditated on the possibility of

death. And discovered a strange thing. After living with the seeds of death in his body day and night for decades, no fear was left in him.

He wanted Sandra and he wanted out, and he meant to find a way to have both.

"You realize, don't you, that nothing can be changed?" he warned her. "You can't save his life. You can't do anything but look. You'll see your father and he'll be going to his death and *you can't help him.*"

She smiled wanly and gestured at the park, the old people, the amahs, the children.

"However bad our world is, it's full of real people, and I could never destroy them. I'm a simple animal, Maks. I don't want to tell him who I am, or even talk to him. I just want to take one look and that's all."

She hesitated, not wanting to sound melodramatic or silly. But this was what she felt, so she touched his arm lightly and said, "I want to be healed."

He nodded, thinking: *So do I.* They embraced. He kissed her ear. To all appearances they were another pair of lovers.

"When, Maks?"

"Soon. I have this medical problem I mentioned. I have to find a way to—"

A shrill, angry buzzing began, audible to Sandra only because they were so close. Maks growled and plunged a hand into his beltpouch.

"Yes?"

"See General Yamashita soonest," exclaimed a wasp's voice.

"Pardon me while I run like hell," he said, kissed her again, and used the commdisk to call for an official hovercar.

Five minutes later she watched him lift off, turn and bank and vanish over the city. She started to walk back to the apartment, feeling so strange, as if everything around her, the park, the dusty sunlight, the strollers, were all unreal as laser-generated figures.

A red ball rolled to her feet and she paused. A toddler followed the ball, seized it, and looked up at her, his plump face radiant with laughter. Watching him scamper away, she thought: *So much to learn. So much to lose, starting with your laughter.*

She walked on alone.

3

"Responsibility for Luna Base is hereby transferred from the Security Forces to the Space Service, effective thirty days from date."

Yamashita was staring at the message grimly when his mashina announced Maks's arrival. An instant later the door slid open and he advanced and saluted.

"Stand at ease," said the general.

Then for a long minute he said nothing at all. Most subordinates visibly wilted under this kind of silent inspection, but Maks seemed to be made of tougher stuff. Like a Darksider—maybe even like a robot—he simply waited. If the general could kill him with a word at any time, why bother to fear him now?

I've bred it out of him, Yamashita thought, pleased with his skill as a molder of the young. Sometimes a young guy needs a sharp lesson. Years had passed with Maks doing his job diligently and bravely, obeying every rule. Once more, he was somebody to trust.

"That fucking gadget of yours," said Yamashita abruptly. "The wormholer. Does it still malfunction over short periods of time?"

"Not as much as it used to. The techs have whittled down the blank period to about twenty-four hours. Shorter spans than that, the logic circuits still get confused over what's 'then' and what's 'now.' "

"I see. Well, I want you to use the wormholer to enter a certain place we can't get into any other way. Admiral Dluga's private quarters, in fact. Sometime when we know she was away."

Always pleased when he could astonish his younger subordinates, he watched Maks goggle, then recover and apply himself to the problem.

"She was at the opera a few nights back. I saw her."

"Good. When you get into her quarters, here's what I want you to do." He explained, then added, "I want this done soonest. An hour from now, I want to be listening in on what she said then."

"Yes, sir."

He saluted; Yama returned the salute. *Took me twenty years*, he thought as the door shut behind Maks, *but I broke myself a good horse. A beast that can take me where no other one can.*

Maybe a beast that can save Luna. And who knows what else besides?

That night, Maks and Sandra were relaxing. She asked him if he'd made a transit after he left her and he said yes, the shortest in history.

She looked at him inquiringly, but he shook his head.

Did he just not want to tell her? she wondered. Or were there now *kloppi* in here, too? Sometimes she wanted to ask him if there was any place in the three hundred occupied worlds that was free of them.

She did not ask the question, and so Maks had no opportunity to answer, as he surely would have, *"Not anymore."*

CHAPTER XXXII

Next day, a smiling Yamashita sat alone in his great office, listening.

If the *klop* in the Admiral's headquarters had been a bust, the one that Maks had planted in her private quarters was yielding pure gold. The words crossing time and space to reach him had been few—the admiral was not a chatterbox—but *very* revealing.

For the third time, Yamashita replayed the most important segment. It was late at night, after the opera, or early the following morning. Presumably Ion was rising from Xian's bed, from that nest of gold-leafed phoenixes that Yamashita had seen only once, during a visit to the Controller when she was ill.

Probably the old woman slept noisily, or—more likely—in drugged silence, while her stallion slipped away to regale himself with livelier partners at the House of Timeless Love.

Had he stopped off at his mother's headquarters? In the recording, a door opened. The admiral was speaking to someone. She said, "Yes, it's going well. But don't get overconfident. Just keep in mind it's like chess in reverse. You play, I suppose?"

An indistinguishable mutter in reply.

"Well, in that game you try to threaten with every move. In this one, you have to make moves without any appearance of threat whatever. Yamashita's the very devil, as you well know. Hence the 'routine redeployment.'"

Yamashita could almost hear the quotation marks enclosing the phrase. Other mutterings followed. Then:

"Yes, the squadron," she said. "It's the most reliable by far. My husband commands it. I made sure of that."

So, he thought. *She wants Luna because anybody who controls it can dominate the Earth.*

He slapped the desk, hard. The petrified wood absorbed the blow, left his palm stinging. A series of phrases spoken by the admiral and her son ran through his mind.

"It'll soon be over" (Ion). "No appearance of threat" (Suzana). "Routine redeployment," in quotes. "The most reliable squadron." And again, "it'll soon be over."

His eyes wandered back to Xian's order. If he knew her—and for all her weaknesses, her great age, her geriatric lust for Dluga Ion—if Yamashita knew her, and he thought he did, the laser would soon be removing some very high-ranking heads. *It does a nice job, too,* he thought. *No mess.*

For the first time in many days he felt secure, dominating a situation that had threatened to spin out of control. He had a month before the transfer of Luna took place. The Deimos squadron would arrive while the Security Forces still controlled the big lunar particle-gun batteries, and then—

His mashina chimed.

"Well, what?"

"Your Honored Wife desires to speak to you, sir."

He almost said, "Tell her I'm busy." Then thought: *if Hariko calls my office, she has a reason.*

"Put her on."

Hariko's small, plain face showed no emotion, yet as soon as Yamashita saw her he knew that something was profoundly wrong.

"Little wife, what is it?"

"Rika has disappeared. Honored husband, I think she may have been stolen. She went out with the amah and a Darksider as guard. They returned but she didn't."

He stared at her, absolutely confounded. Criminals did not, simply did not, touch the family of the Chief of Security.

"Her guard—"

Suddenly, idiot lights flashed on no less than three secure channels. Yamashita, the immovable man, jumped. He knew what sort of information would be coming in.

The first was Yost, looking absolutely baffled. "Honored General, your granddaughter—"

"I know. What happened?"

"She was on an outing with other children of the *fromazhi*. There were thuggi on guard, at least two Darksiders. An officer in Security Forces uniform approached the guards, carrying what appeared to be a written order from you. The guard called your mashina, which confirmed the order. He was to take Rika back to her grandmother's. The guard obeyed, and neither the second man nor Rika has been seen since."

"Well, well? What about the message?"

"Honored General, it's been subjected to every possible test. The message came from you."

2

Like a man in a dream, Yamashita cut the circuit. Lights continued to flash. One, he recognized, was coming in from the *klop* in the Admiral's private quarters.

She did it, he thought. *I don't know how, but she did it.*

"Say!" he barked at the mashina. His big hands tightened into fists; not until later would he find that his nails had cut his flesh and his palms were bleeding.

"How is it possible?" demanded Admiral Dluga. "Who could have taken the girl?"

An atonal voice replied distantly. Automatic voice enhancement brought out only the words, "absolutely no idea."

"Well, tell him to contact me directly."

"... he'll be ..."

A door closed. Presumably the admiral was now alone in her private chambers.

"Great Tao," she demanded of the universe, "what in hell is going on?"

Yamashita sat as before, turned to stone, still not feeling pain in his hands. If not the Admiral, then who could have done this?

More lights were flashing. The usually infallible secretarial software hesitated for a microsecond, unable to decide which message was most important. Then it murmured:

"Honored General, Major Hastings requests an interview."

"Tell him to fucking wait."

The secretary itself then came in for hard words from its owner. "How could you have confirmed an order to take my granddaughter?"

"Honored General, every personal code known only to you was entered along with the command."

"How is that possible?"

The mashina was not intimidated in the least. The thuggi who had let the general's granddaughter be stolen were already in cells at Special Investigations, sweating, fearing *shosho* and the laser. But what did the mashina have to fear?

"The only possible conclusion, Honored General, is that you yourself entered the command into my system."

For once in his life, Yamashita simply gave up. Dully, uncomprehending, he continued to ask questions out of mere habit.

"What have we learned about the kidnapper?"

"He was probably wearing a dermaplast mask. He was big, well-built, and appeared to be wearing an authentic Security Forces uniform. To arrest everyone fitting such a description would entail the self-destruction of the Security Forces."

"What ID did he show?"

"A Colonel Medved, whose presence on Mars at the time

has been confirmed absolutely. Of course, the guards used a pocket scanner to confirm the ID; it was authentic."

The calmness of the atonal voice was driving Yamashita mad. When it remarked that "everything possible is being done," he roared: "I don't give a fuck what's being done! I want results!"

Since this was a typically human and illogical viewpoint, the mashina said nothing at all.

Yamashita jumped up, prowled his office. Lights continued to flash, but he ignored them. Then the door slid open and Hariko entered the office. A Darksider peered after her curiously with unblinking red/black stare.

She waited until the door had closed, then ran to her husband.

"Great Tao," she whispered, "what can we tell our daughter? How can we say her child vanished in our care?"

"Hush, hush, little wife. We'll find the girl."

"Alive or dead?"

"Honored General," said the mashina's flat tones, making them both jump. "Major Hastings Maks states that an absolute emergency compels him to see you this instant. He is waiting outside."

"Tell him to go fuck him—"

Hariko put her finger against his lips.

"No," she said. "You've often told me he's a sensible man. Listen to him."

"What could he possibly contribute?"

"How will you know if you don't listen?"

Yamashita surrendered, but not willingly.

"Let him in," he said, in his grimmest voice.

Maks entered, but stopped in surprise when he saw Hariko.

"Honored General, I've been attempting to see you—"

"Say what you have to say and go."

Glancing again uneasily at Hariko, Maks said, "Honored General, at your command I've just disobeyed the laws dealing with time travel—especially the one that forbids changing the past."

Yamashita shook his head as if to remove dust and cobwebs.

"Why the devil—"

"I did it at your command, Honored General, a command you won't give me for two days—and now, since the past has been changed, a command that you never will give at all. I need your protection, because you yourself declared that you would activate the neurotoxin I carry in my body if I ever violated a rule again."

Yamashita stood as still as the great rock or Zen saint that his wife had recommended. At last he said:

"And that command will be—"

"Honored General, without my action, tomorrow your granddaughter will be kidnapped by unknown persons and vanish. Who knows where? To a room deep in Space Headquarters? To some ship of the Deimos Squadron, which by then will be moored off Luna Base awaiting the changeover of command? Shuttles will be going to and from the fleet, carrying supplies, personnel, perhaps other things. The motive for the crime will be to give your enemies a way of controlling your actions when their plot matures."

Yamashita sat down heavily, and Hariko came and placed her hand on his shoulder.

"Please, Major," she said. "Tell us."

"At that time you'll command me to return to the past and take Rika to a safe place. You'll give me orders and codes to take back with me. Your granddaughter is now in my apartment being cared for by the daughter of your friend the Worldsaver.

"Honored General, this is all I have to tell you. The law has been broken, the wormholer has been misused to alter the past, and Rika is safe."

Yamashita sat staring at Maks, until something almost as incredible as the young man's announcement happened:

Hariko ran to Maks and kissed him, the first time in sixty-eight years of life that she had kissed any man but her father, her sons, or her husband.

Meantime the general roused himself. For a few minutes he spoke in a low voice to his mashina, then he stood up and told Hariko, "Let's go and collect the girl."

To Maks he said in passing, "The activating code on you-know-what has been deleted. I know now that you're completely loyal."

Maks followed him, thinking: *Then it's time for me to betray you.*

CHAPTER XXXIII

At the House of Timeless Love, Dzhun and her second in command, the albino woman, Selina, were making preparations for the visit of Captain Dluga Ion.

"I'll bet," murmured Selina as Dzhun doctored a hundred grams of top-quality Martian kif, "that the honored Controller takes a sleeping pill. Old people sleep so erratically. Or else our little captain slips it to her, giving himself hours off for self-indulgence."

"He's got guts," Dzhun opined. "Or else he's a fool. He's sleeping with a tiger. The Empress, as they call her, cuts off heads as a pastime."

"I think that's enough skopal. You don't want to kill the young man prematurely."

They put a pinch of the doctored kif into a gilded censer, plugged in new hoses, and attached a hygienic mouthpiece still in its plastic wrapper.

"Everything must be the best," Dzhun explained. "Captain Ion has gotten used to that, I imagine, sleeping in the Controller's bed, drinking her wine, sharing her food. When you've lived an ordinary life and you suddenly get rich, it's amazing how quickly the greatest luxury begins to seem like a necessity."

"You should have been a philosopher," said Selina with a touch of irony that was completely lost on her friend.

"Do you know, I think you're right? Trouble is, if I was a philosopher I wouldn't know anything about real life, so my philosophy wouldn't be worth a damn. Now call in those bitches I've assigned to entertain the Captain. I want to make sure they understand their roles. He's to have anything he wants, anything at all. They're to encourage him to smoke, get him to talk but without asking any direct questions that might make him suspicious."

"You think of everything, my dear."

"Well, honey, if you use your head you're more likely to keep it. That's my philosophy, too."

2

At the meeting of the *fromazhi*, Admiral Dluga was reporting on the current military situation in the Solar System.

"Everything's quiet," she said. "Not even any smuggling to speak of. Your hardcopy, Honored Controller, contains a list of recent changes of station and so forth. The big effort is getting ready for the transfer of Luna Base. But that's an administrative problem only."

Ugaitish glanced at Yamashita to see if he was prepared to argue the transfer. He would have opposed it himself, except that he never opposed anything the Controller wanted.

Yamashita said only, "You may rest assured that the Security

Forces will maintain the defenses at peak condition until the transfer occurs."

The admiral said nothing, but gave him a long look. Was that a warning? A threat?

"I've never doubted your efficiency, General," she said.

Xian had fallen asleep in her chair, but now woke. "Ah, General," she murmured. "Your granddaughter. Whatever happened about that crime?"

"The child was playing a prank, Honored Controller. Fortunately, the mass arrests we carried out turned up a number of criminals, so the exercise wasn't wasted."

"Good, kill them all," she yawned.

"Perhaps your excellency should get more sleep," remarked Oleary incautiously.

Fortunately for him, Xian did not hear. She had dozed off again. Sunk in her robes of faux silk and ermine, she looked small and crumpled; despite fortunes in cosmetics and repeated stem-cell replacement therapy, her face still looked much like the mummy Ion had compared it to.

"If no one has any further to report . . ." said Ugaitish, and shortly afterward the councilors gathered up their hardcopy and departed.

At the door Yamashita bowed to the admiral.

"Hope there's no hard feelings about the Luna business," she murmured. She had curious eyes, glassy blue and slightly swollen so that they overfilled the sockets.

"None," said Yamashita. "After all, we're both in the same business, aren't we? Though sometimes on opposite sides."

She watched him go. *How much does he know?* she wondered. *And how did he learn it?*

3

"I've found the way to the general's heart," Maks told Sandra wryly. "He thinks he can use me to control the time process for his own ends. He doesn't seem to realize he's making exactly the same mistake as Dyeva and Loki and Zo Lian. Anyway, for the moment I can do no wrong. So, my love, now's the time to do wrong."

Sandra nodded, trying to smile.

They were approaching the Palace of Justice, walking rather than riding so that they could speak with less danger of being spied upon. It was during the noisy passage of an avtobus with an especially loud compensator that Maks told her for the first time about the poison pellets.

"But—with things like that in you, how could you have hoped to get away?"

"For a long time I couldn't figure a way. You know, I've never been in any danger of being confused with a genius. I was just hoping that if I did everything the general wanted he'd sooner or later relent. Then, after he had me plant the *klop* in the admiral's quarters, I suddenly realized that I could enter his office the same way with a bomb and a timer and destroy his *mashina*."

He smiled, his usual wry smile. "Of course, as soon as I figured that out, the general took me off the hook voluntarily. You never know what'll happen next, do you?"

Sandra stared at him, thinking how little she really knew about Maks. How could he walk with death in his body for twenty years, and then plot to bomb the office of the Chief of Security? Was this the man she'd committed her life to?

She was dreadfully nervous anyway. The adventure she had wanted was at hand, and now she had to face the peril she'd only imagined before or show herself a coward. Under her clothing she wore the latest thermal underwear, which exhaled body heat in the warm city streets but would retain it in the cold of their destination.

At the guard post on the first stage underground, Maks stopped to register her ID.

"I'm taking a friend for a guided tour of the agency. If any question's raised, reference the clearance she's received from the general himself."

He turned to her with a smile and asked, "Ready?"

Except that his smile was a bit rigid, as if he was holding his lips in place with an inner effort, Sandra could see no change in him. *Well,* she thought, taking a deep breath, *I suppose acting brave is the last refuge of a coward. So let me act well.*

"Ready," she said, and preceded him through a steel door into a hallway as blank as any other in a government building. People in uniforms bustled past; some greeted Maks politely, others appeared to see nothing.

He led her through a warren of small offices to a door with SECRET/BEHEADER/NO ENTRY stenciled in red on the bluish nuclear steel. Maks placed his hand into an ID box and a gleam of intense light read his genetic code. The door clicked and slid silently back.

"This was once a torture chamber," he remarked casually, as they stepped inside. "Used to be a metal table in the middle and a blood drain in the floor. I saw it first—oh, a long time ago."

Now the room held only the celebrated device that had done so much to change the world. The wormholer looked like nothing so much as an old-fashioned MRI scanner in some provincial clinic.

"It's not much like the one in the opera," she murmured, disappointed.

"No. And not much like the one that your father and Dyeva used, either. It's smaller, it can take two adults at a time, and it's infinitely more precise. I can land at a particular corner of a particular city at a particular hour of a particular day."

He grinned, held her lightly, kissed her. "Don't be afraid."

"What a silly thing to say," she whispered, "when I'm scared to death. Let's go quickly."

He opened a metal cabinet and pulled out long coats and faux fur hats; for a brief visit in the dark of night, no further disguise was needed. Maks slid out a drawer under the wormholer and extracted two control devices.

"In case something goes wrong," he explained, "this stud returns you through this wormholer into this room. Grip it hard and let the device get to know you, so it won't respond to anybody else by accident."

She did, until the device beeped to let her know that it now recognized its mistress.

"After you," said Maks.

4

"I don't agree with you," said Yost. "There's just no evidence of a military coup in the works. I listen to every word we get out of Space HQ, and I've yet to hear anything to support that idea."

"Perhaps I'm being overly suspicious," said Yamashita.

"There's certainly nothing we can approach the Controller with," Yost went on, querulously. "I agree with you that this whole Dluga clan is deplorable. The admiral's insanely ambitious. Her son's a male whore. We've already lost Luna to them. I don't like any of it, but if there's even a hint of treason, I don't see it.

"Anyway," he added after a moment's thought, "how could we arrest her? She's surrounded by her own guards, including a company of Darksiders. We'd have a battle in the middle of Ulanor, and once the Deimos squadron arrives we might lose."

"The situation's touchy," the general admitted. "There's nobody to threaten our world from the outside, but there's always danger of an implosion. We have to move cautiously, and that's why I want more information. I want more *kloppi* planted, this time inside the admiral's private quarters."

"We've never been able to get in there. My contact simply isn't authorized."

"Who cleans her quarters?"

"Robots."

"Well, prepare a virus to reprogram one of the robots. Surely your goddamn contact can manage to open a cleaning robot's program port and slip in a memory cube with the virus and give the thing a *klop* to plant."

Yost was admiring. "General, you think of the damnedest things."

"Ah," said Yamashita, "that's why I've lasted this long, Yost. I think of everything."

Including, he might have added, *the possibility that my second-in-command is a traitor.*

5

Dluga Ion's well-nourished body ran with sweat. Heart pounding like a rapid-fire *avtomat*, he reached for the kif pipe. One of the women huddled naked across the stained bed, sobbing. The other faced him on all fours and grinned.

A trickle of blood stained her little front teeth and flakes of white makeup had fallen from her face, exposing blotchy skin. At some time in the past her left eye had been replaced, and the plastic flickered blankly as her head wobbled from side to side.

Exhausted as she was, and in pain, she hadn't forgotten her orders. "You're a hell of a man," she panted, still grinning.

Ion had gotten his breath back and he laughed aloud. "You don't have any idea, *suka*." Suka meant bitch.

"I bet you're somebody in real life. I bet you're way up there, maybe in the polizi."

He sprawled back on a cushion, infinitely relaxed. The other woman continued to weep, and the sound soothed him. The tough one crawled up beside him, leaned on her elbows, smiled. Her little tongue flicked and removed a drop of blood from her upper lip.

"I'm the most powerful man in the Solar System," he said, head swimming with the doctored kif. He felt he could say anything, for he lived above the clouds like an eagle and nothing that happened in this sewer could ever reach so high.

"*Vzdor,*" she said. "Bullshit."

He slapped her, casually, just enough to make her head quiver. A few more flakes of white makeup fell off.

"Careful, *suka,* I'll hurt you again."

She changed her approach, touched his face gingerly. "Is it true? Are you so powerful?"

"I fuck the Empress. Know who I mean? She trusts me with everything. When I'm ready I'll nail her up in a box and throw the box in Lake Bai and run things without her. You'll see how powerful I am then—if you live through the fighting."

"Fighting?" she whispered, afraid to interrupt him now that he was babbling his secrets.

In Ion's mind, his mother and father had already been eliminated. The troops, the squadrons of nuclear-steel monitors, and the darting escort destroyers were his to command. Who was that ancient guy, Tsar Caesar, some such name? The one who grabbed power in Rome, then left the senators to make speeches while he ran the State?

Someday, when I have time, Ion thought dreamily, *I just might use the wormholer to run back and take a look at the old guy. Greatness calls to greatness across the ages.*

"I'm a reincarnation of Tsar Caesar," said Ion, and when the *suka* said, "Who?" he slapped her again, lazily, not even causing pain. Instead he smiled blearily.

"You've been fucked by the first emperor of all humanity," he mumbled.

In her boudoir, Dzhun huddled breathlessly with Selina over a receiver whose microtransmitters were embedded in the walls and ceiling of Ion's room. In the queue of Dzhun's mashina a memory cube recorded everything.

They heard sounds of Ion rising, fumbling for his clothes. Muttering to himself as he did so, "Well, back to the palace . . . bloody old mummy . . . ass like a moldy lemon . . ."

"Keep recording," said Dzhun, rising unsteadily. "Yamashita must hear this *now.*"

Selina caught her by the arm.

"Are you sure?" she asked. "This man's talking about civil war. Wouldn't it be safer to tell the polizi we didn't hear anything? That way we could stay out of it completely."

For an instant Dzhun hesitated. She turned slowly around, gazing at the garish Martian brocades that filled the room.

"No," she decided. "I haven't worked hard all these years just to have my beautiful house destroyed in some goddamn war. I'm giving this information to Yamashita and he can have Captain Ion, too. If ever I saw a young man who needed a trip to Special Investigations, he's it! I hope they tear the little bastard limb from limb."

She gave her mashina a secret boxcode.

CHAPTER XXXIV

Snow was falling briskly through the dusk. Yet for long moments Sandra sat on the white ground, frozen not by cold but by astonishment.

People in strange attire hurried past. Bells chimed; nearby, a wheezy musical instrument played a simple tune. People laughed and she heard the chink of glasses.

Somehow, her mind had always refused ultimate belief in the reality of time travel. It was one of those things like black holes that were facts, yet not believable. But there was no mistaking this place, the antique dress of the people, the bitter cold of a younger Earth.

Maks smiled, grunted as he rose to his feet, held out his hands to her.

"Maks, are we—"

He pointed upward. In the last light of dusk, searchlights were coming on, illuminating gold domes. The snow swirled into the lights and vanished again.

"It's the Kremlin," he said quietly. "The Troubles are about to begin. Come on; we haven't much time."

He helped her to her feet.

Clutching his arm, she let him guide her through the shadows. Great black rooks, disturbed by the lights and the crowds, spun cawing overhead.

The music rose from a small group of people who stood apart from the crowds near a cluster of thin birches. A pretty girl whose white wedding dress contrasted with her flushed face was raising a glass of wine. A young man with one arm around her

waist and snow gathering on his stiff black suit laughed and returned her toast.

Then a small, energetic woman emerged from the shadows
and bustled past, her hands thrust deep into the pockets of a
long coat trimmed with faux fur. A tall man followed, not visibly hurrying yet overtaking her simply by the length of his
stride.

Maks gripped Sandra's arms and pulled her against him.

"Oh," she whispered. "Oh, Great Tao."

2

Her father strode past her, his eyes fixed on the woman ahead.
Dyeva had paused at the edge of the crowd, staring at the wedding party.

The people laughed, yet death hung over the scene. Sandra
began to weep. In an instant her father would be dead, Dyeva
would be dead, a whole world would be dead.

In a nearby church a choir was singing—no instrument
played; only the pure bell tones of the human voice, muted by
the thick walls.

Dazed, Sandra allowed Maks to pull her along. Then she
heard a man's voice say, "Dyeva."

The young woman in the long coat half turned to face Steffens Aleksandr. In a flicker of reflected light Sandra caught sight
of a round Tartar face, with high cheekbones and angled eyes.
Her father said something and Dyeva answered, her voice low,
the rhythm of Alspeke recognizable even though her words
were not.

Instead of killing her, he stood there for moments that grew
longer and longer. Sandra whispered, "Kill her, Father!" But the
silence only grew.

The young people in the wedding party now were singing

some popular tune and the guests were sharing the champagne. The Worldsaver, still hesitating, turned his eyes for an instant to look at them. Sandra heard a soft sound, as if Dyeva had coughed.

Her father's body flew backward, shoulders and head almost separated from the rest of him, and struck the snowy ground with a thump. An impact weapon fired again, its sound so puny that no one standing near seemed to notice. Then quite suddenly the body began to break up, lose form, and vanish.

Sandra screamed, tore herself free from Maks, and fell on her knees by the vanishing image. Black blood lay steaming in pools on the snow and she plunged her hands into it. Then Maks had her in his grip again, and the only touch of her father she could ever hope to know was the sticky warm blood left on her skin.

Pulling her along with him, Maks hastened after Dyeva.

"This will be very dangerous," he whispered. "Take your control in your hand and stay in back of me."

They hurried into a thickening crowd, boots squeaking in the fresh snow. Sandra couldn't see Dyeva, but Maks, rising for a moment on his toes, spotted her, and they followed, squeezing through the people, drawing close enough to hear Dyeva murmur apologies. *"Pozhal'sta . . . Prastitye . . . Izvinitye menya . . ."*

Then Sandra heard the sound of engines, and the crowd closed in, people thrusting themselves forward, blocking her view. Maks's foot struck a large stone lying in the snow with some construction rubbish. He turned, slid his hands under Sandra's armpits, and lifted her until she stood on the stone, braced by his arms around her ample hips.

She saw the black-mirror tops of gleaming vehicles, more elegant than any that travelled on the plebeian ground in Ulanor. Somebody was emerging; in a flash of blazing lights she could see a big man's snow-white hair. Among the silhouetted crowd cheers broke out: *"Gurra! Prezident Rostoff!"* The shadowy people moved and shifted, heads and shoulders briefly flickering into sight and back into darkness again. A commotion followed; new and even more brilliant lights flared, wobbling as if held by hand, and for just an instant Sandra saw Dyeva's small taut figure etched in the glare.

Then, almost invisibly, like the opening of a seed, something happened—she couldn't see what. The white-headed man staggered as if he'd been pushed and then, without a sound that she could hear, something horrible happened to his body, the same thing that had happened to her father. A gasp and moan broke from the front of the crowd.

Loud shots, the loudest she'd ever heard, were echoing among the Kremlin palaces. The people surged back, Maks lost his grip on Sandra and suddenly she was falling, her long body striking earth, feeling the cushioned impact of the snowy ground. Maks threw himself over her, shielding her with his body, and his weight drove the breath out of her lungs, blowing a little cloud of crystalline flakes away from her face. People screamed, and bodies and the shadows of bodies slumped together into the snow while another barrage raked overhead.

Commands were shouted. The firing stopped. Maks put his arms around Sandra, first holding her down, then raising her cautiously. There was a charmed, paralyzed moment almost without sound, and then screams, shouts, and the snow-muffled pounding of feet began again. She was weeping helplessly as Maks dragged her upright, his heavy body bearing the impacts as other bodies caromed into him. Shadows in flight were cursing, weeping, making hoarse noises like stampeding animals. Some cried, *"Rostoff myortvy, myortvy!"* and others shouted, *"Yest raneniye!"*

Maks and Sandra were moving, she didn't know where, crossing the paths of the fleeing mob. Maks became a battering ram, thrusting others aside, and she knew that without him the mob would have swept her away or knocked her down and trampled her.

He brought her to the Kremlin wall, where they halted for breath. His face pressed into her hair and she heard him muttering, "He's dead. The president's dead. And so is a world. And a world is born. Our world."

3

The horrible noises continued, but the crowd had scattered and thinned when Maks began to move again, guiding her to a nearby flight of brick steps. Stumbling, trying hard to keep a grip on herself, Sandra climbed with him to the top of the Kremlin wall. There they huddled in the deep shadow of a tall, ornate crenellation.

He whispered, "I'll go first. I want to make damn sure nobody's there to see you emerge from the wormholer. I want you to count to thirty and then press the stud—Sandra? Are you functional?"

"Yes," she whispered. "Oh, Maks, go quick. I'll collapse in a minute, but not till we get back."

He smiled at her, his face pale and smudged as if rubbed with ashes. Then for the second time she watched a man evaporate before her eyes.

When he was gone she waited, counting in Alspeke—*da, tu, tri, fa*—and gazing out over the city, aware that she was counting down to its doom. A dark ribbon of a river wound among pale distant buildings that resembled palaces; bridges wore strings of headlights like pearls. She could hear like a bass note the hum of traffic, interrupted by the braying of horns and occasional metallic collisions.

Down below the wall people were still running, but where were they running to? In the searchlights, rooks wheeled and cawed; some veered off, flying toward a safety they would never reach.

Then, in the distance, a pale glow like a rising moon showed briefly above the horizon. Sandra was so terrifed that she lost count and stood paralyzed. The glow vanished and in its place a pillar of fire rose slowly, majestically, until it mingled with the low-hanging overcast. Forked lightning flickered around it.

Still her hypnosis lingered. As she watched, lips parted, heart beating so loudly that she could hear it, a dull roar pulsed slowly across the city, until the sound of her heart was lost in it. A strong wind began blowing toward the pillar of fire, sweeping along the snowflakes, raising flurries from the white-powdered trees. Suddenly, as if huge carpets were being dropped, the city lights began to go out, district by district.

Then an unimaginable blaze transformed the whole scene. The domes, the towers, the wheeling birds, the Moskva River, the crowded buildings of the city beyond, all suddenly took on the fixed metallic clarity of a landscape revealed by lightning. Reflexively her fingers tightened against the stud on her control. The city vanished, the light intensified, she was lying on cool metal, and it was in motion, sliding her forward and into the arms of Maks, who waited white-faced to receive her.

"I thought something went wrong," he whispered, and she answered, "Oh, it did. It did. Everything went wrong."

4

Seated at his mashina, Yamashita said, "Get Major Hastings to my office now."

"I am trying to locate him."

"Well, where the fuck is he? He's on duty, right?"

"Yes, Honored General. He's showing a visitor through— Ah. Major Hastings."

Maks's face was flushed; he looked shaken. "Sir?"

"Get your ass to my office soonest. What's the matter? Nothing's blown up at Pastplor, has it?"

"No, Honored General."

"Well, something's about to blow up here. So make it quick."

In the transit room, Maks carefully shut down the mashina and joined Sandra at the door.

"I have to leave you again," he whispered. "You'll be all right?"

No, I'll never be all right again, she thought. But she said, "Yes, don't worry about me. Has something else happened?"

He was hustling down the corridor, brushing workers out of the way with his big shoulders, but she thought she heard him say, "Two worlds ending at once."

But he couldn't have said that, could he?

CHAPTER XXXV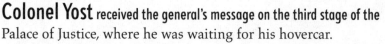

Colonel Yost received the general's message on the third stage of the Palace of Justice, where he was waiting for his hovercar.

He was quiet, expressionless, his tall spare figure neatly if drably uniformed. The shadow of the car drifted over him, and the vehicle had started to settle when an aide ran up to Yost and whispered, "The general wants you in his office at once."

"Did he say why?"

"No, sir."

Yost raised his eyebrows. It wasn't the order that disturbed him, only the timing; his work at the long, tedious process of weaving a beautiful plot was approaching its culmination, and try as he might to be calm, he felt an edge of nervous apprehension that something might still go wrong.

He turned abruptly, saying, "Have the car wait," and hurried back into the building. He ordered up six of his own thuggi, just in case anything unexpected happened. Then he spoke to a security-coded mashina.

"Review the guard station reports and inform me who has seen the general this morning."

A short list of commonplace official visitors appeared. Nothing in that. And nothing for him to do but to go and put his head where it usually was, in the lion's mouth.

Sometimes Yost wondered whether the prospect of supreme power was worth the effort it cost him. But he never wondered for long. He'd waited for twenty years to take over as Chief of Security, and enough was enough. Great Tao, Yamashita might last another thirty, might leave him the job only when Yost was too old to handle it.

Anyway, Yost loved spinning wheels within wheels within wheels. When he got Yamashita's call he'd been headed to Space headquarters to persuade the admiral to launch the coup prematurely, while the Security Forces still controlled Luna. His argument would have been that Yamashita was getting too close, that they must strike now.

His real idea was this: when Yamashita was dead and the Deimos squadron returned to Luna Base after assisting the coup, the lunar batteries would be under Yost's control. They would open up on the squadron and destroy it; Yost would then arrest the admiral, shoot her and her awful son, and emerge as the strongman of the new regime.

That seemed to him a reasonable way to end the affair. A double double cross would give him everything he wanted, make him a hero, and eliminate the tiresomely ambitious Dlugas with their dangerous power and their all-too-likely hope of eventually getting rid of him.

After all, they were allies in the coup purely out of necessity. No love was lost among them, and in the eyes of the prospective Royal Dluga Family, Yost would forever be an outsider.

His party of six thuggi arrived. Yost said, "Check your weapons, make sure a round is chambered, and follow me."

Problems, problems. He sighed, a hardworking man doing his best to get ahead in a difficult world.

2

Yamashita and Major Hastings were waiting for him in the head office, the general sitting at his desk, Maks standing beside him.

"Colonel Yost," said Yamashita coldly, "when I say at once I mean at *once.*"

For a few seconds Yost stood paralyzed, while the nuclear-steel door whispered shut behind him. Ten armed Darksiders were standing at attention along the walls; as usual, their secondary set of hands moved a bit, surreptitiously scratching their chests.

"I'm sorry, General," Yost said, recovering. "I didn't anticipate your call and I was on my way out of the building."

"Read that," said Yamashita. Maks, looking pale, approached and thrust a piece of hardcopy into his hands. It was the transcript of Ion's words in the House of Timeless Love.

Yost read, with a feeling as if some internal gravity compensator had failed and his guts were about to fall out through his anus.

"Great Tao," he whispered.

The plot was blown: there was nothing he could do now except play for time. Either he must kill Yamashita or he must help Yamashita to kill the Dlugas before they could talk.

Yost had conducted too many *shosho* sessions—actually, they were one of his favorite official functions, though he always denied it—not to know what would happen if Captain Ion was once stretched out on a metal table with needles in his spine. The admiral might resist unto death, out of sheer stubbornness. Not her son. Captain Ion would betray everybody and everything, Yost first of all.

Yamashita was saying, "You can see that we must move quickly. But first let me have that paper back. I'm taking it to the Controller."

"Of course, of course," Yost muttered, but Maks must also have been a bit nervous, for the hardcopy fluttered out of his hand and he dropped to his knees to retrieve it. Rising to a crouch, he suddenly launched himself into Yost's midsection, sending him flying with polished boot heels in the air.

At the same instant Yamashita ducked behind his desk, the Darksiders raised their impact weapons, and, announced only by a puny sputter of sound, a hurricane of fire swept across the center of the room. Yost's thuggi seemed to explode, sprays of blood and gobbets of flesh and bone flung out in wide circles as if by a wave dashing itself on rocks.

The door slid open and Yamashita's thuggi rushed in, seized Yost, and locked his neck and wrists into a kang.

"Colonel," said Yamashita, rising to his feet, "I will see you next in a place that you know well."

He gave a few brief orders for removal of the torn bodies and body parts. Then he opened a drawer of his desk, took out a jar of brightly colored candy, and solemnly went down the line of Darksiders, handing out sweets. The big beasts stood quietly, weapons in hand, sucking audibly.

"General," said Yost, struggling for indignation, "I absolutely deny—I had no part in—"

"I wondered why I wasn't getting anything useful from the *kloppi* in the admiral's War Room," said Yamashita, buckling on an impact pistol. "So I set a little trap. I've been getting—never mind how—good stuff from her private quarters. I found a way for you to claim plausibly that you'd put a *klop* in there also. And you know what? The good stuff dried up at once."

He smiled, the most forbidding smile Maks had ever seen on a human face.

"Couldn't wait your turn, eh? Wanted my job enough to offer the Dlugas your services, right? Well, in this game you make only one mistake."

To Maks he said, "I'm going after the *babochka*. I want that pleasure myself. Meanwhile, you go and make all necessary preparations for attacking and killing the admiral yesterday, in her quarters, before she gets wind of anything going wrong."

For an instant he paused, his small bright eyes gleaming at the prospect he saw before him—a new kind of justice: criminals executed before they can commit their crimes by armed thuggi who appear, destroy them, and vanish into thin air. Why hadn't he ever thought of it before?

At last, perfect retribution. Perfect control. *Of course the law's against changing the past,* he thought, *but fuck that. I'll change the law and the past.*

A private lift whisked him seventy-five meters up to the level where Sandra had been held briefly as a prisoner. There he trotted outside onto the third stage of the vast step pyramid that was the Palace of Justice.

A raw wind was blowing, smelling of rain. Hovercars were tuning up engines and compensators; Darksiders in a huge furry clump turned glowing red eyes on their boss. Impact weapons and ammo bandoliers rattled. One Darksider slammed home a clip with a sound like snapping steel. Yamashita beckoned over an officer and gave his orders.

"There's going to be serious trouble," he said. "I've ordered the lunar batteries to open on the Deimos squadron as soon as it's within range. Slap a curfew on the city and shoot anybody who violates it."

Yamashita threw himself into his car. His driver—a human driver; black boxes were all very well for conventional duty, but they had too many built-in inhibitions; only humans could be totally unscrupulous—asked him: "Where to, sir?"

"The Controller's palace," said Yamashita. "We're going to blow a hole in the roof."

The man's jaw dropped. Then he recovered himself, and an instant later the hovercar lifted off.

3

Back in his own office, Maks told Sandra, "It's now or never. The Deimos squadron's close, I don't know just how close. There's going to be fighting in the city. We can escape now and I don't think anyone will even miss us. When they look for us later on, they'll think we were vaporized in the fighting."

Her eyes looked dark and sunken, as if still witnessing the central tragedy of human history. But she answered quietly, "What do we need to take?"

"Oh, a lot of stuff. More clothes, cashcards, that colored hardcopy those people use for money—and you'll have to have a universal vaccination—and we'll have to pick a destination, maybe the English countryside around 2000—Great Tao, I didn't expect everything to happen at once. Yamashita's going to be here in an hour or two with Darksiders and thuggi, ready to commit massacre over at Space HQ yesterday."

"Maks," she said. "I don't want to cause you any more trouble. But there's something else we must do."

"What's that?"

"Save my father. We know now that he didn't kill Dyeva. We can save him and the Troubles will happen and this world will be created. Maks—grant me this one thing and I swear I'll go anywhere, do anything you want. Maks? Will you save him?"

4

Waiting quietly, the maturing of the plot no longer in her hands, the admiral rested in her darkened quarters in the headquarters building.

Only a night-light burned. Brave as she was, the waiting had taken a toll on her nerves; for weeks past, night and day she had been unable to sleep. Yet she feared to take drugs, in case some emergency arose.

She lay on her side, her prominent eyes open, staring balefully at the fingertip-sized *klop* Yost had left with her. It was big, as it had to be to record data and send it out in microsecond bursts through the thick shielded walls.

She recognized the advantage in letting Yamashita hear what he thought were uncensored voices from her lair. Yet the very presence of the thing on her night table made her feel violated, increased her longing for revenge on the Security Forces.

At last admitting she'd have no rest, she rose and wrapped a regulation blue robe around her. She said, "Light," and the room obediently sprang into full view: the gilt case with her medals, holograms of herself at various promotion ceremonies, of her parents—also military people—of her husband Petr as a young man and a grizzled veteran, of Ion as a solemn baby and a strutting young officer receiving his commission.

On a shelf stood her doll collection, a dozen female figures in elaborate costumes of faux silk and ruffles and Martian lace. The dolls filled a mysterious soft spot in Suzana's heart. They smiled blindly and she gave them a brief, fond glance before heading out, past a guard standing rigid at the door.

In her communications room, among blinking devices purring and clicking as they received and routed headquarters message traffic, she sat down at a massive security-coded mashina and opened the most secret channel of all. Ion's virtual head appeared, smiling.

"This is the Controller's office," it said in a rich synthetic voice. "How may I assist you, honored caller?"

Suzana said, "*Novy mir.*" That was the code word they'd selected together: a new world.

A lengthy delay followed. Then Ion himself appeared. He wore a rumpled uniform and a faux silk robe embroidered with yellow dragons. His face was blotchy and his eyes red.

"What've you been up to?" she demanded at once. "You haven't been boozing again, have you?"

"Please, Admiral. The Empress's been in a savage mood, screaming at me about everything and nothing. I had to slip her a pinch of something to knock her out. She's in the next room, snoring."

"What've you been taking?"

"Just some kif. I needed it. And few glasses of wine. I needed that, too."

Suzana's suspicions gradually abated. *He wouldn't go carousing now,* she thought. *Nobody could be that much of a fool.*

"Bear up, my son. Soon you'll be free."

"Admiral, I can't w—"

With a roar the ceiling just behind Ion collapsed and gigantic Darksiders began plunging in among broken shards of steel and stone. A chunk of rubble bounded into the air and struck him on the head and his eyes swiveled and his mouth fell open.

Admiral Dluga Suzana stared, then cut the circuit; unfortunately for himself, Ion had no such easy way out.

5

In Xian Xi-qing's opulent bedroom, a scene absolutely beyond the imagination of living human beings was being played.

Xian crouched on her huge bed supported by gold-leafed phoenixes, her tiny face looking more ancient than that of her idol, the empress Wu, who had ruled China sixteen hundred years before.

In the grip of two Darksiders, Ion had ceased to struggle, merely turning his face from side to side. Spittle flecked his chin; blood trickled from the knot on his skull.

Yet in spite of his helplessness, his dreadful fear, his mind ticked along, obsessed with one thought: how could he survive the necessary minutes or hours until the Deimos squadron struck?

Yamashita strode up and down, slamming one solid fist into the other palm. *Evildoers understand nothing but fear,* he thought; *let's make this little bastard truly afraid.*

"When will Admiral Dluga attempt the military coup?"

"I don't know anything about a coup. Empress! Tell them I'm loyal!"

Xian said nothing. Yamashita had already played her Dzhun's recording of Ion; shown her a voiceprint positively identifying the voice on the memory cube as his; and a lab report identifying the sperm sample collected at the House of Timeless Love.

He had other evidence as well, for he had Yost, already undergoing "special handling," the most severe form of *shosho.*

Darksiders' ears had trouble with the pitch of human voices, and so their human handlers communicated with signs. Yamashita took hold of his left biceps and jerked. The Darksiders nodded, seized Ion's arms, and pulled them out of their sockets. The crack as his shoulders dislocated sounded like the breaking of wood.

"Stop!" he screamed.

"Well, when?"

"When the squadron arrives, Yost will arrest you. The admiral will become Controller, my father will take over the Space Service, and Yost will be her chief of security."

Yamashita raised one palm and the Darksiders gently lowered Ion's arms. Yamashita could not bring himself to look at Xian, now that the treason of her *babochka* was undeniable. Instead, he nodded to the Darksiders and they left the room, dragging their prisoner.

Yamashita approached Xian's bed and sank to his knees like a vassal before his lord.

"Honored Controller," he said thickly, "I would rather have died than do this to you. I am now once again under your command. Kill me if you wish."

Xian had been sitting still, covering her face with her small hands. Now she slowly removed them, struggling to regain her old habit of command.

"All this is true?" she whispered.

"You've heard. You've seen."

"I've lived too long," she said. Her voice sounded remote, the rustle of a dead leaf against a stone. "Suppress this rebellion and kill everyone connected with it. Those are my orders."

She hesitated. He had never seen her look so small, confused, old.

"I suppose all this will have to become known?" she asked in almost a pleading tone.

Yamashita lowered his eyes. Her catastrophic loss of face filled him with embarrassment, as if he'd seen her naked.

"Honored Controller, I don't see how it can be avoided. Soon there'll be fighting in the city."

"Go do your duty, then," she said, adding again: "I've lived too long."

He left her sitting in the middle of her huge bed, in a welter of faux silk sheets, guarded by dully gleaming figures of magical birds.

Neither he nor anyone else saw her rise, pour herself a cup of a fine Siberian vintage, then begin detaching gold leaf from the phoenixes and crumpling the small, thin sheets of metal into the wine.

5

Yamashita's hovercar banked and turned over central Ulanor.

Wide areas were dark. Around the five-sided mass of Space HQ flashing atomlasers and the low mutter of impact weapons filled the night. A column of robot tanks trundled down broad Genghis Khan Allee, firing missiles that burned twisting arcs across the sky as they searched for targets.

Broadcasting a Security Forces signature key, Yamashita's car at first passed through safely. But then a jarring shock sent it spinning.

The driver fought with the controls, righted it, plunged down among the buildings to escape any other hostile missiles. The admiral was fighting back, and clearly she knew how to do it.

The car landed with a bump on the third stage of the Palace of Justice. Subordinates ran to it, hoping to hear orders from somebody who knew what he was doing. The armored door had been bent by the missile; Yamashita kicked it open and emerged shouting.

"Cut off Yost's head! Get me Luna Base!"

Two minutes later he entered his office and demanded information from his mashina. Bad news poured in. Luna Base reported no sign of the Deimos squadron, but its remote monitors had picked up a large blip headed directly for the Earth.

Cursing bitterly, Yamashita watched his world come apart.

He sent a car for Hariko and Rika, wanting them close at hand if worst came to worst.

"When they arrive, send them to Pastplor. I'll be there. Understand?"

He might have been ordering lunch as far as the mashina was concerned.

"The message has been sent, Honored General," said its cool atonal voice. "Do you require anything else?"

But Yamashita was already gone. Automatically, the great office darkened behind him.

CHAPTER XXXVI

In the execution chamber, Yost's headless body slumped to the floor, a puff of steam rising from the stump of its neck.

"Neat," said an admiring thug. "Didn't spill a drop."

"Dumb bastard," said another. "Trying to fight the boss."

"Listen, he was lucky in the end. Without this fucking war, his *shosho* could've gone on for a week."

"Yeah, well, I guess in that sense he was lucky."

2

In her gilded bedroom, Xian Xi-qing fell to the floor, went through a brief convulsion, died. Like a true mandarin of ancient China she'd gone out in the honorable manner, self-strangled with gold leaf.

3

Disorder spread quickly through the city. Crowds poured out of the slums, not to join the perilous fight between the Space Service and the Security Forces, but to loot and burn. That turned out to be dangerous, too.

When a mob tried to sack the Senate building, Darksider guards emerged and began to slaughter them. The smell of blood excited the animals; armed with impact weapons and their own powerful jaws, multiple hands and blunt-clawed feet, they waded into the crowd, butchering everyone. As the people scattered, Darksiders crouched over the bodies, beginning to tear them apart, tasting the smoking meat of their former masters and finding it good.

At Space Headquarters the fighting continued, machine against machine, man against man, Darksider against Darksider. The building was so powerfully built and reinforced, so strengthened with solid masses of nuclear steel, that even Yamashita's micronukes—egg-sized warheads on arm-length missiles—fired by the tanks collapsed the building only a bit at a time. The rising mounds of rubble helped to protect the regions inside, where the admiral directed a seemingly hopeless defense.

"Admiral, we have to surrender," a captain stained with blood and ashes dared to say to her. She gave him one glance and shot him, then shot his corpse.

"If anybody uses that word again," she told her military police chief, who was aiding the battle by killing unenthusiastic defenders, "I want his guts on the floor in five seconds. Understand?

"Universal power or universal ruin!" she shouted over and over to encourage the troops. *Why not fight to the death?* If they surrendered, what did they have to face but *shosho* and the laser?

Then she retreated to her communications room and sat

down by the massive, multicoded mashina. The Security Forces had shut off the city's power grid, but the admiral had installed a laser-fired pure-hydrogen reactor in a subcellar against just that danger. So the red emergency lighting burned without a flicker, turning the faces of the troops to masks of rage, their dark blue uniforms to bloody purple.

Still she couldn't get through to the squadron. Every jamming device under Yamashita's control was blasting away and the shadow box was a chaos of flickering lights. Voices squawked out of the void, but said nothing comprehensible.

"Goddamn it, go through mag space," she commanded the device. "Use all available power! If the lights go out, who cares?"

In fact, the lights dimmed as the mashina diverted almost all the reactor's power to reach the squadron.

Suddenly an image resolved. It was Suzana's husband, a commodore with ferocious mustaches, depilated head, and agate eyes. She greeted him like a loving wife.

"Petr, where the fuck are you?"

"Inside lunar orbit. We're avoiding the moon because our guys haven't taken over there yet. My visual's showing a column of smoke over Ulanor, so I guess the action's started a bit early. What do we hit first?"

She hesitated only a second. "Hit the Palace of Justice. Wait. I have the coordinates."

The commodore stared. "What?"

"You heard me. We're protected from the radiation by all this rubble. Hit it now! We've got to take out their command post. That's an order, my dear."

For perhaps five seconds the commodore stared at her. Then grinned broadly.

"Ah, my Suzana, only you know how to win a war. Always go the enemy one better, eh? Now," he told her, "give me the exact coordinates and hold your breath!"

4

In the corridors of Pastplor, Yamashita raced for the wormholer. He was carrying Rika in his arms, while a ferociously armed Darksider bore Hariko, holding her tiny nose in his great mass of stinking fur.

Where the devil was Maks? *Could he have been killed?* Yamashita bellowed his questions at everybody he saw, but no one would admit to knowing anything.

The rooms were full of Pastplor workers, cowering here with their families, Yamashita noted with displeasure, instead of joining the battle. The news that the Deimos squadron had arrived meant hard, tough fighting—impossible fighting, if the cruisers used their big thermal torpedoes.

But surely they wouldn't? Surely an order to bombard the Worldcity would set off a mutiny? Even in a time of revolution, would a Russian battleship of old have bombarded the gorgeous temples of Saint Petersburg?

Uneasily, Yamashita remembered from some bygone history lesson that the Russian fleet had done exactly that to ensure the triumph of the Reds, whoever the Reds had been. Revolutionaries would do *anything,* because they had nothing to lose. Cursing, he hurried on, holding his granddaughter close.

"Can you operate the wormholer?" he roared at a technician.

"Yes, General."

"Then lead me to it."

Suddenly the man halted, bewildered.

"What's the matter?"

The tech pointed. A nuclear steel door stood open. Inside, the wormholer quivered slightly despite its weight; it was in operation.

"I never thought it of him," muttered Yamashita.

"Husband, what's wrong?"

The Darksider set Hariko down; she approached the worm-holer, taking Rika from her husband's arms.

"It looks as if he's run away from the battle. Where and when is he?"

The tech leaned over the monitor.

"Moscow, 2091," he said.

"Can you trace his exact position?"

"Yes, sir. He's got a—no, he's three controls with him. Huh: one hundred twenty-seven and a half kilos went through. Two people. He's in the Kremlin with another surfer."

"Who?"

"Let me check the roster." The man shook his head. "Nobody at all's supposed to be absent. I don't get it."

"The bloody coward ran away and took his woman with him!"

"Husband, that's not reasonable," Hariko put in. "Why would they run from a mere insurrection to the Time of Troubles?"

He stared at her. Why indeed?

"Perhaps he's on a secret project," the tech suggested.

"No projects are secret from me," snapped Yamashita. "We're wasting time. The squadron may be attacking the city at this moment. I need him and I'm going after him."

He checked his impact pistol, then lay down on the metal slide. Sensors alerted by his weight began to move him inside the massive coils. The surfer thrust a control into his free hand.

At the last moment, Hariko scooped up Rika in her arms and laid her beside him.

"Just in case something goes wrong here," she whispered.

Being Yamashita, he continued to shout orders until the moment that his body dislimned and vanished.

"Close that door! Admit nobody! Rika, lie still!"

Hariko smiled wanly at the tech.

"Silence at last," she said, and finding a chair, sat down quietly to await whatever fate might have in store.

5

For the second time, Maks and Sandra hastened across the shadowy, snow-lightened grounds of the Kremlin. Everything was just as before, the searchlights, the cawing rooks, the murmur of a distant but still peaceful crowd.

Maybe the wormholer had been affected by fluctuations in the power supply caused by the fighting in Ulanor. In any case, they arrived a good hundred meters from their last entry point, near a gigantic antique cannon that loomed threateningly out of the darkness.

As before, faint notes of music piped through the chilly air. They heard the sweet unearthly singing from the cathedral; the wheezy notes of accordion music from the wedding party; tipsy young voices beginning to take up a popular tune.

Maks led her quickly along curving paths, past the shimmering bulk of white buildings, among the leafless trees.

"We don't have much time," he warned. "Have you got the third control?"

"Yes."

"Don't turn it on until we find him. It's got to recognize him alone."

People were emerging from the church. Louder notes of music followed them through the open doors. Maks and Sandra stationed themselves by a tree whose bare trunk had patches of snow clinging to it. Dark figures bustled past, small clouds jetting from their nostrils.

"There!" Sandra whispered. The small, energetic figure of Dyeva again was striding toward them.

"So!" said a deep voice in Alspeke, and Yamashita's strong hand clamped on Maks's shoulder.

"What the devil are you doing here?" he hissed.

He put Rika down to free himself while he confronted Maks, drawing the impact pistol from his beltpouch.

"General—"

"Father!" Sandra cried suddenly. She ran into the path and seized a tall, lean figure by the lapels of his coat.

He tried to push her away, but she clung, exclaiming in Alspeke, "Father, Father, you don't have to kill her! I'm your daughter, yours and Dzhun's, and I've come to—"

"Great Tao," Yamashita gasped, "which is Dyeva?"

Maks pointed at the now rapidly retreating small figure.

"There, General, but—"

"She'll get away! She'll destroy our world!"

Yamashita sprang after Dyeva. Maks, after an instant of paralyzed astonishment, followed shouting, "General! No!"

The small sound *phut!* brought him to a frozen halt. Among the Russians streaming from the church he heard shouts of *"Shto? Shto?"*

Then a woman's scream. Then shadowy figures grappling with Yamashita. *"Pozovitye vracha! Militsiya!"*

Maks swung back and grabbed Stef to stop him from mixing into the brawl.

"This woman really is your daughter. And those people, they're calling for a doctor, for the police."

"I know," said Stef, pulling a small button from his left ear. "This thing's a translator. Is that old guy Yamashita? What's he doing here?"

The small group struggling with Yamashita at first acted like a black hole, sucking in more and more people. Men in uniform were arriving at a run, hefting primitive weapons. Yamashita's pistol spoke twice more. Then a fusillade of shots, shockingly loud, caromed off the walls of palaces and churches, provoking hysteria among people on the ground and in the birds wheeling above.

Suddenly people were running from the brawl, not toward it, and for an instant Sandra, Maks and Stef saw Yamashita struggling in the grip of huge Russian militiamen.

"We have to get away," said Sandra. She thrust the extra control they'd brought with them into Stef's hand. "Don't use yours," she gasped. "Come back with us—"

Yamashita and the men he struggled with had vanished again in a multitude of shadows. Then the crowd parted once more and they saw him for the last time—saw him sag, sink to his knees, and when the Russians released him, fall facedown in the snow.

They stood stock-still: they were stunned as if a colossus had fallen. Then Rika began to cry and Sandra took her into her arms.

"Where's Grandpa?" the child wailed.

"Oh, Great Tao," Maks whispered, "did he kill Dyeva before they got him?"

Slowly, as in a dream, he pressed the return stud of his control. Nothing happened.

Sandra tried hers. Stef tried the new control they'd given him, then the old one he'd brought with him. And again nothing happened. The world they'd come from had never been created and no longer existed in any possible future.

6

With Sandra hugging Rika, they turned and strayed away. They moved with the random, stunned steps of refugees escaping a bombed city, or like starving cattle, stumbling on roots, small stones, and the edges of walks.

Whether they'd hated their world or loved it—and in truth,

they'd done both—it had shaped them, defined them, and its annihilation left them lost as no people had ever been.

Then Stef put his hand on Sandra's arm and said, "Tell me."

She explained what had happened, how they came to this place, how Dyeva would not now cause the Time of Troubles, how everything would be different.

Stef kept making her repeat different parts of the tale, trying to grasp this astonishing revision of reality.

"And . . . you're really my daughter?"

"Yes."

"What is Dzhun like now?" he whispered in her ear. The question was in the wrong tense, but Sandra didn't notice. She was wondering how to answer.

"Very beautiful," she lied. "And kind. She was always very good and generous to me."

"That's a surprise. She used to be a mean bitch."

He grinned at her, and she thought: *why, what a cynical devil my old man was. Is.*

Is, she repeated to herself. *Is.*

They had almost reached Trinity Gate. A guard was explaining to a small crowd of people that the president's scheduled address had been cancelled, because of a disturbance on the Kremlin grounds.

"What kind of disturbance?" someone wanted to know.

"Some guy shot a woman and the *militsiya* killed him. Don't ask me any more because I don't know."

They passed through the brick guardhouse, over the bridge spanning the sunken garden, into the bustle of wide Vladimir Putin Prospekt.

"It's so hard to believe," said Sandra. "I cut my teeth on stories about the Time of Troubles. We all did. And now it won't happen at all."

"Don't be too sure," her father told her. "Minister Destruction is still in power, restrained only by the president. And I don't doubt there are crazies in other countries ready to try the same thing. The bad news is that the possibilities are infinite."

Sandra tried to smile. "And what's the good news?"

"That the possibilities are infinite."

"Are you taking me to Grandpa?" Rika asked, and Sandra said, "He'll catch up with us later, honey," to quiet her fears.

For a time the four of them stood at the curb, staring like nervous bumpkins into the frenzy of surface traffic that thundered along, horns braying. Hordes of people rushed past in the headlong Russian way, sometimes colliding and caroming off one another. The clatter of primitive rotary flying machines filled the darkness overhead. Above pale old marble buildings a half moon was rising.

"I've got a few rubles," Stef muttered. "After that I don't know how we'll live."

"Don't worry," said Sandra, trying to smile. "I'm all set to become the greatest scientist of the age."

All this time Maks had said nothing. The moon held his eyes like a hypnotist's light. Sandi, his lost son, a citizen of Luna. Since they parted, Maks had aged twenty years, Sandi only a few weeks—another of the mysteries of time. How would the little boy react when a middle-aged man found and embraced him? And how would he tell Maia that she had once again been superseded by a newer love?

Then a sudden thought made his knees weak. Almost certainly Maia called the boy Alexander Steffens. Could Stef be his descendant? If so, was it possible for Maks to commit incest at a distance of ten or twelve generations? He almost laughed out loud, thinking of the reunion that lay ahead, of middle-aged Stef meeting the little boy who was his forebear, of little Rika being introduced to the frowning, ill-natured boy who was hers.

As he stood there, smiling at the marvelous absurdity of things, church bells began to ring out over Moscow, here, there, and everywhere. How intoxicating it all was. Any notion he'd ever had of a safe and unchanging world order had vanished with the Worldcity that embodied it. Time, witty and heartless time, had made a fool of everyone who tried to control it. Was time, in fact, the Great Tao that everybody invoked and nobody understood? If so, the gifts of the Tao were life and death and—above all—perpetual surprise.

"How about looking for dinner and a place to sleep?" Sandra asked.

Rika had fallen asleep, and Maks took the child in his arms. She lay against his chest, breathing softly. At last he found his voice.

"Shall we go?" he asked formally, and since no other course was possible they joined the swift-flowing throng, whose only time travel lay in the tremulous ever-changing present and whose ultimate goal was as unknowable as their own.

The End